MISSING

MISSING

The Darrowdale Community was meant to be an idyllic haven where Laura and Terry Richardson could raise their two children. One summer's day, however, Laura went missing, never to be seen again. Traumatised by her mother's disappearance Caitlin has become estranged from her remaining family, and has a private life where no-one knows about her past. Almost twenty years after her mother's disappearance, her world is shattered when she receives a chilling note *'I know where she is. Your mother.'* Is the writer of the letter more interested with a brutal rewriting of history rather than bringing the truth to light?...

MISSING

by

Susan Hepburn

Magna Large Print Books
Long Preston, North Yorkshire,
BD23 4ND, England.

British Library Cataloguing in Publication Data.

Hepburn, Susan
    Missing.

    A catalogue record of this book is
    available from the British Library

    ISBN   0-7505-1887-1

First published in Great Britain in 2001 by
Judy Piatkus (Publishers) Ltd.

Copyright © 2001 by Susan Hepburn

Cover illustration © Anthony Monaghan

The moral right of the author has been asserted

Published in Large Print 2002 by arrangement with
Piatkus Books Ltd.

Magna Large Print is an imprint of Library Magna Books Ltd.

Printed and bound in Great Britain by
T.J. (International) Ltd., Cornwall, PL28 8RW

For Matthew.

In memory of Amy.

And to Peter McDonagh – you were right!

Special thanks to Dr Jane Moss, for enthusiasm and constructive feedback; to Lystra Maisey of the *Gloucestershire Echo* – any errors are mine! To Vanda Woodcock, for unwavering faith; and, above all, to my agent, Jane Conway-Gordon.

Chapter One

The Turning Point
Darrowdale Community
July, nineteen years ago

The thirteen-year-old girl knew only that it was a glorious day, golden and blue and green, heat-haze shimmering between earth and sky like life-force made visible. Walking along the dusty path beside the winding dry-stone wall, she knew it, felt it, throbbed with it. Momentarily, she closed her eyes in sheer pleasure as the warm air rushed over her face and caressed the slender, coltish arms and legs clad only in flimsy shorts and tee-shirt.

Scents came to her, summer scents of grass and sheep and ripening fruit. Sounds came, too: the murmuring of far distant engines, the rush of wings, the humming of bees. Suddenly startled by a scrabbling sound behind the wall, she ran up and down the bank in rhythmic steps to hide her fright and rid herself of excess adrenaline. It was silly. Just a dog or a fox or a cat. She was used to animals, surrounded by them in her day to day life.

Soon she was back in her reverie. The school holidays. Weeks of freedom to roam, to write, to play. She was preparing for a play, was going to be an actress, as famous one day as the actress who lived here and taught her. Her mind danced in time to the steps of her feet and her skin was covered in a sheen of perspiration as she entered the welcome coolness of the Community Craft Shop. The shop was connected to the Tea Room and Mrs Walters was in charge of both.

'Hello, Caitlin.'

'Hello, Mrs Walters.'

The woman looked beyond the girl, then back at her, expectantly. 'Where's your mum? Unloading the car?' Funny she hadn't heard it.

Caitlin realised she hadn't seen the car.

'Oh, I thought she'd be here. She said to meet her. We're going swimming after she's delivered her work to you.'

'And you walked down the track? Never mind. Perhaps she's running a little late today.'

'Or I could be early,' Caitlin suggested, looking at her watch. No, she was on time. Mum had said to meet her at half past three.

'Would you like some squash? On the house. You're looking rather hot.'

'Yes, please. I am.'

'Nothing but dry-stone walls the way you came. No wonder!'

Veronica Walters shepherded the girl into the Tea Room before phoning Laura Richardson to let her know her daughter had arrived. There was no reply. She must be on her way.

She didn't worry when Caitlin wanted to leave. There was no harm in it and she understood the impatience of the young. She knew the child would walk back along the route her mother would take to come to the shop, so it wasn't as if they could miss each other.

So Caitlin left at ten to four. It wasn't like Mum to be late for anything, and especially not this late. But still. Mrs Walters had said not to worry. She'd probably just got caught up in something. She retraced her steps, this time with the taste of summer fruits on her lips. Once more, rhythmic steps took her up and down the grassy banks beneath the wall and she smiled at a sight still some distance away, where the trees began. Adults! They were so *weird*. Acting like kids didn't know about sex. As if to prove her point, the figures disappeared.

She moved to the opposite side of the track. What was it Gran had said? Something about tact and diplomacy. She'd heard her say it to Mum once, along with something about how it was better than using a sledgehammer to crack a nut. They'd stopped talking when they'd seen her, but still, she thought, she'd got the gist of what Gran meant. *I shall be diplomatic, then. And I shall be tactful. And I shall pretend I didn't see.*

And so she'd gone home, but Mum wasn't there. Neither was the car. Caitlin checked to see if she had left a note, but she hadn't. Mothers! Why couldn't they be reliable, like they were supposed to be? She conveniently ignored the fact that her mother had been perfectly reliable until today.

Oh well. She fetched the big red notebook she was using for the play. Might as well get on with something. But she sulked for a while before settling down to write at the kitchen table. She really *had* wanted to go swimming...

13

She was still absorbed in her play-writing when her father came home.

'Hi, there, sweetheart!' Terry Richardson swung his briefcase onto the chair beside her, kissed the top of her head and leaned over her shoulder, looking at what she was doing.

'What's all this then? Katie Shakespeare?'

She laughed and turned to hug him. He smelled of chlorine. Terry held his daughter close, frowning as he realised there was no smell of cooking.

'How did it go, Dad? It was your important meeting today, wasn't it?'

'It sure was, sweetheart!' He ruffled her hair, holding up the carrier bag so far hidden from her sight.

'What's that?'

'This...' He pulled out two bottles of champagne. '...is the makings of a celebration!'

'You got the contract!' Caitlin slipped from the chair in her excitement, scattering pens and crayons in all directions.

'Of course I did! I'm Superdad, remember?' He made aeroplane noises and waggled his arms like wings as he took the bottles to the fridge. Closing the door, he winked at his daughter. 'Where's Mummy?' he asked.

She hadn't realised so much time had passed and felt a stab of anxiety, but when she said she didn't know, he didn't seem too concerned, said she was bound to be home soon. Yet as more time passed, the ticking of the clock seemed to become louder and louder, as if taunting them with its incessant reminder of Mum's absence.

She'd begun to fidget then, trying to shake off the ever-growing anxiety that was looming in her stomach. Dad was still saying there was nothing to worry about, but she knew he was beginning to feel it, too, and when Mum wasn't back in time for her class that evening, he started making phone calls and found that he and Caitlin weren't the only ones who didn't know where Mum was.

No one did.

Chapter Two

The Beginning of the End
Cheltenham, Gloucestershire
Thursday 2 December, the present

```
I know where she is. Your mother.
```

Caitlin O'Connor stared at the piece of paper, shock bringing her heart to her mouth. She turned it over, then back again, bewildered. There was nothing else. Just those seven words.

Pushing her honey-blonde hair behind her left ear, she retrieved the envelope from the waste-paper basket. Of the same grubby white paper as the unsigned note, it offered no further clues beyond a first-class stamp and an illegible post-mark. She smoothed it out, placing it carefully in the centre of the heavy oak desk. Equally carefully, she placed the note itself, no larger than a

15

compliment slip, on top of it.

I know where she is. Your mother.

She reread the words. Typewritten. The letter 'e' dropped slightly. What kind of sick joke was this? Caitlin O'Connor hadn't seen her mother since the day she'd disappeared. Almost twenty years ago.

The letter-writer looked at the clock. A knot of excitement and anticipation tightened a stomach still awaiting breakfast. Caitlin was one of three people written to, but she was by far the most important. She would have received the letter by now. Her postal route had been carefully monitored. She always arrived early at her workplace. The receptionist would have given it to her before her first client arrived. What would she be thinking? Feeling? Long fingers lovingly stroked the space-bar of the ancient typewriter. What would she be *remembering?*

Caitlin had no time to remember. Not with her first client due in less than five minutes. She smoothed the couch linens, an outward sign of her attempts to soothe the turmoil seething in her solar plexus. Oh God! What could it mean? After all this time... She moved swiftly to the glass-fronted cabinet that held her essential oils. Neroli for shock. She sprinkled two drops onto a cotton wool pad and inhaled deeply. Closing her eyes, she tried to calm herself using the techniques she had been taught, visualising herself

16

surrounded by golden light, until she was able to breathe slowly and deeply.

Penny, the receptionist, had to use the internal line to let Caitlin know that Mrs Cowper had arrived. She'd never had to do that before. Caitlin always came, unasked, into reception to greet her clients. She watched, curiously, as Caitlin led Mrs Cowper to the treatment room. She looked, perhaps, a little pale, but it was difficult to tell with blondes. No. She looked the same as always. Tall, slender and coolly immaculate in the white tunic and trousers she wore for her work. Oh, well. Maybe she was having an off-day. Penny frowned at the thought. Caitlin hadn't had an off-day in all the years she'd worked at the Complementary Healthcare Clinic.

Normally, Caitlin was a creature of habit, taking her lunch breaks in the park in summer, at the clinic in winter. Today, she made the five-minute walk to the shopping mall and used the escalator to get to the first-floor restaurant. Soon she was seated at a table with a cup of coffee and a sandwich. The fluttering that had started in her solar plexus earlier had now descended, like a leaden weight, into her stomach. *What am I doing here?* she asked herself. *I have a perfectly good, homemade lunch in the fridge at work.* She was here, she acknowledged, because she wanted to get away from people who might ask questions. She was here because she wanted to look at the note again. It drew her like a magnet, despite the fact that she knew full well that any further examination would be futile. Seven words in the note. Just her name and the clinic address on the envelope. It was burning a hole in her pocket. She had to look at it again. She smoothed it on the laminated surface of the table, her eyes blurring with tears. *Oh, Mummy – where did you go?*

Three tables away, on the opposite side of the aisle, Caitlin was being observed by someone who, to all intents and purposes, was deeply absorbed in a broadsheet newspaper. A smile pulled at the corners of the mouth, not extending to the eyes. The eyes were cold as slate. Caitlin's mother had loved slate. Worked with it. The eyes glistened now, as Caitlin pushed aside her plate and cup. *Lost your appetite, have you? You'll have lost a lot more than that by the time I'm done with you...*

By the end of the day Penny was worried enough about Caitlin to feel she should do something. She couldn't say or do anything herself, of course. It wasn't her place. But Nina Shawcross, perhaps... Nina, the medical herbalist, was a friend of Caitlin's as well as a colleague. Yes. Just a quick word. Just to make sure someone else knew. Caitlin might talk to Nina about whatever it was that was bothering her. Right. She'd do it now.

The letter-writer watched as two women walked down the steps of the clinic. Caitlin was with Nina. Every face in the clinic had been memorised. Child's play. They had a big frame in the

18

hallway, full of colour photographs of their practitioners. 'Rogues Gallery', Penny called it. Penny was the receptionist. Below this frame, a fine old chest, burnished with age, displayed the practitioners' leaflets, detailing their therapies and fees. And to the left of the photographs was a noticeboard advertising evening meetings and classes. Nina taught yoga. Caitlin taught T'ai Chi. The long form. Just as her mother had done.

Nina and Caitlin were separating now. They had stood talking on the pavement, their body language easily readable. Nina was gentle, concerned, her dark hair pushed under a woolly bobble-hat. She laid a hand on Caitlin's arm, asking a question. Caitlin shook her head and stepped away, her body unnaturally stiff. *Tension. It's getting to her. One note and it's getting to her. This is such fun. I can play with her. Cat and mouse. How I shall enjoy this...*

They went their separate ways. Caitlin had pulled herself together, was walking off briskly without a backward glance at her friend. Nina was hesitant, uncertain. Worried about her. She watched Caitlin, concern written all over her face, before turning reluctantly and walking away.

Caitlin was oblivious to everything as she walked home. Oblivious, even on the Promenade, to the crowds around her, crowds of tired workers and shoppers hurrying home after a hard day. Oblivious to the shops themselves, bedecked with Christmas bargains, Christmas decorations. Oblivious to the incessant carols emanating from their scented doorways. And as she let herself into her house, she was oblivious to the person who'd followed her there and who now carried on past without a glance in her direction.

She slumped with exhaustion as she closed the door behind her. This feeling was so alien to her that she felt confused, afraid of what was happening to her. She hadn't felt like this since... *No!* She snapped her mind shut on the memory. It was too painful. Shaking her head, she removed her hat, her coat, her gloves. She hesitated, then went into the kitchen and put the kettle on before running upstairs and stripping off her clothes. She stuffed them into the linen basket before walking naked to the bathroom, where she took a long, hot shower. Moments later, wrapped in her bathrobe, she made a pot of tea and took it into the sitting room. She found herself drawn to the piano. She ran her fingers over the lid, lifted it and stroked the keys, beginning to play. Slowly at first. Softly. As her confidence grew, so did the speed and volume. She was playing Scott Joplin's *The Entertainer*. It was the last thing she'd heard her mother play. This had been her mother's piano.

Later that evening she was in the Butcher's Arms in Cheltenham, her regular Thursday evening haunt. Along with her boyfriend, Josh, Nina, and Nina's husband, Mike, she played skittles with an assortment of people who, like herself, did it just for fun.

'Nice one!' breathed Josh as she sent the pins tumbling yet again.

'You're on good form tonight – you could have

warned us!' shouted a member of the opposing team.

'Better still, you could have stayed at home!' came a further cat-call.

I almost did, thought Caitlin. *Didn't think I'd be up to much. But getting out has done me good.*

She smiled as Mike returned to the table with a tray of drinks, saying, 'Right! Are we going to sort out this weekend away, or what?'

'Or what?' suggested Josh.

'Trust a bloody shrink to have a sense of humour!'

'I'm *not* a shrink, as well you know!'

Caitlin smiled, remembering the first time they'd met, four months ago. She'd been on an ecological clean-up weekend with Mike and Nina and would have had to be blind to have missed him. Over six feet tall, blonde hair falling over his eyes, Josh had been sweating in the shade, a lean figure in jeans, boots and a check shirt, busily shovelling manure. The opportunity had been irresistible.

'So, what do you do when you're not shovelling shit?'

He'd looked up, startled, smiling, not having heard her approach.

'Me?' He'd leaned on the spade and shrugged. 'I'm a psychoanalyst.'

'A *psycho*analyst?' She made him sound like a mass murderer.

God, she has the most kissable mouth I've ever seen...

'So you're what?' she'd asked. 'Clearing out your mental rooms in symbolic form or something?'

'No – just shovelling shit!'

They'd both laughed, and that had been that. Before the weekend was over, he'd asked her out.

'About this weekend...' Mike tried again. Good. He had their attention. 'We have to get it in before Christmas because of Caitlin's duties at the Night Shelter, so what about two weeks' time?'

Diaries were produced, dates debated and finally it was agreed.

'Are you sure it's not a bit close to the end of term, Mike?'

'It's precisely *because* it's the end of term that I want to go then, Caitlin!'

Mike was a lecturer in Environmental Studies at the University. Although they now lived in Cheltenham, Nina had kept her cottage in Oxfordshire when she and Mike had married. They were both glad she had. It provided a welcome haven when they wanted to get away.

Later, in the Ladies', Nina eyed Caitlin's reflection in the mirror as she brushed her hair.

'You're nervous about this weekend away, aren't you?'

Caitlin pulled a face and laughed. 'Is it that obvious?'

'No. I just know you, that's all.'

Caitlin turned to face her. 'Well ... yes. It will be my first time away with Josh. Properly, I mean. Sleeping bags in a village hall on a clean-up doesn't count, does it?'

'I guess not.' Nina knew she had to ask. She just hoped Caitlin wouldn't take offence. She had known her for seven years, but boyfriends – such a stupid word for adult women to use – well,

22

there hadn't been many of those, and never for more than a few weeks. Josh was different. But how different?

She took a deep breath. 'Look, it's not that I'm prying or anything, but I have to know because of the practicalities. You and Josh – sharing, or separate rooms?'

'Separate. Thanks for asking. I was going to bring it up myself.'

Nina followed Caitlin back to the skittle alley. *Sometimes*, she thought, *I get the feeling I don't know you at all*... Still, she was a great believer in holding her own counsel. What people wanted to tell you, they would. Prying was, more often than not, counter-productive, in her opinion. More so with someone like Caitlin. What did she mean by that? She frowned as she walked away, searching for an answer. She'd worked with Caitlin for a long time, yes. Well, not *with* her, exactly. They worked out of the same clinic. It was only in the last two years that they'd really become friends.

Nina had woken up in agony one day. 'Torque neck', Caitlin had called it. Cured it in a few minutes flat, and given her the most wonderful massage she'd ever had. It was as if the cool, distant blonde became someone else when she worked on you, touched you. It was... Nina thought carefully. It was a deeply spiritual experience. Caitlin was not just good, she was gifted. It was as if she connected with something very deep, very warm and powerfully healing. She became alive, vibrant, energised. And those things in her treatment room... That piece of cal-ligraphy, like the open pages of a book. Absolutely beautiful, the letters flowing like water. And the Celtic cross, with ogham decoration. Nina had never seen anything quite like it. It was done on slate, God knows with what, communicating something beyond serenity, something eternal, imbued with life and power.

It had been the first time they'd really talked, and the friendship had grown from there, especially once Caitlin's commitment to the environment had become known. Thinking back to their conversation in the toilet, Nina wondered again how well she really knew her friend. Well enough to know she'd not been quite herself today, even without Penny's expression of concern. There was nothing she could put her finger on. Probably something in her personal life. Nina had to admit that, Josh aside, she knew next to nothing about that. Caitlin really was a very private person.

By the time Caitlin got home, she was feeling much more relaxed. The company had done her good. The note ... well, it was obviously some crank. She couldn't let it affect her. *Mustn't* let it affect her. She had a new life now. *If only I knew what had happened... No. NO. Think of now. Build your own life. You're the only one who can do it, Caitlin. You alone can make it happen. God! I'm sounding like... No. Don't think of that, either. It's in the past. It's over. What do I want now?*

Unbidden, Josh slipped into her mind. Mike and Nina had dropped her off first after skittles. Josh had unfolded himself, with difficulty, from the back seat of Nina's car and walked her to the door, kissed her, said he'd see her for lunch on

24

Saturday. She'd waved as they'd pulled away again, taking him home. What was she going to do about Josh? She'd never been able to sustain a relationship, not since... She took a deep breath. *Not since London.* God knows, she'd tried. So Josh had been something of a shock. A pleasant surprise, but things were becoming ... difficult. What was she going to do? She pushed the question out of her mind, told herself she'd think about it later. For now, she was just glad to be home.

Home. She was lucky to have a home. Especially this one. *If it hadn't been for Gran... Stop it! Even without Gran's help, I'd still be alright. I'd have a little flat or something. I have a good job now, a job I love.* Caitlin had a horror of homelessness, and with good reason. She would never forget what it was like. That was why she had committed herself to helping out at the Night Shelter. *Oh, God. I hope it isn't all going to get stirred up again. Mummy. London. I've worked so hard to forget.* Suddenly, she felt overwhelmed by tiredness. With a heavy heart, she took herself off to bed.

The letter-writer was well satisfied. Caitlin had been followed home today, of course. Not because her address was unknown, but because this was much more the thing. *Stalking.* The word was savoured. Spoken aloud. *You are my prey and I have stalked you to your lair. To what you think is safety. Nothing is safe now, Caitlin. Nowhere is safe for you. This is the beginning of the end. It is only right and fitting that you should die on Christmas Day...*

Chapter Three

Tuesday 7 December

At her desk in the offices of the *Darrowdale Gazette*, Deborah Harvey looked at the pile of newspaper cuttings she'd been given. Pushing her tortoiseshell glasses through the tangle of auburn curls that framed her face, she reached for her mug of coffee and frowned. Old Derek – *Derek Kenny, Editor,* she corrected herself – was probably fobbing her off. Next July would be the twentieth anniversary of the story, which he'd been running for years, and he was giving it to her, so he claimed, because she was his 'cub reporter'. Where did they come up with such terms? What was he, then, a lion? Her mind boggled as she played with the imagery. Hippopotamus was nearer the mark. Too many liquid lunches had done for whatever figure he'd once had. He didn't really expect her to find any new leads, of course. The case was still technically open, having never been solved, and if the police couldn't wrap it up, then how could she?

This was, however, the first decent assignment she'd been given and she was hungry with ambition. Wanted to make a name for herself. Move to one of the London papers. The nationals. She wasn't going to be stuck up here for ever. Not like Derek. And she had a big advantage. She was

coming to the story fresh, with no precon-
ceptions. She would find a different angle. That
alone would get her noticed. At twenty-seven,
she'd come into journalism relatively late and was
still a trainee, anxious to make her mark as
quickly as possible.

She picked up her notebook and pulled the pile
of cuttings towards her. They were in chrono-
logical order, so the first one to hand was the
original newspaper report of Laura Richardson's
disappearance. Deborah read it through silently.

Darrowdale Police are anxious to hear from any-
one who may have seen local artist, Mrs Laura
Richardson, 39, who disappeared from the
Darrowdale Community two days ago.

She was last seen at 1.30 p.m. by her 13-year-old
daughter, Caitlin, when she made arrangements to
meet her at the Community Craft Shop later that
afternoon. The alarm was raised by Mrs Richardson's husband, Terry, 49, when she failed to turn
up to teach her scheduled T'ai Chi evening class.

Despite an extensive search of the grounds, no
sign of Mrs Richardson or her car, a blue Volvo
estate, has been found. The missing woman is
described as being 5ft 8in tall, of slim build and
with shoulder-length blonde hair.

Detective Sergeant Tom Harlow said that both
police and the Community were concerned about
her absence as it was completely out of character.
'If Mrs Richardson left voluntarily we would urge
her to get in touch, simply to let us know she's
safe.'

Husband Terry angrily denied that his wife

would have gone anywhere without letting the family know, saying, 'Laura would never have left the children alone. Never.'

Friends say that the family is distraught with worry. As well as Caitlin, the Richardsons have a son, Daniel, aged 17.

Mr Richardson, an architect, is a founder member of the Community, built to his design some twenty years ago. Despite initial opposition, the Community has become well established and popular with local people as well as visitors from far afield. Its members include a variety of professionals, among them teachers and a doctor, but it is perhaps best known as the home of the celebrated actress, Angela Fielding, and Laura Richardson herself, whose works, particularly those in slate, have received wide recognition.

Anyone with information is asked to contact Darrowdale Police or their local police station. All calls will be treated in strictest confidence.

Deborah wondered if any calls had been made. *Poor kids*, she thought. *Waiting for a mother who never turned up*. She tried to put herself into the daughter's shoes and shuddered. *Thirteen? That would make her what, now? About thirty-two? I wonder where she is? What she's doing?*

Caitlin was eyeing her haggard reflection in the mirror. She had come through the weekend relatively unscathed, she told herself, which was another way of saying there had been no more letters. There had, however, been a nightmare last night. *I thought I'd got away with it. Thought if*

28

I was going to have one it would have been last Thursday, after that bloody letter. But no. It waited for me. Until last night.

All night, with increasing horror, she'd wandered endlessly in the dark, searching for her mother, sick with anxiety, sick with fear of what she might find.

Only because I now know that she never came back, she reminded herself. *Funny. It wasn't like that at the time. Not in the slightest.*

She'd always felt guilty at not having had some sort of premonition. She'd read articles about psychic and emotional bonds between people, about how they knew when a loved one was in danger. *There can't have been a closer bond than between me and Mummy. Mother and daughter. There can't have been. So why didn't I know?*

Silently, she wondered if anything would have been different if she had.

Deep in the countryside, Mags knew it was time to move on. Thanks be to God, though, for disused farm buildings. She stamped her feet as she walked outside, grateful for the near-indestructible boots she was wearing, clapping together hands protected by glove liners with fingerless gloves on top. Good, they were. They had a mitten bit you could fold over and fasten on the back with Velcro, like she had them now.

The morning was bright and frosty, a low white mist curling above the bare fields of fallow earth. Ah well! Life was an adventure, after all. New experiences every day. It wouldn't be doing to be bored, now. That was a killer, boredom. She

29

shivered at the thought, swinging her arms vigorously to drive it from her. Which way should she go? *Well now*, she thought. *Where would I like to be spending Christmas?* She watched and smiled as a pair of magpies winged away, the glinting sun picking out the royal blue feathers in their plumage. *That'll do*, she told herself. *South it is.* Picking up her backpack and swinging it onto her shoulders with practised ease, she set off with a brisk and determined stride.

I know where she is. Your mother.

Christ! Daniel Richardson stared at the note in disbelief. What the hell was this? Snatching up the envelope, he realised it had been sent on from his home address. Home! He was hardly ever there. *I should sell the place. Stupid, keeping two places on. A flat here. A house there. Even though I can afford it.* He looked around his office. Saw the awards. The gold and platinum discs on the walls. *I should sell the Devon house. I will sell it. Tough on Cathy, but hell, I told her it wasn't serious.*

He looked back at the note. Who the hell was bringing all this up again now? He felt physically sick as he remembered how he'd learned of his mother's disappearance. He'd been intercepted by his father before he'd even had chance to set foot in the door.

'Daniel, thank God you're home! Can you sit with your sister a bit? Keep her entertained or something?'

He had bitten off the 'You must be joking!' that would have been his natural response. He knew –

30

whether from his father's voice or body language, he wasn't sure – that something was wrong. Dad had dropped his voice, glancing over his shoulder as he spoke.

'Look, son. God knows, I don't want to worry you, but it's just that, well, we can't find Mum.' Father and son had held eye contact, communicating for that brief moment without words. Daniel had opened his mouth but Dad had cut him off.

'It's probably nothing to worry about. Miscommunication somewhere along the line. Just that we don't quite know where she is.' There was another silence, another shared look.

'Since when, Dad?'

'Since lunchtime.' Dad had led him inside the house where, with a warning glance and wink, he had raised his voice and bellowed, 'Daniel! Where the hell have you been?'

They'd walked into the kitchen together, co-conspirators in Caitlin's protection, Daniel thinking he could hardly tell his father the answer to his mock question. Not all of it, anyway...

And now this. This note. *Christ!* What if Caitlin had had one, too? Cait. 'I wish I could shimmy like my sister, Cait.' How he'd teased her with that when she was little, knowing she hated it. Only he'd called her Cait. Dad had always called her Katie, and Mum... Mum had never called her anything but Caitlin. *Bloody hell! I should do something, I know I should. But how the hell would I find her?* Gran would have known, but Gran was dead. *Died not knowing what had happened to her daughter. Our mother. Christ! If there is an afterlife, then maybe, just maybe, she knows now and can rest in peace. Not like us. How can we rest?*

She must be dead. Mum. She must be. It's just the not knowing. The how, the why, the who? Shit! I have to find Caitlin. She could be married. Divorced. Have kids. She could be... Daniel's thoughts faltered. He didn't want to entertain the possibility that his sister might be dead, too. She could have had a car accident. Christ! He didn't even know whether she could drive. *Of course she can drive. Everybody can drive, for God's sake.*

If only I hadn't gone away to University. What the fuck did I think I was trying to prove? If I'd stayed at home, been there for her, she wouldn't have run away. Dad always blamed me for that. It was always my fault. Like he was the one to talk. Fine fucking father he was. How the hell can I find Cait?

Slowly, Daniel picked up the phone.

'So, how's it going?' Derek Kenny, editor of the *Darrowdale Gazette* addressed Deborah Harvey as she entered his office. He had a gut feeling about this one. He knew he wouldn't be able to keep her. She was destined for better things.

'Good. I have some ideas I'd like to run past you.' She opened her briefcase and withdrew the sheaf of cuttings, placing them on his desk. 'You were here when it happened, Derek. What do you think?' She smiled, suddenly embarrassed. 'I'm just curious, you know.'

He looked at her for a long time before he spoke, lost in thought, in memories. All those interviews. The family. The police. The Community. He didn't particularly like remembering.

There had been stuff they couldn't use. That he'd decided not to use. But he felt he owed Laura Richardson. That was why he'd run an update every year. Not that there was anything new to report, but still, it kept the case in the public eye. Someone, somewhere, knew what had happened that day. Finally, he spoke.

'What do I think?' He smiled slowly, tapping the side of his nose. 'That's for me to know and you to find out...'

Walking downstairs, Deborah was stopped in mid-stride when she heard her name being called.

'Hey, Debs – you've been landed with the Laura Richardson update, right?'

'Right.'

Mandy Stevenson was one of the girls who dealt with advertising. She beckoned Deborah over to her desk.

'We've just had an ad in. Thought you might like advance notice.' Deborah watched as Mandy's fingers flew over the keyboard, bringing the ad up on screen.

**Darrowdale Community Open Day
and Christmas Fayre
Saturday 11th December, 10 a.m.–4 p.m.**

Gifts and Fun for all the family,
including Christmas Carol Concert,
Games and Refreshments.
Free parking. Free crèche.

*Find us off the Heathdown Road, 4 miles past the
Fiveways Roundabout.*

33

'Thanks, Mandy.' Deborah patted the girl's shoulder, digging in her briefcase for her diary.

A couple of minutes later, Derek Kenny watched from the window of his office as Deborah crossed the road to the sandwich bar. Seven months to the anniversary. He'd given her plenty of time to dig. She was a bright girl. Razor sharp. If anyone could find something new, Deborah could. He'd always wanted to crack it himself, but maybe Ronnie had been right. He was too close. Too involved. Couldn't see the wood for the trees.

Derek was not a religious man, but at that moment, in his own way, he prayed. Next year would be his last as editor. Not that he minded, in a way. Everybody had to retire sometime. There was just one thing that haunted him and that was the possibility that the story might not be run again. Oh, it might get a paragraph on page eight if nothing else was happening, but not the front page he'd given it all these years; not the Editor's opinion column, either.

He was still watching as Deborah left the sandwich bar, brown paper bag in hand. He saw her shoot off in the direction of the car park. *You're a bloody fool, man, he told himself. A sentimental old fool.* He recognised that his interest in Deborah went beyond the professional. In her, he saw the daughter he'd never had. Feisty. Keen-minded. Independent. *Daughter!* He snorted. What a waste. Other people had made lives for themselves. Families. Laura had. He muttered to himself angrily, 'Bloody old fool!'

34

'Who is, boss?'

He looked up, startled. Damn the woman! Ellen Walker, his secretary, had come in, silent in her rubber-soled shoes.

'Nobody. Just thinking aloud.'

Oh-oh. Ellen knew that look. Had a name for it. The Thundercloud. She made a mental note to warn the others. When The Thundercloud appeared, he was like a bear with a sore head.

Caitlin knew she would need all the strength she could muster to get through the day. It was a special anniversary. Every year, she thought – hoped – it would get easier, but it didn't. How could it? There was always more to wonder about. Agonise over. There were three days of every year on which Caitlin didn't work: her birthday; the anniversary of her mother's disappearance; and today. No one marked it as an annual absence – why should they? Had she been asked, she would simply have said she was taking a day off to go Christmas shopping.

When the mail dropped through Caitlin's letterbox that morning it was later than usual because of the snow that had fallen in far greater quantities than had been forecast. It would have made no difference had it been on time. She wouldn't have seen it. She had gone out early, trudging through the silent streets in her wellingtons, making her annual pilgrimage of remembrance to the Catholic church of the Sacred Hearts.

The heating was on full blast this morning. Few people came to the earliest Mass of the day, but

Father Bernard had a good feel for weather, regardless of what the forecasters might say, and had taken the appropriate measures. Despite the hundreds of parishioners who passed through his doors each year, he had noticed the woman's annual presence, not at Christmas or Easter, but on this day alone. The woman never received the sacrament but was completely focused, immersed in the Mass, immersed in her own private agony. He knew that when he came back into church once the Mass was over, he would find her lighting a candle before the Black Madonna in the side chapel. He knew she would stay on her knees a long time, tears running down her face. He always hovered unobtrusively in the hope that maybe one year she would speak to him, share with him the grief that was eating at her heart. But never mind if she didn't. Our Lady knew. She would extend a mother's compassion to a daughter so sorely in need.

The letter-writer was perturbed. In place long before the mail was due to be delivered, there had been no sign of Caitlin. And the mail had been late. Late! *I should have taken account of the Christmas disruption. Delivered it myself.* Nonetheless, Caitlin hadn't left the house.

Steadily falling snow had obliterated all trace of her early departure, but the letter-writer was not to know this. Rage seethed in the twisted mind. *How dare she do this! This wasn't how it was supposed to be!* This absence wasn't part of the plan. She couldn't do this! But she had.

Tucked away on the outskirts of London, many people were not aware of the existence of the Abbey. The few who were – the non-Catholics, at least – tended to refer to it as a convent because of the nuns within its walls. 'Abbey' was its correct title, however, given the Benedictine Sisters inside.

Sister Barbara grimaced at the twinge in her knees as she rose to her feet after saying morning prayers. The interior of the chapel was cool and quiet, sacredness hanging in the air like incense. The contemplative life, to which she had come later than most, instilled a sense of timelessness, hours measured by the Daily Office, days by the lives of the Saints, seasons by the cycle of the church's calendar. Yet awareness remained of certain days of significance in the outside world, dates remembered from her earlier life, before she had chosen the contemplative way. Today was one. She would light a candle to Our Lady and pray, as she had done so many times, remembering. Always remembering, always wishing she didn't have to. Memory was her penance, she told herself, knowing that, in comparison to others, she had got off lightly. It could have been so much worse. She could have been in prison. She could have been dead.

Caitlin returned home, face chilled numb by the worsening weather. Forlornly, she let herself into the house, unaware of the frozen figure who watched her with leaping heart. *Right, you bitch! Just wait till you see what's waiting for you!* She picked up the mail from the mat, tossing it onto the hall table. Her mind was elsewhere. Long ago and far away.

Shedding her outer clothing, she stepped into the living room, now bedecked with the flowers she'd bought the previous evening, candles ready for the lighting. She sang softly to herself as she held the taper to each wick, finally seating herself at the piano to play. Slowly, lovingly, and with fresh tears running silently down her face, her fingers traced the melody of a Requiem.

'So, you haven't seen your sister since when?' Chris Farmer leaned back in his chair, eyeing his latest client with open interest. It wasn't every day he had a record producer on his books. Funny how they were still called that when everything was on CD and DVD these days. God knows what they'd come up with next – some way of downloading music directly into the human brain? He shuddered at the thought and turned his attention back to the man in front of him. A man who had demanded – and got – an immediate interview. He had money all right, this one. All Chris's clients needed money. He didn't come cheap. Daniel Richardson had loads of bands under his belt. Bands even Chris had heard of. Bet their record companies loved him.

'I last saw Cait at our grandmother's funeral. That was...' Daniel closed his eyes, thinking. '...That would have been twelve years ago.'

'And where was she living then?'

An embarrassed laugh. 'London, I think.'

'You think?'

Daniel fiddled with the gold cufflinks in his

immaculate white shirt cuffs. Chris wondered if he wore his Versace suits in the recording studio. Daniel shrugged.

'She wasn't very forthcoming. She – she'd run away from home three years earlier. She'd been in touch with Gran for some time.'

'But not with you?'

'Not with anyone else, as far as I know.'

'Who is "anyone else", Mr Richardson? Parents? Other siblings?'

A shadow flickered across Daniel's face. 'There was just me and Cait. And our father. She was living with him when she ran away.'

Ah, thought Farmer. *Now we're getting to it.*

'Your father? What about your mother?'

Daniel Richardson was looking distinctly uncomfortable now.

'My mother...' He cleared his throat, tried again. 'Our mother disappeared nearly twenty years ago.'

Chris Farmer raised his eyebrows. This was going to be more interesting than he'd expected.

It took him some time to get the story out of the man, and even then he knew it wasn't everything. How could it be, when Richardson's mother had never been found? There was more, though. Richardson knew something he wasn't telling. Chris could smell it. He let it lie for the moment, and got to the point.

'What do you think happened to your mother, Mr Richardson?'

Daniel had shrugged, hands gesturing help-lessly. 'I don't know. I simply don't know.'

Chris watched him carefully before asking his

next question.

'Let me put it another way. Do you think she's alive or dead?'

'What kind of question is that?' Chris could see the pain in Richardson's face, the pallor beneath the trim beard, jaw muscles working. Finally, he shook his head. 'I think she's dead.'

Farmer could not have known that this was the first time Daniel had ever articulated the thought aloud.

'She has to be dead. There's no way she would have left me and Cait. Certainly no way she wouldn't at least have got a message to us, saying she was alright.'

Chris gave him a moment before asking, 'What did the police think?'

Daniel gave him a withering glance. 'What do you think they thought? Once they started putting things together, two and two made five. They thought our father had killed her.'

'And do you?' Chris was used to being blunt. It was often the best way.

'No! No way! He couldn't have.' Daniel shook his head and glared at Farmer, guilt kicking in on the wake of his anger. 'Do you seriously think I'd have gone away to University, left my sister living with him if I thought he'd been capable of that?'

I don't know, thought Farmer. *You tell me...*

Chapter Four

Terry Richardson let himself into his house in Barnsley, dumping his small battered suitcases on either side of his legs. Christ, it was cold! He'd been on a special package holiday – three weeks in Cyprus, third week free and no single supplement. It had been glorious and he hadn't wanted to come back. He was more determined than ever to make the break and buy a place abroad, leave this shitty country behind, but the finance... He wasn't badly off – owned his own place, no mortgage and no debts – but he still had to be careful. He'd sat down and worked everything out and with just a little extra cushioning, he wouldn't need to worry. If only he hadn't gone off the rails after Laura had disappeared, he'd be sitting pretty now. Still, he'd go to the shops, get bread and milk and check his lottery tickets. Maybe he'd won while he was away. He savoured the thought for a moment, knowing exactly what he'd do with his new-found wealth, but the chill in the house brought him back to reality.

He shivered, wishing he had asked Father Mac to turn on the heating, ready for his return. There were no other friends or neighbours to do so. Too dangerous. Neighbours were nosy. Friends pried. Friends! There were none left now. Who wants to be friends with a wife-killer? That's what they

41

thought. Judge and jury, though there'd never been a trial. There was always that doubt in their eyes, that lurking fear. He'd learned long ago that it was better to live anonymously. It was a lonely life, but better by far than ostracism and hostility. That's what he loved about his times abroad. Quite apart from the change in climate, he felt like a free man. No one knew or cared about his background. He had a clean slate.

He put the heating and the kettle on before going through the mail. Junk, most of it. That was all he ever got, apart from bills. And stuff from the cuttings agency, he reminded himself. They sent him all the articles about Daniel. *I'm proud of you, son,* he would think as he read of Daniel's achievements. But Caitlin? Darling Katie. What about her?

Sitting down with his cup of tea, Terry leafed through the mail. Bin, bin, bill. Bin, bill, bin, bin, bin. Bill, bin – what was this? With trembling hands, he opened the typewritten envelope. *Oh no. Oh, Jesus, God, no!*

        I know where she is. Your wife.
        And I know what you did...

The letter fluttered silently to the floor as he stumbled, blinded by tears, to the drinks cabinet. His hands were shaking as he reached for the whisky bottle.

Later – not much later – Terry Richardson was drunk. Drunk and crying and shaking. How could it all have started again? Why? Why now? He thought the blackmail had ended years ago.

Why *now!* He smashed his fist into the wall, breaking the whisky glass, cutting his hand. He didn't notice. *Bastard!* BASTARD! If only he knew who it was! But it was the same person, all right. The same dropped lower-case 'e', the same missing bit on the letter 'd'. BASTARD! He tore at the note in a frenzy, pieces falling like confetti. How had his tormentor tracked him down? He'd moved and moved over the years. Not far enough, obviously. *I have to go abroad. No one will find me there.* The resolution was like fire in his gut. Would he go on paying for ever? How much had he paid in the past? Why had it stopped so suddenly all those years ago, only to start again now? He was pacing the room like a caged animal, round and round in circles. Then he fell to the floor, dry sobs racking his thin body. He couldn't go on like this. He just couldn't.

It was a long time before Caitlin got round to opening her mail. Red-eyed, spent from crying, she'd soaked herself in a bath containing essential oils of rose and geranium. It was only as she descended the stairs afterwards that she'd noticed the pile of letters, where she'd left them on the hall table. Silently, uninterestedly, she had flicked through the envelopes, waiting for something to tell her that it needed opening now, rather than later. And there it was. A typewritten envelope with a dropped lower-case 'e' in the name of her street. *Oh God! Why is this happening? Why are such sick bastards allowed to walk this world?* She tore open the envelope.

I know where she is. Your mother.
I can take you to her...

Nina was surprised to hear Caitlin's voice behind her in the kitchen of the clinic. She hadn't heard her come in.

'Nina, I wonder if we could look at our diaries together? I – I'd like a consultation with you as soon as it's convenient.'

Nina was unable to hide her surprise. 'You're not well? And on your day off, too!'

Caitlin was trying to look casual and not succeeding.

That was a stupid question, Nina chided herself. *She looks like shit.*

'I – think I could do with a little help.'

'Sure. Of course.'

Together, they walked the short distance to the reception area, waiting as Penny cast a skilful eye over their diaries. An initial consultation? Nina allowed an hour and a half for that...

'Three o'clock today looks OK.' She smiled brightly at them, so glad she'd had that quiet word with Nina last week. She'd been right. Something must be wrong for Caitlin to make an appointment with Nina. She fervently hoped it was nothing serious. She couldn't ever remember Caitlin being ill.

The two practitioners looked at each other. Caitlin nodded. Three o'clock it was.

There was time to kill before her appointment so she went for a walk, unaware of the gloating tread which followed her. She walked slowly, head down, hands in her pockets, struggling to

44

come to terms with what this consultation would mean. It was a double-bind, really. She was turning to Nina because she trusted her both as a practitioner and as a friend. She couldn't tell all the things she'd have to tell to someone she didn't know. On the other hand, it was extra difficult precisely *because* she knew Nina. What if Nina turned away from her, withdrew her friendship?

Caitlin had had many superficial friendships since she'd left home. She grimaced at the way she'd phrased the thought, corrected herself. *Since I ran away from home.* Yes, they had been superficial. But that meant they hadn't really been friendships at all. Real friendship was about love and trust, things she found enormously difficult. She felt as if she'd lived her entire adult life wrapped in a cloak of invisibility. She simply adjusted it now and then, allowing little chinks of herself to show through. Only the things she wanted to show, of course. That was the point. *She* controlled it. If she were to go through with this appointment with Nina, she would have to rip off that cloak, expose herself. Tell her friend the truth.

Oh, but she's looking pale today! The letter-writer rejoiced at the sight of Caitlin as she made her way back to the clinic. *You are in my power now. I have you. No more running away, upsetting my plans. Oh yes, I have you now. And this is just the beginning...*

The snow hadn't spread as far as Darrowdale,

though a bad weather warning had been issued. Deborah Harvey had a brief word with her editor before setting off.

'...so I thought I'd suss the place out. Incognito. Before the Open Day.'

'And how are you planning to do that?' Derek Kenny eyed her over the top of his glasses.

'The Tea Room. The Gift Shop and Tea Room are open all year round. Just thought I'd get the feel of the place, you know?'

'I do know. It's bloody cold in winter.' He gave her a long look. 'Well, if you're going to the Gift Shop, you might as well talk to Ronnie Walters. Tell her I sent you.'

There were only two customers in the Tea Room when Deborah Harvey made her entrance. A tall, big-boned woman, dark hair streaked with grey, was taking soup and bread to their table. It smelled wonderful, reminding her that she'd missed breakfast, having had to cover a collision between an ambulance and a fire engine. She sank into a chair, grateful for the warmth of the place. Although her car heater worked well, the short walk from the car park to the old stable block housing the Tea Room and Gift Shop had left her open to a biting wind which already carried tiny needles of snow. The land was exposed here, a broad track bounded by dry-stone walls leading away for quite some distance before winter-bare trees became visible.

'Another brave soul, I see! What can I get you?'

'The soup smells wonderful – what is it?'

'Home-made winter vegetable.' The woman

46

had a broad and attractive smile.

'I'll have that then, please. And a pot of tea.'

'We have several varieties...' The woman proffered a menu, pointing out the choices. Deborah chose Assam and watched as the woman walked away. She took off her coat, taking in her surroundings. Dark wood. Gleaming copper. A real log fire. Had it looked like this when the Richardsons lived here? She settled herself, not having long to wait before her order was brought over. She heard a voice call after the woman as she left the kitchen, and looked at her with renewed interest.

'Excuse me. I just heard someone call you Ronnie? Are you by any chance Veronica Walters?'

The thick, dark eyebrows lifted fractionally. 'Indeed I am. But I don't believe we've met?'

'No. I'm Deborah Harvey. I thought you worked in the Gift Shop. Derek Kenny sent me. He said you might talk to me about the Laura Richardson disappearance. I'm researching the story for the twentieth anniversary next year.'

The brown eyes clouded over briefly. Ronnie pulled out a chair at Deborah's table and sat down.

'Poor Derek! One last push before he retires, eh?' She shook her head. 'He never did get over it.'

Deborah's internal radar kicked in, but she kept her voice level.

'So you'll talk to me?'

'Of course I will.' She stood up. 'But not today, I'm afraid. You were right. I usually do work in the Gift Shop but this, believe it or not, is my day off! I'm standing in here until one o'clock – Gina's off visiting her sick mother. Once she's back, I'm making a rare trip into town to do some Christmas shopping.'

'No problem. When would be a convenient time?'

Ronnie thought for a minute. 'We have an Open Day next weekend. How about then? I could give you plenty of time and you'd be ... less conspicuous.' She pulled a face, momentarily embarrassed. 'Some members get fed up with it being raked over every year. Feel it reflects badly on the Community. Especially the ones who weren't here at the time.'

Deborah nodded sympathetically. 'But you don't mind talking to me? You're sure?'

'Laura Richardson was my friend. I'll never rest, not knowing what happened to her.'

On her return to the newspaper offices, Deborah went straight to the archives. Derek had given her all the stuff relating to Laura Richardson's disappearance. What she wanted now was every reference to the Darrowdale Community before and afterwards. *My, my!* she thought as her search bore fruit. *What a lot there is, too...*

Derek smiled to himself when he heard of Deborah's raid on the archives. She would come to him, of course. To ask questions. It would be a relief, truth be told. Nobody had questioned him since Laura disappeared. It had been the police back then, and he hadn't been completely truthful. Maybe now was the time to come clean...

Daniel Richardson was not popular with his girlfriend. He had spent yet another weekend in London and her patience was running thin. She'd phoned him and, grudgingly, he'd agreed to go back to Devon – to her – for the coming one. Daniel ended the conversation, shaking his head in frustration. How had he got into this? *Christ! What the fuck is wrong with me? How many girlfriends? And it always ended like this, with me not being arsed to actually call it a day, so the shit flies and they hate me for it.* What was it Boysie said? He snorted derisively. Boysie was a member of one of the chart-topping bands Daniel worked with. Into all that New Age crap. Said we choose our experiences. Choose the families we're born into. *Bollocks! No one in their right mind would have chosen mine. Mum and Cait, yeah. But Dad? What happened?... Bollocks to the lot of it.*

Josh Middleton loved Christmas. Brought up in a liberal family of mixed Jewish and Christian parentage, he believed he'd had the best of both worlds. Christmas and Hanukkah. A double blaze of light. How he'd loved the light, the stories! *That's the bottom line in any religion*, he thought. *The coming of light. Enlightenment.* He saw his profession in the same way. Bringing light into dark places. That way, healing could come.

He struggled along the High Street, dodging the children, prams, pushchairs and shopping trolleys being wielded like weapons by the harassed pedestrians on all sides. That was one thing he *didn't* like about Christmas. Commercialisation run riot. The shops had been decorated

49

and stuffed with Christmas goods since October. October! They had no respect for the seasons, no thought of light. Just profits. It saddened him to see society so far out of balance. *Selling our inheritance for a mess of pottage*, he thought glumly. *Soul-loss on a huge scale*. How could you help your children have enough of a sense of identity to stand up against all this? To find the light amid so much darkness?

Josh had always wanted children. Wanted to share, to pass on the joy and security of his own childhood. Finding the right woman to have them with was another matter. He'd worked hard, had plenty of love to give, but apart from a couple of false alarms, had never found the woman who wanted to share her life with him. Most women he'd met seemed to fall into two distinct camps where his work was concerned: fascinated game-playing or suspicion bordering on fear; as if he were always analysing them, or at the very least, might. Not Caitlin, though. His heart warmed at the thought of her, bringing him back to his reason for braving the ravening hordes today. He was trying to find a Christmas present for her. He was in a quandary over what to buy. Personal, but not *too* personal. Don't push it.

He was no fool, either personally or pro-fessionally. She was hiding a major trauma, of that he was sure, but he had to gain her trust. She would tell him when she was ready. He was bomb-proof. Came with the territory. Whatever it was, he could handle it. No one could get to Caitlin's age without baggage. She was alive with

50

him. Vibrant. And yet he recognised that degree of personal reticence. The way she never referred to her family. Well, not quite never. Her mother was dead. She had one brother, a famous record producer, but rarely saw him. Lost touch with her father. But that was it. Bare facts. No shared memories. Always skirting round references to them. Coolness. Distance. No warmth there, not like when he talked about his own family.

Josh was skilled enough to know that something had shattered her ability to trust. Trust took time to build, but Josh Middleton was a patient man. He could wait – would wait – as long as necessary.

So what should he buy? It was difficult and frustrating. They'd been seeing one another for four months. Ecological clean-ups. Gigs. Movies. Meals out. Skittles, of course, with Mike and Nina. Not quite as much time on their own as he would have liked. Nothing wrong with her sexual responses, though she hadn't yet committed herself to a full-blown relationship. He had no problem with that, despite his own wants. How often had he counselled clients who had started a relationship on a tidal wave of sexual passion, only to discover they had nothing in common once the initial excitement had passed, as, inevitably, it did? Not abuse, then. Almost certainly not. But it lay in her family background somewhere.

He often talked about his family. It came naturally. His brother in London, his two sisters, one in America, one in Israel. And his parents, of course. He'd hoped to take her to meet them at

51

Christmas, but she was committed at the Night Shelter on Christmas Eve, Christmas Day and Boxing Day. Maybe afterwards, then. He still held out hope for afterwards. For New Year, perhaps. He knew she had time off, no clients until after the fifth. A lot would depend on how things went at Mike and Nina's cottage.

Personal, but not too personal. His mind came back to the search for a Christmas present. It was a bit like walking a tightrope, really. Enough to let her know I care. Not enough to scare her off. Josh was good at balancing acts. He'd find the right thing.

Come on, Physician, get your act together! How much time had he just spent thinking about her? He smiled to himself, coming to a halt by a jeweller's window. Synchronicity at work, and right on the button. *Bugger being sensible. Bugger walking tightropes. I'm in love with Caitlin O'Connor.*

Nina's treatment room fascinated her clients. There was a bookcase, stuffed with tomes on plants and herbalism, and a large desk, like Caitlin's, bearing her treatment forms, a blotter and a box of paper tissues. A telephone hung on the wall beside the desk, calls routed only through Penny or to her answer phone after hours. Beside that was the tapestry Nina had made herself, colours of every hue shining from the healing plants it depicted. On the other side of her desk was the framed calligraphy. She had liked Caitlin's so much, she'd asked where she'd got it, somehow not surprised when Caitlin said

52

she'd done it herself. It had been given to Nina as a birthday gift.

It was obvious, from the day Penny had had a word in her ear, that her friend was troubled, but Nina felt a deeper unease as she looked at the shelves that fascinated her clients the most. A metal racking system held row upon row of brown glass bottles containing the healing tinctures of Nina's craft. Centuries ago, she might have been branded a witch, burned at the stake or crushed to death for being so in touch with nature. Closed minds. Control freaks. Hierarchical structures. Nina had no time for that. Her beliefs didn't have a name, as far as she knew. She wasn't a Wiccan and disliked the term 'Pagan', feeling it was too wide and woolly. Since the advent of New Ageism, it had once again been used in pejorative tones, signalling a new wave of intolerance.

No, it wouldn't do. Her beliefs and practices resisted labelling, even by herself, and she had had them for a long time; not some static abstract code, but a living, ever growing and developing experience and interaction between herself and – what? God? Another word she disliked. Full of Christian, patriarchal associations. She thought of herself in terms of connectedness to all things, to the very Source of Being, whoever or whatever that may be. She had long ago resigned herself to not having answers. Some people had to have answers. Nina accepted mystery; understood herself to be a part of it.

The thought of having Caitlin as a client bothered her. She was so private, so self-contained.

Nina was used to being privy to confidential information. All practitioners were. So why did the thought of Caitlin's confidences disturb her so much? She closed her eyes, sat with the thought, the minutes ticking by, closer to three o'clock. *Because whatever Caitlin is going to tell me, she hasn't told me, yet, as a friend. Something terrible has happened and she doesn't know where else to turn. She has no one else to turn to.* With a compassionate heart, Nina sent out a mental message. *I'm here for you, Caitlin. Whatever it is, I'm here for you. I'm your friend.*

Caitlin arrived a few moments later, taking a seat by the desk. The chair was comfortable, neither too soft nor too hard. For one irrational moment, an image of Goldilocks and the Three Bears paraded through her mind. She was sitting in Baby Bear's chair.

'Right then!' Nina smiled. She'd decided to change her usual routine. Normally, she would first ask the client what the immediate problem was, then take their medical history before proceeding further. She would reverse it with Caitlin, give her time to relax.

'If I can just take your medical history first, Caitlin? Get an overview of your health before we begin?'

Caitlin nodded, mouth dry. It would all have to come out.

She hadn't noticed the teapot until now. Nina was pouring two cups. 'Lime flower. Relaxing without being soporific.' Caitlin took the cup. Nina gave no sign that she'd seen her hands shaking.

'So, routine childhood ailments – measles, mumps, chickenpox?'

'All of them. No problems as far as I know.'

'Good. Anything else? Anything out of the ordinary?'

'Not really. Not as a child. I was disgustingly healthy. Came from living in the country, being outdoors a lot. I – I was brought up in a Community. Sort of like a Commune, but more respectable. Professional people with a common philosophy, pooling resources and stuff. So I had plenty of fresh air and organic food.' Caitlin was babbling, she knew, but couldn't stop herself.

'Right. That sounds good.'

'It was. I loved it.' *Loved it, then hated it. Hated the concerned looks, the whispers. The unspoken thoughts.*

'Any other illnesses?' Nina brought her back to the point. Caitlin was looking at her hands. They lay in her lap, fluttering like butterflies.

'I had pneumonia. Nearly died. I was nineteen. Nineteen and a half.'

'You were hospitalised?'

'Yes.'

'Still living in the Community?'

'No. I was in London.' She took a deep breath. 'I left home ... ran away from home when I was seventeen.'

'Ran away?' Nina spoke softly, letting her pen fall idle.

'Yes. You see, there's something you need to know...'

Nina listened with a growing sense of horror as Caitlin's story unfolded. So much made sense

55

now. No wonder her friend had been reticent. She kept her face calm and her voice gentle, but her heart bled as she coaxed out more.

The letter-writer had gone home. Enough had been seen for one day, and besides, there was always this evening. Caitlin's T'ai-Chi lessons weren't really a risk. They were enjoyable, in fact. Focused the mind, and anyway, there were other things to think of between now and then. Like what to do about the coming weekend.

When Nina got home that evening, she took a shower, her intention fixed on washing away the horror of her friend's story. Who would have imagined such trauma in Caitlin's life? Nina was deeply disturbed, not only by the background, but by the trigger that had led Caitlin to seek help. What sick mind was behind the evil of these letters? And they were evil, she had no doubt of that. Caitlin had brought them with her, passed them to Nina, and as soon as she'd touched them, Nina had known. Caitlin talked about them as though the writer were simply some sick crank, but Nina knew differently. They were dangerous. Whoever was writing them was filled with evil, destructive intent towards her friend.

Nina was still uneasy when she finished her ritual ablutions. Caitlin was in danger and she had to work out the best way to help her. She sighed, wrapping herself in her bathrobe. She'd advised Caitlin to take the letters to the police, but she wouldn't hear of it. Her life had been full of the police when her mother had disappeared, and later, in London, she had had to try to evade them. Nina could understand where she was coming from, but still, she needed protection.

Wiping the condensation from the bathroom mirror, she stared her reflection in the eye. There was more than one way to skin a cat, so the saying went. There was more than one way to protect Caitlin.

Later, and many miles away, Mags was settling down for the night. Thanks be to God – again – for disused farm buildings. She stuffed straw into her sleeping bag. A blizzard was sweeping the country, the likes of which hadn't been seen for years.

'Blessed Mother, keep me safe, please. I should be warm enough here, but food ... that will be a problem if I can't get to a town soon. And towns, as you know, are not very fond of the likes of me.' Her fingers went to the beads around her neck as she settled down to say the rosary.

Chapter Five

Friday 10 December

Veronica Walters squeezed her husband's shoulder as he pored over a pile of correspondence at the kitchen table. He ran his arm up her own, pulling her to him as she looked at the scattered envelopes on his desk.

'How's it going?' she asked. It had been Colin's idea to use the Open Day as an opportunity for former members of the Community to have a reunion.

'Better than expected. Nothing from the remaining Richardsons, of course. God knows where Terry and Caitlin are, but I did track down Daniel. I had hoped, you know... Just about everybody else is coming, though. If this is a success, I thought we might try one in the summer. Maybe after next year.' The memory of a different kind of summer event hung unspoken between them, broken only by the click of the electric kettle. 'I'll make the tea.'

Fancy finding Daniel, Veronica thought, remembering the turbulent teenager she'd last seen so many years ago. She'd heard that he was some kind of hot-shot in the music industry. Probably too busy to come. Probably wouldn't want to come anyway. Why should he? She shuddered at the thought of the memories this place must hold for him.

'You cold, Ronnie?' Colin asked, bearing tea on a tray with a plate of her favourite biscuits. Trust him to do it so nicely! He really was a treasure.

'No love. Someone just walked on my grave.'

The invitation to the Community Open Day had lain in a pile of low-priority mail for days before Daniel had finally come across it. Obviously done on a mail-merge, it was nonetheless personally signed by Colin Walters, one of the founder members of the Community. Daniel remembered him well. Mixed emotions washed over him as he read it. Christ! How long had it been since he was last there?

They'd stuck it out for two years after his mother went missing. He'd never been back. What was the point? It was just a reminder of the most awful time of his life. And yet... There *was* a point, he realised. Right now, there *was* a point. Someone there might know something about Caitlin. Know where she was, or at least have heard from her. *Christ, yes!* He wasn't sure how he'd feel about seeing the place again, but it had to be worth a try. Especially as he'd now had another letter, identical to the first. What if Caitlin were getting letters like that?

The thought of his father being on the receiving end of such missives never crossed his mind. He didn't know where he was and cared even less. He despised his father. Hated him for what he'd done.

Something didn't add up, Chris Farmer told himself, looking at the dates he'd been playing with on an A4 pad. Daniel Richardson had gone to University the year after his mother's disappearance. The father and sister had moved out of the Community the year after that. Caitlin had run away from home the year her brother had completed his degree. He sat back in his chair thoughtfully. Maybe it wasn't her father she was scared of, after all. Maybe it was the thought of big brother coming home that had frightened her away...

Still, at least he had a starting point in his search for Daniel Richardson's sister. He'd

59

tracked down the grandmother's will. The old woman had named Daniel and Caitlin as her only beneficiaries. Not equally divided, though. Mostly cash to Daniel, quite a tidy sum. And an even tidier sum for Caitlin, along with the house. He wondered how Daniel had felt about that. Still, it was a start. He wondered whether Caitlin had ever lived in it, or whether she'd just sold it. He'd soon find out.

Mags was one very happy woman. She'd helped a farmer dig out sheep caught in the blizzard that had descended two days ago, whiting out the landscape for as far as the eye could see. They'd let her stay, fed her, even given her some money. She felt rich beyond compare. The luxury of soaking in a real, hot bath had been over-whelming, warmth flooding through her and soaking into her joints. The farmer's wife, a practical woman, had given her some cast-offs, too. Woollen jumpers and a waterproof jacket. Mags doubted that the latter was really a cast-off at all, but was grateful, accepting the gift in the spirit in which it was given. She had worked hard around the place until the weather lifted, when they had promised to run her into the nearest village.

How good it was to smell sweet, she thought, remembering the way she had sniffed her body appreciatively before dressing in her new clothes. Life was good. Hard, but good. She wondered again where she'd like to be for Christmas. Life had a funny way of turning out, she mused, fingering her rosary beads. She'd be where she was meant to be.

She didn't feel as uncomfortable as usual to find herself among other people. The farmer's wife had dropped her off as promised. Snow still covered the ground but the main roads had been cleared and the sky was blue now. *It must be my appearance*, she thought, stealing a glance at her reflection in a shop window. Clean, and wearing the waterproof jacket over several layers of clothing, she could have passed for a serious walker rather than a lady of the road, which was her usual guise. She thought of stocking up on one or two things before continuing her journey south, but decided against it. She'd wait until the next big town. She hated towns, but supermarkets were so much cheaper.

'Well, I'll be buggered!' Colin Walters put down the phone and called out to his wife. 'Ronnie! Ronnie! You'll never guess who that was!'

Veronica Walters stuck her head round the door, the flour on the end of her nose betraying her activities in the kitchen.

'Who?'

Colin smiled at her, shaking his head in wonder. 'My wish came true, lover. That was Daniel Richardson. He's coming to the Open Day!'

Deborah Harvey had read through everything relating to the Darrowdale Community. The first few articles, covering the intended sale of the land and setting up of the place, had been written by a reporter who had long since moved on. The

NIMBY phenomenon – 'Not In My Backyard' – had been around even then. There was lurid coverage full of scare-mongering hysteria about what the spokesperson for the opposition variously called 'this evil in our midst', 'some Hippie commune' and 'advocates of free lust and irresponsibility'. *So predictable*, thought Deborah, shaking her head. *Some things never change.*

There *had* been a change in the tenor of the articles, however, once a new reporter had come along. A reporter whose by-line had since appeared on every article about the Community. Derek Kenny.

In Gloucestershire, the house had stood empty for almost a year and had come onto the books of Taylor Norris once the executors had given instructions to sell. A lot of people had wanted to view the property in the first couple of months. Curiosity seekers. Ghouls, some of them, simply wanting to see where it had happened. Jarvis Taylor knew it would be a tricky thing to handle. A rational man, it never ceased to amaze him how superstitious some people were about death. While acknowledging that this had not been a natural one, it nonetheless irked him that it had the power, in certain minds at least, to delay the sale of what was, after all, a most eminently desirable property.

The house was set in three acres of grounds on a hill four miles north-east of the town, set back and hidden behind a thick hedge. The only access was through wrought-iron gates that led onto a gravelled drive which wound its way between the flower beds bordering the front lawns. At least the executors had understood the necessity of maintaining the grounds. To have done otherwise would not have been conducive to bringing about a sale.

A low double-garage and boat house lay to the left of the house, with parking space in front for several other vehicles. The house itself, architect-designed some seventeen years ago, was beautiful, light and spacious. The kitchen seemed to be every woman's dream, with its multiplicity of cupboard space, working surfaces and appliances of every kind. The tiled floor, in terracotta shades, gave off a feeling of warmth and was easy to clean. Jarvis Taylor knew this because he'd heard women talking about it. They were not, however, women who would perform this task themselves. Anyone who could afford to buy and run Hermitage House could afford the services of a cleaner.

A walk-in larder and utility room led off one side of the kitchen, a dining room and entrance hall off the other. The entrance hall hid a shower room as well as the door to the cellar, but the eyes of most people were immediately drawn to the imposing staircase leading to the upper level. There were five bedrooms up there, two of them with en-suite facilities, as well as a family bathroom with every fitting imaginable. That was where it had happened. Bloody suicides are never pleasant, but at least the owner, a retired professional, had had the consideration to cut his wrists in the bath. Baths are easy to clean, easy to replace, unlike the case in a sale he had handled some years ago which had necessitated scrubbing floors, replacing carpets and redecorating an entire room. It was sad, really. The owner's wife had died in the summer and it seemed he hadn't got over the loss. But to kill oneself on Christmas Day...

Back in the hall again, one passed through into the sitting room, superbly crafted and with a stunning feature fireplace. Beyond this was the Games Room, a split-level affair, from one side of which a spiral staircase led to the Guest Suite, ingeniously designed and with a skylight built into the ceiling. All the downstairs rooms had full-length, full-width windows at the back, looking out over the patio and swimming pool to the grounds beyond with their maturing plants and trees concealing the summer house, sheds and workshops.

Jarvis Taylor's hopes after the last viewing had finally paid off. They'd loved it. Made an offer which had been accepted. Senior Executive. Company relocation. Very keen. At last, after its season of abandonment, Hermitage House would become a home again.

Caitlin had barely got through the week, despite the absence of further letters. Her care for her clients never faltered, but Nina knew what it was costing her in terms of emotional energy. She had been easily persuaded to get away and spend the weekend – a long weekend, for she did not work Mondays – at Nina's cottage.

'A change of scene will do you good. You'll be undisturbed and able to rest.' Caitlin didn't argue, and Nina didn't voice the relief she felt. Never mind resting – Caitlin would be safe, away from the letter-writer who knew both where she worked and where she lived. *I can't hide her forever*, Nina acknowledged, *but I can do this, giving her a breathing space.* It would also give Nina the chance to take some of the action she'd decided upon. A two-pronged approach, temporal and spiritual. Caitlin had readily agreed to let Nina have a key to her house. If any more letters came, Nina would intercept them first. That in itself was a trouble shared, but it also meant that Nina could put some protection in place.

Angela Fielding had gone into the organic food store only because she had spotted it by accident. *Damn!* she thought. *I would have used it, had I known it were here.* She had been in Cheltenham for over a week, touring in a play which had come to the town's Everyman Theatre. It had been fun. They'd had a good reception, good reviews, and she'd stayed on, using the town as a base for a few days' exploration of the Cotswolds. She was preparing to go home now and had been buying presents for Tony Payne, her partner. She always bought presents when she'd been away, even if only for a short time. But the organic food store gave her an opportunity to buy healthy snacks for the long drive home.

She browsed for a while, impressed by the range of goods on offer, only noticing the presence of the upstairs café as she rounded the end of the aisle from which she had chosen a particularly good vegetarian organic wine. *Why not?* she thought to herself. *Might as well make the most of it.* So she paid for her purchases and made her way up the wide flight of stairs, head down, putting her wallet back into her handbag. Which was why she bumped into someone coming down the stairs.

'I'm sorry!' The words were a reflex. Had she thought about it, she would have realised that the other woman couldn't have been looking where she was going, either. She didn't think about that because she was too busy looking at the woman's face. Good God! It couldn't be? Surely not...

'Caitlin? Is it Caitlin?'

Caitlin stared at her in equal astonishment.

'Angela! What on earth are you doing here?'

'I could ask you the same thing!' Angela drew her to the wall, allowing an elderly man to pass.

'I live here,' Caitlin told her.

'If I'd known, I'd have looked you up! I was at the Everyman for a week and stayed on for a few days. It's *so* good to see you!'

Angela meant it. She had always had a soft spot for Caitlin. She'd been so talented and enthusiastic. Her eyes swept the woman's face, her appearance. Woman! God! She'd been just a girl last time Angela had seen her. Yet it was unmistakably her: taller, older, but still Caitlin Richardson. No wedding ring, she noticed, as the question crossed her mind.

'Please – come and join me for coffee. What are you doing now? I've read about Daniel, of course, but completely lost track of you.'

'I'm sorry, I can't.' Caitlin resisted the pull on

her arm. On top of the events of the past week, she couldn't cope with the shock of yet another ghost from her past coming back to haunt her. She had only popped into the shop to gather a few things before driving to Nina's cottage. 'I have an appointment. I'm so sorry to have missed you – I didn't realise you were in town.' That much, at least, was true. She pulled a business card from her bag. 'Please get in touch with me. I'm so sorry, I really do have to dash.' Hastily, she scribbled her home details on the back of the card before almost running down the stairs.

Angela Fielding watched her leave, dumbstruck, for once in her life. Good Lord! Caitlin Richardson! *Not* Caitlin Richardson, she corrected herself, looking at the business card. Caitlin O'Connor. Oh God! Hadn't that been Laura's maiden name? *Shit! You silly cow,* she chided herself. After her own excitement at seeing Caitlin again, it had only just occurred to her that, for Caitlin, it may not have been an equally pleasant experience. She resumed her ascent of the stairs, found a seat at a table. *God!* she thought. *I'm probably just an unwelcome reminder of her mother's disappearance.*

Then there'd been the other business, of course. She had voted against that. It was all very well people suspecting that Terry had had a hand in his wife's disappearance but... She felt uncomfortable at the memory. Some had come straight out and said they thought he'd killed her. Preposterous! And it wasn't as if he'd been charged with anything. Far more to the point, from Angela's perspective, was the issue of Caitlin and her brother. If one *did* suppose that Terry had harmed Laura, was it not of even greater importance for the Community to exercise responsibility towards the children by keeping them in their midst? They could at least have kept an eye on them. She'd been shot down at the meeting by arguments about how that hadn't helped Laura. While having to admit that was true, she had nonetheless always believed that they could have done more, particularly for Caitlin.

Her worst fears had been realised when the girl herself had gone missing a couple of years later. There had been a very ugly scene when Terry had turned up at the Community, convinced they were hiding her. The police had had a field day. First the wife, now the daughter. But Caitlin had made contact with her grandmother a few days later, refusing to give details of her whereabouts, simply assuring her that she was safe. God! She must have been in the middle of A Levels when she'd done a runner. That must have screwed up her chances of University. Angela had often wondered where she had gone and what she had made of herself. Aromatherapy? She would never have put her down for that kind of career, had always assumed she'd write or act. She had certainly had the talent. *Maybe she tried and it didn't work out. But still. Aromatherapy!* She tucked the card away. At least now she'd have some up-to-date news to share when she got home.

Terry Richardson was in a maudlin mood.

Christmas was fast approaching, and how he hated Christmas! So different from the old days when his family had been intact. He'd loved it then. Absolutely loved it. His eyes blurred with tears as he turned the pages of the photograph albums. Caitlin, skipping in the garden, a gap-toothed grin across her face; Daniel, hanging upside down from a tree; Laura, shrieking as the children threw buckets of water over her at the seaside.

One picture in particular, Terry stared at for a long time. It had been taken just a week before Laura disappeared. There weren't many photographs of the four of them together. So who had taken this one, then? He frowned, trying to remember, then laughed out loud. Doc had taken it to mark the occasion of Daniel passing his driving test. They were all clustered around Laura's car and he'd come along and offered to take a photo. Caitlin was sitting on the roof, and he and Laura were standing either side of Daniel, who had been captured tossing his 'L' plates into the air. There it was, frozen in time, a piece of family history. Irrevocable as the line that had intersected their lives a week later. There was no photograph to mark that event. The defining event, dividing his life into unequal measures. Before Laura. After Laura. Even things like the Berlin Wall had been knocked down. This was something that could never be erased.

Where did it all go wrong? How many times had he asked himself that question over the years? He shook his head and blew his nose noisily. *It was all my fault. I must have been crazy.*

One moment of madness, never thinking of the consequences, and it cost me everything, destroyed all I ever worked for. He shook his head again. He had made up his mind. If there was one more letter, he would kill himself.

Josh was disappointed at the prospect of Caitlin's absence for the weekend. She hadn't even said where she was going, just that she had to get away for a few days. Even Nina, when he'd seen her, was unusually quiet. He wondered if she knew something he didn't. Caitlin had sounded tired, and that wasn't like her. He hoped she wasn't sickening for something. He hoped, above all, that she wasn't growing tired of him...

Mags was grateful for out-of-town supermarkets. They didn't suit everyone, she knew, but it saved her having to go right into the heart of a place, with all the noise and dirt, traffic and people. No, out-of-towns were much better for her. Straight in, straight out, and skirt the town itself. She was still clean enough to avoid the attention she had come to fear and, with a shopping list long since formed in her head, was able to gather the few things she needed with relative ease. It was only when she reached the check-out that she saw the poster on the noticeboard behind it. An Open Day at the Darrowdale Community. The Darrowdale Community! *Saints in Heaven!*

She felt a sudden rush of blood to her head. *Oh, don't let that start again! Not the headaches! I haven't had the headaches for years!* But Darrowdale... Visions of Terry and Caitlin and Daniel

70

swam and blurred through her mind.

'Are you alright?' An arm around her shoulder. It was the woman standing behind her in the queue. And now the boy at the check-out was asking if he should call an ambulance.

'No, no! Really, I'm alright. It will pass.'

They led her to a chair beneath the poster, where she sat, head between her knees, the weight of the world upon her shoulders. Worse than that. Guilt. Unexpiated guilt. How long did it take to expiate guilt such as hers? The floor manager had arrived now. They were talking about her as if she weren't there. Holy Mother! She had to get away! Get outside. If they took her to hospital there'd be forms and questions, endless questions, and she couldn't cope with that. She had to get out of here. Was she mad? What had happened to her sense of direction, her powers of observation? How in God's name had she come to be near that place once more? She had never thought to see it again in her life. When she had left, it had been for good. It took her a while to work out that it must have been almost twenty years ago.

Late that night, Daniel Richardson tossed restlessly in his bed, halfway between waking and sleeping. He seldom slept alone, and the experience discomfited him. Women were his lifeline, his link to sanity. His mind drifted between anticipation and apprehension at the thought of returning to his childhood home. Would *it* still be there? The image of *it* floated into his brain, inviting him to remember what he had been

71

doing that afternoon. The day his mother had disappeared. To remember what it was he had been unable to tell his father when he went home...

God, was he glad to get rid of Cait! He was lucky, he knew. Several of his friends had younger sisters and they were a real pain. Cait was a just a pain. A real pain was having a kid sister who wanted to go everywhere with you, do everything with you. At least she didn't try that! She always had her head stuck in books or mooched around like she could talk to the trees or clouds or something. Sometimes he wondered if she was quite right in the head. He, on the other hand, liked to be where the action was, and action-a-plenty there would be this afternoon. As always. Regular as clockwork.

He felt himself grow hard at the thought. Christ! How he loved his dick! He rubbed it furtively through his jeans, heading off to the trees as it swelled and bulged against the coarse fabric, begging to be let out. Oh, Christ! What must it be like to be inside a woman? He imagined the softness, the all-enveloping slipperiness...

Crashing through the undergrowth, he ripped down his zip, letting it out, letting it breathe. He sucked air through his nose, steadying himself. He wanted to see it, feel it, play with it, make it last as long as possible before it spurted forth its milky whiteness. Oh yes ... yes... In the safety of a bush, he groaned as he gripped it in his left hand, mind rerunning the scenes, the live action he watched every week with his friends.

Who had found it first? It had been the summer prior to his mother's disappearance. Ah yes. One of the kids who stayed at the Community during the summer holidays. Stumbled on it by chance. Daniel had wondered what he'd been doing out on that part of the land, anyway. It wasn't so much that it was off-limits to the kids – 'junior members of the Community' – but that it was so far out, at the border furthest from the hub of houses and Community activity. It bordered, in fact, further wild acreage owned by a small community of monks.

That far piece of their own land was due to be cleared and would have appeared impenetrable to anyone with an ounce of sense. Which cut out the weird kid as well as Will Dutton, a fellow child of the Community, who'd been with him at the time. Misfits, both of them, and no mistake. Daniel and his friends hadn't wanted either of them around, which was probably why they'd hung out together. So they'd gone there and found it. Found *them,* and come running back to tell the other boys .

They couldn't believe it when they arrived, red-faced, sweating, and Will with cum all over the front of his trousers. He started babbling and they didn't believe him at first. Teasing him, calling him a little wanker. He cried, saying he hadn't been wanking, it had just happened when the man had shoved his dick in the woman's cunt.

'You saw that? You actually saw it?' Daniel knew he wasn't the only one getting hard, hearing that. And so they told them. Gave them a blow-by-blow account, so to speak. There was no way they could be making it up. They'd seen it, alright. Seen the fluffy triangle of pubic hair, seen the woman rubbing herself, then the man kneel down and lick her. Lick her! Christ! And

73

then the man had stood up and turned, his giant dick gleaming and wobbling. It was huge, Will said. Really huge. Daniel wasn't sure he believed that. Will Dutton was a runt of a kid, so he probably had a mini-dick to match.

They made them tell the rest of it, then, how the woman had lain down and spread her legs, so that the peepers could see the wetness round her cunt, and how the man had knelt above her, holding his dick, shoving it into her, then in and out, in and out, clenched buttocks straining with each thrust.

Every boy listening was rock hard now, watching Will Dutton's face, the glazed look in his eyes as the story poured out of him. And the noises they'd described! Moaning, grunting, groaning... Justin Smith hadn't cared about the presence of the others, then, just got his knob out, veins bulging blue against the purple-hued tumescence in his grip.

The peepers continued to talk. About slurping noises, slapping noises, of how she'd bucked under him, wrapping her legs around his arse, crying out when she came.

The boys looked at each other furtively when the story finished. When they finished.

'What?' laughed Daniel, who had whooped triumphantly as his own spunk had spurted and soared. 'We live in a Community, don't we? What's wrong with a communal wank?'

In Nina's cottage, Caitlin hadn't wanted to go to bed. She had been busy making arrangements to visit a friend, a real friend she hadn't seen for some time but with whom she still corresponded regularly. Why hadn't she thought of it before?

74

This friend knew her from the old days, knew everything about her past, unlike Nina, who'd been told only the bare essentials necessary to explain her reaction to that initial letter. So tomorrow she was going down to see Sheila. A jumble of emotions fought for recognition. *So much for trying to put my feelings on hold.* She took a deep breath. *It will be alright. Things can't possibly get any worse.*

She'd thought again about what she'd told Nina. About the day she'd run away. God! The things we do! So much wouldn't have happened had she stayed at home. But it hadn't been home any more. She'd hated the move. Dad had said it was for the best, that it would be much easier for her when she was old enough for Sixth Form, but she knew that wasn't the real reason. She wasn't stupid. She knew even then what people thought. What she herself had wondered and feared. Guilt. Her life had become one huge mess of guilt. How could she even think that, for a second? She had hated the whispers behind her back. And she had come to hate her father. She didn't know him any more. He frightened her, with his drinking and mood swings.

The thinking had unsettled her and she had lain awake for more than two hours, memories churning through her mind, afraid to go to sleep in case she dreamed of that day when he'd cracked and she'd cracked and the pieces had been beyond repair. She was right to be afraid. When she could fight sleep no longer, the images had whirled and twisted inside an age-old fog, finally breaking free.

The kitchen was dark and yet she could see in the dark, and understood this ability to be common to cats and her seventeen-year-old self. Her father lurched through the door like Frankenstein's monster, matches propping open his eyelids, yellow, dried-out eyes staring above the dark bags that seemed to grow blacker and bigger even as she looked at him. His clothes, shoddy and rumpled, were highlighted by a malodorous glow, a luminosity that extended to the drip attached to his body, its tubes coiling around him like living, writhing snakes which fed alcohol directly into his sunken veins.

The door of the cuckoo-clock snapped back, its occupant calling, 'Look at the door! Look at the door!', but her father didn't hear it, too busy muttering to himself, unsteady hands grasping at the kitchen table as he went round and round, bare, filthy feet gouging a circle in the floor that became wider and deeper until it seemed like an empty moat, incalculable in depth and yet into which he did not sink, turning, instead, to grab her by the shoulders.

'Don't lose your head! Don't lose your head!' The cuckoo had turned into a parrot now, a living one which fluffed its plumage as it spoke.

The milk bottle in her hand fell to the floor as her father began to shake her like a rag doll, yet she did not feel the shaking, was somehow curiously detached, her sight focused and acute, watching as the glass shattered, as the milk spread across the tiles before being sucked into the moat where it churned and rolled before gathering itself into a slowly building wave which hung, unmoving, waiting – she knew it was waiting, but did not know for what, or why or how it did so.

76

The shaking continued and she tried to loosen her father's grip, but his hands were like claws, nails like talons, digging deeper and deeper into her screaming flesh until she was sure the bones would show and the blood – drip, drip – why did it drip so slowly? – rush towards the milky tidal wave and turn it into frothing, crimson foam. And when she thought she could bear it no longer, he let go. Stopped. And she realised that he'd lifted her off the floor only as she fell, broken glass and blood and milk crushing into her arms and legs and buttocks as she hit the ground, staring after his retreating back. And the snakes around him hissed, 'Daniel!', and the cuckoo and the parrot together mimicked them and mocked her. 'Where's Daniel? Where's Daniel? Where's Daniel?' And the other noises started then, crashing, breaking, roaring noises, and she was aware, even as she went after her father, of the tidal wave beginning to move, to creep along behind her and she opened her mouth to shout for Mummy and Daniel but no sound came. It was locked inside her chest and no matter how she tried, she couldn't let it out. All she could see was wreckage. All she could hear was wreckage, but suddenly, and yet in slow motion, her father had no more possessions to smash. Only she was left and he looked at her and knew and the tidal wave – when had it changed from creep to rush? – the tidal wave engulfed them both and she was drowning, drowning, drowning...

Chapter Six

Saturday 11 December

As Caitlin boarded the coach, she wondered again why she had chosen this means for her journey. On one level, at least, it was easy to rationalise; it saved her the hassle of driving and having to find a parking space when she got to London. She was uneasy, however, recognising that other levels had come into play. She had taken the coach to London the day she had run away from home, fifteen years ago, and after her nightmare she needed no salt rubbing into the wound.

Back then, it had been summer. Perhaps that was as well. She had been unprepared in many ways and doubted she would have found the city as hospitable had she arrived in conditions as bleak and wintry as today's.

She settled back in her seat and closed her eyes. She didn't want to think about it, but lulled by the motion and warmth of the overheated coach, found the memories impossible to shake.

It had been terrible that day. The start of it was bad enough, Dad being drunk and Daniel not being at home. But when Dad had lost it... She shuddered, experiencing again the sheer terror she had felt when he had started smashing up the house. He was like a madman, and she had found herself drowning in a jumble of emotions which had crashed over her like a tidal wave. The fear had been palpable. Not just the fear of what he was doing then, but seeing him in that light, suddenly crazy, a side of his nature previously unknown to her, had reawakened the fear she had so long repressed, the fear that he *was* responsible for Mum's disappearance, *had* done something to her. That he might even have killed her...

The scene before her eyes had been all the more terrifying because of the silence. Not that what he was doing was silent, of course – you can't hurl furniture and smash things to pieces without noise. It was the fact that *he* was silent, never said a word while he was throwing himself around like a man possessed; himself and anything he could get hold of, and that had included her when she'd tried to intervene.

Had he done something similar to Mum? She remembered the total sense of shock when he had first hit her, sending her flying across the room with the force of his blow. It had seemed totally unreal. Unbelievable. Yet he *had* done it, had gone on doing it, not content with one strike. It was as if all the pent-up rage he had felt about Daniel's absence had been unleashed on her. How she had even managed to scream, she wasn't sure. The shock seemed to paralyse her voice as well as her body to begin with, but it had soon become apparent that there was no one around to hear her. More to the point, rather than shocking Dad into stopping the beating, it seemed only to enrage him further.

Even now, after all this time, Caitlin felt physically sick as she remembered her desperate bid to crawl away from him, her right arm stretching out to clutch at the nearest thing she could reach. She'd never been entirely sure what it was she'd hit her father with. Most likely a broken chair leg. But hit him she had, again and again, raining blows on his head and body until he had finally let go of her, reeling backwards, stumbling among the wreckage he had created before falling to the floor.

She had thought at first that she had killed him. Panic had stabbed at her, washed through her, and she had rushed for the phone, only to find it dead, torn from its socket. *Oh God, oh God, I have to get away!* That had been her only thought. It had then crystallised into going to Gran's, but she had dismissed the idea as quickly as it had arisen, knowing it was the first place the police would look for her. What could she do? She had hesitated, hearing her father moan, then run up the stairs and thrown things – her things, her clothes – into a holdall, willy-nilly. Not entirely willy-nilly, though. Somehow she had had the sense to put her Post Office Savings Book in there. She had some cash from her Saturday job and – she was ashamed to think of it now – she had gone back to her semi-conscious father, telling herself she was simply checking that he was all right, as in not dead, or at least not *yet*, and taken money from the wallet in his jacket pocket.

Satisfied that he was, at least, still breathing, she had left the house, feeling horribly vulnerable and conspicuous as she had hurried down the road to catch the bus into the town centre. She had felt that everyone must be able to see what she had done as clearly as if her forehead had been branded. She was a thief. She might even be a murderer. Who was she even to think that Dad might have killed Mum when she herself had possibly killed her own father?

Guilt had gnawed at her so relentlessly that, just before boarding the London-bound coach, she had made an anonymous phone call to the ambulance service, only afterwards asking herself how she would know what had happened. She hadn't wanted to think about it then, and pushed it from her mind on the long journey south, forcing herself to make a plan of survival for when she reached the city and, please God, anonymity. In her own mind she had stepped so far beyond the boundaries of acceptable behaviour that she knew there was no going back. Even if Dad was all right, she could never live with him again. And Daniel – what about Daniel? She had cried silently, averting her face and pretending to sleep, thinking about the brother she had loved so much, yet who had not been there when she had needed him most. He was an adult now, with his own life. He certainly wouldn't be going back to live with Dad now that he'd completed his University course. She supposed he would get some sort of job, though she couldn't think what or where. She was on her own.

It was with mixed feelings that Caitlin, brought back to the present by the arrival of the bus at Heathrow Airport, finally got off the coach at

81

Victoria. Today, she was smartly dressed in a trouser suit, fashionable coat and hat. Back then, she had been wearing jeans, tee-shirt and a thin jacket. As she left Victoria, she remembered how, fifteen years ago, she had gone straight to the Ladies' toilet on arrival, and the shock she had experienced on seeing her reflection in the mirror. There may have been no mark of Cain on her forehead, but bruises and a cut lip were sadly in evidence. She had done quite a job on herself, thanking God that, along with clothes, she had packed her make-up. She had forced herself to walk to a café some distance away before stopping for a cup of tea and allowing herself to sit down and think about what to do next. She had been afraid that if she stayed at Victoria for too long, the police might swoop, looking for her. God, it hardly bore thinking about! Now, she could rationalise, look back and know that she had acted in self-defence. Back then, she had felt only guilt and fear, not recognising that she had, in fact, been lucky to leave the house alive.

Overcome with emotion, Caitlin took herself off, as she had done all those years earlier, to a café before continuing her journey. Sitting with a cup of coffee, she realised just how lucky she had been, and was amazed at the strong survival instinct she had shown as a naïve seventeen-year-old. She had, of course, looked older, especially after that judicious application of make-up. That was what had got her into a cheap hotel for her first night in the big city. She remembered the shock of finding herself in Soho at one point on her travels, staring in disbelief at signs in squalid doorways advertising the attentions of 'busty model, no rush' and 'massage with every extra a gentleman could wish for'. She had made sure she was well away from there before seeking out shelter for the night.

It had been another two days before she had plucked up the courage to phone Gran. It was awful to recognise, with hindsight, that it hadn't even crossed her mind that Gran or anyone else might be worried about her. Her primary motive in calling had been to ascertain the extent of her father's injuries, not out of concern for him, but because she had to know – she absolutely *had* to – whether or not she was a murderer. How on earth had Gran coped so well? Her voice had been full of relief, but she hadn't gone berserk or burst into tears as Caitlin had feared she might. The memory of their conversation still haunted her. The shock of hearing that Daniel had arrived before the ambulance was bad enough, but when Gran had told her that he had called the police because he was afraid Dad had killed *her*, she had been speechless. Gran had had to say, 'Caitlin, are you still there?' several times before she could bring herself to reply. Then she had nearly run out of money and – dear God, how *had* Gran remained so calm? – had had to be persuaded to give Gran the number of the phone box so that she could call her back. Caitlin had almost panicked at that point, begging Gran not to tell the police or her father where she was. Gran had promised, of course, saying, 'But darling, you haven't done anything wrong. Why would the police want to catch you?' And when Gran had phoned her straight back, Caitlin had cried, saying she was afraid she'd killed Dad, that she hadn't meant to do it, that she'd had to keep hitting him to make him stop. Gran had been so cool about it all, telling her that was nonsense, and no, she hadn't killed him, more's the pity, and serve him right if she had. She had talked about self-defence, told her that she and Daniel had been out of their minds with worry and asked when she was coming home.

Home! Caitlin had told her that she could never come home, that she never wanted to see her father again. Gran had said that she meant home with *her* – of course Caitlin couldn't live with her father any more. And yet, no matter how her Gran had tried, she had not been able to persuade Caitlin to go back. It was as if, once she was away, a wave of revulsion had swept over her, revulsion not only against her father but the whole thought of her previous life since Mum had disappeared. She didn't want any more reminders. It was all too painful. Gran had tried very hard to get her to change her mind, and had plugged the school angle particularly well.

'You've only one more year in Sixth Form, darling. Just one year, and then you can go to University and make a new life for yourself, a career, everything you've ever wanted.'

No I can't, Caitlin had thought. *What I want most of all is to have Mummy back.* And did she really want to go to University? Drama School was her real ambition, and the best ones were right here in London. No. She was staying where she was. So Gran had had to give in, making

Caitlin promise to phone her, especially if she needed money. She had been very concerned about that. 'Where will you stay, Caitlin? What will you do?' And she, with the blind faith of youth had said, 'Don't worry, Gran, I'll be alright. I've got a place to stay and tomorrow I'm going to look for a job.'

Caitlin had not learned until many years later that Gran had been so incensed by her father's behaviour that she had waited a further three days before telling the police that Caitlin was safe and well. Now more convinced than ever that he had killed Caitlin's mother, her own daughter, she had believed that a few more days grilling about Caitlin's whereabouts might lead to a confession to Laura's murder.

Back in the present, Caitlin had to make a conscious effort to put the past behind her and continue the journey to keep her appointment. She made two Tube journeys and took a taxi for the final leg to the Benedictine Abbey. Things would have been so different if she'd gone to live with Gran. So much would never have happened. She certainly wouldn't be coming here, now, to see this particular woman.

She was led into the guest parlour by a novice and waited anxiously for the few minutes it took for Sheila to arrive. *No, no,* she chided herself. *I shouldn't think of her as Sheila. She's Sister Barbara now. She's not been Sheila for what? Eleven years? Twelve years? Must be something like that, because of when Nick and I–*

'Caitlin! How wonderful to see you!' The familiar voice broke into her thoughts and Caitlin turned to be enveloped in a hug. The nun held her at arm's length, shaking her head. 'I've been praying for you – the anniversary and all... Is that why you've come?' Although they corresponded regularly, Caitlin kept visits to a minimum. The Benedictines were, after all, an enclosed Order.

'Not exactly. Not at all, really. It's something else...' She waited until a tray of tea had been provided before opening her bag and handing over the letters. 'What do you make of these?'

'Good Lord, Caitlin! After all this time?' She shook her head. 'You poor thing – how awful. Have you taken them to the police?'

Caitlin shrugged. 'For what? There's not exactly a contact name and phone number, is there?'

The nun pulled a face. 'I was thinking more in the way of forensic evidence.'

'Ah. I've probably ruined whatever there might have been. I didn't think.'

'Reacting from the gut, eh? Let me offer your question back – what do *you* think?'

Seconds ticked by as Caitlin considered her response. 'Probably just a crank.'

'But?'

'Does there have to be a "but"?'

'You're here, aren't you? And this is me you're talking to! No pulling the wool over my eyes, even if I wear the habit these days.'

The two women stared at each other, then burst out laughing.

'What's so funny?' Caitlin asked.

'No, you first. What made you laugh?'

Caitlin shook her head. 'Your reference to

86

wearing the habit. Bit different to when I first met you. Sorry – I shouldn't bring up your past.'

'Why be sorry? The good Lord loves us, warts and all.'

The corners of Caitlin's mouth were twitching. '*Snakes* and all?'

'Absolutely.'

It was no good. Neither of them could keep a straight face. When at last she was able to get her breath, Caitlin gasped, 'God, I feel better for that! Seems like the first time I've laughed in I don't know how long!'

'Then you needed to come, and not before time.' Sister Barbara handed back the letters. 'This business is getting you down. Understandable enough. But what are you going to do about it?'

It was one of Sister Barbara's catchphrases, and the first time Caitlin had heard her say it was not to her, but to the gang of youths who were trying to rob her at knifepoint. She had never been so frightened in her life. In London less than a month, in trouble and too proud to phone Gran as promised, she had strayed off the beaten track late one night and into what seemed to be a nightmare. They had her against a wall. She was crying, having no money to hand over and dreading the reaction that might provoke.

'Ah! Poor baby! She'll be calling for her Mummy next!' one of the youths had jibed. That had set Caitlin wailing. The rest of the gang had cheered.

'Hey, Vinnie, if she's this bad now, what will she do when you shake your snake, man?'

87

'Bite it off, if she's any sense.' The voice was controlled. All had turned to look at the new arrival, who stepped between them and their intended victim.

'Well, well – the Caped Crusader!'

Caitlin had gulped air and was trying not to hiccup. The strange woman, tall and heavily made-up, seemed, indeed, to be wearing a cape.

'And what if I am? What are you going to do about it?'

Derisory noises from the gang. The woman held up a hand.

'Going to shake the snake at her, were you? Tell you what – you show me yours and I'll show you mine.' Her face was deadpan.

'Oh yeah? Since when does a bitch like you have a trouser python?'

The woman shrugged. 'Since when do I need trousers?' She opened the cloak. Caitlin, behind her, saw nothing, and was astonished when her assailants fled, calling the woman a crazy bitch. The woman did not turn round until they were out of sight, merely asking in a conversational tone, 'What's your name, girl?'

'Cait – Caitlin Richardson.'

'Well, Caitlin Richardson, my name is Sheila Mason and this is Silent Sam.' She turned and gave the cloak a flourish. Caitlin's jaw dropped at the sight of the snake. 'Wouldn't harm a fly, but they weren't to know that.' Seeing the question in the girl's eyes, she laughed. 'Me and Sam are partners. I'm an exotic dancer.'

It had been the start of a friendship that had saved Caitlin's life in more ways than one, and on more than one occasion.

For Sheila, getting the story out of the girl had been easy. She had been too proud, once money ran out, to ask her grandmother for more and had wound up sleeping rough. Having no fixed address, she had been unable to get work. She was frightened, desperate, and still nowhere near as street-wise as she needed to be.

It was a good thing I found her. What if it had been someone else, someone less scrupulous? Oh, I was a whore as well as an exotic dancer, but she didn't need to know that. Not to begin with. And it was precisely because I was a whore that I didn't want her to end up as one. So I took her home. Got her to contact her grandmother and found her a place to live just a few doors away. Warned off anybody likely to want to mess with her. So they didn't. Not just because of Sam, but because I had a minder – a minder, mark you, not a pimp – and nobody, but nobody, wanted to tangle with Louis.

It had marked a new beginning for Caitlin Richardson. Cleaned up and with somewhere to stay, albeit a dingy bedsit, she had got herself a job in a bookshop, changing it for something more flexible once she started acting lessons, so that she could take time off for auditions. It had been at an audition, around a year later, that she had met Nick. Instant attraction. Instant passion, on all levels. Within a month, they'd moved in together, swept off their feet, all set to become the stars of the future...

Chapter Seven

Darrowdale Community Open Day

The weather was overcast for the start of the Open Day but the snow had ceased and the roads were open. The entrance to the Community was festooned with balloons and banners, with signs in place directing drivers to the car park. The Gift Shop and Tea Room were closed, their goods and facilities moved to the Old Barn and the Main House, from which wafted the sharp, warm smell of the spices used in mince pies and mulled wine. The hearty aroma of soup, freshly made in giant pans, fought for attention beside its more seasonal competitors, and the huge farmhouse kitchen gleamed with the promise of food, warmth and comfort.

In the upstairs of the barn, timbers creaked as portable heaters worked overtime to warm the air. It was used by the Community as a multi-faith chapel, a mandala painted on the far wall the only clue to its designated use. Here, too, yoga, meditation and T'ai Chi were practised. Today, it was filled with trestle tables laden with examples of the arts and crafts for which the Community had become famous.

Deborah had decided not to arrive too early. Ronnie Walters had made a good point about blending in and not being conspicuous. She wanted to mingle, get a sense of the atmosphere before talking to her, but was worried in case there wasn't much of a turnout.

Her concern was needless, she could see that as soon as she turned towards the car park. If the number of vehicles already in evidence was anything to go by, there were plenty of visitors. She locked her car and followed the signs to the heart of the Community, already able to hear Christmas music and other sounds of activity. Deborah was pleased with herself. Now she'd be able to really start digging, to break down the surface of bare facts, times and dates, and put them, and the people involved, into context. This was where things would start to come alive.

The letter-writer had arrived before Deborah and was taking stock. Faces known. Faces unknown. It was easy to pick out Community members. They wore badges, so the visiting hordes could be passed over quickly. But there were new faces even among the Community members these days. Things had changed a lot. People changed, too. Just look at Will Dutton. What a runt he'd been! A skinny, undeveloped, snot-nosed runt. Look at him now! Who would ever have believed it? *Bet he's still thick, though. Some things never change...* The letter-writer moved unobtrusively through the crowd to say hello.

Ronnie Walters managed to organise enough of a break to take Deborah back to her home, where they could talk in private.

'Quite a turnout!' Deborah commented as they

91

made their escape.

'Better than we anticipated, given the weather.' Ronnie was debating whether or not to tell her that Daniel was here. 'That's where the Richardsons lived.' She pointed to a single-storey wooden home surrounded by trees. Deborah had both a good eye and a good imagination.

'Must be beautiful in the summer.'

'It is.'

Deborah had spent quite some time in the barn, browsing, buying gifts and visualising the T'ai Chi classes that Laura Richardson had taught there. She followed Ronnie into her home, glad to shed her coat, and waited until the tea had been made before asking further questions.

'What was she like, Laura Richardson?'

Ronnie smiled before allowing her eyes to become unfocused with remembrance .

'She was an enigma. One of those rare people who can balance creativity and practicality. Like the still eye of a storm. It didn't matter how much chaos was going on around her, she managed to stay centred.'

'How?' Ronnie's answer had not been what Deborah was expecting.

'Her spiritual practice, I believe.'

'She was a religious woman?'

Ronnie frowned. 'Not in the conventional sense of the word. She certainly wasn't super-serious, or pious or stuffy.' She shook her head. 'Full of life, joy ... she had real strength about her. God knows the right kind of label to give her. She somehow combined Catholicism with ... something else. I'm not sure what. But it – the other thing – was strongest. She had no time for hierarchy, papal teaching on birth control, that sort of stuff. She was radical without being a fanatic, if you know what I mean.' She thought for a moment. 'I don't think she would have remained a Catholic.' Deborah noted the surprise in Ronnie's voice and on her face. It was as if she'd only just realised it herself. 'I'm sorry – it's hard to describe.'

'You were close to her?'

'Very. I met her when we were seventeen, when my family moved up here.'

'So you knew her before she was married?'

'Good Lord, yes! I knew her when she was going out with Derek.'

There had been no further communication from the letter-writer when Nina arrived at Caitlin's house. She was relieved. She wanted to cleanse it, put some protection in place before the evil tried to strike again. She took her time, settling down to seek specific guidance before she began, allowing the house to speak to her, consulting her allies in the spirit world. Her guidance so far had been to use a Native American smudging ceremony, and she performed it now, mindfully, reverently. The sweet smell of sage mingled with the bitterness of juniper and other herbs to permeate the house as she moved from room to room. She was led on to do other things, feeling the power rise, feeling it move into place. When she was finished, she prayed, first silently, then aloud. 'Is there anything else I need to know or need to do?'

She was drawn, like a magnet, to the piano. Music was not one of Nina's natural gifts, but she allowed her hands to stroke the wood, to lift the lid. She sat at the stool, eyes closed, felt her fingers move across the keys. She sensed the hours of practice and of pleasure. There was joy here, laughter. Nina sensed both mother and daughter clearly. There was so much love between them. Where had Laura gone? Why would she leave such love behind?

'Ohhh!' Nina groaned aloud as a crushing pain seared through the back of her skull. Shaken, struggling to breathe, her hands flew from the keyboard as if she'd been scalded. She pushed back the stool, forcing herself to stand on legs suddenly weak, disconnecting herself from the experience. What the hell was going on?

Mags had made her escape from the supermarket the previous day by the skin of her teeth. They hadn't been happy letting her go, had urged her to see a doctor. Doctors! She had no time for them. Treated herself, on the rare occasions she needed to, with natural remedies. Much better. Besides, there was nothing wrong with her, nothing that a doctor could treat. It was just the shock of the poster, of realising where she was. She had decided to move on as quickly as possible. Not that anyone would recognise her now, not after all these years. She felt a sudden panic at the near-conventionality of her new appearance. No one looked twice at a tramp. They might at a woman walker. The first field she came to, she would muddy herself up a bit. Just till she was well past Darrowdale.

The letter-writer was surprised to see Daniel at the Open Day. More than surprised. Taken aback. How dare he show his face here? This could be disastrous. He must have received the two letters by now. *Coming here was not the reaction I'd anticipated.* And what was Veronica Walters talking to him about so quietly, so earnestly? Daniel's face was flushed. The letter-writer couldn't make it out. Anger? Embarrassment? They were unaware of the narrowed eyes watching them as Veronica continued to talk, her hand on Daniel's arm. He was looking pensive now, speaking himself.

The letter-writer followed the glance they threw across the room. Who was she? An auburn-haired woman, pale-skinned, like one of those pre-Raphaelite paintings. She was talking to a new member of the Community, but not wearing a badge herself. A visitor, then. So what was her connection with Daniel? Slowly, carefully, the letter-writer moved through the throng, smiling a smile that never quite reached the eyes that devoured Deborah Harvey's face.

Derek Kenny was remembering the last time he'd seen Laura Richardson. Two days before her disappearance. The day she was to give him her decision. Would she leave Terry? Would things have been different if she'd changed her mind? Could he have done something – anything – to prevent it happening? Although it was nearly

95

twenty years ago, time had done nothing to dim the memory of that day. Quite the contrary. He had revisited it so many times, it had become burnished with indelible brightness in his mind, her every word, every gesture, taking on an unbearable clarity.

They had met in the White Hart at Elmridge. He had been late, held up longer than anticipated by an interview with the leader of a campaign to put in a crossing where a child had been knocked down and killed by a lorry in the spring. She had waited for him, knowing that if he said he'd be there, he'd be there. He'd looked different then, of course. Still had a full head of hair, didn't need glasses and certainly hadn't been carrying the belly that he'd developed since. He'd been an attractive man back then, even if he did say so himself.

And Laura – what would she be like now? Middle-age spread? Grey hair? Wrinkles? Derek didn't care. He would still have loved her. But she was frozen now, frozen into an everlasting snapshot that neither faded nor aged with the passing of the years that had been stolen from her, from him, from everyone who'd known her. He felt cheated of all the time that could have been theirs, *should* have been theirs. *I feel cheated? I'm still the same selfish bastard*, he rebuked himself. *What about Laura?* There was the real cheating. Cheated of life itself. At least he was still living and breathing. He'd always believed she was dead, from the first moment he'd heard she was missing. She would never have left her children. Never.

So they'd met at the White Hart and she'd looked as beautiful as ever, despite the concern in her eyes.

'Laura! I'm sorry I'm late – you know how it is...'

'I know. Sit down, you're all out of breath.'

He'd thrown his jacket onto the bench beside her, where her portfolio lay, and they'd talked, trying to make the most of their stolen hours together. Terry had taken the children camping for the weekend. She'd excused herself from the trip because of the amount of work she had to do to fill an order for two days' time. With the school holidays started, she needed to get on. Yet here she was, with him. Could he allow himself to hope? He looked at her carefully. She met his gaze evenly but there was sadness in her eyes. And then, suddenly, she'd pulled herself together and started talking, not about them, but about something completely different. It had startled him, caught him off guard.

'I'm sorry, Derek, this isn't a delaying tactic, I promise. I've made my decision and we'll talk it through in a minute. I'm talking to you as a reporter, now. There's something going on in the Community and I'm really worried about it.' She fiddled with the pepper pot, eyes lowered. It seemed a very long moment before she looked at him again. 'I know this sounds crazy, but...'

Daniel went for a long walk, thinking about what Veronica Walters had told him. Christ! Would it never rest? A journalist. At least Veronica hadn't told her he was here yet. She'd get to know, though. It was inevitable. The place was buzzing. *I feel like a fucking freak show*. Hands deep in his pockets, he walked far beyond the houses, unconscious of where he was going. If only he could find Caitlin! He stopped and closed his eyes, suddenly swamped by memories and emotions. It was being here. He should have expected it. It was terrible when Mum disappeared. The pain. The bewilderment. Your mother doesn't just disappear. She can't. But she had.

He remembered the search. The first one. Just the members of the Community. Veronica had come over to their house to stay with Caitlin. Caitlin wasn't supposed to know about the search. Dad had wanted to keep it quiet. Didn't want to panic her. But she'd known. He'd seen it in her eyes. It was electric. He would never forget the look that had passed between them. It marked a turning point in his relationship with her. Up until then, she'd just been a nuisance of a kid sister. With that look, that knowing, something had changed inside him. He had become her protector.

He'd gone with the search party. There was still plenty of light. Mum couldn't have gone far. Despite the light, the experience had had a dreamlike quality, as if it were not really happening. Even when the police had been called in, he'd felt sure they'd find her then. It had been a nightmare, and you always thought there was nothing worse than a nightmare, but you were wrong. It had got infinitely worse. The way they'd taken Dad for questioning. The haunted look that had appeared in his eyes. The terrible realisation that the police thought Dad was involved in it. And 'it' was the possibility that Mum was dead.

Deborah was present when Angela dropped her bombshell. Most of the day visitors had taken their leave by then, so it was largely a group of past and present Community members who were left, enjoying a drink. She almost missed it, too, discreetly eyeing up a hugely attractive man she'd spotted earlier. *Very nice. Very tasty.* Tall. Brown hair. Blue eyes. Lean but muscular. *Just how I like them. Must ask Ronnie who he is.* Her priority, however, was with Daniel. Ronnie had told her of his presence, persuaded her to let them broker a meeting with him, rather than approaching Daniel directly herself. She dragged her attention back just as Angela's voice cut through her thoughts.

'Daniel! I can't believe it! I don't see either of you for years, and now I see both you and Caitlin in the space of two days!' She was fishing in her bag and missed the expression on Daniel's face. Deborah, however, did not.

So this is the man, she observed curiously. *And he looks like he's just been pole-axed.* For a moment, Deborah thought he was about to faint. White as a sheet.

'Here, look! She gave me her card.' She handed it to Daniel. 'I was in Cheltenham, doing a play there.' She turned to the group nearby, seeking out one particular face. 'Didn't you say that's your neck of the woods?'

The letter-writer returned her smile, disguising

99

a stab of fear. But it was all right. Daniel was looking the other way. 'Yes. Sorry to have missed your play.' Other faces were watching now. Including the pre-Raphaelite beauty. She was still there. *Deborah Harvey. I heard your name mentioned. I'll have to find out about you. Veronica hasn't explained you or your connection with Daniel, and I can't have that. Any connection to that family is my business.* Community members were looked at. *Brazen it out. They don't remember me. They don't remember me at all. Why should they? I look so different now. That's good. Good for me. Bad for them. But I would rather not be seen by Daniel. Not when he's showing such an interesting reaction to news of his sister.*

Daniel was walking away with Colin Walters. Inwardly, the letter-writer gave a sigh. Outwardly, an eloquent shrug, a friendly smile. No one would notice that it did not extend as far as the slate eyes. 'Please, let me introduce myself...'

Chapter Eight

Sleep eluded Daniel. Being back in the Community after so long was disturbing him far more than he had anticipated. It should have been a hit-and-run visit, especially now he had Cait's details, but it wasn't working out like that at all. It wasn't just the being here, he acknowledged, though God knows, that was bad enough because of his mother's disappearance. It was

100

other things – connected things – like the last time he'd seen Cait. *No. That was Gran's funeral.* It was the last time he'd *meant* to see Cait, and that was a different matter. *How much difference would it have made if I'd gone home as originally planned? When I was supposed to. I never dreamed...* He shook his head. He had assumed everything was all right. Cait had given him no reason to believe otherwise, but then, she hadn't written that often, had she? *Steeped in her A Levels, or so I believed. Wanted to believe, because I'd got away and she would have, too, if only... If only...* But it hadn't worked out that way.

He remembered it as if it were yesterday. The day had started with a warm bed and the even warmer body of Linda James. They were lying together like spoons and she had murmured sleepily, pressing her buttocks into his hardening cock as he'd slid his hand over her hip and between her thighs. She was wet in seconds, turning towards him, reaching between his legs. And that was when the phone had rung. She'd giggled then, changed her tactics. No light brushing now. She had his cock tightly grasped, starting a slow, firm pumping, up and down, up and down, as his fingers entered her, matching her movements. What a laugh! Could he talk on the phone without betraying the fire in his loins, the burgeoning ache in his belly? He nibbled her ear as he lifted the receiver. Christ, she was really wet now! More than ready for him. Better get rid of whoever was on the phone quickly. He wanted to come inside her, not all over the sheets.

'Yeah?'

'Daniel, you bastard! Why aren't you home? Don't you know what today is? Have you no respect for your mother?'

Linda faltered in confusion as the velvety hardness became limp.

'Christ, Dad! I told you – I can't get away yet. It's the first time, for fuck's sake!'

'Don't you use that kind of language with me! You should *be* here!'

Daniel rolled away from Linda, swinging his legs over the edge of the bed to sit up. The realisation hit him that his father was drunk and his scalp prickled with unease.

'Look, Dad, you know I've finished my finals. The results will be up soon. I–'

'Bullshit! Bullshit, you snivelling bastard! They'll send the results in the post. Your place is here with me and your sister!'

'How is Cait?'

'You'd know if you were here, wouldn't you?'

'Let me speak to her, Dad. Maybe I–'

'Maybe nothing! You can talk to her when you come home. Get yourself home! Now! Do you hear me?'

'Shit!' Daniel slammed the receiver down. 'Shit!' he repeated, jumping to his feet. Linda looked at him. Naked and shaking, he slammed into the kitchenette. Uncertainly, she followed him, clutching a sheet around her.

'Danny...'

'He's lost it, Linda. He's fucking lost it!' He stared at her blindly, jaw working, running his hands distractedly through his hair. Linda knew next to nothing about his family. He never spoke of his mother and what little he'd said about his father made it clear that he didn't much like him. Well, that was the polite way of putting it. The only person he really seemed to care about was his sister.

'What about Cait, Danny?'

He pushed past her, back into the bedroom where he started throwing clothes onto the bed, nearly pulling drawers off their runners in his temper.

'One more year, Linda. Just one more year in Sixth Form and she can get away from the bastard.'

'You're going home, then.' It wasn't a question. He hopped on one foot, pulling on his under-pants.

'I have to. I can't leave her on her own with him like this.' He turned his back abruptly, afraid to let her see the fear in his face. What the hell had happened to Dad? He tried to tell himself that Caitlin was safe. Dad wouldn't hurt her. He hadn't killed Mum. He couldn't have. Shit! Mum wasn't dead. She couldn't be dead. Even if she were... No! Dad wouldn't hurt Cait. Not Katie. Never in a million years...

He'd had plenty of time to think as he made the long drive north. Where had it all gone wrong? Not the Mum thing. Between him and Dad. They'd been so close. Even more so after Mum's disappearance. There had been a silent conspiracy between them to protect Caitlin, cushion her as much as possible. What the hell had happened? What the *hell* had happened? Daniel grimaced. The camping trip. That's what had happened.

Dad had arranged it a couple of months after Mum had disappeared. Caitlin hadn't wanted to go, so she'd stayed with Colin and Ronnie Walters. Daniel had jumped at the chance, though. A few days alone with Dad, just the two of them together. It was just what they'd needed. Two men together. Although he had only been seventeen, Mum's disappearance – the shock of it, and trying to protect Caitlin – had marked a turning point for Daniel. He had made the transition from boy to man almost unconsciously, and his relationship with his father had deepened in a way he found difficult to explain. Dad had been so strong, even when the police had kept questioning him. Daniel had been sick with fear, engulfed by a growing sense of horror as it dawned on him that the police were treating Dad as a suspect. He couldn't face the thought that Dad might have done something to Mum. *Killed her.* He felt guilty even allowing the thought to float in his head. Mum couldn't be dead. She just couldn't be. And no way would Dad... No. It just didn't bear thinking about. He thought he'd kept his anguish hidden but Dad must have seen it somehow, understood what was going through his mind. So he'd suggested the camping trip and Daniel suddenly realised with a jolt that his father had, in fact, manipulated things so that Caitlin wouldn't *want* to go. He'd planned all along that it should be just the two of them, himself and Daniel, precisely so that they could talk, man to man.

The site had also been chosen carefully, away from holidaymakers in a part of Corton Wood well off the beaten track. They'd left in the afternoon, Cait hugging them both fiercely. Dad had made a big thing about how grown-up she was being, how it was right that she should concentrate on the forthcoming play.

'It'll be good for you to have us out from under your feet, Katie Shakespeare. The show must go on, and you're going to be brilliant!'

Ronnie Walters, standing behind Cait as her father had said this, had winked at Daniel, another co-conspirator, another adult acknowledging Daniel's entry into the grownup world. Daniel had smiled awkwardly at her, feeling himself blush at her acknowledgement of his new status. And so they'd left Cait behind and made their journey together.

It was over the camp fire that night that Dad had raised the business that was burdening Daniel's mind.

'Daniel, you've not said much, but I know you must be worried about the way the police keep asking me questions about Mum's disappearance.'

Daniel had choked over his coffee, trying to deny it, but Dad had cut him off, patting his shoulder.

'It's all right, son. You don't need to say anything. It's natural to feel worried. This is a terrible thing that's happened and the worst part is the not knowing. They're just doing their job. They have to ask. It's an unfortunate fact of life that, in situations like these, the husband is always the chief suspect.'

Daniel had tried to protest, but his father had

shaken his head.

'No, son, listen to me. Statistics back that up. But I'm telling you now, and telling you the truth – I don't know where your mum is, and I had nothing to do with whatever has happened to her.'

'But why do they keep on asking you when you've already told them that?'

Dad had poured more coffee before he'd answered. 'They're concerned, Daniel, because I don't have a cast-iron alibi between leaving home that morning and coming back again.'

'But you don't need one, Dad! Cait saw Mum – had lunch with her – at half past one. Surely they don't think *she's* lying.'

'No they don't, son, and that's the trouble. You see, my meeting for the Sowerby contract was over by then – lunchtime – but I didn't get home until half past six. They want to know what I was doing during that time.'

'What *were* you doing?' Daniel had been somehow afraid to ask, yet knew he had to.

Dad had sighed. Daniel had never heard him make a sound quite like that before. It wasn't weariness, but quite what it was, he didn't know.

'I was elated to get that contract, Daniel. Over the moon. You know how important it is – all the things we'll be able to do in the Community as a result of it. I went to a pub and had lunch, had a drink. Went shopping and bought champagne to celebrate. And I went swimming before I came home. Needed to burn off some pent-up energy, you know?'

'So what's the problem?'

Dad had shaken his head again. 'There was no

one with me once I left the meeting, Daniel. No one to vouch for me being where I said I was, when I said I was.'

Daniel had blinked at his father, not understanding. 'But didn't they ask at the pub and stuff?'

'Oh yes. And I had the receipt for the champagne and the ticket for the swimming baths. Unfortunately, there's a gap between the two and theoretically' – Dad had emphasised that word – *'theoretically* I would have had time to come home, do something to Mum and go back again.'

Daniel's heart had burned with indignation. 'But that's ridiculous! Why would you do such a thing?'

'I wouldn't, son. You know that and I know that, but the police don't. I love your mother, Daniel. I would never do anything to hurt her.'

The flickering flames of the camp fire had reflected the sheen of tears in Dad's eyes. Daniel had swallowed hard. He had never in his life seen his father cry. Not even that day when they couldn't find Mum. Silently, he had moved towards him, awkwardly stretching out an arm around Dad's shoulders. Dad had clutched at him then, like a drowning man reaching for a life belt. They'd both cried for a long time.

It wasn't until the following day that the bombshell had dropped. The morning had started well. Perhaps the tears of the previous evening had been cathartic for both of them. They had slept soundly and there had been no awkwardness between them as they had set about preparing breakfast.

'It's going to be a scorcher!' Dad had observed. 'Looks like we're in for an Indian Summer after all!'

They had eaten at leisure, setting off mid-morning on their planned walk, Dad enthusiastic with his camera, pointing things out, reminding Daniel to watch out for any adders basking in the sun. Daniel had always admired his father's knowledge of trees and plants, thinking it somehow odd for an architect to know such things. Dad had laughed when Daniel had first admitted that some years ago, saying it was precisely *because* he was an architect that he knew. It had to do with architects dealing with both soft and hard something-or-another – landscapes, maybe. Daniel couldn't remember what. Anyway, he had enjoyed the walk, grateful to retreat periodically into the shade of the woods for relief from the seemingly relentless heat which had beaten down upon them as they crossed fields and exposed footpaths.

'God! What I wouldn't give for a cold shower!' Daniel had moaned.

They were crossing a steeply inclined field at the time, the parched grass with its bright clusters of flowers alive with the hum of insects, what little pathway there was puffing up bone-dry dust with their every footstep. Dad, walking ahead of him, had turned and grinned, saying, 'I've something better than that lined up, son!'

Daniel, wiping his shirt sleeve across his brow, had wondered if the heat was getting to his father's brain – they were miles from anywhere that might offer the luxury of running water.

Ahead of them, the field appeared to end abruptly in a sheer drop. Daniel had watched and followed as his father veered sharply to the right. To his relief, the ground had soon levelled, leading in turn to a gentle slope, broad of path and framed on either side by a profusion of bushes. Dad had sat down on a tree stump, watching his own sweaty approach.

'All right there, son? It'll be worth it, you'll see!' They had stopped for a few moments, catching their breaths and drinking from their water bottles before starting down the slope into the welcome coolness of the ever-deepening wood-land. Beside their own soft footfalls and the singing of birds, there was no other sound, not even the sigh of leaves, for the air was still. And yet, and yet...

Daniel had very gradually become aware of a murmuring, so soft at first, so faint, he had thought it simply his imagination. It was only when his father had called softly, 'Do you hear that, Daniel?' that he had known that his ears were not, after all, deceiving him. They had walked onwards, the sound becoming steadily louder and, it had seemed, multi-layered. The murmuring was there, as before, but with a bub-bling sound playing above it, their two rhythms intertwined.

Daniel had become aware of goose-bumps, of the hair on his arms standing up and his scalp prickling, this time not from the discomfort of heat and sweat. He had had to increase his pace as his father had turned suddenly, leaving the path to plunge down between thickly growing trees. Slipping and sliding down the slope after him, Daniel had dug in the heels of his walking boots to stop himself spiralling out of control, coming to a stop as his father, throwing off his hat and unbuttoning his shirt, had said, 'There now – what did I tell you?'

Daniel had stood up slowly, awed by the beauty spread out before him. Away to their right, a waterfall cascaded down a rock face to pour into the stream below. This stream had bubbled over rocks made smooth by many years of such action, flowing toward them and into the pool by which they now sat, tearing off their clothes. Dad had already been in the water by the time Daniel had disentangled himself from the shirt and tee-shirt pulled too swiftly over his head, and was splashing about and hollering at him to get a move on. Daniel had hesitated before taking off his underpants but, seeing his father's lying on top of the pile of clothing nearby, whipped them off and plunged in. Skinny-dipping with Dad was something he had never done before.

They had swum in a circle for a while, then converging, had splashed and ducked each other, laughing and shaking water from their hair and eyes like dogs caught in a downpour.

'Is this better than that cold shower you were after?' Dad had grinned.

'Is it ever!' Daniel had whooped for the sheer hell of it, then rolled on his back to float, staring up at a sky that was surely more blue and beautiful than any he had seen in his life before this moment. How long he had allowed himself to drift, he didn't know, but his reverie was interrupted by his father's shout.

'Time for lunch, I reckon!'

Daniel had turned and trodden water in answer to his father's voice, raising an arm in acknowledgement, watching him as he stood naked by the pile of clothes they had left at the side of the pool. Dad had waved to him before turning his back and bending to pull something out of his rucksack. And that moment, thought Daniel, was when he had seen it. The birth-mark on his buttock. Time had seemed irrelevant. He had been caught in a freeze-frame, struggling to believe his eyes. He had felt as though his very heart had stopped as his eyes and brain, in an instant of terrible recognition, communicated the knowledge of who and what his father really was...

Jolted back to the present by the blare of a car horn, Daniel had realised that his motorway exit was looming. Christ, he must have been driving on automatic pilot! Never mind the bloody camping trip – the problem was *now*, with Dad drunk and Cait at home on her own with him. The memory of the camping trip, however, had evoked a fury which had, after that day in the woods, been kept tightly concealed, and he drove the last few miles home with barely controlled rage, an assortment of awful possibilities flashing through his mind.

None could have prepared him for what he had found as he finally raced up the path and through the front door of his father's house. He stood, brought up short by the chaos that met his eyes. The hall looked like ground zero, everything smashed, even the light fitting ripped from the ceiling. *Oh, Christ, no!* An icy chill swept over Daniel.

'Dad? Cait?' He trod cautiously, pushing open the kitchen door before venturing inside. Jesus Christ! Broken crockery crunched beneath his feet. Milk, water and God only knew what else was splashed all over the floor, leaking from the fridge which sat, overturned, on its side, its door open.

'Dad! Cait!' Daniel backtracked, almost slipping, trying to keep the panic from his voice as he stumbled towards the living room.

'Cait? Cait – where are you?' He saw nothing at first beyond devastation. The TV smashed. Furniture broken. Pictures ripped from the wall. He struggled to swallow, mouth dry with fear. And then he saw him. His father. Huddled in the corner, muttering under his breath. Incoherent. Rambling .

'Dad?' He seemed completely oblivious. Picking his way towards him, Daniel's gut knotted as he saw the blood. *Whose* blood? His father seemed covered in it.

'Dad!' Galvanised into action now, Daniel grabbed him by his shirt-front and, in one swift move, had him off the floor and slammed against the wall. The bleary eyes made an attempt to focus.

'Daniel? I didn't mean... I never...'

Christ, he stinks! Daniel averted his face from the foul breath and shook him until his teeth rattled.

'What the fuck have you done with Cait?' He shook him again, screaming at him now.

'WHERE'S CAIT?'

He was pathetic. Even worse than on that day of the camping trip when they'd wound up at Gresswell Falls.

It probably wouldn't have happened if it had been planned. If we'd had swimming trunks. Terry had not had eyes in the back of his head, had no idea of what was coming when Daniel had seen him naked.

'You! It was you!' Daniel had yanked his father upright so suddenly, Terry had had to struggle to keep his feet.

'You bastard!' *Daniel screamed the words, swinging Terry round only to send him sprawling backwards with an explosive left hook. Terry had had no time to react. I almost beat him to a pulp. It was only rolling together into the water that saved him. Ironic, given that I was trying so hard to drown the bastard. And then... I don't know how he did it, but he got me in some sort of headlock, dragged me out of the water and threw me onto the bank. I got up, but not fast enough. He just landed one on me. A snap punch that sent me backwards in a spray of snot and blood. It was surreal.*

They were both shaking, both breathing in ragged gasps, eyeing each other for what seemed like an eternity before either of them could speak.

'All right, son. You want to tell me what all that was about?'

'It was you! "Big Boy", we called you. You bastard! You fucking bastard!' *Daniel sat up, pulling at a clump of grass and using it to wipe his face. His father stared at him, face blank with incomprehension.*

'What the hell are you talking about?'

'You! Shagging women in the derelict croft. You bastard!'

113

Daniel watched as the blood drained from his father's face, not giving him a chance to speak. He was remembering only what he had been told the night before. '"I love your mother, Daniel,"' the boy mimicked. '"I would never do anything to hurt her."' He was shaking with anger, spitting out the words. 'Right! Playing happy families. Teaching Cait and me to have respect, and all the time you're shagging women – fucking other women – right behind Mum's back. Oh, we know there's more than one. Different coloured pubic hair.' He struggled to his feet, staring straight into his father's face. 'Did Mum find out? Did she? Is that why you killed her?'

Chapter Nine

Sunday 12 December

It was still dark when Daniel awoke. He lay still, listening to the silence, realising for the first time that that was the reason he hated staying in his Devon house. It reminded him of this place. The Community. He breathed deeply as a welter of emotions stirred, shocking him with their intensity. *Christ! I never thought I'd see this place again. Never wanted to, after Dad and Cait left.* He sat up abruptly, getting out of bed and pulling on his clothes, aware now of the smell of fresh coffee. Someone else was up.

The sound of the shower was audible as Daniel passed the bathroom door. Must be Ronnie, he

114

thought, catching sight of Colin in the kitchen.

Colin smiled as Daniel entered. 'Coffee?'

'Thanks.'

'Help yourself to milk and sugar.' *He doesn't look as if he's slept well*, Colin thought, noting the bags under Daniel's eyes and the pallor of his skin beneath the beard.

'Rough night?'

Daniel grimaced as he spooned sugar into black coffee.

'Stirred up a lot memories, being here. Do you mind if I take this outside for a minute? I need to clear my head.'

'Sure. Take your time.'

Daniel stepped out into the morning, steam rising from his mug as it met the chill outdoor air. He moved slowly along the path, drawn like a magnet to that part of it from which he could see what used to be his home. Who lived there these days? He was sure Ronnie had told him yesterday, but couldn't for the life of him remember.

The sky was getting lighter now, sun rising in a fiery glow behind the distant black silhouette of Highcroft Hill. *Christ, this was hardly where I planned to be this weekend.*

'Oh shit!' Daniel spoke the words aloud, remembering, far too late, where he *had* said he would be. Damn! He'd have to phone Cathy and apologise. *Christ, I'll be as popular as a pork chop in Jerusalem.* She wouldn't believe a word. *Oh fuck!* Daniel knew he would have to sort it out. Not just this weekend. The whole thing between him and Cathy. He took a gulp of his coffee, now almost cold, and threw the dregs onto the

115

garden. *I should have worn my jacket,* he thought, realising that he was shivering. *It's bloody freezing.*

Going back into the kitchen, he did his best to appear sociable. It had been good of Colin and Ronnie to put him up at such short notice. More to the point, they had been genuinely pleased to see him after so many years, and it had been a shock to know that their friendliness was sincere. Daniel was unused to genuine people after so long in an industry that was, as his Gran used to say, 'all mouth and trousers'. Smile to your face and stab you in the back without even blinking. He'd grown cynical, aware of how he was valued only for what he could do, judged only on how good the last album had been. These people liked him – valued him – simply for who he was.

'More coffee? You look frozen!' Ronnie, hair still damp from the shower, had been forewarned about Daniel's fragile appearance.

'I am. Should have taken my jacket. Thanks, Ronnie.' He sat down as she refilled his mug. It still seemed odd, calling them by their Christian names after so many years of having called them 'Mr and Mrs Walters'.

Ronnie sat at the table with him, pushing the sugar bowl in his direction.

'Heavy going, Daniel?'

He nodded. 'I never expected to come here again.'

'No one could blame you for that. It can't be easy – must be stirring up some pretty hideous memories.'

'It is.' They sat in silence for a second.

'How do you feel about Deborah Harvey's

116

anniversary piece about your mum?' Ronnie was acting as go-between, having told Daniel about it yesterday. He had promised to contact Deborah after thinking it over.

He sighed. 'It's probably better to talk to her than not. I'd prefer to talk to Cait about it first, though. She needs to know.'

'And your father?'

He shook his head. 'I neither know nor care what my father thinks.'

Colin, himself fresh from the shower, joined them at the table and glanced at his wife before speaking.

'You don't think...'

'...that he killed Mum? No, I don't. But the way he treated Cait was abominable. I've had nothing to do with him since then.'

'You mean since she ran away?'

'Yes. I would never have left her with him if I'd known he was drinking like that.'

Colin stirred his coffee, playing with the spoon. 'These things are never as black and white as they seem, Daniel. Terry must have been in a hell of a state. And Caitlin should have told you. Told someone.'

'You're not a mind reader, Daniel,' Ronnie put in. 'If anyone was at fault, it was this Community. We should never have asked Terry to leave.'

'He was *asked* to leave?' Daniel was aghast.

'Why yes. You mean you didn't know?'

'Christ, no! He told me he'd moved because it would be better for Cait when she went to Sixth Form.' Daniel pushed back his chair, paced the floor and turned to look at them. 'You're telling

117

me – what? You threw him out? Threw Cait out?'

'It wasn't like that. And Colin and I – and a couple of others – voted against it. We felt they'd be better off here, where we could keep an eye on them, make sure they were properly supported. That's the whole point of a Community. But what good are principles if you don't live them, can't put them into action?'

Both men were struck by the bitterness of Ronnie's words. Colin cleared his throat. 'One of the founding principles of this Community was that decisions should be taken democratically. You must remember how all issues were voted on?'

'Like when the Latimers came? Yes. But... Christ!'

'I know. Because something is done democratically doesn't mean it's right. We should have learned that from the fact that Hitler was democratically elected.'

'You let them do that? And you stayed?'

'Yes, we did.' It was Ronnie who spoke. 'It was a democratic decision and, as Colin said, one of the reasons we chose to live here was that everything was done democratically. But you're right. The decision was wrong, and I don't just say that because of what happened. We should have supported them and we didn't. We made our feelings well known and were in regular touch with Terry and Caitlin. Even so, we didn't know about his drinking. I'm sorry.'

'Bloody hell!' Daniel stood up. 'I can't believe this. I can't believe Dad didn't tell me.' As soon as he said the words, he knew that he *could* believe it. He'd barely given his father the time of day after that camping trip, was glad to go to University and get away from him. He shook his head. 'I'm sorry. You obviously did the best you could, and I'm grateful for that. None of us can change the past.' There was silence.

'You said you wanted to talk to Caitlin? About Deborah Harvey?'

Daniel nodded. 'I need to call home as well. I'm not popular with my girlfriend at present.' He pulled a mobile from his shirt pocket. 'I think I'll take a walk while I do this.'

'I did give you Caitlin's numbers?' Colin asked.

They had heard, over a tea break the previous afternoon, of how Daniel had not seen his sister since their grandmother's funeral. 'It was such a shock, hearing that Angela had seen her – and got her business card.' Daniel had ended.

'And you want her details. Without having to say why you don't know them.' Colin had spoken quietly, intuitively understanding Daniel's reluctance to go over the story with yet more people. 'Leave it to me.' He had chatted with Angela during the communal supper that marked the end of the Open Day.

'Fantastic having Daniel back after all these years! And fancy you seeing Caitlin! Can I borrow that business card and put her details into my database. We'll maybe get her, too, next year.'

'Well, Daniel can tell you, surely.'

'Yes, right.' Colin had laughed and pointed to the end of the table, where Daniel was barely visible. 'He's surrounded by his contemporaries and I don't know if we can talk him into staying over. Best be on the safe side, eh?'

Angela had smiled and handed over the card. Had she been taken in by the story? Colin wasn't sure, but right then, he didn't care. Let her think what she liked. She was one of the good guys, anyway. He remembered her own ferocious defence of Terry and Caitlin when that bloody vote had been taken.

'She's written her address on the back.'

Colin had grunted in reply as he wrote everything down. He handed back the card.

'Not like you to come armed with pen and paper...' Angela smiled again as she turned back to a couple of visitors. Colin smiled, too. No use trying to bamboozle that one.

Back in the Walters' kitchen, Daniel nodded in answer to Colin's question. 'I programmed them straight into the mobile. And wrote down her address. Thanks.'

'Sure you don't want breakfast before making your calls?' Ronnie asked.

'No. I might feel more like it afterwards.'

'I'll have something ready.'

This time, when he left the house, Daniel wore his coat.

Terry Richardson had slept late that morning, and better than he had done in a long time. There seemed to be no logical reason for this. He didn't understand it at all, but gave a cautious welcome to the lift in his mood. He showered and shaved, feeling better still as a result, and was pleasantly surprised to find he was ravenously hungry.

120

Neither fridge nor cupboards yielded anything even remotely appetising. They were, in fact, nearly bare. Terry's stomach rumbled. What he really fancied was a good, old-fashioned fry-up. Who would be open on a Sunday? Plenty of places, he realised. There was both Sunday opening and even twenty-four-hour opening nowadays. He felt as if everything had passed him by in a daze, and that suddenly he'd caught up with it all.

An hour later, his kitchen was sizzling with the sounds and smells of cooking food. He'd been to a supermarket and bought the biggest load of groceries he'd had in ages. He felt a sense of satisfaction as he put his purchases away. He really should take better care of himself, he knew. Still, he'd been off the booze for a while – discounting his lapse on receiving the letter – and that was a miracle. It was eating and sleeping that were the problems – he didn't do enough of either. There didn't seem to be much he could do about sleep, but eating was another matter. He could make an effort. Like now. As he sat at the kitchen table, he savoured the feast he had prepared – sausage, bacon, eggs, tomatoes and mushrooms, with four thick wedges of toast and lashings of butter. How long had it been since he'd eaten like this at home? He couldn't remember. He'd eaten well on holiday, however, largely because he'd eaten out or at the hotel, where everything had been prepared for him. He'd been lucky to find that bargain. It was one of those deals sold direct. All the conventional travel agents were still prehistoric, with their

121

bloody single supplements pushing the prices up two or three times more than the ones advertised as being 'based on two sharing'. Mind you, chance would be a fine thing.

He poured himself a second cup of tea and pushed his plate away. God, that meal had been good! He surrendered to the moment. It was a long time since he'd felt like this. What was the word he was looking for? Not happy. That would be too much to ask. Normal? Sort of, though nothing had been normal since Laura had disappeared. Content, then. Maybe that was the word. Content. Clear-headed.

He thought of the letter that had been waiting for him on his return from holiday. God, that had thrown him and no mistake! Brought it all back. Not just Laura, but the blackmail. He shook his head and got up to make another pot of tea, frowning as he tried to make sense of things. The point was, this new letter *wasn't* blackmail. Not yet, at least. He hadn't made any payments for years. He left the kettle to boil and went through to the living room where he pulled the offending item from the bureau drawer. Sometimes, he doubted his sanity, and remembering the state he'd been catapulted into on first reading it, he wanted to check. *I really lost it. Something snapped and I wound up in the abyss. Bloody drinking again. After all this time.* He focused on the piece of paper and read it carefully. No. He wasn't going mad. It really was the same typewriter, he'd swear to that. He hadn't imagined it. So what was this nonsense?

I know where she is. Your wife.
And I know what you did...

It sounded threatening, to be sure, but there was no demand for money, no instructions on how or where payment was to be made. Maybe that would come later. His stomach knotted at the thought. Damn it, he wouldn't pay if it did turn to blackmail. It didn't matter now, for God's sake. Or did it? Shit, it might. The police would go to town on it. On him. It would start all over again.

He walked back to the kitchen and reboiled the kettle, pouring water over the fresh leaves. He'd never taken to tea bags. A hangover from his time with Laura. He smoothed the letter out on the table, frowning. This was different somehow. Quite different. He thought back to the first blackmail letter. It had arrived just one week after Laura had disappeared. He could remember the shock of it even now. More than that – he could still feel it. He stared at the paper again. Whatever this meant, it did not bode well.

Mags had not slept well and it had had nothing to do with being cold or damp. She had, in fact – thanks be to God again – found warm, dry shelter once more. She coughed as she unzipped her sleeping bag, startled by the rattle in her chest, the wheezing as she tried to get her breath. *Holy Mother of God! Please don't let me be ill!* This did not feel like a simple cold. *Oh, dear Mother, please, I mustn't be sick – I can't be sick. Please, you've kept me all these years. Do not fail me now.*

123

Packing her bedding away, Mags thought about the dreams she had had. They were the reason she hadn't slept well. She hadn't had dreams like these in a long, long time. She thought she'd put all that behind her. The Community. Terry and Daniel and Caitlin. But, oh God, they had come back to haunt her. It was the children who afflicted her most. *What I did was an act of betrayal. I betrayed their trust.* The dreams – nightmares, really – had returned because of the shock of discovering how close she'd come to Darrowdale the other day. *Being there was a mistake, Holy Mother. I swear it was a mistake. I promised you – and myself – I would never go back again, and I never have. And you know why. I repented. Turned my back on my sins and walked away. I have repented. Truly I have.*

It was horribly cold. Bone-achingly cold. The ground was white with frost, withered grass as stiff as a board. A low mist hung above the fields. Was it mist or was it fog? Mags felt uneasy. There were no magpies to give her a sign today. She was on her own. *No, no,* she chided herself. *Our Lady is with me. She knows the expiation I have made – am still making – for my sins. She will not abandon me. Warmth is what I need. Just a couple of days of proper warmth.* That would be enough to shake off the cough, she was sure. Then she could think again about where she wanted to be for Christmas.

Daniel was replete with the late lunch he had shared with Colin and Ronnie after being roped into the tidy-up session to deal with the aftermath of Saturday's Open Day. *Odd,* he thought. *Yesterday, I felt like a freak show. Today, I feel more normal than I've felt in years. Accepted. Just part of the furniture.* That felt good.

The round-up for work duty had come immediately after breakfast. Daniel had barely had time to eat, having put his off to make his phone calls, so it wasn't until he had made his escape with the Walters that he'd had time or privacy enough to discuss the outcome. He had, in fact, made three calls, not two, but Colin and Ronnie didn't need to know that.

'I got a dead tone when I phoned home,' he told Colin and Ronnie. 'Tried it several times, but no go.'

'Bad weather, do you think? Snow brought the lines down or something? I take it you still have lines in rural Devon?' Colin asked.

'More than likely.' Daniel laughed. He had never really thought about it. 'If I can't get through by morning, I'll report it out of order.'

'You're not going back there tonight?'

'No. Back to London. Work calls.'

'But did you get through to Caitlin?' Ronnie asked, impatient for news.

Daniel shook his head. 'She wasn't there. Or was still in bed. But I got her answering machine.' He stopped, overcome by the recollection of hearing her voice for the first time in twelve years. He'd phoned her home number, figuring that even aromatherapists didn't work on Sundays. He'd wanted to cry with relief as she spoke her message.

'Hi. Sorry I can't come to the phone right now.

Please leave your name and number and I'll get back to you.' Perhaps it was as well she hadn't answered herself. He hadn't expected to be so strongly affected. At least now he was fore-warned.

'Did you leave a message?' Ronnie asked.

'Yes. Though I wasn't quite sure what to say.'

'So what did you say?'

Daniel shrugged with embarrassment. 'I said, "Hi, Cait. This is Daniel. Your brother. Please call me." And I left my mobile number, office number and the number for the London flat. I'm hardly ever in Devon, so it would have been pointless leaving her that one.'

'She'll ring you, I'm sure.' Ronnie smiled.

'It's been a long time, Ronnie.' Daniel didn't share her certainty.

'All the more reason why she should. Will you let us know?'

'I will.' He meant what he said. He had promised to keep in touch with them, even if it was only a card at Christmas. They walked out to the car with him.

'At least you have a couple of hours of daylight left before it gets dark, and the forecast's not too bad,' Colin told him.

Daniel shrugged. 'I don't mind night driving, and it's all straightforward once I hit the motor-way.' He stood for a moment, then, pushing awkwardness aside, hugged them both. 'Thank you again. For everything.'

'Our pleasure. Take care of yourself, Daniel. And say hello to Caitlin for us. Give her our love.' Colin thumped him lightly on the shoulder.

126

'I will. If she phones.'

'She'll phone.'

'You must have a degree in eternal optimism, Ronnie!'

'No. I just know she'll phone.'

'Woman's intuition. Don't knock it,' Colin said.

Daniel got into the car, laughing. They waved as he pulled away. He watched them in the rearview mirror as he swung onto the drive leading to the main road. They continued waving until he was out of sight.

Chapter Ten

The letter-writer had stayed overnight in Darrowdale before starting the drive back to Cheltenham, and had now decided to take a break at a motorway service station. Nursing a cup of coffee, a mixture of emotions fermented in the disturbed mind. *I must stay calm. Don't let it get to me. Seeing that damned place again. I have gained more insight, and seeing Daniel turned out to be a real bonus.* The thought faltered. Daniel had not seemed unduly affected by the letters, which he must have received by now. *Bluffing. He must have been bluffing. Putting up a front for them.* Surprise filtered through. *Like I did. We have something in common, then.*

A laugh rose, unbidden, and had to be suppressed. This was a public place. Other people were here. *I must appear perfectly normal and in control. Which, of course, I am.*

Memories of the Open Day were further sifted. *So much has changed since I was last there. The swimming pool. Greater diversity and expansion. I suppose they work with whatever talents they have at any given time, depending on who lives there. Some, they have lost. Talents and people.* Names came to mind, but the letter-writer refused to give them mental articulation. *Think only of what you saw.* What had been seen? Normality. Despite all that had happened nineteen years ago and since, they carried on as if it didn't matter. *Maybe they should pay the price, too. The whole Community.* The thought was held while curiosity explored its potential. *Now that would be a statement. A very public statement. I must think further on this. But not now. Not yet.* The fate of the remainder of Laura Richardson's family had to be uppermost at this time.

Did Caitlin really think she could fool me by changing her name? Did she really think she could hide? From me? I know where they are. I know where they all are. Nothing and no one is hidden from me. The light shines and reveals all that would be hidden. The light shines in the dark places, in the midst of the darkness, and reveals the puny beings who think they can hide. They may think they are safe, but they are not. They shall be no more, for I know their secrets. Their secret words and deeds, even their secret names. This is what gives me my power. And they shall pay the price for their iniquities.

More than one possibility sprang to mind for Daniel. How co-operative of him to work in the music industry. It could be made to look like suicide or even an accident. Drink and drugs were still commonplace in the circles he inhabited. The letter-writer smiled into the coffee cup so that no one else would see. An accidental overdose, perhaps. It would make a change from last time. *The last one, at Hermitage House, looked like suicide, which is precisely as I planned. He couldn't live without his wife. Everyone knew that. They accepted that. The Coroner had accepted it...*

Daniel, then, would be an accident. It wouldn't even have to be an overdose, come to think of it. He could be run over. Fall under a train. Plunge from one of the higher levels of a multi-storey car park. *I shall have fun with that one.*

The mind moved on. What about Terry? How will he die? *I don't need to think of that yet. He will be the last of the three. But Caitlin... Caitlin will be the first...* Rage began to seethe, pumping adrenaline through the body of the letter-writer. It had been simmering in a cauldron of hatred for many years. *Caitlin will truly suffer. She has to suffer. No swift and easy death for her. No slipping into unconsciousness, oblivious of her appointment with death. She must be aware of her pain. She must be aware of mine. She must know that she is going to die and I shall show her no mercy. Where was mercy when I needed it...?*

It took a great effort of will for the letter-writer to regain control. *Rational. I must be cool and rational. Until I take her to her fate. Then is the time for the fire. Not until then, when I have her alone. Then, it can all be loosed... All shall be revealed. All shall at last come into the light.* She had seen too much the day her mother had disappeared.

129

Caused panic. It was all her fault...

The letter-writer coughed, forcing a change of mental direction. *The Open Day. Go back to the Open Day... Who is Deborah Harvey? She was friendly with Veronica. Interested in Daniel. Much too interested. Why?* She *didn't miss the expression on his face when Angela produced his sister's business card. She observed his face as acutely as I did. I asked her about herself and she told me nothing. I asked her about Daniel and she pretended not to know him. She lied to me. Why?* Several possibilities were gone through. Ahhh...

The letter-writer's memory had not failed. *The photographer from the newspaper. He knew her. More to the point, she knew him. I should have talked to him, but got waylaid by another visitor. By the time I broke free, he'd gone. He didn't stay long and I made sure he got no pictures of me. But he knew her and she knew him, and she brushed him off, pretended not to know him. Now why should she do that?* This time, as the possible answer slipped into the letter-writer's mind, the smile was not hidden.

That must be it. It has to be. I shall make a phone call in the morning. Deborah Harvey, just like the Richardsons, cannot hide from me. Feeling much better now, the letter-writer rose to leave, another idea finding form. *Tonight, I shall pay a visit to Caitlin. See what she's been up to while I've been away. Perhaps it's time to turn up the heat. Just a little. The more frightened she is, the better. And the longer she feels fear before I take her, the better. She has to suffer. In suffering is redemption.*

'Suffering' was one of the letter-writer's favourite words.

Back at Nina's cottage, Caitlin lay awake, unable to get back to sleep but not yet wanting to get out of bed. Yesterday, she had been to see Sister Barbara. Tomorrow – tomorrow afternoon – she would go back to Cheltenham. Until then, she had the luxury of more time on her own. *How awful not to want to be at home*, she thought. Since the first anonymous letter, she had felt that her privacy had been invaded, that her home was somehow no longer secure .

She shivered at the thought, hugging the duvet to her body and plumping the pillows restlessly. Her life had been on an even keel for so long, and now – what? Everything seemed to be falling apart, all kinds of unwelcome memories surfacing, as a result of some unknown, malicious letter-writer.

What was she going to do? Twice, now, she had been given advice she didn't want to take, namely, go to the police. Hell's teeth! This was no good. She couldn't settle. Might as well get up. Dutifully, she took the medicine Nina had prescribed while preparing breakfast, shocked to notice the time on the kitchen clock. *This is not breakfast – it's brunch*, she corrected herself. *And what's in this potion, anyway? Eye of newt and tongue of frog?* She laughed at herself and spoke out loud. 'Got out of bed on the wrong side, did we?'

The heating was on but the kitchen was chilly. The temperature must have plummeted during the night. Caitlin found a tray and, loading it with the tea, toast, orange juice and cereal she had prepared, carried it through to the living room, where she turned on the gas fire, feeling better for sitting close to the warmth.

Having eaten, she reached for the phone. Normally content with her own company, what she needed right now was the sound of Josh's voice.

Josh had decided to eat out. Heading for the door, he almost didn't answer the phone when it rang.

'Cait! How are you?' The warmth in his voice gave her a glow.

'I'm fine – how about you?'

'Missing you.'

'Really?'

'Really. So how are you enjoying the peace and quiet?'

'A lot. I feel more relaxed than I've done in ages. What are you up to?'

'I was just about to go out for lunch.'

'Oh, sorry, don't let me hold you up.'

'You're not. I'd far rather talk to you.'

Caitlin laughed. 'Where were you thinking of going?'

'I didn't have any particular place in mind. Just thought I'd drive until I spotted somewhere that looked inviting.'

'I know a really good place.'

'You do?'

'I don't know if you'd want to drive that far, though.'

'How far is "far"?'

'Well ... there's this little cottage deep in the Oxfordshire countryside...'

Josh chuckled. He didn't need asking twice.

By the time he arrived, Caitlin had raided the freezer and prepared lunch.

'Mmm, looks almost as good as you!'

She laughed as he nuzzled her neck. 'Well, you know what they say, the proof of the pudding is in the eating. Not that I made a pudding.'

'I'll do that later.'

'Oh yes?'

'I'm a dab hand with desserts, remember? You're looking good, Cait. I was worried you were going down with something.'

'Not as worried as I was.' As they sat down to eat, Caitlin started to tell him what had been happening.

Later, as they sat mulling over all that she had said, Caitlin tried to lighten the atmosphere.

'We never did get that dessert, did we?'

'Damn! I forgot all about it!' Josh jumped up and started rooting around in the larder. 'What do you fancy?'

Caitlin, leaning in the doorway, looked at him steadily and took a deep breath. 'You,' she said.

It was early evening when Nina got the urge to go back to Caitlin's house. *This is silly*, she told herself. *I went yesterday and there were no more letters.* But the feeling persisted. What was to stop the letter-writer from hand-delivering the next message? It could be sitting on the mat now. Or what about the answer phone? Suppose the writer had got hold of Caitlin's phone number? That would be easy enough – she wasn't ex-directory.

133

I can check in the morning. That would be far more sensible. It'll be light and there'll be people around. It bothered Nina to realise that she was afraid. *All the more reason to leave it until tomorrow. Why go now? In the dark?*

Because I have to, she answered herself.

Mike was out so she left a note for him by the kettle. It was always the first place he made for on coming home. *I won't be long, anyway,* she told herself. *I'll be back before he is.* Picking up her car keys, she headed for the front door.

The letter-writer glanced at the clock. Much refreshed by being back home, everything had been planned now, right down to the smallest detail. Time to pay Caitlin another visit...

Before, I had the overview. Now every i has been dotted, every t crossed. A gentle simmer is all we need. For now. We don't want complications at this point. The weather had turned much colder. *Shall I take the car or shall I walk? Perhaps I'll toss a coin.*

Decision made, the only sound in the room was the ticking of the clock as the door swung shut.

This really is silly, Nina told herself. She had known, the minute she walked into Caitlin's house, that all was well, everything as it should be. There was no hand-delivered message from the letter-writer, just a free newspaper and a couple of fliers for take-away food services. *Probably pushed through the letterbox after I left yesterday.* She hadn't checked the answer phone yet – she'd do it on her way out. She drew the curtains and turned on the lights downstairs, being careful to avoid physical contact with the piano. The memory of her encounter with it was still vivid. It did not bode well, she acknowledged. Much as she wanted to think otherwise, she knew in her heart that what she had felt as she had run her fingers over the keys was what Caitlin's mother had felt. She had been dealt a crushing blow to the back of her skull, and Nina had no desire to relive that experience .

There was a name for it, she knew, this ability to pick up on other people's emotions and experiences through contact with an object they'd touched or clothing they'd worn. She hadn't known about it for a long time, and when she did find out, it had come as a great relief. It meant that other people were like her. She was not the total freak she had believed herself to be. It was something she had been able to do all her life, or rather, something that happened to her frequently. She would enter a room, or handle an object, and sense the physical and emotional feelings of people who had lived there, or who had held those same objects. Once, in an anatomy and physiology class, bones had been passed around the group. Some were plastic reproductions, but some had been the genuine article. Nina had recoiled on handling a femur, experiencing a palpable sense of strangulation.

'Where did you get these bones?' she had asked the tutor, doing her best to make the question sound casual.

'Oh, they were dug up some years ago. The police had to be called in, of course, but it was soon established that they were hundreds of

135

years old. It's thought the site may have been a prison at one time, or a place of execution.'

The hanged man, Nina had thought. After that, she had avoided genuine bones as much as possible.

So, she thought, bringing herself back to the reality of Caitlin's living room. *Caitlin's mother was hit on the head. Did she die from that blow or was she merely knocked unconscious? How much damage would it have done? More to the point, perhaps – who had hit her, and why?*

Her thoughts were interrupted by a sound so unexpected, she almost jumped out of her skin. It was the chiming of a bell. There was somebody at the door...

Chapter Eleven

Monday 13 December

Twelve messages had been left on Chris Farmer's answer machine over the weekend. One in particular intrigued him. 'Chris, it's Daniel Richardson, 8.30 a.m. Sunday morning. I've found my sister, but that hasn't made you redundant. There's at least one other matter I want you to look into. Call me on my mobile to arrange a meeting – we need to talk.'

A mile and a half away, in another London district, the red light was blinking on Daniel

Richardson's answer phone with an altogether less measured message from his girlfriend buried among his business calls.

The morning briefing was over and Derek Kenny was having a quick cup of coffee before getting on with his other tasks as editor of a newspaper. Before he could turn to any of that, however, he wanted to speak to Deborah Harvey about her visit to the Community Open Day. She had said she wanted to see him as a result of information picked up there in connection with the Laura Richardson special. His interest, naturally, was piqued. There was a knock at his door at the appointed time and in she came.

'What have you got then, Deborah?'

'Probably more than you bargained for,' she grinned. 'Certainly more than I did.'

'Oh?'

'Mmm. Guess who was there for the first time since leaving the place?'

Derek was caught off guard and unable to answer. She didn't, in any case, give him time.

'Daniel Richardson.' She pronounced the name with all the flourish of a magician producing a rabbit from a hat.

'Daniel?' The only thing that would have impressed Derek more would have been for Deborah to have said 'Laura' .

'The very same. Stuck close by Ronnie and her husband much of the time and looked distinctly uncomfortable when he got collared – as he frequently did – by people who knew him when he lived there.' She thought for a moment.

'Actually, to be fair, he did relax a bit later on. But between those two points, something very interesting happened. Something that, I swear to God, nearly caused him to faint.' She paused dramatically.

'Well, what, for God's sake?' Derek could quite cheerfully have shaken her.

'One of the old guard – Angela Fielding, the actress – was over the moon to see him and made a big fuss. All the more so, because she'd seen his sister, Caitlin, just the day before.'

'What? At the Community? I mean, I thought...'

'No. In Cheltenham, of all places. That's apparently where she lives nowadays. The point is, that's when Daniel looked like he was about to faint. Actually, I tell a lie.' Deborah was thinking again, forcing herself to be precise. 'He was shocked, yes, but the point at which he went as white as a sheet was when Angela was babbling on about having Caitlin's business card. He had it out of her hand at the speed of light. Devoured every detail.'

'He what?'

'Exactly. That's what I thought. Why should he be so keen to see it and hear about her if he was already in contact with her? I don't think he had a clue where she was or what she was doing. More to the point, he seemed to be desperate to get that information ... desperate to contact his sister.'

'Aren't you jumping to conclusions?'

Deborah shook her head. 'Oh, I don't think so. Particularly given that Ronnie's husband made up some cock and bull story later to get the card off her and copy the details "for his database records".' She grinned at her editor.

'I don't know, Deborah.' Derek grimaced. 'You do know that Caitlin ran away from home a few years after her mother disappeared? Maybe they've never been in touch since.'

'Of course I know that. I've virtually lived in the archives since you gave me this story. You'd have had to have been there, boss. Seen the expression on his face. Sure, I know what you're saying, but it was as if he were ... looking for her. Anyway–'

'You say she's living in Cheltenham? What's she doing there?' Derek interrupted.

'An aromatherapist, would you believe? Funny, that. One of the people in the group was from there but didn't know she was living in the same place.'

'One of the old members? Or a visitor?'

Deborah screwed up her face, remembering with pleasure, the man who had taken her fancy. Had he been wearing a badge? She hadn't been paying attention to such details at the time and cursed herself for it now.

'Probably a visitor. Certainly too young to be one of the old guard. About ten years older than me?' She hazarded a guess, noting ruefully that however gorgeous he was, he was too old for her own interest in him. 'Funny though – he seemed to know who they were talking about.'

'Then it must have been a past member. Or child thereof.'

Deborah just shrugged. 'As I was trying to explain before you side-tracked me, I hope to get

139

to the bottom of this business about Daniel's reaction to the news about Caitlin.'

'And how are you going to do that?'

'You're going to love this. Ronnie promised to speak to Daniel on my – well, the newspaper's – behalf. See if he'll be interviewed about his mother's disappearance.'

'You didn't ask him yourself?' Derek's cup clattered as he slammed it onto the saucer.

'Hold your horses! I was there incognito, remember? Ronnie went to a lot of trouble to keep my connection with the paper under wraps. Besides, as I said, I think there's more going on than meets the eye. I didn't want to blow my cover – though Rod nearly did that, the prat, when he came to take the pictures. I had to give him the brush-off in no uncertain terms. Bloody idiot! I felt like something out of a James Bond spoof, hissing at him and telling him to piss off, we didn't know each other.'

Derek shook his head and tried not to laugh. Rod was awfully gung-ho and as thick-skinned as they come. 'He got the message, then?'

'Oh yes. Anyway, Ronnie's spoken to Daniel and he's going to give me a ring, whether it's yea or nay.'

'And if it's nay, you will, of course, change his mind?' Derek raised his eyebrows.

'But of course.'

'Well done. I can see you're thinking up a whole new angle on all of this. Let me know as soon as he rings.' Derek rose and came to the front of his desk, obviously thinking their conversation was at an end. Deborah stood up, too, but made no move to leave.

'There is one other thing.'

'Oh?'

'Yes.' She took a deep breath. If she handled this the wrong way, she could get more than a flea in her ear. She could be out of a job, and she was far too interested in this case to let that happen. 'You put me onto this because you wanted to find out the truth, right?'

'Right.'

'The *whole* truth? Warts and all?'

'But of course. Why do you think I've kept this story going all these years?'

'Well, I had wondered about that. Do you know how many missing persons cases there have been in our circulation area over the past twenty years?' Deborah held up her hand as Derek opened his mouth. 'I do. She was far from being the only one. And that set me wondering. Why *this* story? Why *this* particular woman?' She smiled suddenly. 'But then, it was you who encouraged me to talk to Ronnie, and she just happened to mention, as you must have known she might, that when she first met Laura, Laura was going out with you. In today's parlance, you and she were an item. So if I'm to do this job properly, I need to know all there is to know about your relationship with Laura Richardson.'

She held her breath. They stood, eye to eye, for what seemed like an awfully long time. A slow smile crept across Derek's face.

'I knew you were the right person for this story. What kept you so long?'

Two floors below them, someone else was making enquiries about relationships. Specifically, Deborah Harvey's relationship with the newspaper. It was so easy, the letter-writer thought. No challenge at all, which was a shame, really. *I like a good challenge. Always have. That's why I came to understand my mission.*

All so simple. One telephone call. One quick question, brisk and businesslike. 'I was trying to contact someone who I think covered a story I'm interested in – Deborah Harvey. Is she still a reporter with you?'

'Trainee reporter, yes. Did you want–?'

The letter-writer cut the connection. 'Yes' had been enough. *I was right. It was just as I suspected. My theory has been vindicated. One more piece of the jigsaw puzzle fits into place...*

Josh Middleton took a long lunch break, still reeling from the revelations Caitlin had made to him yesterday. On all fronts. He grinned, thinking how odd he must have looked, screeching up to his house this morning to brush his teeth and collect his briefcase. Their love-making had been better than he could ever have imagined. Sheer abandonment. *I thought I'd died and gone to heaven.* He caught his breath at the memory of her softness, her warmth, her perfume. The touch of her skin, her lips, her hair. *Dear God, I've got it bad...*

He had listened intently as she told him of her mother's disappearance, sensing an initial tension, but then she'd just taken a deep breath and been matter-of-fact, moving through the

142

trouble with her father, separation from her brother, a few years in London and onto what she termed 'the bombshell' of the letters she'd started receiving. She hadn't gone into a lot of detail about any of it and he hadn't asked her to expand.

He leaned back in his seat, stretching out his long legs as he moved mentally from lover to analyst. What a nightmare she had lived through. So much trauma at such a pivotal age, and no resolution, no closure of the underlying problem. What in God's name had happened to Caitlin's mother? The letters she'd talked about didn't make sense.

'Do you have any idea who might be sending them?' he'd asked.

She'd shaken her head. 'No. I can't even begin to think. It all happened so long ago. And that's something else I don't understand – why now? And what does this person mean, "I know where she is"?'

'Where do you think she is, Caitlin?'

'I don't know where she is, in the sense of a geographical location. But I believe she's dead. I just can't believe she would voluntarily vanish and not at least let someone know she was still alive. Even I did that when I went to London. Besides, I can't believe that she would have left us. Daniel and I. She was a good mother, Josh. I'm not making this up, or looking at the past through rose-tinted glasses. She loved us. And we loved her.'

It was a mystery, all right. Unease stirred in Josh's mind. Who would write such letters, and why? And, as Caitlin had rightly asked, why *now?* He had asked to see them, even though she had told him their contents. There was a warped mind at work here. Not by any stretch of the imagination could this be perceived as a practical joke. So what was the connection between the letter-writer and Caitlin? Between the letter-writer and Caitlin's mother? Josh knew he would need more to go on in order to build up a psychological profile, but even on the little he knew so far, he didn't like the look of things. Caitlin had readily admitted that Nina was taking the letters seriously, and Josh was relieved about that. At least he had an ally there. It might be an idea to talk to her as soon as possible. Preferably before Caitlin came home .

It was sheer fluke that Mags saw the newspaper. For a start, she hadn't realised she was still so close to Darrowdale. And secondly, it was a gust of wind that blew it into her legs as she rounded the corner that would lead her out of the village. Anyone else might have thrown it away, but Mags knew that newspapers – especially nice dry ones – have a variety of uses for a lady of the road. She was about to put it into the side pocket of her rucksack when something caught her eye. Whether the caption or the photograph registered first, she wasn't sure. It didn't matter, anyway. All she knew was that she found herself face to face with an account of the Darrowdale Community's Open Day.

Holy Mother! And here I am, trying to get away from all that! She looked around her, anxious to reorient herself. There was no bench to sit on, and no sign of a café. There was, however, a pub, and it had one of those A-Boards outside, advertising the fact that it was open all day and offered afternoon tea, morning coffee and all-day breakfasts. Mags felt a sudden sense of confusion. Pubs never used to do things like that, and it was years since she had been in one. Dare she go in now? Was she clean enough? Did she have enough money for a cup of tea? *Well, of course I do,* she chided herself. *I'm not completely destitute. Not quite. Not yet.*

She approached the pub with a firm stride, her heart leaping as she noticed a toilet block to the left of it. Yes! Not only could she check her appearance, she would be able to use the lavatory and, hopefully, have hot water in which to wash.

Fifteen minutes later, she was sitting in the pub nursing a pot of tea. What luxury! A proper china pot with a pleasing abstract design, and a proper china cup and saucer to match. A milk jug, too, and a pot of hot water. Did people realise how much they took for granted, she wondered? A string and label hung over the side of the teapot from beneath the lid. Tea bags. She'd never liked them much herself. You couldn't beat proper leaf tea, but still, to be fair, that was for homes. It made sense, she supposed, for establishments such as this to use bags. Less waste. She forced herself to stay calm, noting the few people also present, sussing out through intuition born of long experience that no one here was a threat. Her heart rate slowed. She found conversation difficult, being on her own for so much of the time, but had carried this one well. She had been greeted cheerfully, small talk made about the unsuitability of the weather for hiking at this time of year. She knew she had pitched her reply just right, and had even managed a smile. Now, please God, she would be left alone to make the most of her tea. And read the newspaper.

She poured a cup carefully, recognising that she was using the almost ritual movements as a prevarication before getting to the task in hand. Should she be doing this at all? She had promised Our Lady... *Then why did this particular newspaper just happen to choose to come to me, if not to read it?*

It could be a temptation...

She dismissed the thought abruptly. *To what? What might I be tempted to do? Go back there? After all this time?* Her heart beat violently at the thought, and she coughed, trying to keep it as quiet as possible. She would never go back there. Wild horses couldn't drag her.

She smoothed out the paper, taking a deep drink of her tea to steady herself. Her hands weren't shaking. Good. So, this was what had happened at the Open Day, and thanks be to God that she hadn't blundered into it. She read the account carefully, having to adjust the distance at which she held the newspaper from her eyes. She didn't often get the chance to read nowadays, of course, and that was a shame in itself, but if she did – if she had a normal life – she knew she would need glasses to do so. Her distance vision was fine, but her close vision was a different matter. What was it she'd heard someone say once? They had been referring to something else, but it was applicable all the same – that was it – 'if you don't use it, lose it'. That was the problem, all right. Too little practice over too many years.

Her eyes now adjusted, she read the article. There wasn't much of it, really. It told what had happened and when, and said the Day had been a great success with a record number of visitors despite the weather. There had also been a reunion of former members of the Community. Mother of God! And what was this? Colin and Veronica Walters, speaking on behalf of the Community, said they were pleased to see so many faces from the past and were hoping to hold a bigger reunion the following summer. Colin and Ronnie! Still there. They must be senior members now. How many of the originals were left? Oh – Angela, too. No one ever referred to her simply by her name, of course. *Even when I lived there, she was 'the actress, Angela Fielding'.* Like a second mother to Caitlin, she was, Caitlin being so fired up about drama and writing and all. Caitlin … Mags scanned the photograph, but there was no sign of anyone who looked like her. *Would I even recognise her now? Of course I would.*

She looked at the photograph more carefully. Colin and Ronnie. They'd aged well. Ronnie a bit grey, by the look of it, and Colin a bit thin on top, but it was definitely them. Angela, of course, looking remarkably the same, and – Saints preserve us – with the same man, by the look of it! What was his name? Mags shook her head, frustrated. *I should know it. I should remember it.*

147

Why, she argued with herself, *when I've spent so many years trying to forget?*

There were other faces she recognised, too, and a few she didn't. What was this? 'For more pictures of the Open Day, turn to centre spread'. She turned the pages and caught her breath. It was as if everything were put into context. In the middle of the pages, across the crease, was a picture of the public entrance to the Community, showing the Tea Room and Gift Shop. Oh God! How it brought it all back! And clustered around this picture were photos of activities that had taken place on the day. People buying handicrafts. Mags had to fight to stop herself from moaning as she recognised the Chapel in the upstairs of the Great Barn. *I shouldn't have looked at this. I should have thrown it away.* She forced herself to carry on. People enjoying hot soup and crusty bread. *Don't think about food.* People sampling wine and mince pies.

Oh no. No. It can't be. She squinted at the photograph, not because it was small, but because she wanted to get the best possible look at it, the clearest view. She had to be sure. It couldn't be. Daniel? The beard might have thrown her, and he'd certainly put on weight, but – *was* it really him? She stared. She remembered the time Terry had grown a beard. Hadn't kept it long because no-one liked it really, but ... it *was* Daniel. She put the paper down. Added hot water to the teapot. Stirred it. Poured herself another cup. This time, the tremor in her hands was unmistakable.

What in God's name was he doing there? The

place must be to him what it was to her, surely? A place best forgotten, holding memories of trauma and pain. Did he go back every year? She picked up the paper again and checked every picture. There was definitely no sign of Caitlin or Terry. *That doesn't mean they weren't there,* she told herself. *They could have been there, but not in the photographs.* But why would they go? Why did Daniel go? Surely the link would be too much to bear. She looked again at the picture. He looks as if he's done well for himself. I wonder what he does for a living? She remembered the last time she'd seen him. Nineteen years ago. The day – *that* day...

Abruptly, Mags got up, folding the paper and thrusting it firmly in the side pocket of her rucksack. Just as she'd originally planned. *Just as I should have done, without looking at the thing. It's all coming back to haunt me. Will it never go away?* Sick at heart, she left the pub and strode down the road as if aiming to break a speed record. All she knew was that she had to put as much distance as possible between herself and that accursed place.

Chapter Twelve

Nina was pleasantly surprised to receive the phone call from Josh and relieved by his account of the time he'd spent with Caitlin. At least someone else was in the know and, professionally

149

as well as personally, it was good to have him on board. More weight was building up behind the idea of Caitlin going to the police, and, as far as Nina was concerned, that could only be a good thing. Josh was equally pleased.

'She told me you knew about it – the background as well as the letters. Said you were the only one who knew, apart from me. We have to help her, Nina. It's knowing how that's the problem. We need to get together.'

'I agree. But a couple of other things have happened since yesterday. Things she doesn't know about yet. Let me talk to her first. I'll come back to you.'

Nina had sat for a moment before picking up the phone again, this time to call Caitlin. What was the best way to break this to her? Not over the phone. She had to see her, tell her face to face. Above all, Caitlin mustn't go back to the house first. Her mind finally made up, Nina began to dial, praying that Caitlin had not yet left the Oxford cottage.

Daniel Richardson had just retrieved his fifth answer phone message. Still nothing from Cait. Please God, let her phone. He cursed himself for having left things so long. Suppose she didn't want to get in touch? *Why should she, for Christ's sake? It was bad enough that I let her down the way I did, but why the fuck didn't I just tell her at Gran's funeral? Say I was sorry. Explain about Dad. Maybe it's just too late to put things right. Too much water under the bridge.* He snatched up the phone when it rang, heart hammering in the hope that it

150

might be his sister. It was Chris Farmer.

'You found your sister? Good news.'

'Well, I've found her and I haven't. I know where she is, and I've left a message on her machine. I haven't actually talked to her yet.'

'But you say this doesn't make me redundant? What is it you want me to do exactly?'

Daniel scratched at his beard absently. 'Rather a lot. We need to meet. I want to run something past you, sound you out on the possibilities, but I don't want to give you the full go-ahead until I've talked to Cait.'

'OK. Where and when do you want to meet?'

'Are you free today?' The men arranged a mutually convenient time and Daniel chose the place. Small, intimate and exclusive, the restaurant would combine the privacy they needed with first rate food.

There were more messages to retrieve. The next one was not business. It was Cathy, his girlfriend. A demented Cathy.

'Bastard! Bastard! Think you can dangle me forever, do you? Well *fuck you!* Fuck your house! See how you like it! I'm out of here, out of your miserable fucking existence and I *never* want to see you again!'

Daniel stared at the phone, his face a moving picture as a mixture of emotions ran over it. Finally, he laughed, running both hands through his hair. *Shit! I never would have thought she had it in her! Well, saves me the trouble of ditching her. What did she mean about the house, though...?*

Caitlin had been more than happy to take Nina

151

up on her offer of a late lunch, even though it meant leaving the cottage earlier than she had originally planned. That didn't matter now, though. She had needed and welcomed the isolation when she had gone away. Since seeing Josh, however, she had felt strengthened and ready for contact with her friends. She had thought of dropping the car off at home first, checking that everything was all right, but Nina had her heart set on the Citrus Grove, a vegetarian restaurant on the other side of town, so Caitlin had driven straight there. It was one of their favourite places, with stripped floorboards stencilled with orange and lemon trees, the walls hung with works by local artists and photographers, all of them for sale. They played great jazz tapes there, too.

'Hi – it's so good to see you!'

'You've not been away that long!' Nina returned Caitlin's hug.

'I know – but I feel a million times better than when I went. Thanks, Nina.'

'None needed.' Their orders taken, the two friends fell into a silence while waiting for their food to arrive. Nina twirled her elderflower spritzer, wondering again how she was going to break the news.

'Caitlin, I have a confession to make. I deliberately chose this place so you wouldn't go home first.'

'Oh God, not another letter? Or something worse? My house has been fire-bombed?'

'Don't even joke about it!' Nina was sharper than she had intended. 'I'm sorry. There *has* been another letter, as it happens, but that's not the point. We'll come to that in a minute.' She paused, uncertain how to continue. 'Look, I don't know quite how you're going to take this, whether what I'm about to tell you is good news or bad, so I'll just give it to you straight, OK?'

Caitlin said nothing, her eyes fixed on Nina's face. The moment hung in the air, prolonged by the arrival of their starters. Nina waited until the waitress moved away before continuing .

'You had a visitor last night. Your brother, Daniel.'

'Daniel?' Caitlin looked shell-shocked. 'But ... how did he find me?'

'I'll come to that in a minute. You see–'

'Daniel...' A flood of emotion washed over Caitlin's face and she grasped Nina's hand. 'Tell me from the beginning. What happened?'

'It frightened the pants off me, to be honest. I was at your place, just checking things out, when the doorbell rang.' Nina grimaced. 'I know it sounds stupid, but for one awful moment I thought, what if it was your letter-writer? I put the chain on and peered round the door, and there's this man asking for you, claiming to be your brother. Obviously, I wouldn't know him from Adam, and gave him a hard time, making him show me ID. He must have thought I was crazy. I said you were away and I was a friend, looking after the house. He said he was desperate to get in touch with you – had left a message on your answer phone – and was worried in case you'd been getting – what was the phrase he used – "disturbing letters"?'

153

'He's getting them too?' Caitlin's fork clattered onto her plate.

'So it seems. Started around the same time, wording the same.' Nina shook her head. 'I had two choices at that point. Either this really was your brother, or it was the letter-writer pretending to be him. So I asked him some questions – still from behind the chained door. It's a good thing you told me what you did the other day, Caitlin. About your mother disappearing, you running away from home.'

'God, I don't blame you for not letting him in. You must have been scared stiff.'

'Just common sense precautions. I soon got the feel of him, and no way was he the person writing the letters. Troubled, yes. Worried about you, yes. He was on his way back to London after visiting the Community where you were brought up. That's how he traced you – you gave your card to Angela Fielding?'

'That's right! God! It really is Daniel! You said there was another letter?'

'Yes. Not when I was there last night. I found it when I checked the house this morning, so whether it came after I left or sometime today, I'm not sure.' Nina's alarm bells were ringing overtime on this one.

'Well it must have been this morning. There's no post on a Sunday.'

'That's the point, Caitlin. This one didn't come in the post. It was delivered by hand.'

'Oh my God.' It was one thing to know that the letter-writer knew where she lived; something else again to know that he or she had actually

154

been to her house. Caitlin pushed her plate away. 'I don't believe this.'

'Something needs to be done, Caitlin. You can't go on like this. Please will you go to the police now? Please?'

Caitlin said nothing. Chewing her lower lip, she stared, unfocused, at a photograph on the wall, an atmospheric winter landscape in black and white.

'Daniel's getting them too, you said?' she asked.

Damn it! Nina cursed inwardly. *She's evading the issue.* Sighing, Nina picked up on Caitlin's reference to her brother. Maybe she could be persuaded to take some action there. And maybe he could persuade her to call in the police.

'He left three numbers for you to phone him on. Will you call him?'

Caitlin moved her eyes back to Nina's face, focused again. Silently, she nodded.

'What a fucking day!' Daniel slammed the door behind him as he entered his London flat. Unbelievable! First he'd had his cleaning lady – one very upset cleaning lady – on the phone to say there was no sign of Cathy and the house was completely trashed. Then he'd had the police on his back, suspecting murder because – Christ, he still couldn't believe it – Cathy had cut herself while slashing his clothes. They'd found her and checked everything out, but Christ, he really didn't need this shit. Not now.

So why didn't I press charges? I could have done. He answered his own question. *Yeah. Great publicity. Besides, I probably deserved it. And at least*

I don't have to speak to the stupid cow again.

Agnes Harrison, his cleaning lady – Mrs H, he always called her – had taken more than a bit of placating. He'd called her back, once murder was out of the picture, and while she said she didn't mind the clearing up, the blood bothered her. Didn't want to touch it, even wearing rubber gloves and wielding a bleaching agent strong enough to wipe out every germ known to humankind. Probably worried about the risk of HIV, Daniel recognised. Not that he had it, but he couldn't blame the woman for being cautious. He hadn't bothered trying to talk her round. Just sent her a cheque for her fright and inconvenience, thanked her profusely for calling the police, and told her to go back the following week as usual, by which time the place would be presentable. To achieve that, he had phoned a cleaning crew he knew who were used to clearing up after the excesses of some of the more notorious rock bands he'd worked with. They'd get rid of any damage and blitz the place in no time.

Shit, what a mess! It had pissed him off more than he cared to admit, provoking him into cancelling the few non-working commitments he had before Christmas. Easily done – there was nothing major – but Cathy's rampage, on top of the business of the anonymous letters, had left him feeling decidedly unsettled. Still, at least things were moving. His meeting with Chris Farmer had gone well and Chris had agreed the next stage of Daniel's plan with no problem. Said it should be a relatively simple matter and he

156

would get onto it right away. Personally. No underlings involved, which suited Daniel perfectly. Keep things discreet.

God, I'm exhausted! Daniel headed for the bathroom, thinking in terms of a quick shower before going out to eat. Padding across the floor, he sighed with irritation as the phone rang. Now what? Let the machine take care of it.

The voice was hesitant, unsure. 'Daniel? Ah – I'm sorry you're not there. It's Cait, returning your call...' He almost ripped the phone out of the socket in his haste to pick it up.

Deborah Harvey took a deep breath before ringing the doorbell. It was strange enough to be formally interviewing her own boss, but to be interviewing him at his home was something else again. The house was a large, old-fashioned end-of-terrace, solidly built of red brick and showing signs of being well cared for. Her eyes had run over the short path, tiny front garden, windows and door in an instant appraisal. No peeling paint. Everything neat. Even the net curtains were whiter-than-white. Funny. She'd never thought of Derek as a homebody. Most single men of his age had a reputation for not knowing how to work domestic appliances and living off take-aways. She smiled to herself as she finally rang the bell, determining to keep a straight face if he produced an instant meal. At least that would show he knew how to use a microwave...

Two minutes later, she was wondering just how wrong she could be. Derek had greeted her, taken her coat and hung it in the hall, then

157

invited her to follow him into the kitchen to pour herself a drink while he finished off the cooking. Not a microwave in sight, and the most delicious-smelling lasagne she'd ever seen being taken from the oven. Home-made. Definitely home-made. God!

Most women she knew would kill for a kitchen like this. Lots of space, lots of cupboards; the spice racks alone made for interesting reading. What did they tell her about her boss? That the hippo-like appearance might have more to do with a liking for good food rather than liquid refreshment. That he was an experienced and accomplished cook, who, if those spice racks were to be believed, was equally at home with everything from Thai to Italian, with several continents thrown in along the way. Green glass jars and bottles held rice, pasta, cous-cous – *cous-cous*, for God's sake!

The kitchen utensils were stainless steel, the chopping boards expensive and marked separately for meat, fish and vegetables, and the wooden block held cleavers and knives that could quite cheerfully hold up their heads in Raymond Blanc's kitchen.

'Quite the little housewife, aren't I? Bet you weren't expecting this.'

Deborah blinked and shook her head. What could she say, other than the truth? 'You're right. I wasn't.'

'Just don't tell the buggers back at the ranch, eh? Wouldn't do much for my street cred.'

She laughed and followed him as he led the way into the dining room. 'Take a seat, lass. I'm just

158

serving up.'

Deborah sat at the dining table, large, oval and beautifully polished, her eyes flickering to the framed photographs on the walls. Oh my *God...*! Deborah took a large gulp of her wine, hastily topping it up from the bottle she'd carried through with her. *Tempranillo. Argentinian. Hmm. Never had Argentinian wine before ... Stop digressing!* She was mentally sharp with herself, looking again at what had disturbed her, fervently hoping Derek's clankings in the kitchen would give her time to take it all in. There was no wonder she'd felt the need for a good belt of wine. Nothing so far had been as she'd expected, but this – the dining room – was icing on the cake. She flashed a glance towards the kitchen door. He was still pottering. She'd risk it. Swiftly, she left the table to look more closely at the photographs. There was no way she could be mistaken, of course – how many pictures of Laura Richardson had she seen since she'd been put on this case? Even so... She moved quickly, eyes sucking information from them. Laura by herself. Laura with Derek. Both before she was married, by the look of them. Laura with her children. Bloody hell! Where did he get them? Who took them? More pictures of Laura with her children, older now. *That one*, she thought, peering more closely, *can't have been taken long before she disappeared.* None of them had been run in the paper.

'Er, you couldn't open the door for me, could you? Got my hands a bit full here!'

'Sorry!' Deborah had it open in a flash. Derek,

wearing a pair of oversized zebra-head oven gloves, proudly placed the earthenware lasagne dish on a large woven mat in the centre of the table, disappearing again to return with a huge bowl of salad. His final run produced iced water and a second bottle of wine, already opened to let it breathe. Deborah sat inwardly mesmerised, but outwardly effusive about the meal spread out before her.

'I'm sorry, I should have asked – is there anything I can do to help?'

'Not a thing besides eat and ask questions. And enjoy yourself, of course.'

He was teasing her. No doubt about it. Deborah had suspected, when he'd extended the invitation, that he wanted to be on his own turf because he would feel more comfortable. If he really were going to open up about his relationship with Laura Richardson, it would make sense. She regarded Derek with even greater respect. *He's taken a real risk. Letting me see this. Letting me see a completely different side to him. Made himself completely vulnerable.* Derek was steady under her gaze, didn't flinch from the eye contact. Suddenly, he was serious, back to business.

'You're good, Deborah. Really good. Your face never betrayed a thing and I deliberately left you in here on your own for a few minutes. But you already know that. I know that you must have clocked that these pictures...' His arm swept an arc around the room. '...are not just a sign of my obsession with the case. You're quite right, of course. I was in love with Laura Richardson.'

160

Chapter Thirteen

Jarvis Taylor, of Taylor Norris, Estate Agents & Auctioneers, would immediately have recognised the photograph in the hands of the letter-writer, having only recently sold the property.

Hermitage House, in this particular 5" x 7" image, was awash with summer sunshine. The letter-writer was thinking about the last visit. *The* visit. It hadn't been summer then. Oh no. It had been Christmas Day. Last year. Precisely the reason why Caitlin had to die on Christmas Day *this* year. *Christmas presents to myself. The lives of those who've fucked me over. Fucked me up. And the Richardsons – the whole bloody lot of them: once they're dead, I shall at last be free.*

Slate eyes flickered over photographs pinned to the wall. They were divided into two sections. The Dead Pool and Death Row. The Richardsons were on Death Row. The photographs were old, stolen from the Community years ago. *Just like you stole my life. My happiness. There will be no one to commute your sentence. No pardon. No Court of Appeal. I am Judge, Jury and Executioner. Vengeance is mine. Vengeance, vengeance...*

The eyes settled on the Dead Pool, those already despatched. *My so-called family. The Stepmother from Hell. My father.* Mother was missing. The letter-writer's head was shaken in regret. Surely she should have been the first, had

161

there been any justice. Maybe then, none of the others would have been necessary.

Yes, they would. They all sinned. They all had to pay. Pain gnawed in the gut. *Yet Mother didn't pay. Not by my hand. It was cancer that took her in the end. Cancer! And madness before then. Of a kind. I did inflict that.* The mind wandered back to the attempt. To the interruption. The letter-writer's chest felt like it would explode. *Breathe! Breathe!* Control was regained.

Eyes flickered to the stepfather's photograph. It had been surprisingly easy to kill him. The owner of Hermitage House. At last it had been done. After all those years. And yet ... it hadn't been enough. *Why* hadn't it been enough? That one death should have settled the score, made everything all right. But it hadn't. The feelings hadn't gone away. *Wouldn't* go away. Once that realisation had hit home, the decision had been taken to kill the Richardsons. It was the only thing left to do.

Caitlin would die on Christmas Day, the anniversary of the death at Hermitage House. Daniel would meet his fate at Easter. Terry at Pentecost. Religious Festivals. Feast Days, they used to be called. *And I shall feast on my freedom.* The mind slipped back to Pentecost. *I shall kill Terry then. If he doesn't kill himself first...*

The latter thought slipped unbidden into the letter-writer's mind. Slate eyes flickered. Terry had been unstable since Laura's disappearance. A frown hovered around the strangely immobile face. He couldn't be allowed to take things into his own hands. End things just because he felt

162

sorry for himself. *He* felt sorry? Outrageous! He didn't know the meaning of the word. Couldn't begin to. *But I'll make him understand...* The frown was allowed to settle, etching lines of granite to complement the slate eyes. This would not do. Terry's suicide was a distinct possibility. Especially if, as originally planned, Caitlin and Daniel were killed first. Weak. The man was weak. Would never hold up under that kind of strain. And with Caitlin being first... She was his favourite. 'Katie', he'd called her. 'My darling Katie.' Fathers, supposedly, were often like that. Close to their daughters. Some of them went too far. Touched them. Screwed them. A hot flash of sexual excitement surged through the letter-writer's body at the thought. Had Terry done that with Caitlin? No. She had been a skinny little thing back then, and he'd liked his women rather more voluptuous, and the more the merrier. A memory stirred. Watching Terry perform in that old disused whatever-they-called-it. His cock had glistened with pussy-juice. He was an expert with women, you could tell from the surety with which he handled their bodies, the way he shafted them. How they'd moaned and squealed with pleasure.

The letter-writer's head was shaken to clear the sights and sounds. The sexual tension was higher now, much higher. Time to masturbate. No. Not yet. Terry's suicide couldn't be allowed. So what to do? The fingers of the letter-writer's hand beat a brisk tattoo on the table. He would have to be dealt with before his children.

The idea of a simple reordering – *Terry* on

163

Christmas Day, Caitlin at Easter, Daniel at Pentecost – was so fleeting, it barely registered. Even had it become conscious, it would have been instantly discarded. Caitlin *had* to be the one to die on Christmas Day. It would make a symmetry of a sort. Besides, she had seen. Had been seen. It *had* to be then. The anniversary of *his* death.

Air escaped the letter-writer's lips in a long hiss. This was no good at all. A real inconvenience with Caitlin's death so close. No matter. The left hand slapped the table, chair scraping the wooden floor as it was pushed back abruptly. A *minor* inconvenience. Nothing more. Terry, logically, would have to die first. In the next few days. Simple.

Caitlin turned up on Josh's doorstep in a state of excitement. 'Josh, I couldn't wait to tell you – I've spoken to Daniel!'

He ushered her indoors, where they kissed hungrily. Finally disentangling themselves, he smiled and said, 'That's great. How did it go?'

'Really well. I mean, it was a bit awkward at first, you know? It's been a long time. But once we got going... God, Josh, I didn't realise just how much I'd missed him. Sounds crazy, doesn't it? It was so good to hear his voice.'

'It's not crazy at all. You've had to put your feelings on hold for a long time. It was the worst kind of situation – no resolution, no sense of closure. Now you have an opportunity to move forward, those feelings can come out of the freezer and breathe.'

'We've so much catching up to do.' Caitlin was pacing the hallway as she spoke, mind buzzing with fragments of conversation. 'He's hired a private investigator.'

'What?'

'Originally, it was to find me – once he started getting those letters. Now, he's got him looking into Mum's disappearance.'

'He's not been to the police?'

'No need with this man on the case. Daniel said he probably stands a better chance than the police of getting to the bottom of it.'

Damn! Josh cursed silently. He and Nina had been hoping that Daniel would talk Caitlin into getting the police involved. Still, to be fair, what the hell could the police do? There was probably nothing to go on. Josh grimaced. *I would just have felt better about it, that's all.* He nodded, manoeuvring her towards the kitchen.

'Coffee?'

'Mmm, please. Josh – Daniel and I are getting together to talk things through.'

'With the private investigator?'

'No, just me and Daniel. He's doing a couple of days' work at Real World Studios this week – it's in Bath. Or near Bath, I can't remember. Anyway, he's going to stay on in Bath and I'm going to drive down and meet him in the Cricket Club car park.'

'He plays cricket?'

She laughed. 'No. Well, I don't know! I suppose he might. In the summer, anyway. He just said it's a good place to park, and with me not knowing Bath...'

165

'Sure. So when are you doing this?'

'Day after tomorrow. I thought ... if it goes well ... I might invite him to the weekend at Nina's cottage?' It was a definite question, despite the phrasing.

'Just play it by ear, Cait. Don't push anything, and try not to have too many expectations. As you said yourself, it's been a long time. A lot has happened to both of you and there's a whole lot of unfinished business following on from your mother's disappearance. This is likely to stir up a lot of emotion, some of it quite raw. Take it easy, huh?'

'I will. Thanks, Josh.'

'For what?'

'For listening. For the advice. For being here.' Caitlin laughed suddenly. 'I think you'd better send me a bill!'

'I think not!' He put his arms around her, kissed the top of her head. She pulled free, eyes twinkling as she looked from him to the coffee.

'Do you have any dessert to go with this?'

A slow smile crept across Josh's face. 'What did you have in mind?'

This must be the most bizarre interview ever, Deborah thought, as she settled into the deep armchair with a cup of coffee. *We've had a fantastic meal, washed up – how's that for cosy domesticity! – and now we're ready to get down to business. He's been psyching himself up all night. For years, really. And now it's time.*

'So, all set?' Derek sat in the chair opposite, positioning the cafetière on the low coffee table,

166

then pushing it away to his left, leaving only carpet between them. *Bloody hell*, thought Deborah. *The perfect enactment of taking down the barriers.*

'Ready when you are.' She was poised with her notebook and tape recorder. Derek had made it plain he was speaking on the record and with no holds barred.

'Where to start, then?' He took a long pull on his coffee, apparently looking at her over the top of the mug, but his gaze was unfocused, his memory engaged in finding that opening point. When he finally finished talking, over two hours later, Deborah was agog.

The photograph album lay on the table, loose pictures scattered, spilling from its dog-eared pages. The letter-writer, focused on one particular image, either didn't notice the mess or didn't care. This was not Hermitage House. This was a far earlier image of a childhood home haunted by memories too painful to endure. The letter-writer seldom gave conscious thought to that time for that reason, yet, unconsciously, it gnawed like a captive rat in the gut. How had it all gone so wrong?

Mummy went away. Mummies are not supposed to do such things. Even the ones that do, take their children with them. She didn't take me. She left me with him. Why didn't she take me? Because she didn't love me... If she had loved me, she would have taken me with her. Why, why didn't she love me? She left me with him. It was frightening, no longer having Mummy, and Daddy was very, very cross. It wasn't

167

natural. *She wasn't natural, leaving her child. And he said I was the same – unnatural. Abnormal. A bommunashun. How old was I before I realised he meant that I was an abomination?* The Italian International Banker had married an English Rose. He thought his genes would dominate. I was supposed to be beautiful. And what did he get? An abomination. That's what he called me because I was small and skinny and pale-skinned and ginger-haired.

Dark moods were remembered. Dark days. Even darker nights. *I was always afraid of the dark. Afraid of the bogeyman. Afraid that he – it – would come out of the cupboard in my bedroom. I was a child. But Daddy didn't understand that. He wasn't afraid of anything.*

Things had settled after a while. It should have been all right. *Maybe I would have adjusted to it. Just me and Daddy. Oh God, maybe I could have had a normal life. But then* she *came. And she became the Stepmother from Hell. How many times was I sent to my room? How many times did I cry with hunger because I was deprived of food as a punishment? Oh,* she *pretended. To begin with. 'How cute!' 'How sweet!' 'What a darling child!' And he fell for it. Fell for her. But I knew. I saw the looks she gave me when Daddy wasn't in the room, or when his back was turned. I saw the loathing in her eyes. When did it turn to fear? After that night when he beat me. Really beat me. Not the usual slipper on the bottom. Not a belt. Not a stick. AaaarrrGGGHHH!*

The letter-writer's body trembled as the experience was relived. *How could he have done that? My own* father? *I hadn't done anything to her. Well, not much. Not yet. And I only tried on some of*

168

the clothes that Mummy left behind because I wanted to be beautiful. I thought if I were beautiful, things would be all right. I didn't know it was wrong... Why was it wrong? Why?

And after that night... *She wouldn't meet my eye at breakfast. Avoided looking at me. But I made her. And when she did look, all I did was smile. And that's when the fear started. Her fear. But I was afraid, too. Simply refused to show it, after that. But how often did I cry myself to sleep? How often did I pray, begging for rescue? And then I had the idea. I wrote to Mummy. Daddy thought I didn't know where she was, but I'd seen the letters – bitter, acrimonious – I wouldn't have known those words then, though. But I knew where to write. And I told her. Told her about* her *and told her what Daddy had done. Mummy would help. She would have to do something now. The truth had been told. Rescue would come. I was sick with fear, sneaking into the village to post that letter. Threw up on the way there and on the way back* and *when I finally got back to my room, undetected. And I cried. Cried hot tears – they were physically hot – hot tears of hope, truly believing that help would come, that I could at last leave that wretched place behind.*

The photograph album was scooped up, pictures cascading to the ground. *There is no God. She never came. Never even replied.* Hands grasped the pictures savagely, stuffing them back willy-nilly. The Hermitage House picture again. The letter-writer thought bitterly of the last conversation with its owner. *I always blamed him for Mummy's death. And it turned out that he blamed me. Me! He was ranting that evening. What was it he*

169

said? The shocking words still had the power to wound, to cause blood to run like ice. Or was it fire? *Icy fire,* perhaps.

'Why do you think she didn't take you with her when she left your father for me? What did he tell you? That *I* didn't want you? Not true, though I'd never met you. *She* didn't want you! She knew, you stupid shit – she knew even back then that you weren't right! And how old were you? Seven? Eight? And that first summer at the Community – do you think we wanted you? Why do you think you were booked in the way you were? That no one was to know of the relationship between you and your mother? She didn't want you any more than I did, though back then, I was willing to give you a go.' The speaker had shaken his head. 'It was only because of what happened to your stepmother. I was soft. You were so much older then. I thought your mother had been exaggerating. Just like you, in that pathetic letter you sent just after your father remarried.'

I thought my heart would burst out of my throat at that moment. 'She did get the letter, then?' *How did I keep my voice so quiet, so casual?*

'Of course she didn't. You don't think I was going to let her see that drivel, set her off again.'

'You read it? You opened her mail? Kept it from her? It was the truth!' *Even then, he didn't pick up the warning in my voice.*

'Was it, buggery! You were just an attention-seeking kid. Missing Mummy. Didn't like Daddy's new bit of skirt. That happens all the time. It's normal. People get over it. *Should* get over it. Anyway...' The owner of Hermitage

House had turned his back, moved to pour a drink. '...even if it *were* true, you probably deserved it.'

He had taken a long time to die. The letter-writer had made sure he was aware of every minute.

When Deborah Harvey finally got home, head still whirling from Derek's revelations, the light was blinking on her answering machine.

'Deborah – Daniel Richardson. I'm meeting my sister on Wednesday. I'll come back to you when I've broached the subject with her.'

Oh yes! Oh God, let me pull this off! I've got the brother. I've got the sister. All we need now is Dad. Deborah erased the message and put down the things she'd brought back from Derek's. Notebook. Tape recorder. A portfolio of Laura's work. She was buzzing, her head whirling from wine, conversation and the scent of success. She'd have to switch off for now. Heavy schedule tomorrow and – she looked guiltily at the pile of books on the table – she really couldn't afford to let her studies slip. Exams next month. Law and Public Affairs. Local Government. At least Central Government wasn't until June. *Bugger it! I'm hot – I can feel it. I know I'm on the right track. Whatever that is...* She shook her head. Her thoughts weren't making sense. Which meant the sensible thing to do was get some sleep.

Terry Richardson was humming to himself as he prepared for bed. He stopped and spoke, though his visitor was long gone. 'I've really done it.

171

Taken the first steps in sorting out my life. One day at a time. Leave the past behind. I can't change the past, but I can change my future, starting right now.'

He spoke the words aloud so he could hear them, like a litany. Positive thinking was called for. Positive speaking. He saw himself as a drowning man who had been thrown a lifeline. 'A fresh start. That's what I'm getting. That's what I'm giving myself. One step at a time. Everything will be alright.' He repeated the words, recognising his inability to really believe them. Perhaps if he said them often enough, the belief would come.

He recognised the root of the problem. That was something in his favour, he supposed. For years he hadn't allowed himself to admit it. It was an issue of guilt, of being unable to forgive himself. Things had been getting messy when Laura had disappeared.

What a bloody fool I was. Talk about shitting on my own doorstep. If I'd kept my bloody cock zipped up that day, there would have been so much less hassle. Sure, they would have suspected me. They always suspect family, especially husbands in cases like that. But at least I wouldn't have had to worry about an alibi. And I wouldn't have been paying bloody blackmail money for years.

Yes, it had been risky. And stupid. But he'd wanted her so much and, by Christ, she'd wanted him, too. He was amazed to find himself growing hard at the remembrance of that last fuck with her. *God – laying off the booze must be working.* He almost laughed aloud. When was the last time he'd had a hard-on? He wasn't being cynical and sexist, either; not being the stereotypical male by thinking in terms of fucking while the woman thought of making love. No, she always called him her 'little fucker'.

'That's not quite right, though, is it, darling?' she would say, stroking his bulging loins. 'Nothing little about you, Terry. Not where it matters, that is...' And then she would unzip him, go down on him, kneeling to take him in her mouth. God, was she ever good at giving head... And she'd know just when to stop, exactly when, because he didn't want to come in her mouth, he wanted to come in her cunt, deep inside that deliciously tight pussy. Jesus God, she'd make him work for it, too. What didn't he have to do to pleasure her before she'd finally let him in, mocking, knowing he would have got on his knees and begged for entry? Not like a couple of the others. They really were a quick shag. Not her, though. How she would tease him, laying on her back, big-eyed and languorous, taking her time as one of her own hands pulled at her nipples, the other sliding between her thighs, rubbing, rubbing, before she would take her hand away and smile, holding up a finger – one finger – before pushing it into herself. Her hips would start to move then. Jesus God, he could still see her, as clear as if it were only yesterday. Then she'd take that finger out, smile again, squeeze her breasts, before slowly, slowly, licking it. *Christ, years since I've had a hard-on and now I'm almost coming in my fucking pants...* Then she'd hold up two fingers and, eyes mocking, say, 'Think you can do better than

173

this?' And then she'd slide them inside herself, bring herself off right in front of him.

Only then, only when she arched her back and cried out, could he prise her legs apart and shove himself into her. Jesus God, in those early days he'd come almost the moment he was inside her. She'd spent a long time teaching him how to last and was it ever worth it! She could come and come and come. All he had to do was stay hard for as long as possible. Not easy to begin with. Sheer fucking magic! He'd never believed sex could be like that. She was like something out of the Kama bloody Sutra. She'd taught him so much. Positions, techniques... How to stop himself coming, how to come and keep it coming. How to get hard again fast, service her again. And again.

'You're the best fuck I've ever had, Terry – you know that? Now, if that husband of mine had half the cock and half the stamina and took half the pleasure' – she'd licked his balls as she said that – 'in fucking me as you do ... well, I wouldn't need to stray, would I?'

It was unbearable now. Without further ado, Terry dropped his trousers and jacked off.

Daniel listened to Chris Farmer's message with mixed feelings. So he'd tracked the old man down. He blew air through his mouth, a sign of indecision. Did he really want to go through with this? He could call it off now. Farmer wouldn't worry. He'd get his fee whatever the outcome. *Pull yourself together!* He'd gone too far to back out now, especially with the meeting with Cait looming. *Hold your nerve. You can handle it. Let Farmer do what he's being paid for.*

Hours later and miles away, Mags was miserable. The cough was worse, keeping her awake now, and tonight she had not found shelter. *Could Our Lady be deserting me? After all this time? No, no, no!* She went into a choking fit as she breathed out, effort and panic bringing tears to her eyes. *The newspaper. I should never have looked at that newspaper.* One picture in particular floated into her head, clear as day. *Stupid! Stupid!* She was sheltering in a wooded hollow. The night was pitch black, cold and damp. How, then, could she see that God-forsaken place? In colour? Even the newspaper picture had been black and white. Was it *so* imprinted on her memory? She moaned, struggling for breath. No wonder Our Lady had abandoned her.

Oh God, don't let me die! Not like this! The coughing spasm passed and she drew breath, shivering. There had been two photos in the newspaper that had shown glimpses of where the old disused croft had stood. Before and after. She'd never seen the 'after', of course. After her time. She rocked backwards and forwards now, emitting a low, keening wail. *Is it not enough that I'm going to die? Am I to go mad as well?*

She would never forget that day. What in God's name had possessed her to go there? It wasn't as if... How close had she been when she'd first heard the noise? She couldn't remember. She could remember the shock, though. Surely it couldn't be ... but she'd known it was. Moans

175

and gasps like that could be nothing but sex. If only she had walked away then. In fact, she thought that was what she had been about to do when she'd noticed the trail among the brambles. A well-worn trail leading to a peephole. *I should never have looked through it. God should have blinded me first, because, God knows, I've never been able to get it out of my head since. Terry. Thrusting into another woman. Loving it. Fucking someone else. Stark bollock naked inside another woman.*

She'd long suspected, of course, but to see it – to actually see it with her own eyes... The shock. The betrayal. Unbidden sobbing brought on another coughing fit. *Oh God, my lungs will come out of my mouth if I go on like this. How could I ever have thought he truly loved me...?*

Chapter Fourteen

Tuesday 14 December

Penny, the receptionist at the Complementary Health Care Clinic, was beaming. My goodness, what a change in Caitlin! It was satisfying to know that she had done the right thing in confiding her fears to Nina. Whatever had ailed Caitlin seemed to be over. Amazing. Nina had always said that herbal medicine took a while to work, but that was obviously not the case here. Fast and efficacious. Singularly impressed, Penny decided that if she ever got sick, she would beat a path to Nina's door.

Nina, meanwhile, on a break between clients, was listening to Caitlin's account of her phone call with Daniel.

'God, it's bizarre!' Caitlin shook her head. 'I mean, it's worse than a first date or something. Fancy being nervous of meeting your own brother!'

'It's been a long time, Caitlin.'

'Too long. Look, I'll have to see how things go tomorrow, of course, and he may not be able to. But if he *could* make the weekend...'

'That's a marvellous idea! I'm sure we've room for one more – we can shunt around.'

'No need. Josh and I will be sharing.'

'Oh.' Nina raised her eyebrows and smiled. 'So what are you doing about tomorrow's clients?'

'I've rescheduled them. I didn't have too many, so it wasn't as bad as it might have been. One was desperate, so I've sent her to Marcia Howard.' Caitlin glanced at her watch. 'Must get a move on. I finish at four today, but I've got the cheese and wine to sort out for this evening.'

It was the final T'ai Chi class of term, and Caitlin had extended her hire time of the room at the clinic to have a social gathering afterwards.

'I wouldn't mind coming to that. I was thinking of enrolling on your next beginners' course.'

'Seriously?'

'Mmm. I thought it might complement my Yoga.'

'Great! See you at seven-thirty then!'

'Let me get this straight.' Deborah Harvey, on

177

her knees on Ronnie Walters' living room floor, moved the A3 piece of paper to a different angle. She stabbed at the outlines of houses with her pencil as she spoke. 'The Richardsons lived here, you and Colin, obviously, are still here ... Angela Fielding lives here–'

'She does now, but she didn't then.' Ronnie interrupted. 'They originally had this unit, and that's where they were living when the Richardsons were here. They moved to where they are now after the Wilkersons left.'

'And that was after Terry was voted out?'

'That's right.'

'God! Am I ever going to get this straight?'

'Of course! But what you need are two copies of the plan – one showing who lived where then, and one with who lives where now. I'll get Colin to run you off another copy.' Ronnie rose to her feet and disappeared with the paper while Deborah flopped onto the sofa. She was tired after her late night with Derek and had worked long and hard today. She could have done with a quiet evening in, but was prepared to work as late as it took because she felt compelled to get as much information as possible on the Richardson case before speaking to Daniel. She *would* be speaking to Daniel. He *would* agree to an interview. Being turned down was not an option.

An hour later, Deborah was happy that she'd got the picture straight. The two plans were neatly marked, she'd checked with Ronnie, and was finally satisfied that what she had was accurate. She leaned back on her heels and stared at the sheets for a moment, reaching for her notebook.

'So, the Wilkersons left because they disagreed with the decision to oust Terry.'

Ronnie winced. 'Yes. They took it particularly hard because their daughter, Tildy, was a good friend of Caitlin's. Angela's protégés, the pair of them. Always in plays and shows.'

'Were they any good?'

'The girls? Caitlin was brilliant – we really thought she'd be an actress or a writer. Tildy was OK on the acting front, but her real talent was for singing. Very musical. As was Daniel, of course, but he'd got to the stage where he was more interested in being in a band than doing musicals.'

'He went into the right business, then. You know he's a record producer?'

'So I understand, though I've never actually understood what record producers *do*. But yes – at least he's in the music business.'

Deborah brought the conversation back to the Community. 'And the Wilkersons – did they stay in touch?'

'Regularly, for a while. Then it dropped off a bit, apart from Tildy, who kept up contact with Angela for years.' Ronnie shrugged. 'You know how things go. We still get a Christmas Card.'

Shorthand squiggles covered the page and Deborah looked up. 'But the first to leave was Rosie Dwyer?'

'Yes. That had nothing to do with the Richardsons, though. Rosie was the only single person here and left to go to a Community of mostly single people.'

179

'Better chance of catching herself a husband?'

Ronnie looked surprised. 'I never thought of that. Maybe so.'

'OK. So Rosie was the first. Did she stay in touch?'

'Not for long. We had a few postcards, that was all.'

'OK. So who was next to leave?'

'The Latimers, unfortunately. He was the doctor here.' Ronnie pulled a face. 'It was a big blow for us, and it took a long time to get a replacement. Adverse publicity and all that.'

'You mean that was why they left, or that was why it was hard to get someone else?'

'Both, really. Doc was in private practice before he came to us – Harley Street or whatever. Very highly respected. Operated a "Robin Hood" system here – still saw private patients for his speciality, but ploughed money into the Community and treated us on the NHS.'

'What was his speciality?'

'Eating disorders – and that was when they were not so well recognised, don't forget. People paid a fortune to come here in privacy and be treated by an expert in beautiful, peaceful surroundings.'

'But not after Laura disappeared?'

Ronnie raised her eyebrows and grimaced. 'Can you blame them? We had the press camped on our doorstep, lurid investigations into our private lives... No, I can't say I blame them. And Helen Latimer wasn't well even before Laura went missing. That just about finished things off.'

'What was wrong with her?'

180

There was a thud as the living room door opened to admit Colin, bearing a tray of tea and biscuits. 'Thought you might be ready for these!'

'Thanks.' The women gratefully took a break. Colin returned to his own tasks.

'Helen Latimer,' Deborah prompted through a mouthful of oatmeal. 'You said she wasn't well.'

'Yes, but – you can't use that. It's private.'

'Off the record. I'm just trying to understand what was happening and why.'

Ronnie looked dubious.

'Honestly, it doesn't get written up at all.'

'Well, it was sad, really. She and Doc had badly wanted children but ... it was just one miscarriage after another.' Ronnie looked grieved. 'I've always wondered ... if Laura hadn't disappeared; if there hadn't been all the upset...' She looked up. 'She lost a baby the day that Laura disappeared. A lot of us thought it was the shock that caused it.'

A frown flickered across Deborah's face. 'Was she younger than him, then? I mean, if he was a Harley Street practitioner...'

Ronnie blinked rapidly. 'No. They'd been married for years. The baby just never happened. It got worse as she got older.' She shrugged. 'Some people just don't give up, do they? I've always thought it was a bit silly, myself. Added risk of deformity once you pass a certain age, but there you go. It wouldn't do for me, but they weren't me, and kept trying.'

'So she was in hospital the day Laura disappeared and while the first search got underway?'

'No. Doc looked after her here.'

'Why *were* the grounds searched? I could understand it if Laura had disappeared and her car was still here, but the car being gone, too...?'

Ronnie shook her head. 'Terry's first thought – all of ours, I think, once we knew – was that she'd had an accident in the car. That was the first thing Terry did when she wasn't here for her T'ai Chi class – phone the police to ask about accidents. Then, well, God knows. It's hard to explain what goes through your mind. Had she broken down somewhere? Was she walking back? But all the time, in the back of your mind, you're wondering, fearing. It gave us something to do. Something concrete, rather than sitting by our phones all night, worrying.'

Deborah nodded. 'Right.' She glanced at her notes. 'The Latimers left next, you said. Did they stay in touch?'

Ronnie appeared to give the matter some thought. 'It was a while before we heard from them, then we had two or three letters a year. Doc had gone back to private practice. That kept up until, oh, must be ... a couple of years ago?' She nodded, answering her own question. 'Haven't heard from them since. They were thinking of retiring abroad, so probably decided to make a clean break of it.' She sighed. 'We had such aspirations for this place. It just seems so awful that it's been a source of pain and bad memories for so many people.'

'And how long, when Laura disappeared, had you known about Terry's womanising?' The shock of the question caught Ronnie off guard, exactly as Deborah had planned. 'Come on, Ronnie, Laura was your best friend – she must have confided in you.'

'I ... how...? There was never anything in the papers about that.'

'No, because Derek kept it out. But he knew, and talked to Laura just a couple of days before she went missing. And he told me.' It wasn't Terry's womanising that Derek and Laura had talked about, but Ronnie wasn't to know that.

Ronnie put down her cup and walked over to the window. *Hold your nerve, Harvey*, Deborah told herself.

The older woman spoke without turning. 'Derek really told you?'

'Last night. All on the record. He told me a lot of other stuff, too, Ronnie. Don't you think it's time you levelled with me?'

Nina, about to leave the house for Caitlin's T'ai Chi class, had been delayed by a phone call. She hated being late for anything and doubly cursed herself, knowing, as a Yoga teacher, what it was like to have people coming into a class after it had started.

Fortunately, the door to the Long Room didn't creak and she was able to enter unnoticed, especially as the whole of the class was moving away from her as she slipped inside and stood unobtrusively against the back wall.

The atmosphere was powerful and strangely still, despite, or perhaps even because of the slow and graceful movements being executed by Caitlin and her students. No one looked at any-

183

one else, yet the class moved in a fluid unison with barely a sound, baggy clothing and bare feet releasing restriction. She watched in fascination, soothed by the sight, lulled by the slow and regular breathing. No wonder some practitioners referred to T'ai Chi as 'The Dance'.

As the front row neared the far end of the room, the class turned, continuing back towards Nina. Barely an eye flickered in her direction, so total was their concentration. She felt strangely invisible, as though she were an observer from a different dimension, the subjects of her curiosity oblivious to her presence. And Caitlin ... Nina allowed herself to hold her friend in an un-focused gaze, tuning into her energy, and smiled. Strength. Peace. She was centred. The renewed contact with Daniel had been good for her. Please God, their meeting tomorrow would go well.

All too soon, the class was over. Caitlin smiled warmly at her students in appreciation. 'Let's just sit in meditation for a few moments before we get down to the business of food and wine. Nina – would you like to lower the lights while I light a candle?'

Several heads turned to look at her as she moved to do so. They were beginning to form a circle and, deciding to join them, Nina sat between a man and a woman, folding herself easily into the lotus position and closing her eyes. That was when she felt it. Startled, she blinked, casting her gaze swiftly over the group without moving her head. What the hell *was* that? Where was it coming from? More to the point, *who* was

184

it coming from? She realised her heart was pounding and forced herself to breathe from her belly. Every face in the circle was impassive. *Dear God ... it can't be ... not here...*

Nina closed her eyes, surrounding herself with strong, protective white light. To her dismay, she sensed a probing. Forcing herself to stay calm, she resisted the impulse to open her eyes again, kept her breathing slow and even, allowing her protective cocoon to grow in both size and strength. She sensed the people either side of her lose their balance, sensed the same thing happening to others in the circle. Bodies shifted, tried to readjust, but group concentration was gone. Caitlin must have sensed it, and did the right thing in the circumstances.

'I shouldn't have mentioned the food and wine! Put you off your stroke, so to speak. OK. If it's not here already, bring your attention slowly back to the room and your body and, in your own time, get up.' One by one, the group did so.

'Hey – weird or what, Caitlin? I felt like a rope in a tug-of-war!' The speaker was a young man with tousled hair and sharp features spoiled by the remains of adolescent acne.

'It's too close to Christmas, we're tired and, hey, too worldly! Food and wine! Food and wine!' The young woman who had responded, padded as if on automatic pilot to the laden table beneath the window, buttocks followed wistfully by the young man's eyes. 'Shall we get stuck in, Caitlin?' She barely glanced over her shoulder as she asked, lifting the paper tablecloths before Caitlin had time to reply.

'Why not? Peter, would you like to sort out who wants what to drink?' A heavy-set man of about sixty wiggled his eyebrows in response and swiftly took charge. There was red and white wine along with fruit juice and mineral water, and the queue was almost there before he was.

Caitlin smiled happily. 'They've worked hard. Time to let their hair down a bit. I'm so glad you could come!'

'I'm sorry I was late.' Nina deliberately kept her voice light. Caitlin was unaware of anything out of the ordinary having happened and, for the moment at least, Nina wanted to keep it that way. 'Don't eat too much, by the way – you've a late supper invitation.'

'Oh?'

'Tell you later. Why don't you introduce me to some of your students? I was very impressed.'

'Sure.' Caitlin smiled.

The letter-writer, apparently in animated discussion with four other members of class, watched without appearing to as the women chatted briefly. *Well, well! Nina Shawcross is a force to be reckoned with. How bizarre. I've never believed any of that hokum. Not since I was child, at any rate. But she is different. Has power of some sort.*

Slate eyes considered her more carefully. Weighed up the situation. Analysed the possibilities. *She is aware of me, but doesn't know who I am. I must be sure she doesn't find out.* The eyes narrowed. Confidence was questioned, for a split second only. *It will work with her the same as with anyone else. Just be my usual self. The mask. The wall. No-one has ever penetrated that. Why should she be any different?*

'We'd better join the crush, I think.' Caitlin took Nina's arm and steered her towards the table.

'What can I get you?' Peter asked. His hand was hovering over the wine bottles.

'Orange juice, I'm afraid.'

'What? Not letting *your* hair down?' He handed her a glass.

'Not tonight. I've got the car. How do you think I got the food, drink and glasses here!'

'Juggling, as you skipped down the street, Wonderwoman!'

'Right!' Caitlin laughed.

A young woman with plaits shook her head. 'And I thought we'd be partying till all hours!'

Caitlin rolled her eyes in mock despair. 'Don't any of you have jobs to go to in the morning?'

'Yes, but whereas you can't be drunk in charge of naked bodies because they might object, my computer won't.' The speaker was a tall man of about Caitlin's age, with curly brown hair.

'Too much work, you know – you do know that saying, don't you, dear?' An elderly woman, small and birdlike with gleaming eyes, touched Caitlin's arm as she spoke.

'Indeed I do – and you don't need to worry, Mrs Proctor. I may have an early start in the morning, but it's not work for a change. I'm having a day out in Bath, actually. I'm meeting my brother.'

Is she indeed? The letter-writer smiled at her with renewed interest. *Now, what are they going to be talking about, I wonder?* A warm glow of

187

satisfaction set in. *So wise of me to have kept away from Daniel's gaze on Saturday. And it's so nice to know that things are going according to plan. And if she's going away in the morning, I could drop her another little letter...*

'Oh, that's so nice, dear. Give yourself a break. And Bath is such a wonderful city.'

'Aren't you eating, either?' Peter, obviously taking his role as host seriously, was looking at Caitlin in concern.

'Apparently not.' Caitlin flashed a look at Nina and grinned wickedly as she popped a cherry tomato garnish in her mouth. 'Or not too much, anyway. Nina tells me I have a late supper engagement. Perhaps she'd like to enlighten me?'

Nina laughed, but inwardly anxiety was laying heavy on her stomach. 'At Josh's. He's been trying to get hold of you for ages. Thinks your phone might be out of order – you'd better check that.'

'Oh, right!' Caitlin's surprise was followed swiftly by the thought that, if her phone were out of order, Daniel would be unable to contact her about any last minute changes .

Mrs Proctor's eyes were alive with curiosity. 'And who is Josh?'

'My young man.'

A murmur of approval ran through the group. A murmur of disquiet through the letter-writer. *How many more people do I have to check out?*

'And where is he taking you?'

'Now, how do I know that when I haven't spoken to him yet? But I bet Nina does.'

'I do. And he's not. *We* are eating at his house.

As in you, me and Mike.' She turned to Mrs Proctor and smiled. 'Mike is my husband.'

'*Your* young man!'

'Well, I've not heard him called that for a long time, but he suits me very nicely.' Nina took a sip of her fruit juice and looked at Caitlin. 'These are nice glasses. Where did you get them?'

'Borrowed them. One of my clients runs a catering company.'

'Very nice.' Nina picked up a wine glass and held it to the light. 'Mmm. These would be lovely for Christmas lunch.'

'Not quite what we'll get at the Shelter, eh, Caitlin?' Peter laughed. Nina looked at him curiously.

'You're a volunteer there, too?'

'He's cooking Christmas lunch, brave man! He's a chef, supposedly retired.' Caitlin shook her head.

'Good Lord! Christmas lunch for how many?'

'Probably sixtyish, if last year is anything to go by. Not all at once, I hasten to add.' He smiled at Caitlin. 'I do a pretty mean vegetarian version, too.'

'I shan't be there for it, I'm afraid. We just had to rejig the roster and I've pulled the Christmas Eve sleepover instead, so I shall be going home, recovering, and going back on duty later.' She looked at Nina and grinned. 'It may be called a sleepover, but sleep is just about the last thing anyone gets.'

'Hey, give us the sordid details!' The young man with acne, who had heard only the last part of the sentence, was all ears.

'Not what you think!' Caitlin raised her voice. 'But if any of you fancy helping out at the Shelter for the Homeless over the Christmas and New Year period, it would be a great help, even if it's only for the odd hour or two. Between sickness and holidays, a lot of our usual volunteers aren't going to be available and we need all the help we can get.'

Well, well! What a lot of useful information has been gathered this evening. This calls for a slight – a very slight – change of plan on Christmas Day. Thanks for giving me plenty of warning, Caitlin. The slate eyes smiled as the letter-writer became one of the first to respond to Caitlin's appeal for help.

Deborah's mind was reeling as she awoke, startled for no apparent reason, from an unsatisfying sleep. She looked at the clock and rubbed her eyes irritably. *God! How am I going to get any proper sleep when I'm this wound up?* She had done a couple of hours' study this evening but the Richardson case would not leave her alone, running through her mind even as she went to bed. Something was nagging at the back of her mind, tantalisingly eluding recognition. *What? Bloody what?*

Sighing heavily, she got out of bed and tramped into the kitchen. *Coffee? No. Keep me even more awake.* The fridge clicked into action as she opened the door, frowning at its meagre contents. Time to go to Safeways. *What can I have that won't keep me awake? Hot chocolate!* She slammed a pan onto the cooker, poured in the milk and rummaged in the cupboard above the sink until she found an almost empty tin. *I definitely need to go to Safeways.*

Impatient for the milk to heat, she left it to go into the living room and dig out the notebook she had used at Ronnie's. What was it she had said...? Deborah flicked through the pages until she came to the relevant part and read her squiggled shorthand three times before being satisfied that she hadn't got hold of the wrong end of the stick.

The milk! She caught it only just in time, made her drink and flopped down on the sofa, reading her notes again. That couldn't be right, surely? Frowning, she went over to the bureau and dug out the micro-recorder and tapes she had used at Derek's. Setting things up on the sofa arm, she pulled a new notebook onto her lap, set the machine to play and started transcribing the tape in shorthand.

'Laura and I were engaged to be married ... moved to London ... she couldn't handle the separation ... plans for the Community got going ... Terry was the architect – did you know that? That's how she met him. Swept her away ... idealistic, creative ... not a muck-raker like me...'

'Get on with it!' Deborah muttered, snatching up the machine and pressing the fast-forward button. This was it – the bit where he'd met Laura a day or so before her disappearance.

'I'd never made any secret of the fact that I was still in love with her, and gradually, through her disillusionment with Terry, she'd realised that she still loved me. We weren't having an affair – there was nothing sexual, though God knows I wanted it. Wanted her. She wanted me, too. Hard to

191

believe, eh, looking at the fat old bastard I am these days? But she thought of nothing more than those children; the effect things would have on them. "Two wrongs don't make a right", she said.'

There was a pause before Derek had spoken again.

'It was crunch day. I'd told her I was committed. All or nothing. I wanted her to leave Terry and marry me. We met to discuss her answer. She'd made up her mind to leave him, alright, but not until Caitlin had left school. If I still felt the same then, then yes, she would marry me.'

'Did the police know about this?' Deborah's own voice, incredulous.

'What do you think? I'm going to say, "Excuse me, Officer – I had a good reason for kidnapping or killing her – semi-spurned lover and all that"? No, they didn't. But you can print it anyway. I have an alibi for the relevant times, and no, I didn't kill her, and I don't know what happened.'

Deborah stopped the tape and fast-forwarded again, reading her notes from Ronnie's as she did so. She stopped and started the tape a couple of times, increasingly impatient. Ah – this was it! Laura had talked to Derek about something funny going on at the Community. That was the bit. She sat absolutely still, listening as the tape played on. She stopped it, sat in silence and replayed it once, twice, three times more, checking that she'd heard right; checking that she'd transcribed accurately. Finally she switched off the tape and sat back, resting her head against the sofa cushion.

So. Derek said this. Ronnie said that. One of them must have been mistaken. Or one of them was lying...

Terry Richardson let himself back into his house and drew the curtains. He had walked for hours. Oh God. Whatever had possessed him? *How am I supposed to live one day at a time if this madness is still in me?* He sat down, closing his eyes as he thought back to the day Laura had disappeared.

No one had ever heard the whole truth, especially not the police. *Yes, I went to my negotiations. Yes, I got the contract. Bought champagne to celebrate at home. Bought presents for the kids. Bought a ticket for the swimming pool, went swimming – briefly – and collected water from the chlorinated foot thing you had to walk through before going into the pool. Pre-bloody-meditated. So I could splash it on myself later and smell like I'd just come from there. I had it worked out to a fine art.*

I had lunch. I drove back to the Community – almost to the Community. Took the back road across the monk's land. Hid the car under the trees behind the hedge at the back of the field. Made my way on foot to the rendezvous where I had that last glorious shag with my little nympho. Business as usual. And after we'd finished, after she'd gone, I stayed behind, smoking a cigarette before moving on to the next phase prior to going home. And what a bloody shock I got. Confrontation had not been on my agenda...

Terry stood up abruptly, telling himself he did not need a drink just because he was thinking of these things. *Face them! Don't hide. Have a cup of tea instead.* He walked through the kitchen door, remembering the look on her face as she had entered the ruined building.

What must mine have been like? It doesn't bear thinking about. You think you have everything under control, and the women screw it up. No, that's not fair. How the hell did I think I could get away with it for so long? How could I have believed I could keep it all so organised and quiet?

He filled the kettle, thinking of what had happened. All hell had been let loose. *Christ! It should have worked. It* would *have worked except for the fact that on that one day, that same day that I chose to be so devious and so bloody stupid, she had to walk across that field and find me at it. I never meant to hit her. Well, I didn't really – I just sort of pushed her. Was it my bloody fault if she fell and banged her head?*

The letter-writer continued along the London Road when Caitlin and Nina turned off. *Dropping off the glasses before going to 'her young man's'.* It wasn't her 'young man' that the letter-writer was concerned with at that moment. It was her 'old man'. Terry.

Arriving back home and expertly backing the car into the garage, the letter-writer sat for a moment after turning off the engine, fingers drumming on the steering wheel. Walking briskly into the house, the old typewriter was put through its paces once more. *There! That should ruffle a few feathers. Put the cat among the pigeons. Cat! Clever, even if I do say so myself!*

Caitlin's letter out of the way, the letter-writer's thoughts turned back to her father. *Sleep well tonight, Terry. Make the most of comfort. This time*

194

tomorrow, you'll have no further need of a bed...

Ronnie Walters was standing in the darkness of her living room, staring out over the moonlit ground between her own home and the one that had been Laura Richardson's. She couldn't sleep. Had willed and willed herself to, knowing she had to be up early in the morning, but it hadn't come, wouldn't come. How could it, when she had so much on her mind? She had agreed to help with the update on Laura's disappearance, thinking it would be the same old tired stuff – where were you, when did you last see her? *Bugger Derek!* She moved restlessly. *I can't believe Laura told him as much as she did. Didn't realise quite how close they'd become. Or remained. Her and her bloody morals. Black and white. That's all she ever saw things in. Some best friend! Best friends are supposed to tell each other everything!*

She chewed her upper lip, recognising the hypocrisy of her thoughts, of her own anger. *Right. And I told her everything, eh? I think not. What am I going to tell Colin? He'll have to know what I've said, so he can back me up.*

The worst thing was not knowing quite how much Deborah Harvey knew. What if she knew everything? Impossible! It would have come out before, been splashed right across the front page. She and Colin would have been in prison.

God damn your eyes, Laura! Why couldn't you just let things be?

Chapter Fifteen

Wednesday 15 December

Caitlin was nervous. She had tried on three different outfits and was still undecided. *Why am I making such a fuss? He's my brother, for heaven's sake! What do I have to prove?* The thought sobered her. *Rather a lot, really. Like, I've survived without you. Made a life for myself. That I'm a calm and competent woman.* She addressed her reflection in the full-length bedroom mirror. 'Caitlin O'Connor, calm and competent one, you're a pain in the arse and far too serious!'

It worked. Deciding on the brown trouser suit, she finally got herself ready. Time for one more cup of coffee before she set off. *Have I got everything? Have I checked everything?*

It had been a great evening at Josh's house. Everyone was supportive of her meeting up with Daniel, encouraged her to be up front, have confidence. In her happiness, she had almost forgotten the business of the letters. It was only as Josh insisted on accompanying her back home that she realised the underlying worry. He made light of it, of course – wanting to check the phone – and it turned out to be a simple enough matter. He had lifted the receiver, jiggled the connection, then traced the wire to the wall socket, in this case behind the dresser in the hall.

'Ah-ha! Have you been moving furniture lately?'

'What? Oh – I had to pull this out yesterday when I dropped something down the back. Why?'

He had stood up, grinning, looking extraordinarily relieved. 'Pulled the wire from the wall socket.' He picked the phone up, dialled Nina's number and got her to ring back. 'Just to double check. Best be on the safe side.'

He had stayed the night, leaving early in the morning to collect things from home before going on to work. Before then, however, he'd gone up into the loft to fetch down an old suitcase containing something that Caitlin had decided to give to her brother. She looked again at the picture she'd chosen. It was taken from the old album that had come from Gran's and, surprisingly, it hadn't been too painful. It all seemed so distant now. Like another life. As if she were another person. It was a lovely photograph of herself and Daniel. He hadn't yet grown old enough to be embarrassed by his younger sister. She still patently adored him. They were sitting together in the huge old tyre – surely it must have come from a lorry? – that had been used as a swing. She smiled to herself. Yes. This would do nicely. If she left the house now, she could get it copied and framed in town before setting off for Bath. In fact, if she took it to that place on the Lower High Street, there was even a shop a couple of doors up that sold cards and gift wrap. Perfect.

Chris Farmer was playing things by the book. Checking oil, checking water, checking tyre pressure and every other thing he could think of before starting the long drive north to pay his visit to Terry Richardson. Best not take any chances. This car – a BMW M3 – was his pride and joy. The mutt's nuts and twice as frisky. It made a pleasant change to be able to use his own car instead of the inconspicuous clunkers he normally used for undercover work. *This isn't surveillance and Richardson is paying for the petrol. I get to play. We'll eat that motorway in no time.*

Caitlin had reached Stroud by the time the letter-writer slipped the latest missive through her door. It was too early to set off to Terry Richardson's yet. No point getting there before dark, but then... Why not start out, anyway? *I could stop off somewhere interesting on the way.*

A bitter smile twisted the thin lips. *My father always said there was no life beyond Worcester. Only the working classes, and the further north one went, the more uncivilised they became. Did he know how much that frightened me? Did he say it to frighten me? Tales of the plebs, the rustics... I thought they were savages. And then he sent me to boarding school. North of Worcester. Shipped away to the Badlands. I realised that he knew, of course. Perhaps not knew. Suspected. So he sent me away. To keep* her *safe. To get rid of me. I really thought he hoped I would die there. Among the savages. But I didn't. And I had years to plot my revenge. What a pity it didn't quite work.*

The letter-writer glanced backwards, accelerated to join the motorway. *Still, I was a child then. Young, to be making my first attempt at murder. It's been far easier since. Far more successful, too.*

198

Ronnie Walters was rushed off her feet. God, where were they all coming from? It seemed as if everyone for miles around was descending on the Gift Shop to buy Christmas presents, and, having made the trip, wanted to eat there, too. She was desperate to go on her break and, when she did, took it away from the comforting warmth of the premises and walked along the frost-hardened track, hands deep in her pockets. She had to do something, but what? Even Colin had commented on how peaky she was looking this morning. It had taken a major effort not to blurt out the whole thing, tell him what was happening. What *might* happen if Deborah Harvey really knew as much as she was hinting at.

Ronnie kicked viciously at a rock, sending it over the dry-stone wall and into the field. Lack of sleep was making her irrational. When she'd told Colin about the lies this morning, he'd looked at her as if she were mad. What was she thinking of? he'd asked. They weren't lies at all, unless they were someone else's. She'd only repeated what they'd been told. Told back then and stuck to ever since.

I can't tell the difference between truth and lies any more. But I have to remember, so I know what to tell her. More importantly, what not to tell her. Deborah Harvey can't know. If Derek knew, he would have spilled the beans as soon as Laura went missing. He loved her, for Christ's sake. If he had any inkling of anyone having a motive for wanting to get rid of her, he would have been screaming blue murder. The word brought her to an abrupt halt.

Oh God. Oh God. All these years. How could I have let myself be talked out of it? That she was murdered. She has to have been, with what she knew. What she suspected. It would have been better if I'd kept my own mouth shut. If she'd gone straight to Colin. I never realised – not for one moment – what effect that one casual remark would have.

She tried not to think of what had happened that day. Tried not to think of her last conversation with Laura. It was bad enough at the time. It was only later – such a short time later – that her own world had been blown apart.

Daniel Richardson was nervous. He had arrived early at the Cricket Club car park, choosing a space from where he could see any vehicle turning in. What if he didn't recognise her? What if she didn't recognise him? Stupid. It had not been that long. And Angela had recognised both of them. *We can't have changed that much*. He opened the window and lit a cigarette. Not good, he knew. How many times had he tried to stop? But with everything that was going on at present, he needed something. Better this than booze or drugs. He smiled to himself. Was it Mark Twain who had said, 'Giving up smoking is easy – I've done it hundreds of times'? Whoever it was knew what they were talking about. Daniel had worked with several musicians who had had severe drug problems but cleaned up their act. Without exception, those who smoked had said, 'It was easier coming off coke than this – I've never been able to give up the fags.' What a bloody depressing thought.

He glanced at his watch. She should be here soon. He'd told her to allow an hour and a half by the route she'd chosen. What if she didn't come? What if she'd changed her mind? Christ, it was worse than being on a first date! *Please, God, I'm doing the best I can. Help me make it up to her...*

Several cars had pulled in, all containing more than one person. Here, though, was a green Ford Focus with driver only. Daniel watched as it was expertly parked. After a moment, the driver emerged, a woman wearing a brown trouser suit, reaching into the back of the car for a long, stylish overcoat which she shrugged on before locking the vehicle and heading towards the ticket machine. Daniel's heart was in his mouth. Cait! It was Cait! But – Christ – she was the spitting image of Mum...

Chris Farmer had travelled half a mile since the last junction and it had taken him forty minutes. Traffic was now at a complete standstill. What the bloody hell was causing the problem? Much more of this and everyone would be keeling over with carbon monoxide poisoning. He'd meant it as a joke, but snorted, suddenly remembering a newspaper report he'd read some years ago of a Japanese lorry driver who had done exactly that. Not funny. Not a sign of movement, either. Oh well... If things didn't clear up soon, he would have to seriously consider getting off the motor-way at the next available exit. He pulled a map from the glove compartment and looked at it, frowning, estimating. Yes. That might be a better route to take. He drummed his fingers impatiently on the steering wheel. This was doing him no good at all. Wouldn't like to have his blood pressure measured at the moment – probably through the roof by now. The traffic was still rock solid. Surely to God he had something to take his mind off the hold up? He groaned in frustration, not in the mood for music. Suddenly he grinned. Thank God for modern technology. He had a CD-writer at home and had used it to make a copy of one of the presents he'd bought his father for Christmas. He looked at the dashboard, at the controls of his multi-CD player. If he was going to be stuck in traffic indefinitely, he could do with some humour. *Hancock's Half Hour* might be just the ticket...

The letter-writer, too, was caught up in motor-way traffic, albeit in a different place, but, unlike Chris Farmer, was singularly unconcerned by it. *Patience is a virtue and I learned it long ago. Remarkable how one could learn from unpleasant experiences.* A music track was remembered from several years ago. What was the name of the band? Pearl something. Pearl Jam, that was it. *I was almost out of the room when I noticed the lyrics. A revelation.* The track had been called 'Rear View Mirror'. *Someone else knew what I had been through. Someone else understood. I bought the CD for the words of that one track alone. Going to boarding school was rather like that. Seeing things more clearly in the rear-view mirror. With that distance from Daddy and his Wife from Hell, I was able to plan my revenge clearly and dispassionately. Behaving myself when I went home for the holidays.*

Taking my time. Vengeance is definitely better served up cold. I learned her routine. Stayed out of her way. Gave her no cause for concern at all. She never trusted me, though. That's why I had to do it as I did. It had to be an accident, and I pulled it off beautifully. Except for one thing. She *was* supposed to die, not the horse. *Pity. I've always liked animals. You know where you are with them. Not like humans. So, one dead horse. One living-dead stepmother. Crippled. Quadriplegic. Bet that put paid to their sex-life.*

On reflection, the letter-writer thought, it was better than having killed her outright. So bright. So beautiful. So utterly *ruined*. She had walked and run and ridden and fucked. Knew what she was missing. And even dear Daddy had never suspected a thing. *No-one ever saw me. The evidence was removed and by the time anybody found her, I was miles away. With witnesses.*

The impatient honking of a horn broke through the reverie. *Ah! We're moving again. Splendid!* Feeling very pleased at such progress, the letter-writer, cocooned from other ears, broke into a rendition of 'All Things Bright and Beautiful'. All six verses. *Amazing what one remembers from one's school days...*

Any expected awkwardness was thrown to the wind. Caitlin and Daniel enveloped each other in what felt like the biggest bear-hug ever. Neither was completely dry-eyed by the time they let go.

'Cait! God, it's so good to see you! You got here all right?' Daniel flapped his arms and shrugged with embarrassment. 'Of course you did – I'm standing here talking to you!'

'No problems. Your directions were impeccable.'

They looked at each other, both tried to speak at the same time, then laughed, each urging the other to go first. It was Daniel who dived in.

'Cait, I am so sorry. Sorry for letting you down, for not being there when ... and then, at Gran's funeral, I was too ashamed. I am just so sorry. Can you ever forgive me?'

Caitlin watched the struggling emotions in his face, bit her lip to stop herself from crying. 'We've both been bloody idiots, Daniel. Shall we try and start again?'

'I've missed you, Cait.'

'I've missed you, too.'

Their next hug lasted even longer than the first. When they finally disengaged themselves, they left the car park arm-in-arm, turning left to walk along North Parade Road towards the city centre. The air was cold and crisp, the sky clear and blue. It felt somehow fitting that the sun should shine on the day of their reconciliation. Daniel hugged Caitlin's arm with his own as they passed over the river. 'Isn't it beautiful?'

'Everything it's cracked up to be, so far. Is that Pulteney Bridge?' She pointed to their right.

'Yes.' Daniel shook his head, remembering their conversation when they'd arranged to meet. 'I can't believe you've never been here, living only – what is it? Thirty or forty miles away?'

'I know. It's always been one of those places I meant to come to, but somehow I never got round to doing it.'

'Well, we'll do the lot today. I'm just sorry we

204

can't go for coffee at the RPS – no longer here.'

'The what?'

'Royal Photographic Society.'

'Are you into photography?'

'Only as an amateur, but I love it. Love other people's work, if it's good. I'm a great believer in "if you've got it, flaunt it; if you haven't, admire it".' He stopped suddenly. 'There's so much we don't know about each other, isn't there? All those lost years.'

'Well, today's when we start catching up, right?'

'Right!'

As they passed a little tower, Caitlin raised her eyebrows and looked around, hardly trusting her ears.

'Where's that music coming from?'

'In there!' Daniel laughed. 'It's a saxophone school.' Caitlin turned back to have a look, peering into the apparently tiny interior. 'I think they teach upstairs,' Daniel volunteered. 'Be a bit exposed to gawpers like you, otherwise!'

'You obviously know this place well – do you come here often?' They both burst out laughing at the inanity of the question. 'God, it sounds like the classic hideous chat-up line! I can't believe I said that!'

'I know what you mean – and yes. I first came on business some years ago, but I visit often just for pleasure. In fact...' A thought was forming rapidly in Daniel's mind. And with Cathy now out of his life, there was no reason why not... 'I've been thinking of buying a place here.'

'That would be wonderful!' The genuine pleasure on his sister's face warmed Daniel's heart.

'It would, rather, wouldn't it? Come on, let's get that coffee!' He led her swiftly to Milsom Street, pointing out where the RPS used to be, before taking her into a coffee bar nearby.

Caitlin gave him the photograph as they sat at the table together. 'It's from one of Gran's old albums – I thought you might like a copy.'

'God!' Daniel squeezed her hand. 'If I remember rightly, I pushed you off that tyre about two seconds after the photo was taken!'

'So you did!'

'I have something for you, too.' Daniel picked up his shoulder bag, stashed beneath the table, and opened a zippered compartment. He hesitated, hand still inside, overcome by awkwardness. 'I made it for you years ago. Meant to give it to you when I finished University, but, well...' He handed over the package.

Caitlin took her time unwrapping it, trying not to tear the paper, strewn with musical notes. She looked up, flashed a shy smile when she realised that there was another layer, this time of tissue paper. 'Here's one I made earlier,' she quipped, defusing Daniel's tension, if not her own. 'Oh, Daniel...'

Her hand flew to her mouth, heart racing. It had been recognised early on that he had inherited his parents' gifts for drawing, but the likenesses were so perfect, it took her breath away. How many times must he have seen this scene? Often enough for it to be engraved in his memory. Yet never once had Caitlin been aware of him sketching. Tears blurred her vision as she stood to embrace her brother.

'It's beautiful!' The sketch was small, beautifully framed, and showed Caitlin and Laura on an overstuffed sofa, completely absorbed in their story-telling.

Deborah Harvey was at her desk when Derek stuck his head around the door.

'Deborah!' He indicated with a jerk of his head that she should follow him. Back in his office, he said without preamble, 'I got your message – what is it you're so puzzled about?' He looked tired. Looked his age.

I've got to get to the bottom of this. For his sake. For everybody's sake.

'Your last meeting with Laura – when she told you she was worried about something going on in the Community. What exactly did she say – her exact words, if you can remember them. This could be really important.'

He didn't ask questions. Just leaned back in his chair, closed his eyes, as if listening.

'I laughed. Said, "Don't tell me, the kids are running home-grown grass to their school friends."' He opened his eyes. 'She was unusually sharp with me. Said it wasn't funny, it was nothing to do with drugs, and besides, any whiff of drug-taking and Colin would be the first to know. He taught at the Comprehensive. No...' He shook his head. 'She was irritated by my flippancy. Said it definitely wasn't drugs and then clammed up. Changed her mind about telling me – probably because I'd been so bloody flippant. She said she wasn't going to say anything else until she'd spoken to the person concerned. If

207

she couldn't get a satisfactory explanation, *then* she'd tell me.'

Deborah's mind was whirring. 'Are you sure she said *person*? As opposed to people or persons?'

Derek frowned and closed his eyes again. 'Definitely.' In his mind, he was back at that table in the pub, could see her sitting across from him, smell her perfume ... He swallowed. 'Her exact words were, "Look, this was a mistake. I'm not saying anything else until I've spoken to the person concerned." Then she got up and walked out. Took her bag but left the portfolio – it was under my jacket. That's why I've still got it. Or rather, you have now. What do you think?'

Deborah gave an embarrassed shrug. 'I haven't had time to look at it yet, to be honest. But I will. And I'll give it straight back to you. So you're sure she said "person"?'

He nodded emphatically. 'Person. Singular. Definitely.'

Ronnie Walters went home for lunch, something she didn't usually do. Her frantic morning had degenerated even further, with her last customer really putting the lid on it, bringing back everything she'd tried not to think about on her break. He'd signed the visitors' book, making effusive comments about the range of goods, the service, the welcome. It was as he'd looked up at her that he'd grinned and said it.

'You don't get people signing in as Daffy Duck, then?' She'd laughed, of course, as he'd expected, thanked him, watched him leave. Then she'd closed her eyes, wanted to scream, remembering the day when Laura had walked into her house, looking for Colin.

'Colin about?'

'No, still in town. I think they're having an end of term booze-up. What are you wanting with my husband then?' She'd grinned at her friend, loading the question with innuendo.

'Oh, nothing like that, thanks! No, I wanted to see the guests' book, actually, and as Colin is keeper of the same...'

She hadn't been referring to the 'visitors to the Gift Shop' book, of course. This was different. The guest book kept a record of anyone staying with any of the families for one night or more. Colin had a bee in his bonnet when it came to Health and Safety.

'It's for our own good as well as for the Fire Brigade. God forbid there ever *were* a fire, but at least we'd know how many we're looking for. And bearing in mind that we'd need to at least start fighting a fire ourselves, with the Brigade so far away, well, you can't be too careful.' That was the reason he'd given for starting it. All perfectly logical. Comforting, even.

Ronnie had been surprised by the request, but not bothered. She had no reason to be. Simply went and fetched it for her. 'There you go!' She had watched as Laura flicked through the pages, obviously looking for a particular date.

There! She'd got it! Her finger had stabbed, then run down the page. She was frowning. 'There must be some mistake...'

'What? Is there a problem?' It was an automatic question that, with hindsight, Ronnie wished she had never asked. She wasn't expecting an answer. Not really. Certainly not an affirmative one.

'Yes. That is, I think there might be.' Laura had sighed, straightened up, smiled at her friend. 'It's probably nothing. I'll go and double check.'

'What, Laura? You've got me all intrigued now!'

Laura had hesitated, turned away. 'Like I said, it's probably nothing. But I know what I saw...' Her voice had tailed off. 'Let's just hope I'm wrong, eh? If I'm not, I'll be back later. I'll need to speak to Colin.'

She had come back. And the can of worms had at last been opened.

Chapter Sixteen

Mags had been lucky to find the Shelter and even luckier that it was a place which had a doctor on call. Nonetheless, ill as she was, she was deeply disturbed to be driven to other people by necessity. In a city, no less. How she hated cities.

She was tired. So tired. A few days' rest. That was all she needed, surely? Her body was racked by yet another coughing spasm and she fought for breath. *Holy Mother of God!* She had heard of drowning people having their lives flash before them. Maybe it was her turn to die. Certainly her sins, if not the rest of her life, were flashing before her eyes, in lurid Technicolor and stereophonic sound. They were all that had been on her mind recently.

'That's a nasty touch of bronchitis. I'm going to have to prescribe some antibiotics. Are you allergic to any that you know of?' Mags shook her head. 'Alright then. You need to take all of these, even if you feel better before you've finished them. It's vital you complete the course. You need to take one, three times a day.' The doctor's hand hovered over a prescription pad. 'Do you drink? Alcohol?' A lot of the itinerants did, so it was no use prescribing the type of antibiotic where it had to be avoided. Better something where the only stuff off-limits was dairy products.

Mags had enough breath to reply verbally this time.

'That's never been one of my sins. Teetotal all my life.'

'Hmm.' Kind eyes smiled at her. 'I have to have a name. For the prescription.' Panic flashed for a second. 'It doesn't have to be a real one. But just for the records, you know.'

When was the last time she'd told anyone her name? Mags turned her head away and made one up.

Caitlin could barely contain herself as she drove back to Cheltenham, her headlights cutting a swathe through the countryside over which the sun had set long ago. What a completely wonderful day it had been. Neither of them had wanted to leave and Daniel had jumped at the chance to spend the weekend at Nina's cottage. What a lot she had to tell everyone! She could hardly wait to get home. So much news had been caught up on. So many things they hadn't known, and now they

211

did. And if Daniel really did move to Bath...! They'd even looked in the windows of Estate Agents. Not only was he back in her life, but he would be no more than an hour-and-a-half's drive away. Caitlin felt as if some great weight had been lifted from her shoulders.

'Thank you! Thank you so much!' She spoke the words aloud. If there was a God, she wanted that on record. 'And please don't let anything come between us again.'

The letter-writer had arrived in Barnsley. Driving rain had turned the streets into black pools in which street lights were reflected, their colours seeming to fizz like garish children's drinks. Blaisdon Avenue. Where was that? The car slowed to a crawl and finally came to a halt beside a bedraggled pedestrian. The window was wound down.

'Excuse me? I wonder if you can help...'

On the other side of the city, Chris Farmer pulled into a car park, switched on his interior light and pored over a map, the engine idling. *Right. What was the best way to get there from here? And where exactly is here?* He glanced up, checked the sign by the ticket meter, looked at the map some more.

OK. I'm here. Terry Richardson is there. Providing I don't get fouled up in any one-way systems, the most direct route would seem to be... His finger traced the roads. Finally satisfied, he put the car into gear and pulled away.

The letter-writer peered through the swish of the

212

windscreen wipers in disbelief. *Damn and blast! Someone has beaten me to it!* Slate eyes watched as a tall, well-dressed man was admitted to the house. *I hadn't banked on this. There's nothing for it but to wait.*

The rear-view mirror was checked, slate eyes taking in everything in sight. The street was deserted, rain still teeming down. *At least that's one thing in my favour. It wouldn't do to be conspicuous. Hopefully, no one will come out in this unless they have to. Still, I must be careful.* The engine was cut, the lights extinguished. The letter-writer slid down in the driver's seat. Too risky to put the tape on? Probably. Shame. Some music would have been nice. *But I can hear it in my head. While I wait...*

Nina knew it was her imagination, but the whole room seemed to be aglow with the light from Caitlin's face. Sitting round the kitchen table, they were passing photographs to each other.

'Daniel had this point-and-shoot camera, so he took pictures of me, I took pictures of him and here' – she held up a particular one – 'we got these Japanese tourists to take one of the two of us together!' She smiled at the memory, at the way the couple had bowed, of how she and Daniel had returned the favour for them. 'Thank God for one-hour developing and extra sets of prints! I don't think we could have waited any longer to get the pictures back!'

'You went to the Baths?' Nina stated the obvious as she took a photograph from Caitlin's hand.

213

'It was fantastic.' She turned to Josh. 'You have earphones that go with handsets, like video remotes, and you key in the numbers you come across at various points around the site, and get told all about it.' She was as excited as a child.

'A successful day, then?' Mike asked.

'Oh yes. And so much easier than I'd expected. We just told our life stories, warts and all.'

'Accepted each other, warts and all?' Josh was smiling.

'That, too. There's been a lot of water under a lot of bridges but, at the end of the day, he's still my brother and I'm still his sister. I just wish we'd had the sense to make things up earlier, that's all. We've missed so much that we could have had together.'

'You can't change the past, Caitlin. No one can. But what you've done today is give yourselves a future you wouldn't otherwise have had.'

Caitlin's smile took in everyone at the table. 'That's what I tossed my coin for. When you leave the Baths there's this pool where people used to throw offerings to the Goddess, Minerva Sulis. The sign says the money goes to the Bath Archaeological Society or something now. But I threw mine to the Goddess. As thanks for Daniel and I being together again. And a prayer that everything will be alright.' She pulled a face, suddenly embarrassed. 'I'm getting daft in my old age, eh?'

It was Nina's turn to smile. 'Not at all. It was a symbolic gesture. And the Universe loves symbolic gestures.' *And besides*, she thought to herself, *we need all the help we can get.*

Back at his London flat, Daniel was also looking at the photographs taken that day. She had been such a gangly kid, and look at her now – beautiful! And so like Mum it was untrue. He looked again at the picture the Japanese tourists had taken. He'd get that one enlarged. But for now... He crossed to the bookcase, took down a silver frame and eyed its contents with distaste. It was a portrait of Cathy. Swiftly, he took off the back, removed the print and tore it up, dropping the pieces into the waste-paper bin. There! That was better. He set the frame, now containing the photograph of himself and Cait, back on the shelf, trying out different angles until he was satisfied that he could see it from where he was going to sit. He went back to his seat and picked up a picture of Cait on her own. This was one he'd taken near Pulteney Bridge. *My sister. An aromatherapist.* He shook his head at the memory. They seemed to have walked and talked for hours. Well, not so much walking, maybe, apart from moving between one eating place and another. Coffee had been followed by lunch in a restaurant in George Street. That's when he'd asked her.

'Aromatherapy, Cait? How come you got into that? I always thought you'd write or act.'

She'd pulled a face. 'Didn't everyone? Including me. It's why I stayed in London, I did all the usual things. Took jobs that allowed time off for auditions. Read *The Stage* from cover to cover every week, as if my life depended on it.' She had fallen silent.

'So what changed your mind?'

'Nothing consciously. Not at that point, anyway. I was really going for it.' She'd looked at him then, an odd look, as if she were weighing him up somehow. 'Oh well, in for a penny, in for a pound! You've told me about your mistakes. I'll tell you about mine. It's a bit complicated. I met a man called Nick...'

Daniel had been shocked by what she'd told him. Horrified, by the time she'd finished. *And now? Having had time to take it in? I feel guiltier than ever about her running away from home. Christ! If only we could foresee the consequences of our actions. Or inactions, as the case may be. It seemed like no big deal at the time. I would have gone home in a couple more days, anyway. If only Dad hadn't blown like that, Cait would have stayed and none of that shit would have happened.*

He walked to the window, trying not to think about what might have been. She would have finished A levels. Gone to University or Drama School. Could have really made something of herself. *Aromatherapy! Christ! Is she happy? Really happy?* And no wonder she'd never married. Never even lived with anyone after what had happened with Nick. Still, Cheltenham seemed to be a decent place to live. What had she said? She'd done her training in London but, after Gran had died and her legacy had come through, she'd thought about moving and a colleague had told her about a friend who was setting up a Complementary Health Clinic there. She'd had a look and liked what she'd seen.

The phone rang. He picked it up absently, still

thinking of his sister.

'Daniel? Chris Farmer. There was a bit of a complication, but mission accomplished.'

That's odd, thought Colin Walters as he parked outside his home. The place was in darkness. He hadn't realised that Ronnie was going out, and besides, she always left a light on, even if it was only the one in the porch. He was more than startled, then, to find his wife sitting in the living room when he turned on the light.

'Ronnie? What on earth are you doing, sitting in the dark?' *Oh my God.* She'd been crying. Her face was blotchy, eyes red and puffy. He hurried towards her, arms outstretched.

'Ronnie, love, whatever's the matter?'

She blew her nose noisily, didn't move into his offered embrace. 'It's no good, Colin. She knows too much. We have to talk.'

In Barnsley, a man's body was found. The person who found it was exceedingly sick. So was the first police officer on the scene.

Caitlin had no qualms about entering her house that evening. She had insisted that she did not need an escort home. Nothing had spoiled her day with Daniel and nothing would spoil the end of it. She closed the door behind her, put it on the chain and dropped her coat on the chair in the hall. The answer phone on the dresser was blinking. Three messages. They could wait. First of all, she wanted to sort out a frame for the picture of herself and Daniel. She threw the mail on top of her coat. One of the letters slid off, revealing a typeface on the envelope below that she had come to recognise.

Not again! Now what? More nonsense about Mummy, no doubt. She hesitated, then, angered by its presence, decided to open it now rather than later. *Get it over and done with. Then bin it. OK, don't bin it,* she corrected herself as she slit it open. She had promised Daniel. His private investigator wanted to see everything they received. *Right.* She unfolded the single sheet of paper. Bigger than a compliment slip, this time. That was new. *Oh my God!* Her hand flew to her mouth as she stifled a gasp. This was altogether different...

The hour was late and the residential area of the Retreat House was silent, its corridor lights dimmed to their night setting. Quietly, a door was opened, closed and locked, its occupant, dressed in pyjamas, dressing gown and slippers, padding along the corridor until he reached the double doors on the right that opened onto a flight of stairs. He went down, rather than up, descent leading to the older part of the building, to the large basement with its maze of corridors, exposed pipes and signposts for those unfamiliar with its layout.

He was becoming more familiar now. This was his second day. He walked down the sloping wheelchair access ramp to the lower level, arriving with relief at the kitchenette, open to the corridor. Wow! There was still cake left from this afternoon. He turned back the cling film covering the plate and ate a slice before plugging in the kettle. God, that was good! You had to say that for the place – you certainly didn't starve. Breakfast, lunch and dinner, all provided; good, plain cooking, but loads of it. They certainly didn't stint on portions. Even better, cereal, bread, drink-making facilities, biscuits and cakes were available twenty-four hours a day in the kitchenettes on each floor. This wasn't the one he was supposed to use – not that it mattered – but he'd made it his own because he loved coming down here, going on through the twisting corridors and sitting in the room they called The Undercroft. There were many rooms in which to meditate, as well as the grounds, of course, which were extensive and beautiful, even in the middle of winter, like now. But The Undercroft was his favourite. He was amazed that no one else had used it during his visits. He'd had time completely alone, soaking up the beauty and atmosphere like a sponge. Like an oasis in the desert, it touched some level of primal need that he had been afraid to acknowledge.

He would be going there again in a moment, after he'd drunk his coffee. He pictured it in his mind, felt the pull of it. Thank God he'd found it, and that it was accessible at any hour of the day or night. Sleeping had not been easy here, at first. Strange bed and all that, so perhaps to be expected, but it was the silence that had been so difficult to begin with. A silent retreat! This was a new one, alright. He hadn't been convinced he could handle it, but, apart from the sleeping problems, he had.

I've surprised myself. Somehow it didn't seem odd eating meals in silence any more. The dining room was large and decorated in peaceful colours, all those in the retreat in the same boat. They had respect. It was amazing what could be conveyed by a look, a gesture. 'Would you like water?' 'Can I get you a cup of tea?'

After breakfast, he had his sessions with the spiritual advisor appointed to his care. That was the only time conversation was permitted, except in an emergency. The sessions with Father Richard seemed, so far, to be lasting between twenty minutes and half an hour. He had worried, at first, about what he would say, about what the priest might say to him, but again, he'd been surprised. It was giving him food for thought.

After his sessions, the day had no structure beyond set times for meals. It was up to him what he did. He had worried about what he would do, how he would fill the time, but that, too, had been needless. *How quickly we establish routines for ourselves.* He had taken to walking in the grounds until elevenses time, wrapping up warm against the winter weather, so far finding new paths and gardens every time. After elevenses, he would go down to The Undercroft until lunchtime. He had looked at the other meditation rooms and they were all beautiful in their own way, but this was the one for him. After lunch, back into the grounds, a good walk, then a little nap before the evening meal. Maybe that was why he couldn't sleep at night. It didn't matter.

He washed his coffee mug, carefully placing it back on the hook from which it had hung beneath one of the wall cabinets. His eyes ran over the kitchenette, looking for anything out of place, anything he could do. Nothing. All was well. Satisfied, he set off along the corridor, pulse quickening at the thought of being able to sit in The Undercroft again. He came to a T-junction and turned left, knowing that to his right was the Physical Health and Fitness suite with its exercise machines, sauna and Jacuzzi. He had had a sauna and Jacuzzi both yesterday and today. Planned to do so every day of his stay. They were the only things you paid extra for, but the price was nominal.

Before he knew it, he had arrived at what he called 'the mini-roundabout', a section of corridor dominated by a statue of the Risen Christ. It had unnerved him slightly at first. There were four different ways you could go from here and the eyes of the statue seemed to follow you whichever one you chose. He had thought, to begin with, that it was a trick of the light, but was now inclined to believe that it was some property of the statue itself, of the way the face had been carved, for no matter what time of the day or night he had come down here, no matter what lights were on or off, the eyes still seemed to look at you. He glanced at it now as he passed into the corridor that housed the art rooms, two seminar rooms and, right at the end, the Black Hole, nickname for the one room on the premises where smoking was allowed. He turned left again before he got there, this time into a shorter corridor, passing one of the laundry rooms and the Genesis Room, another place for meditation. Nearly there. The Under-croft would be next.

He paused before opening the door. What if someone else were there? Would he feel able to stay? *Please, God...* He gripped the heavy iron handle and turned it, pushing open the door just a crack. Darkness. A wave of relief rushed through him. Stepping inside, he reached for the dimmer switch before moving to adjust the downlighters and uplighters scattered through-out the place.

As its name suggested, The Undercroft was a room, no doubt originally part of a huge cellar, that was divided into three sections by brickwork arches, now whitewashed. This meant, effect-ively, that it was three shrines in one. All were simple. Just inside the door was the plainest of the three. A large hand-crafted pot containing dried flowers was the focal point here. Pass through the first arch, and another area was set aside, this one with a large Bible, ornately decorated with illuminated letters and fantastic figures as its centre point. Pass beyond that, under another arch, into the deepest recess of the room, and you came to the Holy of Holies. Such was the effect it had had on him, that it was the only way he could think of it now.

He stood before the white gauze curtains, bowing his head and praying silently. A minute or more passed before he stepped forward, stepped through the veil, into the presence of the Mother of God. He sat, cross-legged, hands palm-up on his thighs, thumbs and index fingers curled into a loose 'o' shape. He gazed into the face of the icon before him, feeling himself wrapped in the warmth of its colours, its shadows, its mystery. Awe overcame him. A sense of love so powerful it felt like a tidal wave about to engulf him. Time and space were irrelevant as he floated in the very heart of Eternity.

It was much later when he left. How much later, he couldn't have said. Wouldn't have wanted to. He didn't even glance at his watch. There was no need. He felt calm and refreshed, yet also knew that his body was tired enough, relaxed enough, to sleep now. For that reason, he took a shorter route back to the residential quarters, turning left by the statue of the Risen Christ to go up two short flights of stairs which seemed to fold back on themselves. A large door with glass-panelled panes opened into the reception area of the Hall where the offices and noticeboards were the hub of activity during the day. He had only to pass through this area to reach the corridor where his room was situated. He moved quietly, even though there was no one around to be disturbed, glancing automatically at the occupants' noticeboard as he approached. Messages were left here for them, sometimes from their spiritual director, sometimes from home. He stopped, curious to see a folded piece of paper secured by a drawing-pin, bearing his own name. Could that be right? Who would leave a message for him? He peered at it more closely. Yes. It was his name all right. Terry Richardson.

It was Colin Walters' turn to be unable to sleep. He had sat up long after his wife had gone to bed, and later still, in desperation, had slipped outside in the vain hope that fresh air would clear his head. The air may have been fresh but it was bone-numbingly cold and he wound up shivering and, for a while at least, even less able to collect his scattered thoughts. What a God-awful mess. It had been bad enough back then, when Laura had disappeared, but now...

He recognised that they had been lulled into a false sense of security. It had all happened so long ago. They'd kept things quiet, even in the face of the police investigation. His blood ran cold at the newly revealed knowledge of what Laura had shared with Derek Kenny. If he'd said anything at the time, it could have put the kibosh on everything, ripped the whole business apart.

Colin forced himself to slow down, stand still. Even with a torch, it was not wise to charge around the Community at this time of night. Derek hadn't said anything at the time. Hold on to that. If he'd known anything really important, he would have spilled the beans, done anything to help the investigation. So either he didn't know as much as Deborah was hinting, or he had reasons of his own for having kept shtumm for so long.

God, this is getting us nowhere! Try and think straight. The point was, Derek may have known something that didn't seem important at the time. Now, with hindsight or whatever... No. Forget Derek. It was *Deborah* who was the problem. She was the one putting two and two together, if Ronnie could be believed. But what sum was she going to come up with? How much did she really know?

He had tried to reassure Ronnie, telling her that a lot of it was bluff and supposition. Fishing. Throw out the bait. Panic people into spilling the beans. They simply had to hold their nerve. They'd got away with it back then. Surely to God, that was all there was to it now.

Frustrated, Colin started to walk again, this time stopping to light a cigarette, having to open his jacket and form a shelter against the wind to prevent the tired flame of his lighter being extinguished. *She can't know,* he told himself, inhaling deeply. *Bloody hell, even we don't know what happened to Laura.* He exhaled now, breath and smoke frosty in the moonlight. *Oh God...* His shoulders sagged as he slumped down on a tree stump. Momentarily, his train of thought was distracted by physical discomfort. *'Does your bath bite your bottom?'* He'd seen an advert in the paper. Never mind the bath. This bloody tree stump was making a good job of it between the cold and the. roughness of its surface. Haemorrhoids. His father had always told him never to sit on cold surfaces because it gave you haemorrhoids. Load of bollocks, of course, but still...

He stood up, briefly rubbing his backside. *Think, Colin, think!* He didn't want to think. Didn't want to trace things back to the beginning because that would mean acknowledging his own crucial role in the course of events. Not that it had seemed like that at the time. *I was only trying to help. Doing a favour. Showing compassion, for Christ's sake. I never dreamed it would lead to all this.*

He had never forgotten that night. Phillip

225

coming to him in a panic, begging for help. Unbelievable. He remembered the shock, the outrage he had felt to learn that his good friend, also a teacher, had been sleeping with one of his own underage pupils. More to the point, had got her pregnant. Even more to the point still, the poor girl had tried to get herself an abortion through illegal channels rather than the NHS, and the bloody thing had been botched. She was ill and bleeding and Phillip was in a panic, thinking she would die.

'You've got to help me, Colin. Got to help *her*.'

'You bloody fool...'

But I was the bloody fool, looking back on it. Should have left them to it. Well, no, I couldn't have done that. But I should just have driven them to the nearest Casualty Department and left Phillip to face the consequences. Only I didn't.

Whatever had made him do it? Why in God's name did he ever think of bringing them here, to the Community? Doc was just that – a doctor, not a surgeon. All right, he acted as their GP and obviously knew first aid, but Colin was asking him to cover up both an illegal relationship and an illegal operation. He remembered the devious route he'd taken, parking away from prying eyes. Remembered Phillip, nearly hysterical by then, pleading with him to hurry up. Remembered his private, urgent talk with Doc. The relief when Doc had agreed to help. Even greater relief when it had all turned out alright. And that should have been the end of it.

Everything alright? Yes.

Until Doc had decided it was payback time...

226

Chapter Seventeen

Payback had been the girl. When had that been? April? She'd been and gone and that was the end of it as far as Colin was concerned. Until Ronnie shouted through to him that Saturday evening in July.

'Colin – Laura to see you!'

He'd walked through, a smile on his face. 'To what do I owe this pleasure? Life too boring with Terry and the kids away? Don't tell me, you've decided to do A Level Physics!'

'I think not!' Laura couldn't help but smile. Science was not her strong point, as Colin knew all too well. 'No, I'm afraid it may be a bit more serious.' She sat at the dining table, a newspaper in front of her. 'I came over and saw Ronnie earlier. It should have been straightforward, but it isn't. Look at this.'

She opened the paper at an article on missing persons. Ronnie leaned over Colin's shoulder to look at it. He frowned, wondering what on earth Laura was on about, scanned it, and froze at the sight of one particular face. He composed his features as best he could, took a breath to steady his voice, but his heart was hammering.

'I don't understand...'

'It's this girl – young woman, I should say.' Laura pointed at the face. 'Isabella Harvey-Hewington. If you read the piece about when she

227

went missing – well, the point is, she was here. In the Community. I was all excited, thought we could pass on some news to her parents. Then I thought I'd better check, and came over and looked at the guest book. She wasn't booked in.'

Silence. Ronnie looked puzzled. Colin's mind was racing.

'Hold on a minute. You say she was here, but not booked in. What are you getting at? I mean, anyone staying here goes in the book. I see to that.'

'Exactly. And that's why I'm worried.'

'You've lost me,' Ronnie said, looking between the two of them. 'If she's not in the book, she wasn't here, surely.'

'Precisely,' Colin put in. 'So what makes you think she *was* here?' He picked up the paper as if scrutinising the picture more closely. Not that he needed to. He remembered all too well the night Doc had brought her here. She wasn't the kind of face you forget. Something fluttered to the floor from between its pages. Laura bent to pick it up.

'This does. I don't just think, I know. I sketched her.' She produced her evidence. The likeness was uncanny. Colin's mouth was dry.

'Oh my God...' Ronnie breathed.

'See the date?' Laura pointed it out. She always signed and dated even her rough sketches. 'There's no mistake. I was having trouble with the latest designs for the slate work and did what I usually do – went for a walk with the sketch pad. It always seems to work for me; I go and do something else creative and while my mind is apparently absorbed with that, the answer to the difficulty seems to present itself. I was actually heading for the top meadow, but as I went through the orchard, that's when I caught sight of her, upstairs at the back of the farmhouse.'

'So she was at Doc's?' Ronnie looked at the sketch again and Colin did likewise, even though he didn't need to. Stupid question. Of course she was. Laura had placed her *in situ*, and even though done in close-up, as it were, that window of the farmhouse was unmistakable.

Colin's stomach was churning. *How the hell do I handle this...? As if I know nothing. Make her spell it out.* He spoke slowly. 'So what are you saying, Laura?'

She laid her hand over his. 'Well, there are two problems, as I see it. The first is that Doc brought – smuggled, effectively – someone into the Community without going through procedures. Why? We know he has private patients. So why not just book her in as usual? Secondly – and far more serious, at least potentially – is what happened to this girl. She never went home.'

There was silence again as the three of them thought through the implications. Colin cleared his throat. 'Are you saying Doc ... *did* something to her?' He forced himself to meet Laura's eyes.

'No. That is – I don't know. I don't know what I'm saying. What I do know is she was here, unbeknown to the rest of us, and was never seen again. I think we need to have a word with Doc, don't you?'

Colin nodded slowly. *Jesus! Let me get a word in before she does!* 'It will have to wait till Monday, Laura. They're away for the weekend.'

On the Sunday night, Colin had nearly smoked himself sick in the apple orchard by the time Doc Latimer's car drew up outside the farmhouse. He stubbed out his latest cigarette, then wished he hadn't, as he watched its occupants get out and move to the door. He'd have to give them time to unpack and get inside. It wouldn't do to just go charging in, in front of the others. He lit another cigarette and stayed concealed in the darkness. Just a few minutes. He prayed fervently, wondering what the hell he would do if Laura turned up. She was determined to have a showdown over this, and it would be just like her not to leave it until the morning, even though she had said she would ring him then to arrange a meeting. *Come on, God, give me a break. I've got to talk to him first.* Unable to wait any longer, he strode to the door and knocked.

It was Doc himself who answered it. 'Good God, Colin! Do you know what time of night it is?' He was his usual jovial self, but his profession was at the fore as he immediately went on, 'Not a medical emergency, I hope?'

Colin heard Helen, Doc's wife, call, 'Who is it, Stephen?'

Doc turned and called over his shoulder, 'It's alright, dear – it's for me.'

Colin's impatience could be held in check no longer. He pushed past Doc, saying, 'It's not medical, but it is an emergency. We have to talk. Right now.'

Doc looked surprised but said nothing until they were alone in his private first floor office. 'Right. Do you want to tell me what this is about?'

'I want you to tell me.' Colin took a deep breath. 'That girl – the one you asked me not to book in.'

'As a return for the favour I did for you. Yes.' Doc's voice was sharp.

Colin looked at him steadily. 'There was an article in the paper. About how–'

'Ah yes. I saw that while we were away.'

'Well, the point is, not only do *I* want to know what happened to her – so does Laura Richardson.'

'Laura? But we agreed to say nothing to anyone about her presence here.' An angry red flush was creeping up Doc's neck.

'And I didn't.' Colin shook his head, lit another cigarette despite Doc's No Smoking policy. 'The bloody woman sketched her.'

'That's impossible. She never left the house.'

'She didn't need to. Laura was heading for the meadow and noticed her standing at the window. Stood out there in the orchard and sketched her. Not only that, she dated the bloody thing, and you realise what that means – she knows not only that she was here, but when. What the fuck happened?'

'Nothing happened.' Doc crossed the room and handed Colin a large tumbler of whisky. 'She came here as planned. I did what needed doing, then she left. Alive, and well.'

'An abortion, was it?'

'The reason she came here is completely confidential, you know that.'

'Right. How bloody convenient. And can you prove that she left here? Alive and well?'

'I don't see that I need to.'

'Then you're bloody blind. And if you can't convince Laura, she'll go to the police. She's pissed off enough by the fact that she wasn't registered. That in itself is enough to make her think you're up to no good. And I can hardly tell her about the favours without dropping myself in the shit.'

'I see.' Doc sat at his desk. 'What, precisely, is she planning to do?'

'The plan is that she phones you in the morning and arranges to meet you, shows you the article and sketch and asks for an explanation. Not just of why she wasn't booked in, but of what happened to her.'

Doc ran his tongue along his upper lip, slowly shaking his head. 'The implication is that I ... *did* something to her? Like what? Killed her?'

Colin shifted uneasily in his chair. 'An accident, of course. No one is accusing you of ... well, murder or anything. It's just – if, hypothetically, she had come here for an abortion, say – well, something could have gone wrong.'

'You really believe that?' Doc's face was pinched with anger now. 'You really believe I would perform a surgical procedure for which I am unqualified, and then cover up the resulting death?'

'I didn't say that.'

'But you're thinking it. Along with Laura Richardson.' Abruptly, he swung round in his chair and stood up. 'Who else knows about this?'

'Ronnie.'

'Oh great. So I have her to appease as well, do I?'

'Look, you have to admit the whole thing looks bloody suspicious. In fact, it stinks. What the fuck happened to that girl?'

'I've already told you, Colin. She left. Alive and well.' Doc's voice was dangerously quiet.

'Yes. Right.' Colin drained his glass and stood up. 'Let's see what Laura has to say tomorrow after she's seen you, OK?' He turned on his heel and left the room.

And he'd never seen Laura again.

Chapter Eighteen

Thursday 16 December

Nina stood wordlessly as Caitlin handed over the latest letter. She sensed the fear in her friend, but stronger even than that was her anger.

```
          I know where she is
          I know where you are
        Caitlin-cat, Hellcat
     You thought it was over
          but it's just begun
     I sleep not nor slumber
        till everything's won
     But do not try thinking
        that you can outrun,
       for vengeance is mine,
          little hellcat
```

She frowned as she read it, having to make a conscious effort to allow the letter-writer's aura into her own. Her instinct was to shut it out, but the contamination had to be allowed. She had to feel what he or she was up to. She shivered. What was wrong? *Younger.* The word – not quite a word, more an impression – floated into her mind. Younger? What did that mean? Nothing was making sense. Nina felt sick. She shut herself off, brought her attention back to Caitlin, who was gabbling now. *I must have missed something. I don't understand what she's saying.*

'...so I won't be driving down with you to-morrow night – I'll come early on Saturday morning.'

'What?'

'Oh, Nina! Aren't you listening to what I'm saying? I'm going to see Barbara again – Sister Barbara.'

'But why? You've only just been.'

Caitlin sighed in exasperation. 'You weren't listening, were you? I have to see her. When I went before, I didn't know who was writing the letters. Now I do.'

The letter-writer had given no thought to Caitlin's reaction to the latest missive. The mind was on yesterday's excursion. *Whoever would have thought that I would kill a priest? Not I.* To begin with, something close to panic had set in. That was worrying. Thoughts were remembered. *Am I really spinning out of control? This wasn't planned. It was Terry I wanted.* But Terry hadn't been there. *Not that I realised it, even when the two men came* out of the house. I assumed it was Terry with his visitor. *Right size and age, and, let's face it, all those years ago, it was hardly Terry Richardson's face I was familiar with.* Slate eyes had watched as both men had walked to the visitor's car. Nice car. BMW M3. The visitor had got in, let down the window and chatted for a moment before driving away. Who did Terry know with that kind of money? *I thought he would go back in the house, then. Was all prepared. But as the car pulled away, he walked off down the street.* Jaunty. That had been the word for his gait. As if he were pleased with something. *I couldn't have that. Why should Terry Richardson be happy?*

The letter-writer had got out of the car, walked swiftly and silently at a distance until the figure had turned into an alleyway. *A logical place to make my move, although I was having to think rapidly how to get him back to the house to carry out my plan. My plan!* Long fingers clenched into a fist at the thought of the meticulous effort and attention to detail that had been ruined by what had happened next. *The alley was empty. Perfect. The heavily falling rain, coupled with my stealth, meant he never heard my approach.*

A strangled attempt at laughter broke from the letter-writer's lips. *Dear God! I had to raise my voice to get his attention! 'Excuse me? EXCUSE ME? Mr Richardson?' The figure had turned then. And it wasn't Terry. It wasn't Terry at all. It was this* thing *in a dog-collar. A Roman collar. He'd smiled, the idiot. Smiled at me. I backed off, made that lovely, fluttery gesture so common to women that always placates people, makes them feel safe. Gives them a*

false sense of security. I apologised for my mistake,
said I was looking for Terry and assumed, when he
had come out of the house...

'So sorry, Father.' *And I smiled when I said it.*
Father! How I hate that word! Hated the man, the
very concept. And here was a man who dressed in
skirts for his rituals, without reproach, forswears sex
and calls himself a father! Such mockery could not go
unpunished. But I needed a response first; inform-
ation, if possible.

'Lord! Two of you looking for him in one night!
He's Mr Popular at the moment, to be sure. Well
now, he's away for a few days. Did you want me
to pass on a message?'

What could I do with an invitation like that? I
wouldn't want to disappoint a priest, would I? So I
gave him a message. For Terry, for himself and for his
non-existent God. Vengeance is mine, not the Lord's...

Mags seemed to have done nothing but sleep
since her arrival at the Shelter. Well, yes, she'd
eaten, too, and taken her antibiotics, but, by and
large, she was simply sleeping. It was as if years'
worth of it were catching up with her. The
weakness of her body bothered her greatly. All
her strength seemed to have drained away, and
even the short walk to the bathroom and back
exhausted her. Her head was hurting again, too,
though that wasn't the bronchitis. It was
punishment, she felt sure. They had said, though,
that she would start to feel better in a few days.
She certainly hoped so. They were nice people
here. Kind. Caring. But she didn't want to stay.
Still too close to Darrowdale. *Holy Mother! What*

if one of them helped out here? Turned up for a shift and recognised me? It was just the sort of thing they'd be likely to do, with their social consciences and commitment. What was that phrase? 'Think globally; act locally'. It was no good. She had to get well. She had to get away.

Father Richard, Terry Richardson's spiritual advisor, smiled as he stepped onto the landing at the top of the staircase.

'You're eager this morning, Terry.' He knew from the man's body language that it was agitation rather than eagerness, but had experience enough to keep things casual. Terry would unburden himself if he wanted to, and from the look of things, that would be in the next few minutes. He turned the key in the lock and held open the door. 'Come on in.'

The room faced east and early morning sunlight was already filling it with light, if not warmth. That was provided by an ancient radiator system that occasionally hissed and clanked but otherwise seemed to be working OK. Father Richard made himself comfortable in the old-fashioned armchair behind the door, leaving Terry to the more comfortable seat opposite. He didn't take it. Instead, he shoved a piece of paper into the priest's hands and stood before him, trembling. Had he been drinking? He wasn't even properly dressed – still in his worn-out old carpet slippers.

'Oh, God, Father, I could barely sleep. Went back down to The Undercroft. This message – you don't know what it means.' He swallowed convulsively. 'I tried to phone him before breakfast. Three times.' He was literally wringing his hands. 'Couldn't do it. I just chickened out.'

The priest rose and led him to the chair, got him to sit, then moved to the power point below the window where he switched on an electric kettle. 'You take a couple of deep breaths, now, and tell me all about it. Let's have a cup of coffee, shall we? Stimulate the grey cells.' He lifted two mugs down from the bookcase, spooning freeze-dried coffee into them.

'You know I told you about ... all that bother? My wife – how I went to pot – what happened with the children? Daniel is my son. I haven't spoken to him since the day Katie left home.' He was crying now, and blew his nose noisily. 'I can't tell you how much I've longed for this, prayed for it. Contact. And now he's made the move.' He took the mug of coffee from the priest with shaking hands.

'So what's the problem?'

'I'm scared to death that something bad has happened.' The scalding liquid burned Terry's lips as he tried to drink it. With a shudder, he placed the mug on the floor.

'Like what? What's your worst fear in all this, Terry?' He watched as the man's Adam's apple worked furiously before he was able to speak.

'Katie. That's something's happened to Katie ... that she's dead.'

Father Richard smiled. 'No, Terry. Look at the message again. What does it say?' He handed back the piece of paper.

Terry looked at it blindly before composing

himself enough to read aloud. 'Father Mac-Donald phoned to say that Daniel is trying to get in touch. It's not bad news, but please contact him a.s.a.p. on the following number.' His face crumpled with relief. 'Oh God, why didn't I see that?'

'Too much emotional investment. And there you are, then. Katie's death would be bad news of the worst kind. It says it's not bad news, therefore she's not dead.' The priest stretched forward to touch Terry's hand. 'Go and phone him now. We can meet again later and you can tell me all about it then – if you want to, of course.'

Terry stood up. The priest had put on his glasses and was looking at his diary. 'How about straight after lunch?'

'Yes. Yes, that's fine. Thank you, Father.' Terry was out of the door in a flash, almost tripping in his haste to get downstairs.

'Watch those slippers, now! And get plenty of change from the office, Terry!' Father Richard called after him. 'That's a mobile number you'll be calling.'

Ronnie Walters was feeling better that morning. She and Colin had had a long talk before she'd come to work and he'd convinced her that Deborah Harvey didn't know half as much as she was making out.

'So she's baiting the line – casting it at us. It doesn't mean we have to bite. Hold our nerve, girl, that's what we have to do. Just like last time. When it happened, I mean. And for Christ's sake, let's not lose sight of the fact that, at the end of the day, we don't know what happened to Laura. No one does.'

Someone does, she had thought, although she didn't speak it. *And we may not know, but we have a lurking suspicion...* She pulled herself together. Be positive. Like Colin said, Deborah Harvey couldn't know anything that mattered, however much she might like them to think so. And at least now they'd talked it through, they could meet her with a united front. They'd got their story sorted out – just like last time; all they had to do was stick to it. She felt an inordinate sense of relief. Dear God, before Colin had given her that talking to, she'd been half off her head with worry. Must have been, to have entertained the wild thoughts that had come into her mind.

Hold our nerve. This won't – can't – go on forever. Once Derek's out of the way, once the twentieth anniversary has passed, it will all die a death. No one will be interested anymore.

'Ronnie – phone.' Abby Dewsbury was working with her today, and smiled as she squeezed against the counter to allow Ronnie to pass through to the alcove where the phone hung on the wall.

I must have been miles away. Didn't even hear it ring. She picked up the receiver. 'Ronnie Walters.'

'Hi, Ronnie, it's Deborah.' Ronnie felt an involuntary spasm in her stomach at the sound of her voice. *Speak of the devil ... or think, in my case.* 'I'm sorry to mess you about, but I'm not going to be able to make this evening. Car trouble. The head gasket's blown.'

'Sounds expensive.' Her first thought had been one of relief. Now, picturing her face, hearing again those questions ... she was like a dog that wouldn't let go. All her confidence evaporated.

'Yes, but I do need to get it fixed. I depend on my car a lot in this job.'

'Oh dear, what a shame. Look...' Ronnie's mind was in overdrive now. She could call Colin on the mobile. '...we'd got the bits and pieces ready for you, so – well, Colin's in town today, anyway. Why don't I get him to pick you up? He could drive you up here – you could have supper with us...' Dear God, how on earth was she managing to sound so enthusiastic? '...and I'd be quite happy to drive you home.'

'That's very kind, but really, I couldn't. I don't want to put you out.'

'Not at all. We're anxious to help all we can, you know that. Why not come? It's no trouble at all, really.'

'Well, if you're really sure...'

'Of course I'm sure. Are you at the newspaper offices? Colin can easily pick you up from there. What would be a good time?'

Colin can pick you up. I can take you home. Home. It couldn't really hurt to know where she lived. Just in case...

'Daniel ... it's Dad.'

'Give me your number and I'll call you straight back.'

It was hardly the greeting Terry had expected and he stared at the information on the pay phone in confusion, only managing to locate and repeat the number at the expense of further coins. He replaced the handset and stood waiting for the phone to ring, feeling as if he had a nest of snakes curling in the pit of his stomach. There had been no warmth in Daniel's voice at all.

What did you expect? he chided himself bitterly. *All these years and everything that's happened, and suddenly it's going to be happy families again?*

He snatched up the receiver on the first ring. 'Hello?'

'Dad...' The word sounded strange on Daniel's lips, as if he had difficulty getting the word out. 'Have you been getting funny letters connected to Mum's disappearance?'

Oh Christ! 'What sort of letters?'

'Don't piss me about – yes or no?'

'Yes.'

'Right. We need to meet, then. Have you still got them?'

'What?'

'The letters.'

'Yes – except one. But, Daniel...'

'No buts, Dad. Bring them with you. Where are you, by the way? The priest told my investigator that you were away, that's all. Wouldn't say where.'

Investigator? Oh, Jesus... Terry struggled to keep his voice steady. 'I'm on a kind of retreat. For recovering alcoholics.'

'That's what you call yourself, is it?' Daniel sighed. 'And how long does this retreat last?'

'I can leave at any time. Especially if it's about the letters.' Terry's mind was clearing now. Obviously Daniel had been getting them, too.

Oh, shit... 'Daniel – has – has your sister been getting them as well? I mean, are you in touch with her at all?'

'Yes and yes. I'm spending the weekend with her. Monday, I need to keep free – there's someone I may or may not be seeing. Tuesday, then. How does that sound?'

'Fine, son. That's fine. Just name the place and time.'

'That will depend on how the weekend goes. I'll ring you Sunday night or Monday morning to finalise.'

God, he's going to hang up on me. 'Then you'll need my home number. I'll have to go home first – to get the letters.'

'Not a problem. My investigator will pick you up and run you there, then bring you to meet me. Give me the address of this Retreat place. I've got a pen – shoot.'

Terry spelled it out slowly, desperate for a way to prolong the conversation. 'Ah, Daniel – I just want to say how pleased I am – your career and all – I've kept track of what you've been doing.'

'Really? I'll give you a ring, like I said.'

The line went dead. Terry stood holding the handset for a long moment before finally laying it back to rest.

The afternoon's end had come quicker than Colin Walters could have imagined. He glanced at his watch as he waited for Deborah Harvey. What was Ronnie thinking of? He would far sooner have put her off. She wouldn't have minded – certainly wouldn't have been sus-

243

picious. After all, it was nearly Christmas. Still...
He could see Ronnie's point, and he'd been the
one going on at her to hold her nerve and act
normally. 'The more helpful we look, the better,'
she'd said, and she was probably right. Damn it,
though, why hadn't she suggested a later time?
That way, he could have picked her up from
home. Despite his pep talk – which had secretly
been as much for his own benefit as Ronnie's –
he couldn't help wondering what to do if things
didn't go according to plan. Stupid idea, really.
Just for back-up, of course, finding out where she
lived. It wouldn't really come to that...

Terry Richardson had little appetite that evening,
but forced himself to eat and to face up to what
had happened. He had been upset at his lunchtime meeting with Father Richard, recounting
Daniel's coldness almost in a state of shock. 'He
wouldn't have contacted me at all, but for these
letters.'

The priest had asked about them, of course,
and Terry had found himself explaining not only
the recent communications, but the blackmail
letters he had received for so many years, inwardly squirming at how unbelievably tacky
everything sounded. It was as if, in telling the
story to another person, he was hearing it himself
for the first time, and it was a painful experience.

The priest had listened, patient and dispassionate – at least outwardly. Terry wondered what
he was really thinking. When he spoke, it had
been with firmness and compassion. Like Father
Mac, he had urged Terry to make reconciliation

244

with the church through full confession and Holy Communion, stressing that this was no light matter, not an outward following of form, but an inner conversion requiring true repentance.

'Repentance isn't a problem, Father. I've had years to repent, and believe me, I have.'

They'd talked about the meaning of repentance then, and Terry recognised that what he'd felt more than anything was guilt and self-pity, which were not the same thing. He'd had to concede that, certainly back then, all that had really bothered him was the fact that he had been found out. How on earth was he ever going to put any of this to rights?

And that's where Father Richard had been most helpful. He had been kind, but had not minced his words. It was what Terry needed. He asked Terry to put himself in Daniel's shoes, think about things from his perspective. How would he feel about the situation then? He had pointed out, as Terry had recognised during that phone call, that things couldn't simply be swept under the carpet.

'You can't pick up this relationship as if nothing ever happened. A lot of things happened, for most of which you do bear responsibility.' So they had talked then of facing up to one's responsibilities and the consequences of one's actions, whether those actions had been intentional or unintentional. Consequences are consequences, and Daniel's phone call – the reasons for it and his coldness towards his father – were consequences .

Terry knew the priest was right, that he had to stop thinking only of himself and try to make amends. He and Daniel may never get on. He may never see Caitlin again – why should she *want* to see him, after what he'd done? But at least he could help with the letters. Just do what he could and bow out. The rest was in God's hands.

So absorbed was he in his thoughts, so slow in eating his evening meal, that he didn't notice Father Richard's face peer round the doorway and withdraw.

Father Richard, for his part, was also recalling their earlier conversation and had a good idea of the pain Terry would be suffering as a result. He knew that what he had to say – the message he had to pass on – would only add to it, so decided to let the man eat his meal in peace. It was only as Terry left the dining room, therefore, that the priest stepped forward and took his arm. 'I've some bad news, I'm afraid, Terry. About Father Mac...'

Deborah Harvey was giving serious consideration to learning to cook. The meal at Derek's had been superb, and Colin and Ronnie Walters were close to matching it this evening. Her taste buds would never again believe that micro-waveable ready-meals were the height of culinary achievement. Still ... she brought her mind back to more important matters as she accepted a second helping of carrots and potatoes. Was it her imagination or were the Walters being just a little too bright and considerate this evening? They were certainly being liberal with the wine, though it must be said, only when it came to her glass. Neither of them was drinking very much. *Trying to loosen my tongue, maybe? I thought the idea was for me to loosen theirs...*

The conversation flowed easily enough over supper, but was largely inconsequential. Only after the plates were cleared away and coffee served did it turn to the matter in hand: Laura Richardson's disappearance. Then the flow decreased to a dribble, certainly as far as any new information was concerned. Things looked up, however, when Colin produced the photograph albums.

'Started out informally, but I soon decided to keep a pictorial record of the Community's progress over the years. You can use whatever you like, of course, but please – don't lose anything. I don't have negatives for all of these.'

'No problem. I'll guard them with my life, get them scanned and return them to you straight away.' Deborah took her time looking through the pages, asking a lot of questions, mainly along the lines of 'Who's this?', 'When did they come?', 'When did they leave?' The Richardson family she already knew well from the newspaper picture library, but it was good to be able to put faces to other names at last. Ronnie and Colin seemed more relaxed and willing to chat now. On firmer ground, perhaps? *Then where's the quicksand they're afraid of?*

Deborah smiled, made notes, chose which photographs she wanted to take. *Well,* she thought, as the Walters laughed at some long-ago embarrassment, a memory provoked by a picture, *it worked once before with Ronnie. Let's try it again...*

247

'Ronnie, Derek says that the business Laura was worried about wasn't drugs at all. Said she was quite specific on that point.'

The laughter froze, along with their faces. *Even if they don't say a word, it's enough to tell me that they* do *know what was bothering her. Now why don't they want to tell me?*

'What?' Colin looked thunderstruck.

'Oh, I never told you at the time, but Laura confided – a couple of days before she disappeared, I think it was – that she was worried about the possibility of drugs among the children.' Ronnie shrugged at him. 'I told her straight away there was nothing to be concerned about. Any whiff of drugs and you'd have known in an instant. Being at the school, and all.'

'There certainly were no drugs. Never have been. We had enough opposition as it was, and that was precisely the kind of ammunition our detractors would have loved. We've always kept things clean.'

'I'm not arguing with you,' Deborah said mildly. 'What I *am* saying is that Laura told Ronnie she was worried about drugs, but Laura told Derek it *wasn't* drugs she was worried about. It was something else.' She let the statement hang, watching their reaction. Their faces seemed frozen, and Deborah noticed that both of them were holding their breath. It was Colin who broke the impasse.

'Like what?'

Deborah made no response.

He tried again. 'But why would she do that? Say one thing to Ronnie and something else to

Derek? It doesn't make sense.'

'No, it doesn't, does it? Any chance of another coffee?'

Ronnie chattered a great deal as she drove Deborah back home. Strange – it was more personal stuff, like how long had Deborah been up here, where was she from originally, and what were her ambitions beyond what Ronnie referred to as 'Derek's rag'? Deborah assumed that Ronnie was desperate to stay off the conversation stopper of Laura Richardson. *OK,* she thought. *Give her a bit of rope and let her hang herself. I've enough to be going on with for now.* So she answered, hoping to lull the woman into believing that she wasn't suspicious about a thing.

'It's really good of you to run me back like this. I do hope I haven't put you out too much.'

'Oh, not at all. Colin and I can usually work things out to accommodate a sudden crisis. Comes of being married for so long, I suppose. Are you seeing anyone? A boyfriend? Sorry – that's so personal. I'm just nosy!'

'That's OK. Not at the moment, no. Too busy with the job.' Deborah's mind was sharp as a razor. *That was an interesting turn of phrase. They can work things out to accommodate a sudden crisis, eh? So what crisis arose when Laura disappeared and what did they do about it? Methinks you made a Freudian slip there, Ronnie...*

Ronnie needed clear-cut directions to get to Deborah's flat, especially once they got into the St Mark's area of the town. She smiled as she pulled up outside the building, a refurbished one-time tenement block. 'Which floor are you on, then? Not the top, hopefully!'

'Thank God, no, because there isn't a lift! That one's mine.' Deborah pointed out the front ground-floor apartment.

Ronnie did her best to keep her voice easy and conversational. 'Looks like your flatmate's home anyway.' She was referring to the light in the window.

'Good Lord, I couldn't share with anyone! More to the point, no one would put up with me! Thanks again for the lift.' Deborah got out of the car, brandishing the large envelope she was carrying in Ronnie's face before closing the passenger door. 'I'll take good care of these, I promise. Get them back to you a.s.a.p.'

Ronnie watched her run up the steps and put the key in the door. Natural enough. Dropping off a single woman, you could never be too careful. Sensible to make sure they got inside OK. Deborah waved before closing the front door. Ronnie waved back, a litany going through her head. 31 Northfield Terrace... 31 Northfield Terrace... 31 Northfield Terrace...

The evening was at last coming to a close, everything ironed out to everyone's satisfaction. Rod Challoner, the driving force behind the Cheltenham Shelter and its Christmas initiative, put his arm around Caitlin's shoulder as they walked to the kitchen, ready for a cup of tea.

'Well, that's gone perfectly! Better than I thought possible.' Donations of food, clothing and money were well up on the previous year and now, despite the apparent calamity of the past few

250

days, there was no shortage of volunteers either.

'That newspaper SOS certainly didn't hurt.'

'No, though I'm hoping to persuade them, when they do the follow-up in the New Year, to lay it on thick so that people don't just think we're here at Christmas and that's the end of it.'

Caitlin nodded. People were more aware of need at this time of year, but the Shelter also provided breakfasts and lunches every weekend, and breakfasts most weekdays. Along with bathing facilities and, wherever it could, clothing. 'That's the problem, alright. Christmas is high profile. Day in, day out, week after week, isn't.'

Rod rolled up the shutter above the counter between the kitchen and the rest of the church hall. 'We could do so much more if we had the volunteers for day in, day out, every week.' The ones he had were doing sterling work, but there was always room for more. 'Still, your T'ai Chi class has done us proud. That young lassie with the plaits reckons she could do one morning a week while she's still at college.'

'Good.' Caitlin had been surprised to see two more members of her class turn up, asking if there was anything they could do. Funny how things are sparked, she thought. Just a few words at the party after her last class, a query from Nina, and suddenly the whole group had become aware of the Shelter and what it was trying to do.

The boiler in the kitchen had been chuntering away while the volunteers had gone over the rosters and sorted out their duties. Cups and saucers were laid out ready and, with Caitlin and Rod on pouring duty, it wasn't long before the

251

hall was buzzing with conversation and laughter. Caitlin soon found herself among one of the groups of people scattered around the hall. She glanced round automatically, feeling more able to do so now that people were mingling rather than sitting in a circle, talking business. All the old stalwarts were here, but a number of new faces were apparent, which was always heart-warming. Ordinary people *can* make a difference. Many of them were retired, a number unemployed, and there always seemed to be a few students.

'So, Caitlin, what did you give up to have the pleasure of our company this evening?'

She smiled at the elderly man who had addressed her. 'Skittles, Noel.' She pulled a face and did an exaggerated shudder. 'My team is probably being decimated, even as we speak!'

'That good, are you? We'll have to watch this! Where do you play?' She told him. Two of the people from her T'ai Chi class wandered over.

'Did you have a good day with your brother?'

'Wonderful, thanks! Nice to see you here.'

'Only too happy to help. One week to go, eh? To Christmas Eve.'

'Yes.' Rod popped his head into the midst of their conversation. 'Get all the rest you can in the meantime – you'll need it!'

'Any chance of that, do you reckon?'

'What, rest? Me personally?' Caitlin smiled. 'Oh, I should think so. I'm visiting an old friend tomorrow, then off to Oxfordshire for the weekend.'

'Alright for some!'

'Don't knock it – there's some beautiful

countryside there!' Rod smiled. 'Make the most of it, Caitlin, that's what I say!'

By the time the evening broke up, the letter-writer had made another slight change of plan. *Knowing as much as I do about her whereabouts over the next few days, I can afford to go back up north. There's still a little unfinished business there...*

In the Butcher's Arms, Josh, Mike and Nina, with a substitute for Caitlin, had not been trounced quite so thoroughly as she would have liked to believe. As they walked to the car park, Nina laid her hand on Josh's arm as she told him of the morning's conversation.

'I don't know what's come over her. She was so angry, which is maybe not such a bad thing, but I wish she wouldn't be so damned secretive.' She stopped, trying to find the right words. 'It's as if she's just kicked into gear, or something. I'm worried she might be going into overdrive.'

'But she still won't go to the police?'

'Quite the opposite.' Nina shook her head. 'She made me handle the damned letter by the edges and put it in a plastic bag when I'd finished. Said she *will* be going to the police, once she's seen Sister Barbara again. But that was all I could get out of her.'

Josh thought for a moment. 'Sister Barbara is the ex-prostitute who looked after Caitlin when she ran away to London, right? And when she had some sort of trouble with a boyfriend?'

Nina looked at him carefully. 'How much do you know about that?'

'Not a lot.' He considered the question further. 'I felt that what she told me was the bare bones. The fact that she told me anything at all was a major achievement, and I didn't want to push it. You think it's connected?'

'No. No, I don't. I mean, it is to *her*. She didn't say so outright, but I think she's convinced – why, I don't know – that Nick, this ex-boyfriend, is behind the letters.'

'But you don't think so?'

Nina looked up at him, her face sombre. 'No. It's all wrong, Josh. Call it intuition, call it whatever you like. My gut tells me that it's somebody far worse than Nick.'

'You two finished chatting each other up yet?' Mike called good-naturedly from the bonnet of the car, where he'd sat huddled like a vulture for the past few minutes. Nina looked at him, startled.

'You've got the keys,' he told her, sliding off it, 'and I don't know about anyone else, but I'm freezing my nuts off.'

Chapter Nineteen

Friday 17 December

Deborah Harvey had said nothing to the Walters about the meeting she had just arrived for. Save it and use it as another bombshell, had been her attitude. She doubted that Daniel Richardson would have said anything to them about it. From what she could gather, he had simply used them as a means to trace his sister. What would they think if they knew he had a private investigator on the case, though? *More to the point – what do I think about that?* It was odd, to say the least. *Nearly twenty years since his mother disappeared, yet he's suddenly decided to look into it? Why now?* Hopefully, she would find out in the next few minutes.

Daniel had phoned her, told her about Chris Farmer and suggested she meet with him. What was it he'd said? 'I believe it could be to our mutual advantage.' Really? She'd raised a very cynical eyebrow at that point, but kept her thoughts out of her voice as she agreed to the meeting. So here she was, like someone out of a spy movie, wearing a pre-arranged outfit for easy identification, knowing that Chris would be doing likewise. Daniel had given her a good description, anyway. *All we need is a carnation in a buttonhole or a copy of some obscure novel, held upside down, and we'd be straight out of John le Carré.*

Moments later, she and Chris Farmer, identities established, had moved from the foyer of the Hotel through to the inside terrace of the Grand Salon, where a tea-dance was taking place. 'Good God, I didn't know this kind of thing still went on!'

'It does here.' The Grand Hotel really *was* grand, one of the oldest hotels in the town, and it prided itself on a long-established reputation for old-fashioned service. Deborah was pleased she had chosen it for the meeting. The music – from a live band of elderly gentlemen in full evening dress – was not loud enough to prevent conversation, but was adequate to prevent their conversation being overheard. That possibility was made extra unlikely due to the fact that most of the people who came to these dances were there for precisely that reason – they liked to dance, not sit around talking or listening to other people. True, a few of the very elderly ones who weren't quite up to it any more tended to sit and listen, but they were few and far between, their attention focused on the music, not on the much younger couple sitting without a view of the musicians.

'So how can I help?' Deborah asked, taking a bite of angel cake.

Chris looked at her with open interest before making a reply. 'I think it's more a case of working out how we can help each other.'

'Oh?'

'Daniel Richardson originally hired me to find his sister. He found her anyway, through his connections to the Darrowdale Community. You're probably wondering how come he took so long before deciding to look for her; if, perhaps, there was a particular reason for doing so at this time? There was.'

Deborah kept the excitement off her face and merely inclined her head.

Chris smiled at her, amused by her ability to mask her response. 'And that has a direct bearing on your coverage of Laura Richardson's disappearance. We could help each other, Deborah. You're digging in your way. I'm digging in mine.

256

We both have the same aim – to uncover what really happened back then. By pooling information, we stand a better chance and are likely to get there faster. And it goes without saying that you get the story and the glory.'

Deborah leaned back in the Lloyd Loom chair. 'How do I know you have anything worth trading? You could just be trying to get information out of me.'

'How do I know you have anything worth offering? I don't. You don't. We have to establish some trust, Deborah. Now, how might we do that?'

Deborah held his eye. It was like being a kid again. *You show me yours and I'll show you mine.* Someone had to go first.

Chris continued speaking, unfazed by her silence. 'It seems to me that you might like to hear things from the horse's mouth, so to speak. You had asked the Walters to try and broker an interview with Daniel, and so far he's prevaricated, wanting to consult his sister, right?'

'Right.'

It was Chris's turn to incline his head now, mirroring Deborah's own body language.

'Well, Daniel will speak to you – answer questions – whether Caitlin agrees to co-operate or not. He will also tell you what provoked his sudden interest in reopening the case. Are you free on Monday?'

'I can be.'

'Good. He's willing to talk to you then. In depth.'

'Where and when?'

Chris took a notebook from the inside pocket of his jacket and started to write. 'It would be a long way for either of you to travel to meet the other on home turf. How does somewhere in the middle sound? Say, Nottingham?' He ripped the page from the book and handed it over. Deborah looked at it and nodded.

'No problem.' She tucked it into her shoulder bag. 'Tell me something. Why didn't he just phone and suggest this himself?'

'It was important for us to meet – you and I. To get the measure of each other. If we can come to an agreement, Daniel will only be in the background. It will be the two of us on the front line. We're the ones who have to be able to work together, right?'

'Right.' She nodded.

'I know you agreed to lay off Caitlin until Daniel had spoken to her. What about Terry?'

'What about him?'

'Have you tracked him down yet?'

Should she lie or should she tell the truth? 'Not yet,' she conceded. 'But I will.'

'Then let me save you some time and effort.' Chris handed over another piece of paper, already prepared. 'He's away at the moment, but Daniel's spoken to him.'

Deborah tucked that one away, too. 'Are you up here for long?'

'As long as I need to be.'

'Alright. You doubtless have a business card with a mobile number?'

They both smiled then and carried out an exchange. 'Let me talk to my editor and I'll come

258

back to you.'

As they made their way across the Grand Salon, their meeting at an end, Deborah, watching the couples swaying and gliding in time to the music, wondered if Derek had ever whirled Laura around the floor here...

Despite the chill air coming through the open window of his old Land Rover, Colin Walters was sweating as he drove, for the second time, past Deborah Harvey's flat. God, what a performance it had been trying to get the address from Ronnie when she'd come home last night. Colin was not used to being devious with his wife. The only time he'd done it before was that business with Doc. *And that*, he thought bitterly, *is why I'm having to be devious again. I mean, I could hardly say to her, Ronnie, I need to know where she lives because I'm preparing to take desperate measures if necessary, could I?* So he'd been vague, wondering what journalists earned nowadays, whereabouts they could afford to live. Infuriatingly, Ronnie had been vague in return, obviously hadn't been paying attention at all.

'Oh ... St Luke's, I think. You know, past where they built the new supermarket? Somewhere off the Poet's Corner area – Northfield Road? No, might have been the Terrace ... Northfield Terrace. Yes. I think that was it.'

He'd teased her then – made out he was teasing her, at any rate, although inside he'd been screaming for more precise information.

'Bloody hell, Ronnie, to think you used to brag about how observant you are, and how I never noticed anything unless it was shoved under my nose! At one time, you would have come home, told me the number, the colour of the door and how long she'd been living with her boyfriend!'

She'd fallen for it. Screwed up her eyes in concentration, told him it was number thirty-one, ground floor, the door was green and she didn't live with anyone, thank you, let alone a boyfriend.

He'd been so relieved, he'd wanted to punch the air and shout 'Yes!' He coughed and shook his head, turning back towards the supermarket. *And that wouldn't have been a give-away, eh?* Instead, he'd laughed and said, 'God – you were having me on! I thought for a minute you'd lost it, girl!' Then he'd made her a cup of tea, massaged her feet and told her that Deborah Harvey didn't know Jack Shit. Everything would be alright. Just wait and see.

On the outskirts of London, Caitlin, far from having rushed to her meeting with Sister Barbara, had pulled off the road and was sitting with her head slumped against the steering wheel. She had had a nightmare last night, one that used to be recurring but hadn't reared its head for several years. Now, even in the light of day, it was still alive and vivid, as if its absence for so long had given it added power, its return to her nocturnal world now spilling over into waking consciousness. Despite her best efforts, it reran itself, in her gut as much as her head, like a video on a loop. Blow after blow. Bone-shattering pain. Suffocation. Looking down on her own body, as if she were somehow floating up against the ceiling. Seeing the blood running down her legs...

She raised her head, wiping her nose on the back of her hand, slowly coming back to the present. Less than a mile to go to the Abbey. She restarted the engine, forcing herself to overcome her revulsion to focus on Nick. He'd gone too far this time. Much too far. He may have got away with it then. He wasn't going to get away with it now.

Derek listened with undisguised excitement as Deborah recounted her conversation with Chris Farmer. A private investigator, eh? Dear God, between Deborah's digging and his... Maybe, just maybe, at long last they would get to the bottom of all this.

'So, am I OK to confirm this meeting with Daniel on Monday?'

'Absolutely. Don't worry about a thing.' He was doing rapid calculations in his head. 'I can put somebody else on what you would have been doing. You're not indispensable, you know.' He grinned suddenly, unable to conceal his feelings. 'Except on the Laura Richardson story!'

'Thanks!'

He leaned forward, serious again, tapping a pencil on the blotter on his desk. 'Play it by ear – stay longer if you need to. Just stay in touch and keep me informed, alright?'

'Shit!' Deborah smacked her head with the heel of her hand.

'What?'

'I forgot! My car's knackered – the head gasket.

261

They can't look at it until next Tuesday.'

'So what do you think trains are for?'

'Trains!'

'Those big things that run on tracks and take longer nowadays to reach their destinations than they did at the end of the nineteenth century. Count yourself lucky – in my day...'

'Don't tell me,' Deborah groaned. 'You'd have had to walk.'

'How old do you think I am? That's really taking the piss! We did have bicycles.' He smiled again, having wound her up nicely. 'Stop worrying – we'll hire a car.'

Deborah rose to leave. 'Oh, it just crossed my mind – I wondered – did you ever take Laura to the Grand? Dancing?'

Derek looked at her over the top of his glasses, eyebrows threatening to fly off his balding head. 'Are you kidding? You may think I'm old, but back then we were mere bloody striplings. The Grand? Much too sedate. We did our bopping at the Palais...'

Mags leaned against the sink as she waited for the kettle to boil. She was feeling much better, but the weakness still seemed to pervade her body. She was taking the antibiotics religiously, willing them to work quickly, praying for a full recovery. *And, above all, Holy Mother, quickly. I need to get away from here.*

Mick, one of the wardens, a man in his thirties with a ponytail, came through and watched her as she made herself a drink.

'You're not happy here, are you, Mags?'

262

Mags bit her lip, tried to stop the tears coming to her eyes. *What's wrong with me, that I'm crying or on the verge of tears all the time? It's worse than the Change.*

'It's not that,' she told him, awkwardly. 'You've been very good to me here, and as God is my witness, I'm more grateful than I can tell you.'

'But?' Mick prompted.

'But...' She shook her head, almost in despair. How could she put it? 'It's not *here* I'm unhappy with. If this Hostel was elsewhere in the country, I'd be happy as Larry. It's the area. It's too close to...' She struggled for words. 'I have unhappy memories, let's put it that way.'

'So where would you like to be?'

'South, I don't care as long as I can move south.'

Mick considered her for a moment or two. In the days she'd been with them, it had become quite obvious that she didn't have a drink or drug problem. She'd been cooperative and was doing everything the doctor had told her to. She was quiet, too. Most of the people who came here – guests was the way Mick liked to think of them – poured out their life stories in no time. The delivery varied according to the state of their mental health. Some poured, some mumbled, some rambled. Terrible stories they were, too, for the most part. Mick had early on become a firm believer in 'There but for the grace of God...' But Mags? Nothing. He was no wiser now than when she had first arrived.

'South, eh?' he said at last. 'Well, it just so happens I'm going that way myself. I have family

263

in Bristol, and I'm going down in time for Christmas.' He smiled. 'I did Christmas here last year, so I'm being let off for good behaviour. So how about I give you a lift? I can drop you off anywhere along the way, if you don't want to go that far. I'd be happier, though, if I knew it was a place with a Hostel or Shelter.'

'Oh, thanks be to God!' Her cry was heartfelt. 'And thank you! I can contribute to the cost of your petrol,' she added.

'You certainly will not! And I'll take no argument,' he emphasised as she opened her mouth in protest. 'This is the season of goodwill, remember? Take it as a Christmas present.'

The window of Father Richard's office looked out over a lawn and path that led to a lake, almost hidden by reeds and trees. Almost, but not quite. Even in summer, with everything in full foliage, the water could be glimpsed. In winter, the bare branches would be silhouetted by the setting sun. Today was a winter's day but the sun had set hours ago. It was the moon that cast its silvery light across the darkened landscape. Father Richard often turned out the light and stood for a few moments before leaving the room to take in its beauty, for it was the beauty of the scene that had long ago impressed him. This evening, however, something different had caught his attention and he drew a sharp intake of breath as he focused on the solitary figure by the water's edge. He couldn't be sure from this distance, of course, but his instincts told him it was Terry Richardson. Offering up an urgent prayer, he turned on his heel and left the room, mind already racing ahead to the quickest exit from the building in order to get to him in time.

His heart was hammering as he stumbled his way in moon-filtered darkness along the path leading to the lake. There had only ever been one suicide at the Retreat House since it had opened, and that had been a man who had hanged himself from a tree close to where Terry Richardson had been standing. Had he had anything in his hands? Darkness and the distance of his view from the window meant he could not be sure. Oh dear Lord! The most logical way would be to throw himself into the lake. Maybe he had already done so. Father Richard felt sure he would have heard the splash, but there had been the time it had taken him to get outside... Hurriedly, he threw off his jacket and kicked his slippers from his feet. One of the older priests had told him off about those slippers, said they should only be worn for visiting the bathroom at night, that he needed to watch his slovenly habits. He broke into a run, unable to see Terry because of the bushes and trees on either side of the path, which snaked along, deliberately designed to encourage peaceful meanderings in the grounds, rather than supplying the shortest route from A to B. The dirt path was hard under his feet, compacted from long years of use as well as the more immediate cold of the evening. It was littered, he knew, with stones and twigs, yet his feet did not register them as he loped along, his socked feet creating only padded footfalls as he moved inexorably closer to his goal. He dared not cry out, for fear of precipitating rash action on Terry's part, had he not already taken it. One last bend–

'Jesus, Father!' The priest was caught in a spray of urine as Terry turned round, startled by the sudden sound of undergrowth rustling behind him. 'You scared the pants off me!'

Chapter Twenty

The letter-writer drove steadily north. 'All Things Bright and Beautiful' was no longer the tune for the day. That day had passed, swallowed in the river of time. Today's rendition was 'The Way We Were'. After a while, however, the voice faltered and tailed off.

I remember the way we were, alright. When I first arrived at the Community. What was I feeling? What was I expecting, hoping for? The mind looped back, trawled through years of memories. *I wanted her to acknowledge me. Welcome me back. Stupid! Stupid! How long was it since I'd seen her?* A low moan escaped from thin lips. *I had such hope, then. But he told me – last year, before I killed him – that they hadn't wanted to have me. It was only because* she – *the Stepmother from Hell – was dying and they wanted to give my father a break. And, as I also found out later, because my father had said I was normal, was doing well...*

The moan turned into a harsh impersonation of a laugh. *What the fuck is normal? Who decides?*

So they'd had a progress report. *I had completed my first year at Uni. Stuck it out and was thriving. Computers are so much better than people. For once, I didn't stick out like a sore thumb. I was good at something. So off I went, just for a couple of weeks until* she'd *got her dying over with. Then I could go home, get a job through the summer vac. Oh, he always liked to rub that in, my father. The work ethic. The Protestant work ethic. Pretty funny coming from an Italian Catholic who had hardly had to work a day in his life. International Banking? Money laundering, more like, and he loved every minute of it.* The mouth twisted into a grimace of contempt. *So off I went. Like a lamb to the slaughter.*

Tears started to prick the eyes now. Not a good idea in the fast lane of the motorway. It was so contemptible. The reason for the tears. *I hadn't seen my mother for years. Had never even met my stepfather. And what happens?* He *was the one who was kind. She barely even acknowledged me. He wasn't* really *kind, though. He must have been pretending, though he did it very well. I never knew then that he hadn't wanted me, even if it was obvious from the word go that she didn't. What was I? An embarrassment? A reminder of her failed first marriage?*

He had made all the conversation. She had barely said a word. *She was hardly ever there. Avoiding me. Even when she was there, she hardly ever looked at me. Not directly, anyway. Oh, she looked when she thought I wasn't looking, when she thought I didn't know. I caught her at it several times.* The mind struggled to put a word to those looks. Bewilderment? Hatred? What was it?

So. It was difficult for me. I got there before the local

schools broke up. There was no one to mix with for most of the daytime. No one of my own age, although a few of them were close. There I was, in a beautiful place with nothing to do. So I made my own entertainment. Roamed the place like it was my own private territory, but never so that people could see. Well. Hardly ever. And then the worry set in. About my mother. I spoke to him. Asked him about her. Said how concerned I was. Asked if she were ill? What was it he said? 'She has her problems, I'm afraid.' He never explained what, though. Even when I – in a rare rush of weakness – asked if it was because I was there. And he looked astonished and said, 'Bless you, no! You mustn't think that. She's had these ... difficulties for years.' So I spent my time there wondering whether she was a drug addict or an alcoholic. Those were the worst things I could think of. Until I found out...

Alone in his London flat, Daniel spent the whole evening dredging up every possible memory he could of the day his mother had disappeared. *What did I do first thing that day? And then? And after that?* He sat at his PC, tapping the keys steadily, adding to his list things that came to mind about the time immediately afterwards. Things other people had said or done, or said they had done. Soon, he had a headache. He told himself that he probably needed glasses, but couldn't avoid acknowledging that it was more to do with painful recollection than eye strain. He would need two, possibly three copies of this, he thought, as he pulled up the print controls. One for Cait – they would be comparing notes over

268

the weekend. At least, he hoped they would, once he'd explained what he was getting Chris to do. One copy for Chris, of course. And the third? He wavered. Deborah Harvey? He wasn't sure about that. It wouldn't do to let a journalist have *all* the details. Maybe Dad, then. *Christ!* He didn't even need to articulate the word before it made him want to choke. Dad was a bloody big problem, both then and now. He pinched the bridge of his nose and rubbed his eyes while he thought about it. *I really, really hoped never to see the bastard again.* He printed a third copy, anyway. The important thing now was to clear his head and get some rest before going up to Oxfordshire tomorrow. Dad, he'd think about later.

The nun sat with her eyes closed, listening in disbelief as Caitlin poured out her anger.

'...he's made a real mistake with this one, Barbara. The others were too short – how could you tell anything from those, right? But this ... he's given himself away. I knew as soon as I read it that it had to be him! He always said he'd come back and get me, and "Hellcat" – well, you heard him call me that on God knows how many occasions. I just don't understand why he's left it so long.' Caitlin puffed out air in exasperation. 'I was so stupid. So naïve. I wish I'd never told him about my mother. And, of course, I changed my name as soon as I was eighteen and old enough to do so. What a bastard!'

'It isn't Nick, Caitlin.' The nun spoke quietly. Throughout her tirade, Caitlin had been so self-absorbed that she hadn't seen the pain etching itself on Sister Barbara's face.

'What?'

'It isn't Nick, Caitlin. It can't be. He's dead.'

'Dead? No. No way. This is *him*, Barbara – it's got his stamp all over it.'

'Will you listen to what I'm telling you, Caitlin? He's dead. Beyond any shadow of a doubt.' She drew in a deep breath. 'I identified the body.'

Caitlin stared at her. This wasn't making sense. She had been so sure.

'When? I mean – how can he be dead?'

The nun gave a bitter half smile. 'Quite easily, Caitlin. I killed him.'

None of it should have happened. They were so perfect. The Golden Couple. Happy. Common goals. So right *together. Two years. Everyone thought Caitlin and Nick seemed destined to live happily ever after. But then Caitlin fell pregnant. The rows! Dear God ... Caitlin had been shell-shocked. Young and naïve enough to think they could have a baby and pursue their careers, she had been outraged when Nick had demanded she 'get rid of it'. And the fights became physical and she moved in with me while she was trying to find somewhere else to live. And Nick found her. And I wasn't there...*

The nun cleared her throat, forced herself to speak. 'After he nearly killed you ... after I found you ... he legged it, of course.' The colloquialism seemed strange coming from the lips of a nun, but Caitlin realised that it wasn't the nun who was telling the story. It was the old Sheila, the hooker, her friend.

'He blamed me for the fact – for not being able to finish the job, I suppose. Blamed me for interfering. He laid low for a while. We were all stupid back then, Caitlin, me included.' She looked her friend in the eye. 'None of us knew who did it, right? Random attack by some nutter who mistakenly thought you were one of us – a hooker.' She shook her head. 'I really thought he'd just disappear. Sorry – your mother and all...' Caitlin said nothing, hardly appearing to breathe. 'Anyway, you were in hospital and the rest of us – I suppose we forgot about the threats. Thought he'd just buggered off and wouldn't come back. He wouldn't, if he'd had any sense. But you know Nick...'

Seconds ticked by. 'I was working when he found me. Chewy's place – you remember?'

Caitlin nodded.

'So there I was – on the job – when the door bursts open and in comes Nick, raving like a lunatic. God knows what he was on. He pulled the punter off me – fat bastard, is all I remember – and threw him down the stairs. That was probably what saved my life. I tried to scream, but he had me by the throat. I managed to hammer on the wall a couple of times, but Louis was already up and running – he'd heard the commotion when the punter went arse over tit on the staircase.' Caitlin remembered Louis well. Unofficial minder to the girls using Chewy's place. Built like a brick shithouse.

'Nick was screaming at me, saying he was going to kill me, teach me a lesson, called me...' The nun in Barbara reasserted herself and she paused. 'He called me a lot of things. And he tried to cut my left breast off.' Caitlin gasped.

271

'But Louis ... Louis made his entrance – took the door clean off its hinges. Dragged him off. They had a fight, brief, but to the point, and Nick had to run away again. Was lucky Louis didn't kill him. And then I said it. I was crying, screaming, convinced my breast was hanging off – there was blood everywhere...' She fell silent.

Caitlin waited, waited, then asked, 'You said what, Barbara?'

The nun's lips were pressed together. She produced a white cotton handkerchief from some hidden pocket and wiped her face before she spoke. 'It's like Thomas à Becket. "Who will rid me of this meddlesome priest?" What I said was, "It's time someone taught that fucker a lesson. Someone his own size".'

Caitlin felt as if an icy hand had gripped her heart. 'Oh Barbara...'

'Don't you wish you could take things back? Unsay them? Did you do that as a kid? You know, someone says something horrible to you and you say, "You take that back!"? But they can't. You can't. God knows, I wish I'd never said it.'

Sister Barbara stood up, started to pace the small parlour which had been set aside for her meeting with Caitlin. She turned to face her. 'Louis took me literally. He always had a crush on me. Went and found a couple of mates. Told them what I'd said. Said, "What Sheila wants, Sheila gets, right?"' She shook her head. It seemed strange to be referring to herself by her old name after so long in her new identity.

'I didn't know this until afterwards, of course. He was shaking when he told me. Said they were

272

sure Nick was alive when he went into the water, so they hadn't actually killed him. Said it was his own stupid fault – Nick's, I mean. "The stupid prick was so pissed, he couldn't run straight".'

In her mind's eye, Louis was standing in front of her. He'd put his hands on her shoulders, looked her straight in the face. 'It was his own fault, Sheila. If he'd have taken his beating like a man, none of it would have happened. Well, the beating would have – that was the whole point, wasn't it? But dying – that was down to him.' Nick had broken free, he told her. 'Not that we was finished, mind. Pegged it along, pulled 'imself up on the parapet, see, and just sort of swayed, like. Called us a bunch of pussy-whipped wankers. Then he fell off. Honest to God, Sheila, we didn't touch 'im. One minute he was there, teetering on the edge, laughing at us; the next minute he was gone. They had heard the splash, raced to the parapet and looked over.

'Didn't you try to fish him out?' Sheila had asked.

'What? No! Left the fucker to it. Marco seen him at the pool, regular. He could swim.'

'Apparently not this time,' she had said. They thought she was being droll. Laughed like it was the best joke in the world.

She looked at Caitlin. 'They thought it was funny. All I felt was panic. Nick was dead. Dead! Sure, I hated him. Sure, I wanted him beaten up. He deserved it. But *beaten up* – not dead. They weren't worried at all. I was the one with the guilty conscience. I was the one waiting for the police to call, because it was all my fault. But they never did. Not to arrest me, anyway. Just asked me to identify him, because he'd been a neighbour and they had no details of next-of-kin. Nick was still bruised from his fight with you. He'd also been involved in a brawl in the pub where he'd been drinking before Louis and the lads got to him. He'd been thrown out of there – that's when they'd spotted him. But nobody had noticed them following him down the road. Perfect, wasn't it? Certainly good enough for the police and the Coroner. Nick had got drunk, got into a fight and apparently fallen, some time later, while still under the influence of alcohol, into the river and drowned. An unfortunate accident. That's what the Coroner said. And I didn't enlighten him.'

She cried then, short gasping barks of pain. Silently, Caitlin walked towards her, arms outstretched.

Stillness and silence hung in the darkness over Nina's cottage like a blanket. It was more than an hour since they had finally gone to bed, Josh to his own room, Mike and Nina to theirs. Beside her, she could hear Mike's breathing, slow and regular, but Nina couldn't sleep. She had taken herself back to her experience on Tuesday, at Caitlin's T'ai Chi class. Dear God, it couldn't really be? Surely not?

Stop avoiding it, Nina! Yes, it bloody was! Denial was going to get no one anywhere. Her intuition had never let her down before. Whoever was writing the letters had been in that room. They were one of Caitlin's students. But who? *Who?*

274

She reran the evening through her mind, seeing the faces again. Nothing. Absolutely nothing. She tried once more, thinking back to when she had first felt the warning bells, what had happened afterwards. She was forced to the conclusion that, somehow, whoever it was had recognised that she was picking up the psychic signature they were putting out and had made attempts to block it.

She couldn't put it off any longer. She would have to speak to Caitlin about it. But how? If her behaviour since then had been anything to go by, a direct approach would not be well received, especially since she was so convinced that her ex-boyfriend was responsible. She lay still for several minutes, keeping her breathing slow and even, letting her unconscious search for an answer. Finally, it came. Thank God she hadn't been able to arrange a Christmas social evening for her Yoga class!

Carefully, she slipped out from under the duvet and padded downstairs to the living room. On the desk by the back window was Mike's old computer, the one he kept here for working in peace and quiet on the rare occasions he managed to get away during term-time. She switched it on, its whirrings and beepings seeming loud enough to waken the dead in the stillness that hung in folds around her. She glanced at the door, moved swiftly across the room to shut it, hoping to God she wouldn't wake the men. Passwords ... passwords ... oh yes. Finally she was in.

She sat for a moment, thinking about the

information she needed, what she'd have to do to get it. She double-clicked Word, which duly obliged her with a new document. Slowly at first, then with increasing speed, she began to type.

Chapter Twenty-one

Saturday 18 December

The letter-writer's finger moved down the page, searching, searching... There had been two Ds and one D.A. Harvey in the phone book and none of them had been the D. Harvey being sought. Now the Electoral Register was being checked. Ah-ha! Here was a Deborah Jane. The details were written down, compared with the Telephone Directory. Didn't match. No one paid any attention to the figure leaving the Public Library. There was a telephone box right outside. *How convenient.* The call was made. The suspicion confirmed. The Deborah Jane Harvey who lived at Flat 2, 31 Northfield Terrace, was ex-directory.

Daniel Richardson received a warm welcome when he arrived at the Oxfordshire cottage. Nina, of course, he had met before when he had decided to stop off at Caitlin's house on the way back from his visit to the Community. Mike was her husband, he learned from the introduction, and Josh he had already heard about from Cait herself. So this was the boyfriend. The two men eyed each other up. Mike was busy admiring Daniel's car and Nina had gone to the kitchen to put the kettle on.

'No Cait?' Daniel asked.

Josh raised his eyebrows. Knowing he wasn't the only one who'd been left in the dark made him feel only marginally better. 'She didn't tell you either? Probably wanted to come back with a *fait accompli*. Apparently, she believes she knows who's writing the letters...'

'What?'

'My reaction exactly. She's gone off to check it out.'

'Christ! On her own?' Daniel looked set to turn straight round and go after her.

'No, no – not like that. Checking it out with an old friend who might know where he is.'

'But who, for Christ's sake? Who does she think is doing it?'

'Some guy named Nick. An ex-boyfriend.' Josh shook his head and shrugged.

'Nick! Jesus Christ – he nearly killed her!' The stricken look on Josh's face brought his outburst to a halt. 'Shit – you don't know about that? When she was in London?'

'She mentioned living with someone after she ran away from home. She never said anything about him trying to kill her.' His face was bleak as he stared at Daniel. *What else hasn't she told me?*

Mags was settled at the kitchen table when Mick stuck his head round the door.

'Hiya, Mags!'

'Hello, Mick.'

He drew up a stool and perched opposite her with a mug of tea. 'Still on for going south?'

'Oh yes. Please.'

He smiled, defusing the anxiety in her face. 'Wednesday evening, then.' He pulled a sheet of paper from his shirt pocket. He knew she could read, had watched her with the newspapers that were left lying around the place. 'I've made a list of places where I know you'll be able to stay warm and dry until you're better.' He slid it across the table to her, capturing her hand in his own. The smile was gone now. His face was serious. 'I'd be a whole lot happier if you'd stay off the road until a couple of weeks after New Year. Give yourself a chance to rest up properly.' He let her go. 'I'm sorry, Mags, I'm just a worrier, that's all. But you've been really ill, and if you don't listen to what your body's telling you, you'll just wind up having a relapse. And that could be serious.'

She nodded. 'I know. I'm listening, believe me.' She picked up the sheet and looked at it, holding it at various distances from her face until she was comfortable reading it. She hoped she wasn't expected to make an instant decision. She flushed slightly. What would he think of her ways of divining what was right?

'Take your time. We can always just stop on the way. Just think about it, eh?'

'I will. Thank you, Mick.'

'My pleasure.'

The letter-writer had bought a map from a little

old-fashioned newsagent and tobacconist shop. Northfield Terrace was easy enough to find; it was understanding the one-way system that had proved the problem. The shortest distance, the logical route, had been unavailable due to its vagaries, but eventually, there it was.

The car crawled along the narrow road clogged by motorists having parked on both sides. There was barely room for a single vehicle to pass between them. *Even that helps me. No one will look twice. Had the road been clear, I might have looked suspicious.* Slate eyes ran ahead, took in the well-kept frontages, the house numbers. *23 ... 25 ... 27 ... 29 ... 31. So that's the one. What's this?* The eyes narrowed. Deborah Harvey was getting out of a car. On the passenger side. The driver, a tall man of about forty, walked with her to the door of her home and followed her inside.

The letter-writer's vehicle came close, then abreast. That car had been seen before. An M3... Of course. Terry Richardson's house. Frown lines etched themselves between the eyebrows. Memory reran the image of the man being let into Terry's house, coming out again with, as it turned out, not Terry but the priest. The letter-writer no longer liked to think about the priest. Attention refocused on the car's driver. *It was dark back then, but today I got a good look at him. Would know him again. To look at, anyway.* The frown deepened. *First at Terry's. Now at Deborah's. On my territory, so to speak. Interested in the same people at the same time. Why? Who is this man?*

Caitlin's arrival at the cottage had everyone jumping to their feet. She looked tired but somehow 'firmed up'. That, at least, was the phrase that came into Nina's mind, though she wasn't sure, at this stage, quite what it meant. There was a strange silence as Caitlin was wrapped in her brother's arms. *She went to him first, not Josh*, Nina noted. Josh's face was impassive. Emerging from her brother's embrace, she walked to Josh, smiled and hugged him. Turning to Mike and Nina, her body language now including everyone, she shook her head sadly.

'I got it wrong, guys.'

Josh and Nina exchanged a look, said nothing.

'Why don't you tell us about it?' Mike was doing 'genial host' duty and steered her towards a chair. She chose, instead, to sit next to Daniel, who had made himself at home on the sofa.

'I could do with a drink first.' She sniffed appreciatively. 'Is that mulled wine I can smell?'

'Your wish is my command...'

Daniel put his arm around her and hugged her. 'The others said you had some idea that Nick was behind the letters.'

'Yes. Thanks, Mike.' Caitlin took the wine from him, curled her fingers round the glass and sniffed deeply. 'This smells wonderful.' She looked at everyone and smiled ruefully. 'Yes. But I was wrong. Nick's dead. Died a matter of weeks after my run-in with him. And as ghosts can't send letters – not that I know of, anyway – that's him out of the frame.'

'What happened to him?' Nina asked quietly. Caitlin lowered her eyes to her glass as she replied.

'He got drunk. Fell in the river and drowned.'

Nina said nothing. Maybe the truth. Certainly not all of it.

'Cait...' Daniel's arm had tightened around her shoulder. 'What made you think it was him? Writing the letters?'

'Oh, I don't know. I mean – why should he? After all this time? But, well, he knew about Mum. Knew about the business with Dad. Even went with me to the solicitor's when I was old enough to change my name, so he knew I was O'Connor. And what really clinched it – because those first letters, there was nothing to give anything away, was there? No clues to the writer's identity. But this one – it was the "hellcat" business. It had been a sort of standing joke between us. That and the business about running and hiding.'

'Can I see this letter?' Daniel asked.

She disengaged his arm, went to her bag and brought it to him. He read it, frowning. 'I don't like the sound of this at all. The others – alright, they were a nuisance. But this is ... almost threatening.'

'That's why I think it's high time you went to the police,' Nina put in firmly.

'Maybe. But I have plans you need to know about first. Things are on the move. In, the meantime...' He looked at his sister, squeezed her hand. 'I don't like the idea of you being at home by yourself. That really does bother me. I know Josh is going home to visit family, so how about letting me move in with you? Till after Christmas, at least. If nothing's sorted by then, I think we may have to go to the police.'

Caitlin's face was alight. 'You'll come and stay? Brilliant!'

'God, that's just the way you said it when you were a kid!' His voice tailed off.

'What is it?' she asked.

Daniel thought, then shook his head. 'I don't know ... something was right on the edge of my memory then. Something about hellcats.' He turned and looked at her. 'Who called you that? Back at the Community?'

She looked at him blankly. 'No one. "Catterbrain, Scatterbrain", yes. But no one called me Cat or Hellcat. Definitely not.'

There was obviously no point in arguing with her. But Daniel was convinced she was wrong.

Later that evening, in the privacy of their room, Josh sat on the edge of the bed and asked quietly, 'Why didn't you tell me about Nick?'

'What? I just did.'

'About him trying to kill you. About the baby.'

Her face was tight as she turned to look at him. 'What business is that of yours? And who told you? They had no right!'

'Daniel told me. He was worried – thought you'd gone to confront him.'

'Bloody hell!' Caitlin threw her jacket onto the floor. 'What is this? Everyone thinking I'm stupid or something? As if I'd go after him by myself! Give me some credit!'

'We were worried, Cait. And I felt stupid. Not knowing.'

'Well poor bloody you! How long have we known each other? And you want my whole life

282

story? You want to know about all the other men I've slept with as well, or is it just Nick you're bothered about? I'm thirty-two years old, Josh. What do you expect – that I'm some bloody vestal virgin? Or am I just another case study? Is that what this is?'

'Cait, no! That's not what I meant. We need to talk rationally about this, that's all.'

'Oh, we do, do we? And since when do you make decisions on my behalf? I don't say anything about anything until I'm ready! Have I made myself quite clear?' She snatched up the jacket and put it back on. 'If you want to talk rationally, don't treat me like a child or a head-case! Bloody well talk rationally to yourself!'

She slammed the door so hard that the window rattled as she left the room.

Chapter Twenty-two

Sunday 19 December

Chris and Deborah pored over the plan of the Community spread across Deborah's kitchen table. She could hardly believe what he'd just told her.

'My God!' Deborah breathed. 'So Terry *was* there after lunch and before Laura was supposed to deliver her work and meet Caitlin. I can't believe Daniel didn't tell the police!'

'Come on, this is his dad we're talking about!

283

Daniel's seventeen, doesn't want more upset and buys the story that Terry couldn't be doing anything to Laura while he's screwing another woman.'

'But it makes it all the more likely that he did! Suppose Laura found them together? Can you imagine it... Big confrontation, tempers lost – I'd say he had even more reason, wouldn't you?' Deborah's voice shook with excitement.

'I'm not disagreeing with you.' Chris left the table to make more coffee. 'Don't forget, though, whoever Terry was screwing would have had a motive, too.'

'But you don't know where this took place – Terry's little session?'

'You'll have to ask Daniel. Take the plan with you tomorrow.'

Deborah nodded, giving it one last look before finally folding it away. 'This could get pretty ugly if Daniel is so determined to blow the whole thing open. Besides, what if Terry won't talk? He didn't back then. Why should he change his mind now?'

Chris stirred the mugs, not answering immediately. He hadn't told Deborah about the letters. Daniel wanted to do that himself. 'Daniel will be able to cast light on that when you see him. But I think there's a good chance Terry will talk now. Assuming for the moment that he *is* innocent, back then he was maybe trying to protect the woman he was with. After so many years, that may not be so important.'

'Any idea who she was?'

Chris shook his head as he handed her a mug.

'No. Neither does Daniel. But he's determined to get it out of his father.'

'Happy families, eh?' Deborah thought for a second. 'I'd say it's a pretty good bet she was someone from the Community, wouldn't you? A stranger up there would have stuck out like a sore thumb.'

'You have some ideas of your own on that score?'

'I don't know... A lot of people have left since. Some of them quite soon after Laura's disappearance, so there's always the possibility that Terry's lover was among them. But the ones still there...' She was thinking of Ronnie's frightened look when she'd asked her about Terry's womanising. 'Let's just say there's someone I can lean on a little harder. Might be worth doing, whether or not Terry agrees to cooperate.'

'Go for it!' Chris smiled.

'It's all so incestuous, somehow.' Frustration was evident in Deborah's voice. 'I mean, the stranger theory is out – sore thumb and all that – so it *had* to be someone there – an inside job. But how the hell do we find out?'

Chris sat tapping his pen on his mug. 'It's the most likely, yes. Logic dictates that. But there is one other possibility.'

'Like what?'

'Visitors. Not the ones who just potter up there to buy stuff, although I still think there's an outside chance...'

'What – Laura catches someone pinching windfalls and he does her in?' Deborah laughed.

'Stranger things have happened.' He shook his

head. 'No, I was thinking ... say you live at the Community. Your sister and her kids want to come and stay. Or your parents. Or whoever.' He shrugged. 'Who keeps a record of that? *Is* a record kept of things like that?'

'Shit! I never thought to ask. It seems a bit far-fetched, though. What the hell would be the motive?'

'I'm not thinking of motive at present – I'm thinking of opportunity. You did a good job with those plans – who lived there then, who lives there now – but surely an equally important question is, who else was there? If anyone, of course. I could be completely off-beam here. It's just a thought.'

'No, you're right. And I don't know if they kept records, but I know a man who would...'

Colin Walters put down the phone but continued to stand with his back to Ronnie. She was hovering anxiously, had handed the call to him, so she knew who it was. She'd been in the middle of preparing Sunday lunch and still had a vegetable knife in her hand.

'Colin, for God's sake! What did she want?'

'The books.'

'What?'

Colin turned to face her. 'Wanted to know if we kept visitors' books and did we ever keep a record of people who stayed here as guests of members and their families...'

'Oh my God.' She clutched the knife convulsively. Blood began to drip onto the floor.

'Love, you've cut yourself. Come on...' He put

his arm around her, led her through into the kitchen and put her hand under the cold tap. She was crying, whether from the pain of the wound or because of Deborah's query, he wasn't sure.

'It'll be alright, lover – you heard what I told her. We didn't keep guest records then, and the visitor books are ditched after seven years – lack of space.'

'But she *knows!*' Ronnie wailed. 'She must do! Why else would she ask about the guest books?'

'Ronnie, get a grip of yourself. She doesn't know. She can't know. And we're not going to tell her, right?' He examined her hand, pulled a clean tea-towel from the drawer and applied pressure. 'We'll give this a few minutes, OK? If it doesn't stop bleeding, you'll have to see a doctor. That's a nasty cut. It might need stitches.' He sat her down. 'Just keep pressure on it. I'll make us a cup of tea.'

'I'd sooner have a brandy.'

She never drank in the day. Just wine with Sunday lunch. Not spirits.

'No, love. Alcohol will make it worse. Maybe later, eh?' What was he going to do? His wife was cracking up and it was all his fault.

'What did you mean about later? On the phone – you said you'd see her later? That woman.' Ronnie couldn't bring herself to say Deborah's name. She was no longer a person. She was quite simply a threat.

'She's coming up to bring the photos back. I told her I'd check to see if we did have any records from the time Laura disappeared. Just to keep her quiet. But like I said, I'd already told her

287

I was sure we hadn't.'

'Where are they, Colin? Where are the books?'

He didn't answer straightaway. His mind was on other things. Finally, he told her. 'In a trunk under the stage. But not for long...'

Sunday morning had started awkwardly at the Oxfordshire cottage. Josh and Caitlin had gone outside early on to try to hammer out their disagreement of the night before, and Daniel was cursing himself for being the source of dissension. Mike and Nina were keeping their own counsel, and Mike had volunteered himself for breakfast duty, saying he had already part-prepared his 'cobbled-together Cajun special'. No more details had been forthcoming, but Nina had laughed, saying it was a knockout dish and they would love it.

Josh and Caitlin eventually came back, apparently reconciled, and Daniel took his sister aside to apologise for his part in the proceedings.

'I would never have let the cat out of the bag except for worry, Cait. I'm sorry – it was out of order.' He shook his head. 'Shit, the last thing I wanted to do was come back into your life and stir up more bloody trouble. Especially between you and your man.'

She ran her hands through her hair. 'It's getting to all of us, isn't it? It's not your fault, Daniel. It's not anybody's fault. We're all strung up. I overreacted. What the hell. What's done is done. Let's just try and get on, shall we? Sort this bloody business out.'

They hugged in silence, and Mike, disgustingly

cheerful by anyone's standards, had thrown them all out for a morning walk while he got on in the kitchen. The morning was cold but bright, and they followed the sign-posted way through fields sparkling with frost. Daniel had taken Nina's arm and walked on ahead with her, leaving Caitlin and Josh to follow. With suitable distance between the two pairs, Daniel asked, 'Can you recommend a hotel in Cheltenham? It's for my father – I'm bringing him down on Tuesday but I want him away from Cait.'

'Is that wise?' Nina asked.

'Very. Trust me on this. She's going to like him even less when she hears what I have to tell her later.'

'Mike and I could always put him up for a few days.'

'No.' Daniel was emphatic. 'Thank you, but no. I just want to get him down, get the letters off him – and the information I'm after – and send him home.' He glanced sideways at her. 'I know it sounds harsh, but – really – you don't want to know.'

'Alright.' Nina walked a few more paces before coming up with a suggested place for Terry to stay. 'It's on the other side of town to where Caitlin lives.'

'Which is another point.' He smiled. 'I'm sorry, I'm not making a lot of sense, am I?'

'I'm sure you'll get there in the end.' Nina sensed energy flying off Daniel at a rate of knots. No wonder his thoughts were scattered.

'I'm worried about that latest letter, obviously. Which is why I'm going to stay with her.

Apparently she walks to work?'

Nina nodded. 'It's about a fifteen-minute walk, yes.'

'I thought I'd do it with her. Make sure she gets to work safely. And if you could walk her home...'

'I'd have to drop her off in the car. I live further away. Walking is not an option for me.'

'OK. So I walk her there, you bring her home.'

'I don't think she's going to like it.' Nina's voice was mild, but she could sense trouble brewing.

'I know. But I'm not giving her a choice. There's another favour I need, too.'

'Which is what?'

'I'm supposed to do my spiel after breakfast, right? Which I will. One of the things is, I've arranged to meet a reporter tomorrow to talk about the day our mother disappeared.'

'Good Lord! You can't be serious?' Nina stopped and looked at him.

'It's not as bad as it sounds. Trust me. Christ, I sound like Indiana Jones on a bad day! Just listen when I tell Cait about it, OK? The thing is, I want to take her with me. I've already made the arrangements, but that was before I knew about this latest letter. I'd be a lot happier if I could keep an eye on her.'

Nina puffed out breath, which hung white in the morning air. 'I can't promise, Daniel. Not until I've heard. I'm really not sure that reporters are what you need. In fact, I'd say they were the last thing. I'd be a whole lot happier if you'd just go to the police. I've made that clear to Caitlin from the start.'

'Nina, I promise you – if our father can't shed

light on this, then I *am* going to the police, and stuff the consequences for him. I'd never forgive myself if anything happened to Cait. He should have thought about the consequences before he ever unzipped his bloody fly.'

'What?'

'You'll hear, after breakfast.' Daniel's face was grim. 'I'm just glad she has such a strong support system in you and Mike and Josh.' He turned and Nina followed his gaze. Josh and Caitlin were arm-in-arm, some distance down the sloping field. 'They seem to have sorted themselves out, anyway. Me and my fat mouth. He seems like a decent bloke. What do you think?'

'He is,' she answered simply.

Further down the field, Caitlin turned to Josh. 'I wonder what they're talking about?' She waved to Nina and her brother. 'How slow we are? Whether I'm about to scream at you? If we'll still be talking by the time we get back?'

'Does it matter? And besides, we're not slow – just taking our time. Why rush on a lovely morning like this?'

'Maybe because breakfast will be ready before too long?'

'You could be right!' Josh quickened his pace, squeezing her arm with his own.

The letter-writer opened the car window and breathed deeply. This was a good place to park. *My memory served me well.* The country road twisted and turned here, and the parking area was at the foot of the hill that led up to the Darrowdale Community. Walkers parked here

291

often. Behind the flattened surface was a fence separating off thickly wooded hillside which soared steeply, all part of Hunters' Wood. It was not the wood that the letter-writer was thinking of. It was another spot.

If only I hadn't been there that day. Why couldn't I have arrived afterwards? Or seen nothing? Would it have changed things? Really? This line of thought was no good. *I was* there *and what happened, happened. The important thing now is to follow through, complete my plan.* But something else was important, too, something the letter-writer had not considered until very recently. It was important that the truth be known, that it be *told,* so that the reasons could be understood. Nothing less would do now. *Then ... then, I can slip away to my new life, where no one will know, where I shall live, knowing that I have been avenged. Nothing more to do but enjoy myself. The demons will finally be laid to rest. At last. At last...*

A voice whispered inside the letter-writer's skull. *'You thought that when you killed him. Your stepfather. It was supposed to end there. To make you feel better.'*

No! You can't frighten me now. I didn't understand then. Didn't see the intricacies of the web. That it was *a web. That* every *thread had to be broken. And there are only three more threads to break. Plus the one that will bind them all together in their doom...* It was a shame, of course – the letter-writer observed with some curiosity, a genuine sense of regret – but it had to be. *It is right and proper that my deeds should be recognised. Understood.*

The sound of an engine cut through the silent

air and the letter-writer glanced curiously towards the road. Eyes widened in surprise at the sight of an M3. *That car again...* The decision was made quickly. *Let's just see...* The letter-writer's car purred into action, slipping onto the road behind the other vehicle, following as it twisted and turned, surrounded by bare-branched trees.

As I thought... Slate eyes shone with satisfaction as the M3 turned into the entrance to the Community. *I shall drive on and turn round again at the next convenient place. There's a pub up here, I believe...* Sure enough, there was, and its gravelled car park enabled the manoeuvre to be made. The car was driven in leisurely fashion back to the Hunters' Wood parking area, where the engine was cut. Once again, all was still.

Well, well. Things are moving around here. I shall need to move soon. Make *my move. Not too early, or my plans could be jeopardised. But not too late, either, or there won't be time...* Neurones fired as calculations were estimated. *How much time will it take? How much time will* she *need? I must think about this carefully...*

After breakfast, Daniel finally explained what he knew about his father's actions on the day his mother had disappeared. The air was electric as he finished speaking.

'How *could* you! Daniel! How *could* you have kept that quiet?' Caitlin knocked over her chair as she sprang to her feet. 'Dear God! That's not an alibi, it's a motive! She could have found them! He could have killed her, for Christ's sake!'

'Cait, Cait... What can I say? I believed him.

293

Oddly enough, I think I still do. I was thinking of you at the time. Of what it would do if you found out.'

'How could he do that? The bastard!' She brought her fists down on the table, sending her plate crashing to the floor.

'Please – forgive me. I did what I thought was best at the time. All I can say to you now is, that when I've talked to him, we'll go to the police.'

'What do you mean, when you've talked to him?'

'I'm seeing him on Tuesday. He'll be bringing the letters he's had and I'm going to get more information out of him, even if I have to rattle his teeth to do it. We've got to get to the bottom of this.'

Caitlin paced the floor before righting the chair and sitting down next to Josh. 'If you have any more nasty surprises, I'd sooner you tell me now. Just get it over with, alright?'

'Alright.' Daniel had recomposed himself. He had been more shaken than expected by his sister's anger. He tried not to look at Nina. 'There's something I want you to do. The private investigator – Chris Farmer? Once I'd found you, I set him onto looking into what happened to Mum.' How far could he stretch the truth? 'He's working closely with someone who would very much like to talk to both of us.'

'And who is this someone?'

Shit! She was really defensive. This was the last thing he needed. He took a breath. 'Her name is Deborah Harvey. She's a reporter on the *Darrowdale Gazette*.'

'Are you mad?' Caitlin was on her feet again.

Daniel left his seat, caught her by the shoulders. 'Caitlin, listen to me!' His use of her full name was enough to make her pause. 'Run with me on this, alright? Uncle Derek – you remember Uncle Derek?' She nodded. He turned to the others. 'Not really our uncle – he was a friend of Mum's before she married Dad. A reporter. Went away and worked all over the place before coming back.' He looked at his sister. 'He's the editor of the paper now. Every year, on the anniversary of her disappearance, he's run a story. You know, "Someone knows what happened to this woman. Justice must be done." That kind of thing.' He had her full attention now, got into the flow. 'He's retiring, right? Wanted to have one last stab at solving it, and he put Deborah onto the story. Fresh perspective. She's doing a lot of digging. All she wants from us is a first person account of that day.' Caitlin opened her mouth to speak but Daniel cut her short. 'She'll do something from that angle with or without our co-operation. I figured it would be best to get her on our side. If something's going to be written, it might as well be the truth.'

Caitlin turned away. No one said a word. Daniel glanced at Nina, raised his eyebrows. She simply raised hers back. Damn the woman! Why wouldn't she help?

'I don't see what we can tell her that isn't already known.'

'Neither do I. But maybe – just maybe – if she gets the information from the horses' mouths it will make sense with something else, someone

295

else's account. As you said, no one knew about Dad back then. That sheds a different light on things, for a start.'

'You're going to tell her about that?'

'Yes. Then he has the option to tell it from his own point of view or leave her to make mincemeat of him.'

Mike and Josh moved uncomfortably in their seats. 'I don't know about that...' Mike began.

'I think it's a good idea.' It was Nina who broke in. 'As Daniel says, better your own version than some distortion. My only stipulation would be that you have to be prepared to see this thing through to the bitter end. Which may – or may not – result in your father being charged with your mother's murder.'

Daniel and Caitlin stood facing one another. Neither of them spoke. The others held their breath as the seconds ticked away. When Caitlin made her decision, she never said a word. Just nodded.

Chapter Twenty-three

Was it Deborah's imagination or did Colin look at her and Chris as if they were as welcome as Death? She glanced at Chris. They had already talked about how they were going to handle this. They followed Colin into the living room, where Ronnie was looking decidedly peaky.

'Sorry, we've had a bit of a day of it – Ronnie

had a nasty accident with a kitchen knife.'

'Oh, I'm sorry.' Deborah turned to Chris. 'Let me introduce you. Chris, this is Colin and Ronnie Walters; Colin and Ronnie, this is Chris Farmer, the private investigator hired by Daniel.'

The silence was electric and just slightly too long. Colin laughed uncomfortably as he shook Chris's hand. 'Good Lord! I thought Daniel'd already found Caitlin!'

'He has. And his father, come to that. No, I'm going back to basics – looking into Laura's disappearance.' Chris smiled broadly, completely at ease.

'Oh dear. He has got the bit between his teeth.'

'You don't approve?'

'No, no – it's not that. It's just – well, without being rude, what can you do that the police couldn't, nineteen years ago?'

'You might be surprised. We have some very promising leads.'

'Which reminds me,' Deborah put in. 'Did you have a look for those records, Colin?'

'I did, yes, but as I told you, we really have nothing going back that far. We didn't keep guest books back then – this is what we do now.' He showed them the latest one apologetically. 'I'm afraid we weren't so Health and Safety conscious in the old days. Or security conscious, I suppose. Laura's ... the business with Laura changed all that.'

'So you brought in guest books and other procedures after she disappeared?' Chris handed the book back to him.

'Yes. Yes, that's right.'

'Shame. Still – you were here at the time? Can you think of any particular guests who were staying then? Or maybe which families had guests?' Chris laid heavy emphasis on the word.

Colin and Ronnie glanced at each other. 'Well, no, not off the top of our heads. We'd have to think about that, wouldn't we, love? Being the school holidays and all that, it was more a case of who *wasn't* here, really. That's what sticks more in my mind. What about you, Ronnie?'

'Yes. I agree. We'd need to sit down and think, after so long.'

'OK. You do that.' Deborah turned to Chris. 'In the meantime, I can ask Daniel for his recollections tomorrow.'

'He agreed ... to meet with you?'

'Yes. Isn't it great?' Deborah smiled at Colin. 'I can't thank you enough for brokering that for me.' She turned to Chris once more. 'I told you, didn't I, that Colin and Ronnie approached Daniel on my behalf? I thought it would work better than a direct approach from me, and sure enough, it did.' The enthusiasm in her voice was quite genuine. 'Anyway,' she flashed a smile at the others, 'it'll give me plenty to sift through when I go home for Christmas.'

'Right. Right, yes. So you're getting Christmas off, eh? Derek not working you to the bone?'

'Thank goodness, no. With any luck, I'll be back from the meeting with Daniel tomorrow evening. Maybe Tuesday. You know Derek – said to stay longer if I need to. But I'd like to be back by Tuesday afternoon because I can go to Mum and Dad's on Tuesday night. That way, I get a

298

decent break for Christmas – I have to be back before New Year. Duty calls and all that.'

'Right. Well, have a good time.'

'Oh, I shall.' She stood up. 'Mustn't forget to give you these, of course! Whole point of coming!' She opened her briefcase, balancing it against her knee and swore as its contents cascaded onto the floor. Colin jumped forward to help pick things up.

'Your photographs–' Deborah began. The expressions on Colin and Ronnie's faces cut her off. *What the hell?*

'Excuse me...' Ronnie ran from the room. Colin watched her go, then held out Deborah's things, fingers lingering on the portfolio in his right hand.

'Like I said, she's been a bit peaky since the accident this morning. Never could cope with blood. This – this gave me a bit of a turn as well, actually. Looks just like the smaller portfolios Laura used.'

'It was hers, yes. I was going to–'

'I didn't know you had that,' Chris cut in. 'Mind if I take a look?'

'Sure. Why not?' Deborah's heart was racing. He was lying. They'd leafed through it not more than an hour ago. She took it from Colin, opened it up, laid the artwork on the sofa. The three of them stood looking at it, silently. Deborah was suddenly aware of Ronnie behind her.

'Look at this, lover!' Colin's voice was strained. 'Long time since we've seen any of Laura's sketches, eh?' He put his arm around his wife.

'Good God! Where did these come from?'

299

Ronnie was as white as a sheet.

'All part of the investigation,' Deborah said, neatly sidestepping the question.

'Yes. Yes. Long time since we've seen these, eh?'

'You've seen these before? These specific drawings?'

'Well, I couldn't swear to that, of course, but Laura often used to show us her work. She had loads of these portfolio cases, you know. Bigger ones, as well.'

'Right.' Deborah turned on a sympathetic smile. 'I do apologise. Being an outsider – new to all this – I tend to forget that it must be stirring up painful memories for you.' She gathered the sheets together, slipped them back into the portfolio and zipped it up. 'Well, we'll leave you to it. Thanks for your help. And I hope you're feeling better soon, Ronnie.'

Ronnie just nodded mutely as Colin led their visitors to the door.

'Bloody hell!' As Chris pulled away and headed down the track to the main road, Deborah fought the impulse to look back at the Walters' house. 'What the hell was all that about?'

'God knows. But we'd better find out.' He was at the junction now, cancelled his left indicator, which would have taken them back to Darrow-dale, and indicated right instead. 'Let's pull off the road a.s.a.p. and take a look through that portfolio again.'

'There's a pub about half a mile down the road – why don't we go there?'

Moments later they were seated in a wooden

cubicle, well away from any prying eyes, with the sketches laid out on the table between them. They looked at the artwork in silence. What was it that had caused such violent reaction from the Walters?

'Well, search me, but I don't see anything of any relevance, do you?'

Chris shook his head. 'All looks straightforward enough.' He split the work into three separate piles. 'Abstract stuff. You said she did this kind of thing on slate?' Deborah nodded. 'And what would you call this everyday stuff? Observational stuff?'

'Something like that.' The work in question was pictorial. Landscapes, mostly of the Community.

Chris's hand moved to the third pile. 'And portraits.' This last pile was the smallest, no more than half-a-dozen sketches .

'Maybe we should have asked them about these,' Deborah said, looking at the pictures more closely. 'Some are obvious – to me, I mean – because of all the photographs I've seen lately.' She stretched out her hand. 'These are Caitlin and Daniel – she was really good. That's Terry, I think, and the others are probably other people who lived in the Community.' They both stared at the unknowns – a woman with pigs, a woman in a window and a woman with three small children hanging on her skirt.

'Why don't you ask your editor? He might know.'

'Yes. Yes, I'll do that when I drop them off.' That was the only reason Deborah had had the portfolio with her on the trip to Colin and Ronnie's – she was going to drop them back to Derek this afternoon before preparing for tomorrow's meeting with Daniel Richardson.

'Are we missing something obvious?' Chris rubbed his chin.

They sat in silence, shuffling the sheets one more time.

'Beats me. The only odd one out, so to speak, is this.' Deborah tapped the sketch of the woman at a window.

'How's that?'

'The date. Look – all the others are June or July. This one is early April.'

They looked at each other, baffled. Chris shrugged. 'Maybe it got mixed up. Or maybe she was going to do something else with it – I don't know – a painting, perhaps. Did she paint?'

'I'll ask Derek.' The sheets were gathered together again, put away. 'Maybe they really were just upset at seeing something so personal to Laura after so long.'

Chris snorted. 'You really believe that? Ronnie looked like she was going to throw up and Colin didn't do much better.'

Deborah smiled. 'Well, no, I don't really believe it. But I don't understand their reaction any more now than I did when we were with them. They're just pictures. What the hell is so significant about them?'

Nina walked into the kitchen of the Oxford cottage carrying a clipboard and pen.

'Caitlin – do you fancy a break from all this heavy stuff?'

'Do I ever! What have you got in mind?'

'Well, as you know, I wasn't able to organise a Christmas bash for my Yoga students – so many of them going away – so I said we'd do something in January instead. I was thinking about it last night and thought, why don't I invite your students as well? Give them a "taster" evening, maybe a cut-price introductory offer for the first term if they want to give Yoga a go as well as the T'ai Chi. Would you mind?'

'Not at all. I could do something reciprocal for your class – we should have thought of it before. What do you need?'

'Names and addresses for the invitation cards.' Nina placed the clipboard in front of Caitlin. The top sheet showed the date of the planned social evening with her own students' names and addresses listed below.

'Sure. Not that I have their addresses on me, of course. In fact, you won't need them, really, will you? If you give the invitations to me, I'll hand them out at my next class.' She started to write.

Nina bit back her disappointment. Names might be enough, if she could tune in properly. They'd *have* to be.

Caitlin finished her list and looked up. 'What a shame that didn't take longer. I've got the *really* heavy stuff next – Daniel and I are going to compare notes on what we remember of the day Mum disappeared.' She handed back the clipboard and smiled. 'At least this was nothing to do with the wretched letter business. I'm getting thoroughly sick of the whole thing.'

The letter-writer allowed some distance to elapse before pulling out of the parking area and following the M3 down the hill as it headed back towards town. Who had they been talking to? And who *was* this man with Deborah Harvey? Terry, Deborah, now the Community ... *I mustn't let it get in the way of my plans. But how best to...? If he's with her, it could get complicated...*

If they were going back to Deborah's flat, they would go straight on at the first set of traffic lights. *Better I should turn off there. Right or left, it doesn't matter. Just so long as they don't know they're being followed. Can't have them* too *alert, now, can we? Forewarned is forearmed, and I'm the only one allowed to have that privilege.*

Chapter Twenty-four

Daniel and Caitlin had completed their notes and recollections of the day their mother had disappeared and were drinking coffee with the others. It had been singularly disappointing as far as Caitlin was concerned.

'So we're back to square one, basically,' she reported. 'Neither of us saw or heard anything remotely pertinent – except Daniel's observation of Dad with whoever she was.' Caitlin flushed slightly. 'And that just makes it more likely that he did something ... awful. Which is precisely what the police thought in the first place.' She pushed herself out of the armchair. 'God, this is depressing. I thought everything about that day was etched on my memory forever. How come there are so many gaps? So many ... I don't know – vague bits? I feel like my head has been wrapped in cotton wool!'

Josh stood and put his arm around her. 'It's not as bad as you think. And quite understandable. It was a huge trauma. The mind has to protect itself. It's a self-defence mechanism – thank God it works.'

'Yes, but not if it stops us getting clues as to what happened to Mum! Is there nothing we can do?'

Josh looked at Daniel before answering her question. 'Cait, in all probability, there was nothing of any significance anyway. It's a long time ago. You were thirteen years old.'

'But ...?' Daniel prompted softly.

'But ... well, gentle hypnosis may – and I stress the may – be able to help. By putting you into a deeply relaxed state, taking you back to that time, it could, just possibly, unlock some hidden detail.'

Daniel and Caitlin exchanged the briefest of glances.

'Let's do it.'

'Are you sure?' Mike asked.

Before either of them could reply, Josh spoke again. 'Technically speaking, I shouldn't be the one to do it, being in a relationship with Caitlin...'

'But you will, because she trusts you and we're here to witness it.' Daniel was talking to Josh, but both men were looking at Caitlin. She shrugged.

'It's fine by me. What do we need?'

305

Moments later, everything was ready. Caitlin sat back in the comfy old armchair by the fireplace, Mike's Dictaphone strategically placed to record whatever she might say, and Josh's voice smoothly and steadily guiding her into a state of relaxation.

'That's right, Cait. You're walking in your favourite place, a light breeze ruffling your hair. Look around you. Take in the beauty of it. Hear the sounds. Are there birds singing? Water? You feel totally relaxed and at peace.'

Her breathing became deeper, steadier, as Josh directed her to a beautiful building with a magnificent staircase. 'You're walking down the stairs, Cait, perfectly at ease, perfectly relaxed. Down you go, back in time...' Further and further back he took her. The stillness in the room became tangible as everyone seemed to be holding their breath as he finally brought her to a date in July almost twenty years ago. 'It's a great day, Caitlin. It's the summer holidays so you can do whatever you like. And your Dad has his big meeting today. If he can pull this off, it will make a big difference to the Community. You're at home, in bed, early in the morning. Can you remember it, Cait? What did you think, when you woke up...?

Yes! Caitlin Richardson beamed as she pulled aside the bedroom curtains and saw the glorious day that greeted her eyes. The sky was a blaze of blue, untouched by cloud, the early morning sun already enlivening the extravagant riot of colour in the garden. Perfect! What perfect weather for the school holidays! She turned and raced out of her room and along the corridor, only to be beaten to the bathroom door by her brother.

'Daniel!'

Four years older than her, at seventeen, Daniel had no time for younger girls, especially not his sister. He pulled a face and stuck out his tongue before locking himself inside, determined to take his time just to annoy the runt.

'Mum! Daniel's being rude! He won't let me in and I need the toilet and he stuck his tongue out!'

'Don't be such a baby, Caitlin! Go and get breakfast. Now!'

Laura's voice may have been soft, but both children knew better than to argue with their mother's 'Now!' She rapped on the bathroom door.

'Daniel – don't take long! I'm timing you…'

Half an hour later, Caitlin was outside in shorts and teeshirt, beyond the garden and into the grounds of the Community in which she lived. The day was going to be a scorcher! Maybe she would go swimming later. Mum might take her after she'd delivered her new batch of work to the Craft Shop. She could meet her there when she dropped it off. She'd ask at lunchtime.

'Good morning, Caitlin! Isn't it a beauty of a day?'

Caitlin smiled at the familiar figure of Rosie Dwyer. Rosie's face was round, like an apple, her skin tanned like old leather from constant exposure to the elements, and her black hair was pulled back from her face in a long, thick plait. She always wore a hat. Straw in summer, felt in winter. How Caitlin loved that plait! She'd told her mother countless times that she wanted to grow her hair like Rosie's, but the reply was always the same, 'Your hair's too fine, Caitlin. It's

307

better off short.'

Rosie looked after the chickens and pigs and was one of the few members of the Community who wasn't married. That was why she lived in a room in the old farmhouse rather than one of the log cabins of various sizes which accommodated couples and children. The old farmhouse, built of brick, had been the only building on site when the Community had bought the land, fifteen years ago. Well, that and the barns and the out-buildings. It seemed a wonderful thing to Caitlin that her parents, with the help of other members of the Community, had built their own home. She had been born there, actually born in her parent's bedroom. It had been a bad winter, roads made impassable by snow, and she had arrived two weeks early, upsetting plans for a hospital delivery. The nearest hospital was twenty-five miles away.

'Might as well have been a thousand, Katie!' her father had said, telling her of the rush to boil water, the call to older women to come and help. There hadn't been a doctor in the Community, then, not like now, with Dr Latimer and his wife. They lived in the old farmhouse, too, even though they were married, but that was because the surgery was there and there were rooms for when his special patients came to stay. They were mostly girls or young women, though sometimes there were older women, too. There had been a Community meeting about it. There had to be meetings to make sure all sides of an argument were heard and to make sure everyone was happy about things. Everyone had been happy about having a doctor and the children had all been briefed on the importance of being kind to Dr Latimer's patients, if they saw them. They needed rest and fresh air and good food. Not

308

questions. *People's health was a private matter. Dr Latimer's patients were to be considered guests of the Community and accorded the privacy and respect given to any member.*

'So what are you going to do with yourself today?' *Rosie's voice broke into Caitlin's wandering thoughts.*

'Oh, you know...' *Caitlin flashed her a smile.* 'Reading. Playing. I'm meeting Glenda and Toni later.'

'Sorting out the new play, eh? Well, that should keep you busy, then!' *Rosie laughed.*

'Not all day,' *Caitlin said solemnly.* 'I might go swimming later, if Mum will take me.' *The town of Darrowdale had a small and ancient indoor swimming pool which everyone referred to as 'the baths', though Caitlin had never understood why.*

'What about your dad? Couldn't he take you? Your mum's delivering work today, so she'll be busy.' *Everyone knew everyone's business in the Community.*

'Not afterwards. And Dad's got a meeting today, so he doesn't know what time he'll be back.' *Caitlin's father was an architect and she'd heard her parents talking about how important this meeting was.* 'I'd better go — there's Sandy. We need her for the play!' *Caitlin waved at her friend and ran down the track, throwing an apologetic look over her shoulder at Rosie.*

Josh's voice came subtly into Caitlin's awareness, leading her gently on towards lunchtime...

Caitlin burst through the door. Hot and sweaty, she made straight for the kitchen sink and gulped down two glasses of water before making herself some squash.

'Good Lord, girl, what have you been up to?'

'Rehearsing. It's hot out there, but it fits what we're doing. Oh, Mum,' she slapped her big notebook down on the kitchen table and flopped onto a seat, 'couldn't we go swimming this afternoon? Please?'

Mum ruffled her hair. 'Why don't you go and get in the shower before we have lunch?'

'But that's not—'

'And yes,' Mum smiled. 'We will go swimming. How about after I drop the work at the Craft Shop this afternoon?'

'Oh, Mum – brilliant!' Caitlin jumped up to hug her.

'Caitlin, will you please go and get yourself in that shower – Now!'

At three o'clock sharp, Caitlin was setting out along a different track. This one led to the main road – what was it Dad called it? The A-something-or-other. Anyway, the public entrance to the Community was there, leading to the Tea Room, Craft Shop and Pottery. Mum had liked the idea of a swim and would meet her there with the car. Normally, if she was going that far, she would have come on her bike, but Mum didn't want it in the boot. Caitlin didn't mind walking. In fact, she loved it. Loved the way the sun felt on her skin, the periodic caress of the warm, scented breeze on her arms and legs and face. She had gone to Tildy Wilkerson's after lunch, to spend time listening to music. Tildy had all the latest hits. Even more than Daniel, but Daniel never let her play his albums. Said she'd damage them, as if she were a baby or something. Brothers! Still, at least she only had one. Sarah Highsmith had four. What a nightmare!

Caitlin pushed all thought of brothers aside. She was happy and determined to stay that way. The play *was coming on brilliantly, working out really well. Angela would be pleased...*

Caitlin's thirteen year old voice filled the room of the Oxford cottage as she relived her day. She was chanting to herself, now.

'*Sun blaze, sun haze, summer sun for summer days. Sun blaze, sun haze, summer sun for summer days.*'

'What are you doing, Cait? I can't see, remember. I need you to be my eyes and ears.'

Her breathing had a different rhythm, now, matching the chant, matching strange half-movements of her arms and legs.

'I'm walking down the track to the Craft Shop. The track between the dry-stone walls.' She chanted again before saying, 'Running up and down the banks. *Sun blaze, sun haze, summer sun for –* shit!' She caught her breath. Everyone's eyes were on her.

'What is it, Cait?'

'Bloody animals! Made me jump, that did!'

'What did? What made you jump?'

'I told you. Animals. Behind the wall.'

'What sort of animals?'

'I don't know. I didn't see. Just heard it.'

'It or them?'

'I don't know!' Her voice was impatient. 'I didn't look, did I?'

'What did it sound like? The noise you heard?'

She shrugged. 'Animals. I told you. Scrabbling. Clawing. Animal noises. Happens all the time. Just made me jump, that's all.' She started chanting again, back on course for her visit to the Craft Shop.

It was lovely and cool inside. The shop was

311

connected to the Tea Room and Mrs Walters was in charge of both.

'Hello, Caitlin.'

'Hello, Mrs Walters.'

'Where's your Mum? Unloading the car?'

Caitlin realised she hadn't seen the car.

'Oh, I thought she'd be here. She said to meet her. We're going swimming after she's delivered her work to you.'

'And you walked down the track? Never mind. Perhaps she's running a little late, today.'

'Or I could be early.' Caitlin suggested, looking at her watch. No, she was on time.

'Would you like some squash, Caitlin? On the house? You're looking rather hot.'

'Yes, please. I am.'

'Nothing but dry-stone walls, the way you came. No wonder!'

Veronica Walters shepherded the girl into the Tea Room before phoning her mum. There was no reply. She must be on her way.

Ten minutes later, she still hadn't arrived. Ten minutes after that, Caitlin decided to leave. She'd walk back the way she came. That way, she wouldn't miss Mum. It wasn't like Mum to be late for anything, and especially not this late. But still, Mrs Walters had said not to worry. She'd probably just got caught up in something. A phone call, maybe. Or Dad coming back from his meeting with good news.

A flicker of apprehension crossed Caitlin's mind at the thought of what other kind of phone call could make Mum so late. What if Gran were ill? She lived in Lower Dell. Only eight miles away. Mum might have rushed off to see her. No. She tossed the thought

312

aside. Gran was really fit and healthy for an old person. And, she told herself triumphantly, Mum would have phoned Mrs Walters to let her know, so she could tell me. Mum wouldn't just go off somewhere, knowing I was waiting for her.

She quickened her step, brightening at the thought of good news from Dad's meeting. She knew it was an important contract he was – what was that word he used? Negotiations. Yes, it was an important contract he was negotiating. She skipped up and down the bank by the drystone wall. It would bring a lot of money into the Community if he got it. There would even be a meeting about building their very own Community swimming pool. Yes! We could swim any time we liked. The adults would take turns life-guarding. No more having to get the bus or finding an adult to drive the twenty-five miles to Darrowdale. Great!

She smiled at a sight still some distance away, where the trees began. Adults! They were so weird. *Acting like kids didn't know about sex. As if to prove her point, the figures disappeared. She pulled the closest expression she could get to a leer – Daniel was quite good at that, she'd noticed – and moved to the opposite side of the track.*

Daniel had signalled to Josh. Josh's nod was almost imperceptible as he asked, 'Who are the adults, Cait? Who can you see?'

'I don't know. Just adults.' She shrugged. Started chanting again.

'Strangers? Or people from the Community?'

She frowned. 'I don't know. I didn't see them properly. Just registered that they were there, before they sank to the ground.'

'Sank to the ground? That's poetic, Cait.'

313

She shrugged again. 'They swayed together and sank down. Lovers. Doing it.'

'Did you see them doing it?'

'Of course not! I pretended I didn't see them and I cut across the field, just before I got to where they were. Tact and diplomacy.'

She'd heard her Gran say it to Mum once, along with something about how it was better than using a sledgehammer to crack a nut. They'd stopped talking when they'd seen her, but still, she thought, she'd got the gist of what Gran meant. I shall be diplomatic, then. And tactful. And I shall pretend I didn't see.

And so she'd gone home, but Mum wasn't there. Neither was the car. Caitlin checked to see if she had left a note, but she hadn't. Mothers! Why couldn't they be reliable, like they were supposed to be? She conveniently ignored the fact that her mother had been perfectly reliable until today.

Oh well. She fetched the big red notebook she was using for the play. Might as well get on with something. But she sulked for a while before settling down to write at the kitchen table. She really had *wanted to go swimming...*

Colin and Ronnie Walters had said little to each other since Chris and Deborah had left. Ronnie had been sick and gone to bed. Colin, left to his own devices, had found his heart hammering, crazy thoughts going through his head. On automatic pilot, he went into the kitchen to make yet more tea. He was awash with the stuff. He leaned against the sink. This was completely out of hand. He couldn't let it go on. He stood with his head bowed, thinking again of the conversation that

314

had taken place. So much emphasis on the guest books. How much did they know? How much?

He could have believed it was coincidence, just a routine question, had it not been for the portfolio. Maybe. Still uncomfortable, but no more than that. Just a matter of holding nerve, repeating the same old stuff. But the portfolio! That changed everything.

Sweet Jesus! Did she stage that for our benefit? Dropping the stuff? If she did, it bloody worked. That was it, then. If she had the portfolio it was only a matter of time before she put two and two together. What if she already had?

No. He shook his head. *She can't have done. Not yet. The police would be all over us. But how long? If she doesn't already know, she has to suspect, otherwise why the big show of it? Trying to break us down. Trying to. But she hasn't. Not yet. And I won't bloody let her.*

He drew a long, shuddering breath, let it out slowly through his nose. When had Deborah said she was going home? Tuesday?

He heard the lavatory flush, the familiar creak of the bedroom door. He made tea and took it through on a tray along with a plate of plain biscuits. Ronnie was looking dreadful. 'Here you go, love.'

She made an effort, sat up and took the cup from him. In a moment of panic, Colin realised how old she looked. She had never looked old. He never thought of her as old. Himself, neither. Right now, he felt as old as Methuselah. He cleared his throat.

'Ronnie, love, I've been thinking. Why don't

315

you go to Nicky and Don's for Christmas?' Nicky was their daughter. Living in the Scottish Highlands, they didn't get to see her as often as they would have liked.

'What? I couldn't possibly. I...' Her face contorted. 'She's got the portfolio, Colin. The picture ... that girl in the window ... the missing girl...'

'Ronnie.' He took her hand in his own, pressed it against his mouth. 'I've never bossed you about, have I? Wouldn't have dared!' He forced himself to smile. 'Just do me a favour, eh? Just this once. This bloody business, it's ... getting you down. You need a break, lover. And you'd be giving them the surprise of their lives – best Christmas present they could have. How many times have they asked, eh, and you wouldn't go without me? Well, now I think you should. You know you'll enjoy it. I can cope with everything here. Please? For me?'

Ronnie looked away. When she finally turned her head to meet his gaze, her eyes were brimming with tears as she agreed.

Chapter Twenty-five

Monday 20 December

Father Richard was disturbed by Terry Richardson's agitated state, but kept his feelings to himself. 'So you're leaving this evening?'

'Yes. Daniel phoned last night. He's sending

someone to pick me up – Chris Farmer, the private investigator. He'll take me home, and tomorrow we go on for this meeting.'

'How do you feel about that?'

Terry was silent, his jaw working while he thought about the question. 'I don't know. Scared, more than anything. All the dirty linen's out. What do you do when your own son despises you?'

'Has he said that?'

'Not in so many words. But I can hear it in his voice.'

'And your daughter? What about her?'

'What about her?' Terry shrugged. 'I've had no contact. Daniel won't even tell me where she lives. I don't know what to do, Father.'

'Recognising that the situation is largely out of your hands is a start. I know it's no comfort, but all you can do is play it by ear. I think the secret is in giving, not asking for anything, Terry. Co-operate all you can and see what develops. Above all' – the priest made sure Terry was looking at him before he continued – 'take it one day at a time, especially where the drink is concerned. You're vulnerable, but you know that. We have a place here for you when this is over. In the meantime, my thoughts and prayers are with you and your family. What time are you being picked up?'

'Straight after dinner.' Terry laughed, a hollow sound even in the small space of Father Richard's office. 'What is it they say? "The condemned man ate a hearty meal?"'

'Come, now. At least no one's sentenced you to death!'

317

'It feels like it. I know – "feelings can be changed". I'm doing my best, Father. I'm just not convinced it's good enough.'

'Let Our Lord be the judge of that.' Terry rose and the priest accompanied him to the door. 'Would you like me to come and see you off?'

'Why, yes.' Terry flushed awkwardly. 'I would very much appreciate that. Thank you.'

Deborah Harvey swore under her breath as she manoeuvred the hire car into the right lane for the motorway. *Bloody hell! I hope I get used to this thing smartish...* It was both longer and wider than her own sick vehicle which, please God, was even now being fixed after a series of frantic phone calls had tracked down a garage that could look at it before tomorrow. She didn't like to think about the bill. At least getting onto the motorway wasn't as bad as she'd anticipated. *Too bloody early for traffic, that's why! Only me and a few other idiots are up at this time of the morning.* She hadn't yet quite made up her mind about whether she was in a good mood or a bad one. Daniel's phone call, changing the venue for the meeting, had come as a shock. So much for meeting her halfway – Cheltenham was a lot further. *But,* she reminded herself, *I'm getting two for the price of one. No longer going to see just Daniel. I get to interview Daniel and Caitlin.* Good mood, therefore, she decided. And the excitement was growing with every passing mile. Maybe Derek was infectious, she mused, realising that 'this case', as she thought of it, had become personal. Just what you shouldn't do – get personally involved. When had that happened? How? She thought about the matter quite seriously. *It wasn't personal until I realised that Ronnie or Colin, or both – I'm convinced it's both – were lying.* Why that made things more personal, she didn't understand. Only that it did. *I don't like people lying to me, anyway, and somehow I now feel I owe it to Laura Richardson to find out the truth...*

Derek Kenny's secretary stuck her head round the office door. 'Boss, got a caller on line two been passed on from downstairs? Someone after Deborah about the Laura Richardson update? Thought you might like to take it?' Derek marvelled at the way she made every sentence into a question. He imagined the whole newspaper being written that way and shuddered. It didn't bear thinking about.

'All right – two seconds.' He spoke into the telephone handset. 'Gerry, let me call you back, will you? Something urgent's come up.' He waited for the call to be put through.

'Hello? Derek Kenny, Editor. I understand you wanted to speak to Deborah?'

'Yes, I'm sorry to trouble you. I was hoping to speak to her personally, but I understand she's away at the moment?'

'Can I help at all? If it's the Laura Richardson story–'

'It is. Which is why I wanted to speak to Deborah – woman to woman, you know?' The voice hesitated. 'It's ... well, shall we just say it's a little *personal?*'

Derek's eyebrows crept up. 'I quite understand.

319

I think it may be better if you try to contact her after Christmas. She may be back in the office tomorrow, but she's due to go to her parents tomorrow evening, so I can't guarantee you'd catch her. I could always ask her to call you, of course.' His hand was poised with a pen.

'Mmm. No. It's not that urgent, and I don't want to bother her if she's going away. After Christmas, you said?'

'She'll be back in the office...' Derek glanced at the wall planner, '...on the twenty-ninth. Can I tell her who called?'

There was a pause. Damn! It was going to be a bloody anonymous job, he could just feel it. He was right.

'No. I'd rather not leave my name. Not at this stage. I'll try her again after Christmas.'

The line went dead.

Mick was worried. He hadn't seen Mags all morning, and when he checked, her rucksack was nowhere to be seen. He stood in the doorway of the dormitory and cursed. Damn and blast! Only two days and he could have had her down south and with a roof over her head.

'Mick.' Mags's voice was slightly breathless. He whirled on his heel.

'Mags!' He smiled with relief. 'Bloody hell, woman, I thought you'd done a runner! You had me going there for a minute or three.'

'Runner?' Mags slid the rucksack from her shoulders and lowered herself onto the bed. She shook her head and closed her eyes briefly. 'I couldn't run to save my life just now. Went for a walk round the block and it nearly killed me.'

'What have we said about taking it easy? And you didn't have to take the rucksack – it must weigh a ton!'

'Feels like more. Dear God, this being sick has taken it out of me more than I thought.'

'Feeling rough?'

'No. No. I feel much better. That's why I tried the walk. Except it was trying to run before I could walk, if you see what I mean. Bless me, I feel like I've done a marathon.'

'Then put your feet up. Still on for Wednesday, then?'

'Thanks be, yes. If nothing else, my little wander has underlined the fact that I couldn't walk it in a million years.'

'Fancy a cuppa?'

'I can't put you to that trouble!'

'No trouble at all.'

By the time he came back, she was fast asleep.

Nina sat in the kitchen at the clinic, head in her hands. Thank God she wouldn't be working after today. The business around Caitlin had taken more out of her than she cared to admit. *And if I feel this bad, what must it be like for her?* She reached into her handbag and, once again, cast her eye over the list of Caitlin's students. She stared at it, willing the right name to jump out at her. It didn't. Nina shook her head. *It's one of these people, I know it is. But who?* Who?

Caitlin and Daniel were preparing themselves for the meeting with Deborah. If it was odd for

Daniel to be with his sister again after so many years, it was odder still, living in her house. It wasn't just that it *was* her house – it was the things in there, reminders of his past, of other people. Like his mother and grandmother. His mother's piano had hit him particularly hard.

'My God! I can't believe it!' Gran had taken it back when Terry and Caitlin had moved out of the Community. Just as well, or it would no doubt have been smashed during his father's rampage. He had sat down, started to play, soon getting into his stride. Caitlin came into the room when he was in full flow, belting out Boogie-Woogie so fast, his fingers seemed to fly over the keys.

'Now you're showing off!' Caitlin laughed, sliding onto the seat beside him and taking over the left hand. 'Too fast!'

'Come on, you wuss! Keep it up!' They fought it out for several minutes before collapsing into a heap, breathless with laughter.

'How many years is it since we did something like this? Don't answer that!' Daniel shook his head. 'Mum hated it if I played Boogie-Woogie, remember? Said it was a cacophony of screaming harpies. Christ, she even pulled the stool from under me that one time!'

'She'd be proud of you now, Daniel. She really would.'

'She'd be proud of both of us, Cait.' They looked at each other in sudden silence, as if the shadow of their mother had somehow passed between them. 'That's why we've got to do this – with Chris and Deborah. For her. It's the not knowing, isn't it? Somehow, we have to lay her to rest.'

'God! I'll be glad when it's all over. *Will* it ever be over?'

'If I have any say in it, it will.' He hugged her. 'Still, we have Christmas to look forward to. Christmas together. Christ, Cait, I can't tell you... And if Mike is as good with Christmas dinner as he was with the food at the weekend, we're in for a whale of a time!'

'Oh, he loves his cooking alright! I just wish Josh could be here.'

'Yes. But he won't be away too long, eh? Now – Christmas Day – do you want to go straight to Mike and Nina's from the Shelter? I could pick you up?'

'Are you kidding?' Caitlin looked at her brother askance. 'Daniel, I'll *stink* by then! I'll need to come home, have a shower. A long one. And you needn't pick me up – one of the volunteers will run me home.'

They had already had a disagreement earlier in the day when Daniel had insisted on driving her to the Shelter on Christmas Eve rather than letting her use her own car, 'just in case anyone tampers with it'. She saw the mulish look on his face again.

'Daniel, I'm no longer a teenager. You're my big brother and I love you, and God knows, I'm so glad we're together again, but come on – I'm a big girl now, remember? Trust me. One of the volunteers will drive me home. No one there is going to hurt me.'

Colin Walters didn't need anyone else to put a name to the way he was feeling. Paranoid. Short

323

and simple. Three times already he had made the trek to the Community entrance and back, searching for any sign of Deborah or – what was his name? – Farmer. Chris Farmer. He hadn't dared begin to destroy the old records yesterday, and today – today, he recognised that he was becoming paranoid. Today, Deborah was off to interview Daniel. At least, that's what she'd *said* she would be doing. What if it were a trick? What if they were watching his every move, waiting for him to make a mistake? Paranoid. This was ridiculous.

Wearily, he made his way back to the house. Ronnie was out. Gone shopping for extra presents and provisions for her trip to Scotland. A strange sensation passed through Colin's body and he sat down abruptly, afraid he was going to pass out. *Dear God! Please – not a heart attack. Don't let me have a heart attack!* He leaned forward, put his head between his knees, breathing deeply in an attempt to stem the rising flood of panic. *If I can breathe, I'm not having a heart attack. I haven't got chest pains. No pain in my arms. Christ, what is this?* The strange sensation hit him again. His whole body quivered. *A bow! That's what I feel like – a bloody bow, so strung up I can't control it.* Blood pounded in his ears. *Breathe! Breathe! Breathe!* Finally, after what seemed like an eternity, the sensation passed. *And I thought Ronnie was cracking up. But it's not just her, is it? It's me as well.* He had to risk it. He picked up the telephone and dialled Daniel Richardson's mobile number.

'Sorry, where were we?' Daniel put the mobile

away. 'I should have switched it off.'

'No problem.' Deborah was curious. She had heard only Daniel's side of the conversation, of course, but it seemed odd to her to say the least. 'Why did Colin want to know if I'd got here safely?'

Daniel shrugged. 'Something about you've had trouble with your car? So – where were we?'

'I was asking...' Deborah drew the plan of the Community towards herself, wondering what Colin Walters was up to. '...sorry, I know this must be embarrassing. Where was the place where you ... um ... observed your father with another woman?'

Daniel leaned across, pointing out an empty spot at the rear boundary of the area. 'It's no longer there, of course. All cleared, later that same year, I think. Some sort of deal with the monks who own the land behind... I'm not sure.'

'But that's where it was?'

'Definitely.'

She examined the plan again, measuring out distance with her fingers. 'That's quite some way from where you lived. Or from the Craft Shop, for that matter.'

'A hell of a distance. Further than it looks. Our mother would have had no reason to have gone there. It's the wrong direction altogether, when she had work to deliver.'

'But that's assuming she didn't know about Dad. What if she'd found out? Decided to confront them?' Caitlin's voice was quiet and well under control. Daniel squeezed her hand.

Deborah looked at the plan, pursing her lips.

325

'Could she have approached the place un-observed?'

'Absolutely. We certainly did. Every week. And we still come back to the problem that we don't yet know who this woman was. Or the others he screwed there.'

'If only you'd been able to see their faces.'

Daniel shook his head. 'The place was a wreck. There were only a couple of points where you could spy on anyone inside without being observed yourself, and what with the under-growth and all... The place was overrun with brambles for the most part. We could have seen, maybe, if they'd moved around more, but there was a corner which they seemed to prefer. They'd made a kind of nest for themselves, I suppose you'd call it, with straw on the ground and a blanket that was hidden away afterwards. When you're spying on someone having sex, you can hardly ask them to move so you can see who they are.' He looked, for the first time, embarrassed. 'It's a bloody disgusting thing to say, but if I'm honest, well – when you're seventeen and spying on someone having sex, it's not exactly their faces you're interested in.' He grimaced at his sister. 'Sorry.'

'So we won't know the identity of these women unless your father decides to tell us.' Deborah did not sound hopeful.

'He'll tell us.' Daniel's voice held certainty. He leaned back in his seat, appraising Deborah. She'd handled this – as far as he was concerned, at any rate – extremely well. Promised not to reveal Caitlin's address, been spot on in her attitude towards her. Caitlin hadn't been too happy about being interviewed at home, but, as Josh had pointed out, backing up Daniel's own argument, she would be more relaxed here. This was *her* turf and any disadvantage would be Deborah's. Also – and this had swayed the argument for Caitlin – she need take only minimal time away from work. Nina was going to run her back to the Clinic and Daniel would continue the interview alone, if necessary. As he'd told Cait, 'It's just a token appearance from you. Brief, on the record, and over with. You were thirteen. She won't expect much, and you're automatically a sympathetic figure for her anyway.' Yes. Deborah Harvey had handled things very well indeed. He smiled at her.

'I'm seeing him tomorrow morning – our father. How would you like to sit in?'

Deborah peered over her glasses, eyebrows shooting up to her hairline. 'Won't he object?'

'Who says he has a choice? We could work something out. You know, like a good cop/bad cop routine.'

'With me, the prying journalist, as the bad cop, no doubt!'

'You couldn't be more wrong. I'm the hardened son, loathe sharing the same air that he breathes. You're the young woman offering sympathy and a listening ear. Between us, we'll get him.'

This was too good an opportunity to miss. 'I wasn't expecting to stay overnight, but – yes, I'd love to be there.'

'Right. Cait ... where's a good hotel, close to here?'

327

'There's one just a couple of streets away. I'll give them a ring, shall I?'

'Thanks.' He watched as his sister left the room. 'You've been really good with Cait. I appreciate that.'

'It's a terrible thing to be dragging up. I just hope to God something good comes out of it.' She stood up, taking off her glasses and rubbing her eyes. 'Do you mind if I go into the garden to use my mobile? I need to call Derek and let him know what's happening.'

'Sure. Go ahead.'

When she came back into the room, Caitlin told her the accommodation was booked.

Terry Richardson had said little on the journey home, beyond admiring Chris's car, so Chris was more than a little surprised when, a few moments after going into the house, Terry turned to him and said, 'You don't like me, do you?'

'I'm not here to like or dislike you, Mr Richardson, and I certainly haven't enough information at this stage to form an opinion. I'm simply being paid to find out what happened to your wife.'

Terry stared at Chris. 'I saw you looking. Casting your eyes all over the place, sizing everything up. What did you expect? That I'd live in a hovel? An old lush with bottles littered everywhere and rotting food?' He was pulling papers out of a bureau. 'I had a problem with the drink yes, but I'm attending a Twelve-Step Programme and the Retreat. Father Mac got me sorted for them. Bloody shame. No justice, is there?'

Chris was not following his train of thought. *What is he babbling about? He thinks it unfair to be on a rehab programme? Why the hell is he doing it then?*

'Knocked me for six when they told me he was dead.'

'What?' Chris's brain came back on track.

'Not just dead. Murdered. Christ, the same night I got the message about Daniel. Not that I knew then.'

Warning bells were ringing in Chris's head. 'Let me get this straight. You're saying that Father Mac was murdered the same night I spoke to him here?'

'Yes. They write down the time and everything when they take a message for you at the Retreat House, so we know he was alive and well then. He phoned from here, of course. Apparently, he was found dead not more than a couple of hours later.'

'Murdered? You're sure?' It had to be coincidence. But Chris wasn't sure he believed in coincidence.

'What else would you call having your throat cut?' Terry shook his head. 'Which is a point. Before we head off – it would be on the way, in any case – I'd like to call in at the Presbytery and offer my condolences. If that's not too much trouble?'

Chris looked at him. 'No trouble at all.'

Chapter Twenty-six

Tuesday 21 December

The letter-writer had found a spot where traffic could be observed turning into Deborah's road from either direction. *There is no way I can miss her.* The merest hint of anxiety chewed inside. No – she could not have gone home to her parents yet. She would have to come here on her return from wherever she had been. *I shall not miss her. The light is shining on my plan.* Sudden confusion. *I do not want the light to shine on my plan. I work best under cover of darkness. Dark! Dark!* A cruel frisson of fear coursed through the letter-writer's body, causing a sudden inability to breathe. The body may have been that of an adult, but the memories and their accompanying emotions were those of a small child.

Why do I think of him now? At a time like this, why do I think of my father? It was not easy, killing him. Not like my stepfather. That was easy. But that was only a year ago. Not quite a year – 361 days, to be precise. My father was ... a long time ago. I was unpractised, then. Unskilled. Had only the botched attempt on my stepmother's life for experience. The Stepmother from Hell! Back where she belongs... I wonder if there is such a place? If so, the bitch deserves to be there. But ... probably it's just a lurid figment of the priests' sick imaginings. To keep the masses in line.

Medieval mumbo-jumbo...

Why wasn't killing my father easy? It was logical. The execution of it – of him *– was simple enough. It was two years after the death of his wife. He was depressed, everyone knew that. They were such a devoted couple, after all, and he'd nursed her for years after that terrible horseriding accident. Pitiful, really. So when he put the shotgun in his mouth – ha! That's what they think! When* I *put the shotgun in his mouth... So. When he died, people were sad, but not really surprised. I was surprised. Later. At the size of my inheritance... I've had such a good life on that money.*

So – what had been hard about it? Slate eyes flickered nervously at the remembrance. Maybe *... That was it. The look. The way he looked at me. I've never let anyone do that to me since. Why do they try? What do they think they'll gain? Pity? Compassion? Mercy? That I'll change my mind and let them go? Oh no. No. The power is mine.*

An image of Deborah Harvey slipped into mind. *And the glory shall be mine, too. Oh yes. I am good at killing now. I have honed my skills. I no longer have to pretend, hiding my light under a bushel. The light shall overcome the darkness! I am the light! The darkness shall not overwhelm me now. No one can ever lock me in a cupboard again...*

Ronnie was being awkward. Why was she being awkward at the last bloody minute? Colin tried desperately to keep any hint of panic out of his voice and off his face. She *had* to go.

'Of course you should go, love, and of course I'll be alright.' He squeezed her shoulder through

331

the open window of her car. 'You can't change your mind now. You're loaded up like Santa Claus Mark II and it's too late to send that stuff by post!'

She clutched at his hand. 'Colin – we have never had a Christmas apart in all the years we've been married.'

'Ronnie, please, I'm only thinking of you, love. It's for your own good. It's much too stressful here – you know that. You need a break. And you know you'll enjoy it once you get there.'

'But it's the busiest time of the year and – you didn't tell them I was going, did you? If I *am* going, you know I want it to be a surprise!'

'No, I didn't tell them, and as for being busy here, it's covered! In the nicest possible way, lover, you're not indispensable! It's time you put your own needs first.' He pulled his hand free and stepped back from the car so she couldn't reach him. He banged briskly on the bonnet and smiled. Reassuring. Encouraging. *Go, Ronnie, go! For Christ's sake go, before I lose my nerve...*

Reluctantly, Ronnie pulled away. He stood, the fixed smile hurting his face, waving until she was out of sight. Only then did he allow his shoulders to slump, the smile to vanish. *Dear God, I've got a headache!* He brought himself up. He shouldn't think of God. Not now. And certainly not after today. Not after he'd been to see Deborah Harvey...

It was early afternoon when Derek picked up the phone and found he had Deborah on the line.

'Hi, boss! Just to let you know that all is well.

Sorry I missed you yesterday.'

'Never mind, lass, I got your message. So how's it going?'

'All done and dusted. Daniel and Caitlin yesterday and – wait for this – the man himself, Terry Richardson today! Not a pleasant experience, I might add.'

'How do you mean?'

'I'll tell you all about it when I see you – I'm on my way back now.'

'Well done, lass! At this rate, you'll get to go to your folks tonight as planned! Which reminds me – though I don't know why – some woman phoned for you about the update and wants to talk to you. Personally. Ah – now I know what reminded me – I told her she'd be better trying to link up with you after Christmas. She reckons she's got two-pennyworth to chip in, but wants to talk to you, woman to woman. A mere man like myself is not good enough to receive her confidences. She must have been screwing Terry, I reckon.'

'Along with half the female population of Britain.' Deborah's voice was dry with distaste, but nonetheless, this could be exciting. Maybe Terry hadn't told them everything they'd needed, after all. This woman could be another piece of the jigsaw. 'Look, boss, I've got to go. I'm at a motorway service station and I need to get back on the road. Hopefully, I'll see you in a couple of hours.'

Nina had made the long, steep climb up the wooded hillside and paused at the top, breathing deeply after her exertions. She resisted the temptation to rest and divest herself of the backpack she was carrying, and stepped forward onto a narrow and ill-defined earthen path. No time to waste. Today was Winter Solstice and she needed to ensure that what she had come to do was completed before the light began to fade. She glanced down the steep slope, now sliding away to her left. It wouldn't do to have to make her descent in the dark. You could break a leg – snap your neck, come to that – if you weren't careful here, and as no one, not even Mike, knew where she was, she figured that would not be a good idea.

She strode briskly onwards, the path familiar beneath her feet, senses alert to everything around her. She took the higher path here, the lower one after the meadow. In spring and summer it would be awash with wild flowers, alive with colour. All that promise was hidden below ground now, waiting to be recalled in the spring. The left fork here, then, quite some distance further on, second right after the gnarled and ancient tree whose convoluted protuberances caused her to see, within its trunk and limbs, the head of a hare, the face of a gnome, a large penis.

The ground was heavy-going and difficult now, hardly ever trodden, so remote was this spot. And here, on the left, so deeply hidden you could walk past it if you didn't know it was there, was the entrance to the Stag Grove.

That was not its real name. Nina wasn't sure it actually had one. It was certainly not marked on any map she'd seen. It was *her* name for the place, given to her through a vision she'd had the first time she'd come here. She approached with care now, with reverence, making herself known to the spirits of the place. Beyond the entrance was a point that, for her, marked the boundary of the sacred space, and she paused there, waiting for permission to enter fully. It came, an unspoken knowing within, and she moved forward, heart and spirit lifted by the welcome she sensed.

It was a magical place, the Stag Grove, a large circular space out of which rose gentle banks, thickly wooded and completely enclosed. It was, Nina thought, as if the veil between the worlds was translucent here, shimmering, pregnant with power. She would have come today anyway, to mark the Solstice. Caitlin's situation had given her added reason, but yesterday... She closed her eyes, breathed deeply, then removed her backpack and laid out its contents on the ground. Sitting cross-legged, she invoked protection, marked out her own sacred circle before allowing thoughts of yesterday to enter her mind again.

She had gone to pick up Caitlin, to take her back to the Clinic, and had been introduced to Deborah Harvey. She had come across as bright, strong and full of energy. Then they had shaken hands. Nina's blood ran cold at the remembrance of the experience. Never had she felt such an overwhelming horror. It had hit her like iced water, flooding her senses. The woman was in urgent, mortal danger.

Nina offered up the memory, the experience, Deborah herself. Only after several more moments had passed was she ready to begin.

'It was, in all probability, a coincidence,' Chris Farmer concluded.

'Right. And that's your professional opinion, is it?' Daniel was shocked by the news of the priest's death.

'As a matter of fact, yes. I was seriously worried to begin with, but the police…'

'Don't know that you were there. Or why. That information might change their opinion.' Caitlin's house was a no smoking zone and Daniel was pacing the garden with his cigarette. 'You're not really telling me it was a random act of violence?'

'There is plenty of reason to believe it was. I had a good talk with the other priest at the Presbytery, Father Lawrence Howard. Father Mac was obviously on his way back after stopping off at your father's house, talking to me and phoning the Retreat with your message. I watched him walk away myself – we left the house together and chatted briefly in the street before I drove off. He'd taken a short cut down an alleyway.'

Chris paused, remembering how Terry had pointed out the place, how they'd walked along it together, both moved by the sight of bunches of flowers, laid in tribute, among the litter of its path. 'I can't say I would have liked to walk down there in the dark by myself, but then, I'm not a local. He obviously felt comfortable doing so. Anyway, that alleyway runs between two rows of terraced houses. There are brick walls either side, set with gates into their rear entrances. The theory – and it's entirely plausible – is that he disturbed a burglary. There's been a spate of B&E in the area and that kind of thing always goes up in frequency at this time of year – people have been buying Christmas presents. And three of the houses in that alleyway were ripped off that night.'

'And a merry fucking Christmas to you, too.' Daniel flicked his cigarette butt away. 'It's a bit bloody extreme, even so. Bastards.'

'It may not have been as calculated as you think.' Chris reran the scenario in his head. 'The priest is walking along, the burglar or burglars are coming out of the back of one of the houses, he remonstrates with them, or starts to give chase … all it takes is a knife whipped out, one panic-driven slash. Probably didn't even mean to hurt him, let alone kill him.' He shrugged. 'It's a bitch, yes, but these things happen.'

'Well they shouldn't. What the fuck are we coming to when Christmas presents are worth killing for? Burglars carrying knives? It makes me want to spit!'

'I couldn't agree with you more, and I have the scars to prove it.'

Daniel looked at him with interest. 'Knife scars? You've been stabbed?'

'Three times. And shot once. In Manchester. Needless to say, that's when I decided to call it quits.'

'Shit!'

'Major shit. I'd had enough. Was grateful to walk away with my life, thank you very much.'

'I don't blame you. Christ! I didn't think it was that bad! So you're going to give a statement to the police?'

'Sure. I told the priest I'd go back after I'd dropped your father off. At least I can tell them what time I saw him. That will maybe narrow the time down a bit as far as the investigation is concerned.'

'Do you have to tell them why you were there?'

'It's of no relevance. Obviously, I'll say I was hoping to see Terry, and Father Mac promised to phone him with the message. Which he did, as Terry can confirm. More than that, I won't say without your consent. As I said, it has no bearing on the case. At least he wasn't killed in your father's house, Daniel. That *would* have worried me.'

On her return, Deborah had stopped off to report to Derek and their meeting had lasted longer than either of them had anticipated. They'd both been excited, but now everything was catching up with her. It was no good. There was no way she could drive to her parents' tonight. She was shattered. Much better not to risk an accident. Even a minor error of judgement at motorway speeds could be fatal, and falling asleep at the wheel didn't bear thinking about. She had lost a friend from University that way, at this time of year, too. No. Her parents would be disappointed, but hell – better to have a live daughter a day or so late, than a dead one who had become another Road Traffic Accident statistic. She phoned them from the office. They were more than understanding and urged her to rest properly before making the drive.

'As long as you're here for Christmas Eve, love.

You just look after yourself.' She felt relieved. The way was clear now. Just go home, have a bath and go to bed. Give herself a breather.

Mags watched the TV news appeal for witnesses or any information relating to the murder of the priest 'affectionately known as Father Mac.' The room at the Hostel was dark, most of the residents preferring to watch the box without the lights on.

'Makes it more like the cinema, dunnit? Years since I been. Gawd Almighty, I can't even remember what film it was! You know what it costs nowadays, girl? A fuckin' fortune, that's what!' Sam, an older man with a nasty cough, cackled as he shared this information with her.

Scandalous, killing a priest, Mags thought. No one would have dared do that in the old days. She winced, feeling herself flush, grateful for the darkness. Despite her devotion to Our Lady and her love of Our Lord, she knew all too well that God's ministers were only human, like the rest of humanity. She shuddered as she remembered a particularly traumatic experience. How she had been harangued! How he had gloated over the fact that she would spend a long, long time in Purgatory – that is, if the Almighty deigned in His goodness not to send her directly to Hell for her sins. Such scarlet, terrible sins. She smothered a laugh, feeling panic as it rose, grateful for the darkness. Eternal Monopoly. That's what had struck her, and the priest had been holding the card, rejoicing as he read, 'Go to Hell, go directly to Hell, do not pass the Pearly Gates and do not collect any remission for your sins.'

What was wrong with her? How could she make a joke of such a thing? She shifted uncomfortably, unused to the luxury of a chair. One more night. Just one more night and she'd be out of here and away from this accursed region.

Deborah was dog tired. She kicked the door shut behind her, flicked on the living room light. Thank God she was home! It may be a rented flat, but it was hers and she loved it. She closed the curtains, comforted by the sight of her own car parked in the street below the window. One of the lads at work had picked it up for her and put the keys through her front door. She tossed them onto the table. *Yes! I'm mobile again. My own wheels, not some other car to get used to!*

At least the hire car was back safe and undamaged. The hire company was only three streets away, so she hadn't had far to walk after dropping it off. She'd only had the overnight bag to carry but, shoulders stiff from long hours of driving, it had felt like a ton weight. She stretched and rotated her neck. Bath first, or food?

She opened the fridge, which merely acted as a reminder that she still hadn't done the necessary shopping. Could it wait until she came back from her parents? Mmm...What could she eat that was quick? Soup. She opened the kitchen cupboard. OK. No soup. Baked beans, though – she had a tin of those. *Did I see cheese in the fridge...?* She checked again. Yes, just a bit, and she'd have to cut that mould off, but it would do for now. *Just grate it in with the beans and bingo – instant nutrition.* Tiredness overwhelmed her. *Oh bugger this. I'll do it in a minute. Bath first.*

She went through to the bathroom, set the taps running and poured in a generous dollop of Radox Muscle Relief. That should do the trick. Going into the bedroom, she started pulling off her clothes. *I'll sleep like a log tonight. There's nothing like your own bed. Might not even bother with the beans. I could always have them for breakfast...* She had just wrapped herself in her green fluffy bathrobe when the doorbell rang.

Terry Richardson sat in his hotel room, eyeing the bottle of Scotch. He had been eyeing it for the last hour and a half, having bought it simply to prove to himself that he could resist temptation. Still seething from the confrontation with Daniel, he was determined to stick it out.

It hadn't just been Daniel, though, had it? No Katie, but while that had been a disappointment, he'd thought at least he could work on that, get her to see him. But no. It hadn't just been Daniel. There'd been someone else there, a woman. A reporter. Jesus God! What the fuck was Daniel thinking of?

He eyed the bottle again, refocusing on its contours while bitterness rose like bile in his throat. The man he'd seen earlier hadn't been Daniel. Not the son he remembered. This bastard was cold and hard and unforgiving. Didn't give a shit about anything but Katie and the letters. That was all he was interested in. *Jesus, I could have posted them if that was all he wanted.* But it hadn't been all. He'd wanted names. A specific name, and Terry had had to give it in the end. God, the humiliation! Terry flushed. And now it would be all over the papers, and Daniel was even talking about going to the police.

Not quite all had come out, though. That's why they'd argued, Terry insisting he'd told them everything, Daniel suspecting – correctly – that he hadn't. No. Fucking Daniel had wanted to know who else he'd been fucking, and Terry wouldn't tell him, said it wasn't relevant, asked him what did he want – a list of every bloody woman he'd ever slept with? That would teach him, the cocky little shit. Who the hell did he think he was, speaking to his father like that?

That hadn't been all they'd argued about. It was Katie. The fact that Terry had asked to see her. *How can a son of mine be so fucking arrogant? I'd brought him everything, too. Not just these latest letters, but what I remembered of the earlier blackmail ones. Told him all about it, was able to swear it was the same fucking typewriter. And he treats me like I'm something that he picked up on the sole of his shoe. Bastard! And all the time, the bloody journalist is sitting there, looking all prim and sympathetic. Fat lot of fucking good sympathy will do me. The police will be all over me again.*

Bugger it! Terry stood up, fists clenched. *Bugger him! Damn and blast his eyes – especially his eyes. Fucking pervert, watching people on the job.*

Terry was no longer eyeing the bottle. He had picked it up and was unscrewing the top.

'You've got to leave us alone! You're destroying us, don't you understand?' Ronnie Walters

342

pushed straight past Deborah Harvey into the living room of her flat and stood like a coiled spring, ready to explode at any moment.

'Ronnie–'

'You've got to drop this! It'll destroy our marriage.'

'Take a seat, why don't you?' Deborah's tone of voice was lost on Ronnie, who continued to stand, trembling with pent-up emotion. Deborah kept her excitement hidden. *My God – this could be the breakthrough we've been waiting for... What's the best tactic?* 'Ronnie – if there's a point to be made, just make it and leave, will you? I've had a long day and...'

'Long day? A long day?' Ronnie's laughter was verging on hysteria. 'We've had a long nineteen years! Have you any idea what it's been like? No. Just like you have no idea what you're doing now.'

'Then why don't you tell me?'

'And have it all over the newspapers?' Ronnie sat down suddenly at the table, head slumped in her arms, and wept.

Deborah closed her eyes, then headed for the kitchen. 'I'll put the kettle on.' Moments later, her voice was soft as she asked, 'What is it you don't want all over the paper, Ronnie?'

The older woman lifted her face, now mottled and tearstained. *Dear God, let me be able to convince her, otherwise there'll be no alternative...* 'How can I tell you that when...'

'Try me. If it's not directly pertinent to Laura's disappearance, it doesn't have to come out.'

Ronnie stared at her for what seemed like a very long time before she spoke. 'I was having an

343

affair with Terry. I was with him that day. Colin doesn't know. He'd...' She stopped at the expression on Deborah's face. Shock. Disbelief. *I've done it! The lie has worked! Thank God!* 'I know it's terrible. Wicked. She was my friend and...' She started to cry again.

Deborah's brain was buzzing. Shit! They must be hiding something big for Ronnie to lie like this. Deborah knew from the interview with Terry earlier that day that the woman he had been seen with by Daniel was Helen Latimer, the doctor's wife. Chris Farmer was tracking them down, even now. Deborah had been as surprised as Daniel by the revelation and had asked, 'Not Ronnie Walters?' The look on Terry's face had spoken volumes. She would bet her life that his reaction had been genuine.

'Ronnie? Are you crazy? Not only was she one of Laura's best friends – she hated my guts.' So what the hell was going on?

The doorbell rang again, startling both women. *Bloody hell! What is this? Clapham Junction?* Deborah stood up.

'I didn't realise you were expecting anyone.' Ronnie got to her feet awkwardly.

'I wasn't.' Deborah shrugged and went to the door, opened it. Her visitor's smile was friendly, the voice kind, the eyes a lovely slatey shade of blue.

'Deborah, I'm sorry to disturb you at home. I wondered if...' The eyes took in the other woman, standing behind her. 'Ronnie, are you alright?' He pushed past Deborah, put a protective arm around Ronnie's shoulders. *Don't mind me,* thought Deborah. She closed the door, resigned now to having her evening interrupted.

'What's happened? Not an accident or anything?' The man turned to look at Deborah.

Hold on a minute... She was running his face through her mind, trying to place where she'd seen him before.

'Have we met? And how do you know where I live?' Warning bells were beginning to sound.

'It was Ronnie I was looking for.' The lie came easily. *How good I am at improvisation.* 'And yes, we have met at the Community Open Day.'

Deborah relaxed. *Of course. Mr Gorgeous with the curly hair. God, I must be tired!* She looked at Ronnie, only to see confusion spread across the other woman's face.

'You were interested in joining the Community. But I...'

'Is that it, Ronnie? Is that all you remember of me?' The voice was silken, sorrowful, and sent a sudden shiver of fear through Deborah. Something was terribly wrong...

Shit! Shit! Shit! She tried to edge towards the door but he intercepted her, still with that arm around Ronnie's shoulders.

'You don't remember me at all, do you, Ronnie? Not really. Not from back then.' He looked at her almost regretfully for a moment, then the arm around her shoulders moved to cover her eyes while the other hand flashed.

He was looking at Deborah Harvey as he cut Ronnie Walters' throat, and as the blood spurted forth, Deborah was too shocked even to scream.

Chapter Twenty-seven

Wednesday 22 December

Eyes. Wherever she looked, a million eyes seemed to hold her in their unblinking gaze. Deborah Harvey lay perfectly still. *Where am I? Am I dead? Am I dreaming? What...?*

A sudden image of Ronnie Walters flashed through her mind. Ronnie with her throat cut. Deborah gave a strangled cry and sat bolt upright as memory flooded back, a jumble of horror, blood and darkness. Being dragged from the house, bundled into the boot of a car. Nausea overwhelmed her. She was going to be sick. She barely made it to the sink in time. She stood shivering, stomach still fluttering on empty. Still, the eyes watched her. Where was she? She took a deep breath to steady herself. The cold water tap worked. She splashed her face, tried to clear vomit from the sink and muddle from her head. *Breathe, Deborah, breathe,* she told herself. *Look. Really look. What can you see?*

She was in a cellar. A very nice cellar, but a cellar nonetheless. Below ground. There was electric light and running water. It was large in size, and apart from the sink unit, there was a mattress and duvet on the floor, a small kitchen table and two straight backed chairs. The walls were covered in paintings and drawings, done on paper in water-colour or pastels. They were held up by Blu-tack. Very little variation on a theme. Trees, almost like an orchard, straggled in the background. In the foreground, huge and monstrous, was another tree, startling in its size and difference from the naturalistic execution of the puny-looking specimens behind it. This tree had neither branches nor leaves of the normal kind. Their parts were taken by peacock feathers, and every feather had a scattering of unblinking human eyes. Goose-bumps rose on Deborah's flesh. Her scalp prickled. She looked from one picture to another. What the hell did it mean?

Her own eyes were drawn suddenly to the space between the pictures – not that there was much of that. She touched the wall tentatively. Where had she seen this kind of interior work before? She racked her brain, closing her eyes to aid concentration. *Come on ... I was interviewing someone ... who was it?*

'You're admiring my handiwork, I see.' She hadn't heard the door open and whirled around, heart in mouth, at the sound of that voice.

'Who are you? What do you want with me?' Her voice was cracked, unsteady. Her skin crawled at the sight of him. Every instinct said 'Back away,' but there was nowhere to go.

'It's an ideal place, don't you think?' He set down a tray on the small table, bearing coffee, cereal and toast. 'Nice and secure. Comfortable, too, I hope. You'll only be here for a few days. And don't waste your breath screaming.' He lifted the edge of one of the pictures, exposed the surface she had been trying to place. 'No-one will

347

hear you. I bought this house from a musician. She had the cellar sound-proofed so that she and her band could practise down here without disturbing the neighbours. Very effective it is, too. No expense spared. Now...' He sat down, gesturing to Deborah to join him. 'To return to your questions. My name is Alessandro di Palma. Not that Caitlin O'Connor knows me by that name. That is, however, the name I was born with, and that is where my story begins. And you, Deborah Harvey, are the chosen one. Chosen to be my scribe.'

He raised the cafetière and smiled. 'Do you take sugar?'

'You've outstayed your welcome. It's time to move on.' Daniel's voice was sour with contempt.

'Oh it is, is it?' his father snapped. 'And what does Katie have to say about that?'

'She doesn't want to see you. Read my lips. You're not welcome.'

'Well fuck you! Think you can just use me to get the letters and that's it? I have a right to see my daughter!'

'Right?' Daniel laughed in disbelief. 'You have no rights! She's an adult woman and doesn't want to see you. Why should she? And why do you think she changed her name? Last time she was in your company, you beat the living day-lights out of her, or don't you remember that? Booze wiped it from your brain?'

'Everyone deserves a second chance!' Terry found himself mumbling, seared with guilt at Daniel's acid reminder.

'Oh, come on? How many have you had? And what about Cait? She deserves to have her wishes respected. All you can think of is yourself! If you really loved her, you'd let her go. Stay away from her.'

Terry said nothing as he sat down on the bed in his hotel room. His eyes had a faraway look.

'I'm paying your bill and booking you out. Go back to your Retreat or Twelve-Step Programme or whatever it is. And leave my sister alone.'

Daniel hadn't planned on seeing his father again. He should have been gone by now. This was Cait's last morning at the Clinic before her Christmas break and she had called Daniel to say that their father had phoned there, insisting on speaking to her. Daniel's mouth curled grimly, remembering what she had said.

'Penny – the receptionist – said there was a man claiming to be my father and sounding upset.' She had paused. 'Penny's very tactful, so I asked her, did she mean upset or was he drunk? She said he was drunk. I'm scared, Daniel.'

'Come on...' Daniel put a hand under Terry's elbow. *This is all my fault. If I hadn't been so paranoid about leaving Cait on her own, I would have seen him on his own turf. He would never have known where she was. Damn Deborah for revealing the fact that she's now an aromatherapist. And damn the Yellow Pages.*

Terry stood up.

'Where's your bag?' Daniel watched as his father rummaged in the bottom of the wardrobe, produced it and started to pack. He hadn't brought much. Should only have been a flying visit.

'That's it?' Daniel asked.

'That's it.' Something in his father's voice made him uneasy.

They walked together to Reception. 'Chris will be here any minute to give you a lift home. Or back to your Retreat. Whatever. And no more pestering Cait. Do you understand?'

'Perfectly.' Terry sat and flicked through a magazine as Daniel settled his bill.

Deborah had been writing for what seemed like hours. Alex – that was the name he insisted she called him – was frightening in his organisation.

'I wasn't sure whether you'd prefer to use a Dictaphone or take shorthand notes, so I provided for both.' He had set everything out for her: the machine, along with a batch of tapes; the pile of spiral-bound reporters' notebooks with a box of pens. He had smiled at her then. 'Are you sitting comfortably? Then I'll begin...'

He was frightening, period. And Deborah grew more and more afraid as he began to tell the story of his life and unveiled his plan for the members of the Richardson family. *How can I even be functioning, listening to all this? He's insane. And he's going to kill me. And here I sit, writing it all down as if I'm on Court Reporter duty. Don't antagonise him. There has to be a way out of this. There has to be...*

'Why are you so set on killing Caitlin on Christmas Day?' She had to ask. Even after Alex's account of killing his stepfather on Christmas Day last year, it hadn't been clear. Not to her, at any rate.

'Isn't it obvious?' There was exasperation in his voice. 'Why do you think I did these?' His sweeping arm took in every picture on the wall. 'It was on Christmas Day that he made me understand the key. *Seeing*. I saw. And Caitlin saw. Caitlin *saw*.'

Deborah nodded, saying nothing, continuing to write. She still didn't understand. Neither did she know as yet what had happened to Laura Richardson. The first part of Alex's story had been reasonably coherent. Up until he'd gone to stay at the Community for the second time, in the summer that Laura had disappeared. After that, it was crazy ramblings about seeing and not seeing and wiping out the Richardsons. Her mouth was dry with fear.

'You look like you need a break. Shall I make tea, or would you prefer coffee?' Alex's voice was genuinely solicitous. 'You may not be staying long, Deborah, but we have to look after your health. You're doing me a great service. The truth shall be known at last. I shall be vindicated, and have peace.'

He had even apologised for not bringing any of her clothes. 'Had you been by yourself, I should have been much more organised, but dear Ronnie rather scuppered that, didn't she? She told me off, you know. For teasing Caitlin. And didn't even remember.' Deborah was confused by his sudden change of tack. 'Never mind. I shall go shopping and get you some things. Toothbrush, washing kit, clothes. You'd better tell me the sizes.'

Deborah wanted to scream at the apparent

351

normality of it all. It was unreal. It was *surreal*. Like his bloody pictures.

'Won't your editor be thrilled when he gets all this? The scoop of the century, Deborah! You will be famous. I shall finally be understood.'

Colin Walters was red-eyed from lack of sleep. *I bottled out. Couldn't go through with it.* He didn't know whether to laugh or cry. Was it a good thing or a bad thing that he had lost his nerve? Sitting in his battered Land Rover, he gazed across wild acres of heathland, miles from home. Tears ran down his cheeks unnoticed until their saltiness touched his dry lips.

How many times had he driven past Deborah Harvey's house last night? Backwards and forwards, backwards and forwards, with the lump hammer burning a heavy hole in his pocket. *What was I thinking of? Smash her head in and make it look like a burglary? I must be off my head! I nearly made a murderer of myself – and for what? We did nothing wrong, me and Ronnie.* He thought again of how the shit had hit the fan when Laura had disappeared. He and Ronnie had been convinced that Doc had lost his head and killed her during their confrontation over the missing girl, but Doc had been demented, had sworn he'd told her the truth and that she'd left the house satisfied. They would never have believed him, of course, had it not been for Janet Wilkerson. That initial newspaper report had been wrong. Caitlin had not been the last person to see her mother. Janet had seen Laura walking past the orchard and said she'd been fine, then. That she'd waved and looked perfectly alright, even to the point of having what she called 'a lightness in her step'. Also, Janet had said that she herself had only happened to look across in that direction because she had the car window open and had heard incredibly loud music coming from the Old Farmhouse. And *that* tied in with Doc's account of how he'd put it on when she left because that was his way of dealing with stress. And, of course, if Laura was walking *away* from the Farmhouse and past the orchard, the logical assumption was that she was going home. Going home, as she'd told Doc, to collect Caitlin's swimming things, jump into the car and drop her delivery down to Ronnie at the Craft Shop. It all made sense. So what in God's name had happened to Laura?

'I swear to God I never touched her!' Doc had insisted. 'Yes, she came to see me. Yes, we talked about Isabella – under protest on my part. I told her that what she was saying had serious implications and put me in a very awkward position – though not for the reasons she may have thought, but because of patient confidentiality.'

'Go on.' Both Colin and Ronnie had been tight-lipped. 'You don't deny she was here, then?'

'Of course not. And I told Laura that.'

'You could hardly tell her anything else when she had a sketch of the girl, could you?'

'Why should I deny it? I did nothing wrong! Laura asked me to explain why Isabella hadn't been officially booked in and, of course, what happened to her.'

'And what did you tell her?' Colin had been standing no more than six inches from Doc when

353

he asked the question and was looking him straight in the eye.

'I told her that she wasn't booked in because it was of vital importance to her that her movements remain untraceable.' They waited. Doc squeezed the bridge of his nose. 'Colin...'

'WHAT HAPPENED TO HER?' Ronnie didn't ask. She yelled.

'*Nothing* happened to her! Dear God...' He paced to the window, swung round and looked at them. 'You have a daughter – Nicky. This article Laura saw ... I take it you've seen it, too?' They nodded. '...It mentioned the fact that she had an older sister who had committed suicide two years before her own disappearance, am I correct?'

'Yes, it did. All the more reason–'

'And it mentioned the grieving parents expressing grave concern because she hadn't coped with that, said they were afraid she might do the same thing?'

'Absolutely.'

Doc stopped pacing, shook his head, flung out his arms in a helpless gesture. 'Dear God, I could be struck off for what I told Laura. What I'm telling you. Disclosing medical information. Breaking confidentiality. You think I killed her or something, right?'

'We don't think anything about her yet. It's Laura we're concerned about. And Laura was concerned about this girl. What did you tell her, Doc?'

Doc closed his eyes, letting go a long breath. 'Isabella's sister, Caroline, killed herself because she was being sexually abused by her father. After

Caroline's death, he turned his attentions to Isabella.' Ronnie opened her mouth, but Doc had carried on. 'She came to me – was sent to me – by someone who wanted to help her disappear. I kept her here for three days and sent her on to someone else, with recommendations for certain aspects of her treatment. Sexual abuse is not my field. As God is my witness, that is the truth.'

'And Laura believed that?' Ronnie's voice was dangerously quiet now.

'As a matter of fact, no. She said, "You seriously expect me to believe that a father who is sexually abusing his own child would lay himself open to a newspaper interview? Why wouldn't she just tell someone? Go to the police? Tell her mother, for God's sake?"' He looked at them heavily. 'So I had to tell her. That her mother knew. Knew and did nothing. It happens more often than people think. We talked further. I made phone calls. Laura spoke to people. And she left my office satisfied.'

Colin opened his eyes, back in the present, stirred and turned on the ignition. Ronnie still hadn't believed Doc. She'd been all for going straight to the police and telling them all about the missing girl. And that's when it had all gone to pot. Doc had told her about the favour he'd done for Colin and his friend with the botched abortion schoolgirl. Told her that Colin had helped smuggle Isabella into the Community, too. Said that if she told, he'd tell. He wasn't going to carry the can for something he hadn't done.

Colin would never forget the look on Ronnie's

face as long as he lived. It had almost finished them. She'd always said Doc must have done something to Laura if he had to resort to threatening Colin that way. Maybe she was right. He'd held his breath, prepared for the worst, until she made her choice. To stay with him. To keep quiet. To believe Doc's account of his conversation with Laura after all.

Colin caught sight of his eyes in the rear-view mirror as the vehicle moved forward. What did he look like? Mess, mess, mess. He would drive about for a bit. Clear his head. Go home and have a shower and a kip. Then he'd think about what to do next. He thought of Ronnie and forced himself to smile. At least she'd have a good time at Nicky and Don's for Christmas.

God, the man was mad! Alex had bought the promised things for Deborah and more besides. Gift-wrapped. He'd had everything gift-wrapped. Even the nappy bucket. He was concerned about hygiene, he said. She had an ordinary bucket to pee in – she could tip that down the sink. He had bought bleach to put down afterwards. *You could blind someone with bleach*, she thought to herself. No chance. He was ahead of her. *He* would keep the bleach upstairs and put it down the sink morning and evening. So much for peeing. As for 'the other', as he so delicately put it, he had provided a nappy bucket with a lid. Again, he would deal with that. He'd thought of everything. Toilet paper. Shampoo. Even sanitary towels.

'I forgot to ask if you might need this sort of thing over the next few days.'

She had steeled herself to ask him. 'And what then? What when you've killed Caitlin? I know you're planning to kill the others, remember? You've already talked about that. So if we send these' – she indicated the notebooks – 'to Derek, he'll know. And then the police will know. They'll stop you.' He looked at her. Her mouth was so dry with fear, she could barely speak. He seemed genuinely puzzled. Hadn't seen the gaping hole in his plan. 'So you can't just kill me as soon as you've killed Caitlin, right? If you want me to chronicle all of this, Alex' – she forced herself to use his name – 'you need me alive until it's over.'

'All right, Mags? Ready to go?'

Mags levered herself out of the armchair, bent to pick up her backpack and started to swing it onto her shoulder in a reflex action.

'No need for that.' Mick stopped her. 'It can go in the boot. Or the back of the car, if you'd prefer.'

Of course. No need to carry it this time. A car. How long had it been since she'd travelled by car? She smiled to herself. She used to drive a car. How good that had seemed! Freedom. Independence. All so long ago now.

It was only as she got into the car and Mick was helping her to fasten the seat belt that he asked the question she'd been waiting for. She'd had to devise a different divination method to have the answer ready for him. No magpies here. None of the other signs in nature that she could read. This had called for something else. She'd torn up his list of places, placed them in an empty container in the kitchen, shaken them up and, eyes closed, pulled a piece out, like at a raffle.

'Have you decided where you'd like to stay over Christmas, Mags?'

'Oh yes,' she told him. 'Cheltenham.'

Alex had been gone for a while. Deborah was worried sick. What if he just abandoned her here? No one would ever find her. She fought down the rising sense of panic as she remembered at least two fictional books she'd read where just such a situation had occurred and the female victims – why were they always female? – had perished in the most terrible fashion.

There *had* to be a way out! Once again, she dragged a chair to the outside wall and stood on it. *No good. And I already knew that.* It was a mark of sheer desperation that she had even bothered looking again. There was only a small part-pane of glass set up near the ceiling. Sure, she could probably break it. Probably. It wasn't ordinary glass, by the look of it. Thick. Like the bottom of a bottle. Even if she could, it wasn't big enough to get through unless you were a cat or a very small dog. *Maybe I could throw things out? I have pen and paper. Messages. Ask for help. But what if he sees them?*

She scrambled down hastily, swinging the chair back into place. At least she could hear him coming now. He'd fitted a padlock to the door, so she was now locked *and* padlocked. No escape. That's what he'd told her. Her heart pounded violently. What if she'd tipped him completely over the edge by exposing the flaw in his plan?

Christ, he was so far over the edge already – what if he just decided to cut his losses? Kill her now? Maybe it wasn't a flaw anyway. He'd just get her to write down the rest of his plans, kill her, then send everything to Derek when it was all over.

He walked into the cellar. 'Try to get some rest. I shall need you to take dictation later.' He smiled, asked if her bucket needed emptying. 'No? Well, I shan't be long. I have to pop out for a while. To visit Caitlin.'

Chapter Twenty-eight

Disappearance Day

He was hiding in the orchard. Not *hiding*, exactly. It was more a case of not wishing to be seen. His body was still awash with strange sensations after the peep show he'd just witnessed. He needed time alone.

They hadn't wanted to let him see, even though he'd been the first to find the place, the previous year. He had followed them, knowing from their furtive behaviour where they were headed. Instinctively silent, like them, on the approach to the dilapidated building, his arrival had startled them and a flurry of gestures had followed, their resentment having to give way to a grudging accommodation which allowed him to partake in their voyeuristic ritual. And it was theirs, now, he knew, because he was still the outsider, the stranger, the visitor. Had it not been for him, they would never have known, never have had this entertainment, but conscious thought passed away as he became absorbed in their peep-show. They were oblivious to his presence now, breathing hard, getting their dicks out and wanking themselves, faces glazed and ecstatic, almost tortured in their necessity to stay silent. His own eyes had flickered between the scene within the ruin and the other boys' dicks. He had felt himself becoming hard, but fought the temptation to expose his own knob to their devouring eyes. Oh God, Oh God – how could he stop himself from coming? He'd wanked himself and other boys at boarding school, been wanked – even sucked – by other boys at boarding school, but he'd never seen a man and woman doing it until he'd come here last year.

His eyes went back to the writhing bodies now, fascinated by her, by the sheer abandonment she revelled in, riding the man like he was a horse, then pulling him on top of her. Jesus, what a prick-tease! Now she'd pushed him off, was rubbing herself down there, legs wide open, and he went in like a puppy, licking her wetness. She'd moved now, was squeezing her breasts while lover boy was bringing her off with his mouth. It was no good. He had to get his own knob out. Only when she'd come from that tonguing was her lover allowed to ride her again. His right hand worked furiously as he watched the buttocks as they thrust into her. Oh God, oh God, oh God...

Now, in the orchard, he was already hard again from remembering it all. He had fantasised, back there, about who they were. They seemed to have a particular corner of the ruin where they liked doing it, and although he'd been able to see their bodies, their faces had never been visible. Still, he now knew who the man was. He had hung around after the other boys had left, catching glimpses of the woman's lacy underwear and floral print dress before she made her own exit. That was when he'd heard someone else approaching and had to hide. It was like one of those bedroom farces. The woman just shagged had left, but another one had turned up and had a blazing row with the man. She'd been watching them at it, too, from a different vantage point, and was giving him what for. Called him a lying, no-good bastard. Got really upset.

'You don't deserve anyone, Terry Richardson! You're nothing but a piece of shit!'

He'd scampered away, then, leaving them to it. And now here he was, hard again, wondering... His thoughts were rudely interrupted by the sound of classical music, playing full belt. His head jerked up. It was coming from the Farmhouse, where he was staying with his mother and stepfather. What the hell...? He peered over the wall. Bloody Norah! It was *Mrs* Richardson, walking away from there, back in the direction of her own place. He had a sudden delicious vision of her screwing his stepfather while her husband was with his mystery woman. Women, plural, if you counted the other one who was all upset. He watched as she waved to someone in a car, going in the opposite direction. The car was soon out of sight, and Mrs Richardson carried on walking.

361

And that's when he heard the voice. His mother's voice, calling to Mrs Richardson. He hid further in his corner, realising that his mother's voice had come from behind and to the left of him. She must be walking through the orchard. Best to lie low so she wouldn't ask him what he'd been doing. He held very still, almost flat on the ground, only raising himself when she'd gone through the gate and started walking towards Mrs Richardson, who was waiting for her. That was when he recognised the floral print dress and the world spun in a red haze around him...

Chapter Twenty-nine

Thursday 23 December

'Not another one!' Daniel stared at Caitlin in disbelief as she handed over the latest missive.

'Yes. Hand-delivered, too.'

'Shit!' Daniel scanned it and looked at her blankly. 'What the hell is this supposed to mean?'

```
      iiiiiiiiiii
      iiiiiiiiiii
     The eyes have it
   It was all your fault
   If you had not seen
It would never have happened
      iiiiiiiiiii
      iiiiiiiiiii
```

Caitlin shook her head. 'I don't know. Maybe I should talk to Josh again – have more hypnotherapy. There must be something we've missed. I'm seeing him later, before he goes to his parents for Christmas and Hanukkah.' She paced for a moment, agitated. 'What the hell is it I'm supposed to have *seen!*' The word burst out in an explosion of frustration.

'God knows. Don't upset yourself, Cait. This is probably just a load of bullshit.' Daniel picked up the envelope from the dresser, where his sister had left it. 'I don't like this hand-delivered business at all, though. Whoever is doing this probably lives near here. You sure you've not had a spat with a neighbour?' He tried to make a joke of it.

'Quite sure. And I've hardly been telling my neighbours about our past.' She looked at Daniel, chewing at her lip. 'It says if I hadn't seen, it would never have happened. Like to put money on what "it" was?'

Brother and sister held each other's gaze, saying nothing.

Alex seated himself comfortably before speaking. 'I've been thinking about what you said, Deborah, and you're quite wrong. All I need is for you to act as scribe, write down my plans, and I've finished with you. I send the story to your boss after everything is done.'

Deborah's mouth was dry. It took every ounce of willpower to look Alex in the face without flinching. 'Not a good idea. What if something goes wrong? If you have to juggle things about – like when Terry wasn't at home? Besides, you don't really need me at all if you want to take that line. Why don't you just write it yourself?'

He looked at her quizzically, then, to her astonishment, burst out laughing.

'Bravo, Deborah! I knew I was right to choose you! You see, I don't want to write it myself. You're a professional journalist. You're also in my power. This way, I'll be believed. If I dealt with it myself, cut you out of the picture, so to speak, who's to say I'm not just some crank trying to take the credit?'

He stepped forward suddenly, stroking the side of her face. She moved backwards, an involuntary reaction, inwardly cursing herself for doing so but unable to hide her revulsion. He gripped her chin hard and looked straight into her eyes.

'You're right to be afraid, Deborah. But do your job well, and I promise yours will be a painless death.'

It was only after he left her that he realised he had been able to look her straight in the eye, to meet the gaze that feared him. A frisson of excitement shot through his body. What could this mean?

Terry Richardson had asked Chris Farmer to drop him at his house yesterday, rather than returning him to his aborted Retreat. He had not, however, stayed there. He was on his way back to Cheltenham, this time by public transport. He wasn't going to give up over Katie without a fight. Daniel was lying. He had to be.

Katie would want to see him. Of course she would. What better time than Christmas to put the past behind them and start again? He'd find a way to get to her.

Colin Walters woke up with a raging headache and a mouth like the bottom of a budgie's cage. He had not returned home until late the previous day and had taken the phone off the hook and fallen into bed in an effort to get himself back together. He made his way to the shower, disgusted with the way he smelt, and spent a long time in there, willing the water to clean his mind and emotions as well as his body. It was only as he was making coffee afterwards that he realised the phone was still off the hook. Guilt overcame him. Whatever would Ronnie think? He hadn't even phoned her. Mind you, it was a hell of a drive. She'd promised to make at least one overnight stop en route, so he hadn't expected to hear from her until after she'd arrived at Nicky and Don's, way up in the Highlands. *Still best if I wait for her to phone me. Don't want to spoil the surprise.*

Mags was settling in fine at the Cheltenham Shelter. A separate area had been set aside for women in the large back room and, so far, there was only one other occupant, whose name was Annie. She was younger than Mags – probably in her late twenties or early thirties – and spent most of her time sleeping. Mags preferred to help out as much as she could, not that there was much to do, really. They had everything very well organised. Masses of food had been donated,

365

along with a generous allowance of cigarettes for those who smoked, and there was a wide variety of clothing to choose from. Mags considered herself pretty well kitted out at present, especially after the generosity of the farmer's wife earlier in the month, but was grateful nonetheless for good socks and, praise be, new underwear. It was a long time since she'd had that luxury. An upstairs office had been allocated for the safe-keeping of valuables and that meant anything that was of any value to its owner, regardless of its monetary worth. That was nice. Thoughtful, too. Not everyone respected other people's property. At one time, maybe, but now, there were so many rootless wanderers, you never knew who you might come up against. The biggest problems were the druggies. Pinch anything to bankroll their next fix. It was a desperate existence, but even so, Mags wanted to safeguard what little she had. The Shelter people had a policy of not turning anyone away unless they were drunk, high or violent. Booze and drugs were strictly off limits in this place. That was fine with Mags.

An elderly lady helper called Celia solemnly took the few things she wanted kept locked away upstairs and issued her with a receipt. Mags watched as she went through the glass door to the stairs, locking it behind her, and tracked her progress along the upstairs corridor until she entered a wooden door and disappeared from view. It was perhaps as well that no guests of the Shelter were allowed up there. There was no telling what Mags' reaction would have been had she seen the duty roster pinned up over the old-fashioned roll-top desk. As it was, she had no idea that Caitlin O'Connor would be on the stayover shift the following evening, and went back to her space beside the sleeping Annie quite content.

Chris Farmer rang Daniel to give him the last routine report before setting off for his Christmas break. He had had his office do some digging while he'd been on the leg-work side of things. 'I'm afraid the Latimers are a dead end – Helen died in the summer of last year and the Doctor killed himself on Christmas Day.'

'Shit! So we still have nothing to corroborate my father's story?'

'No. But do you have any reason to believe he's lying?'

'No. But I don't know... If he *knew* they were dead, it would be a safe bet to say he was screwing Helen. She's hardly in a position to deny it.'

'Umm.'

'Thanks for dropping him back, by the way. What did he settle on – home, or back to his Retreat?'

'Home. Said he didn't want to spend Christmas with strangers.' Daniel made a hrummphing sort of noise that Chris found hard to interpret. 'Anything else before I head off?'

'Nothing urgent. Cait's had another letter – very bizarre. I'll fax it to you. I think we've reached the point where the police will have to be told about them. Cranky is one thing. Threatening is a different ball game.'

'Threatening?'

'Almost. Nothing explicit, but the tone is quite different. I still want you on my mother's disappearance, though. Have a good break, anyway.'

'Sure. You too.'

Caitlin parked her car in Josh's drive and emerged with a carrier bag that was unable to disguise the Christmas presents it struggled to contain. Josh had the door open before she got to it.

'You've boxed me in!'

'Of course! That way, you can't run off before I give you these!' She held out the bag and stretched up to kiss him.

'Mmmm!' He pulled her inside and kicked the door shut. 'What did I do to deserve this?'

'Nothing. Other than getting my pulse racing and being generally gorgeous.'

'Is that all?' He laughed before they kissed again.

Finally breaking apart, Josh peeped into the bag. 'Can I open them now?'

'No, you cannot! They're for Christmas Day itself. You did say your family celebrates Christmas Day as well as Hanukkah?'

'Oh yes. Somewhat adapted, of course, but we stint on nothing.' He led her into the living room where he produced a bag of his own. 'These are for you. And likewise – no peeping. Christmas Day only!'

'Oohh... Can't I just feel them and guess?'

He laughed. 'No! You think I'm going to tell you if you guess correctly? No way, José!'

They stood and hugged, both falling silent. Josh

stroked her hair, breathed in the scent of her. 'How are you doing?'

'OK.' She spoke into his chest. 'I had another letter. Hand-delivered. Weird.' She told him about it. 'Josh, I really think I should be hypnotised again. I must have seen something, or none of this makes sense.'

Josh sat beside her. 'It's a fallacy to think that anything should. Whoever is writing these letters is one very sick person, Caitlin. You probably saw nothing. There was nothing to see. But this latest letter is in a different class to the others. I really think you should go to the police.'

'We are. Once Christmas is over. Daniel says things are getting out of hand.'

'I agree. But when is Christmas over?' These days, he knew, it could effectively run to a three-week break.

She smiled, knowing what he was thinking. 'We're going to the police the day after Boxing Day.'

'Promise?'

'Promise. I don't want this going on for ever.'

Josh felt more relief than he cared to admit. He stood up, pulling her with him. 'You take good care while I'm away, OK?'

'I will. I can't really do otherwise! Between Daniel and Nina, I seem to have personal minders wherever I go! I'll miss you, though.'

'You will?'

'Yes.' She looked at him, suddenly very vulnerable. 'I love you, Josh.'

'I love you, too, Cait.'

Her heart seemed to explode through her

369

chest. Kissing him fiercely, she murmured, 'Any chance of dessert before you set off...'

Deborah could have screamed with frustration. She had examined every inch of the cellar, every item to hand, and had come to the conclusion that the only way she could get out of here was through the door. And that meant she had to get through Alex. She had practised swinging one of the chairs, forcing herself to picture the way it would slam into him. The way it would *have* to slam into him. Should she go for his head or his body? Or what about his legs? Would that be the best way to disable him? She had to really go for it. No hesitation. Full force. There would be no second chance. It was him or her, and she had already seen the merciless way he had dealt with Ronnie Walters. She daren't think far beyond the basic necessity of getting through the door. She ran it through her mind. He comes in. Maybe even carrying food, so his hands would be full. Slam him with the chair. Leg it out of the door. This was where she faltered. She didn't know what was on the other side. Obviously, a flight of stairs. But what if there were a locked door when she got to the top? What if he kept the keys on him, and she had to go back to get them and he killed her?

A sound caught her attention and she frowned, straining to hear it more clearly. What the...? This was not a sound she had heard here before. It was... Oh God, it was the sound of a woman's shoes – high heeled shoes – and they were coming down the cellar stairs...

She almost cried with relief when the door opened. A woman stood, looking at her in disbelief. 'What on earth–?'

Deborah ran forward. 'Please – you have to help me! I'm being held prisoner. Please – I have to get out of here!' She pushed past the woman, legs rubbery with shock.

'Not *just* yet, darling!'

Her arm was caught in a vice-like grip. She was pulled backwards, feet slipping from the stairs, her stairway to freedom. She screamed with all her might. The whole house couldn't be sound-proof. 'Help me! Help me!'

Pushed back into the cellar, she flailed at the woman as the door was closed. 'How can you do this! He'll kill me! You have to let me go!'

She was knocked backwards by a blow, stared at the woman from her new position, sprawled on the floor.

'I don't think so.'

Deborah watched in horrified fascination as the woman took off her wig and started to remove her clothes.

'I thought it was time you met Aless, my alter ego. Had you completely fooled, didn't I?' Alex/Aless stared at his/her reflection in the mirror above the sink. 'I must take off my make-up before we go any further. Can't risk clogging my pores...'

Deborah heard herself screaming and, even knowing that no one could hear, couldn't seem to make herself stop for a very long time.

Later, she was frantic, for altogether different reasons. Trying to keep up with his rantings seemed impossible. He was completely manic. Anyone else, and she would have thought they were taking drugs. Her time with him, albeit short, had made her realise that drugs were something he had no need of. His plan for the extermination of the Richardson family was quite sufficient.

He was back to being Alex again. Aless had been short-lived, something for him to crow about. She still could not believe how completely he had had her fooled. The way he held himself, the way he spoke, his voice, make-up – all was perfection.

'This is not a perversion, you know,' he'd told her, 'and I'm not gay, either. Aless started as ... how can I put it? An act of defiance. I was beaten for dressing up in my mother's clothes when I was small. Small and defenceless. Well, once I'd left home – certainly once I'd killed my father – who was to stop me? No one. I didn't bother with it again for years. Then ... then it became a challenge. Could I pass myself off as a woman? I found to my delight that I could.'

It was Aless, he had told her, who had killed the priest. 'It's so much easier to get close to people when you're a woman. People are stupid. They don't see women as a threat. But we are, dear, aren't we? And it suddenly struck me the other day – Terry having such an eye for the ladies – that going as Aless, he'd be far more likely to let me in. I could say my car had broken down and ask to use the phone. I could have come up with a hundred-and-one scenarios. He wouldn't be listening. Just seeing a woman. Not seeing the danger.'

He had sat talking to her, carefully removing his makeup, telling her about his blackmail letters to Terry, and, to Deborah's amazement, to his own stepfather. 'I bought an ancient typewriter from a junk shop the minute I got home – one of the old "sit-up-and-beg" things, weighs a ton. Made a fortune out of them over the years. Could have made more, but I got tired of it in the end. I even sent them to myself – phoned Doc, absolutely frantic. I was still at University, remember, so not supposed to have much money of my own. But I get ahead of myself.'

He told her, then, of how he had run from the orchard to the Farmhouse and burst in on Doc. Told Deborah what he had told him.

'Laura Richardson attacked your mother?!' Deborah was incredulous.

'Don't you think she had reason to? My mother was screwing her husband, when all is said and done.'

He smiled at her then, the kind of smile that made her blood run cold.

'Only kidding. That's what I *told* Doc. What actually happened was rather different.'

He was waiting for her to ask. Challenging her. Could it be she was really about to hear the truth? To finally know what had happened to Laura Richardson?

She knew it was a game. Knew she had to play it.

'So what actually *did* happen, Alex?'

He smiled again. And told her.

'It's all in the detail, isn't it?' He shook his head, mind faraway, reliving the moments after he had

373

burst from his hiding place.

'Red. Red. That's all I could see. Like a haze over everything. And I just picked up this thing – a tree-branch, I believe it was – and hit her. My mother. Thwack! Right on the back of the head. She never knew what hit her. Certainly never knew it was me. The thwack – it was satisfying. Dull and heavy. And she gave this scream. No, I must be accurate. More of a – let me think – an involuntary, gasping cry. Yes, that was it. And I hit her again as she went down. And then – and then...'

He glared at Deborah, still affronted by the memory. 'I heard a voice. Laura bloody Richardson. She'd seen. She'd heard. And she came running over. At first I couldn't make out what she was saying – there was a kind of roaring in my ears, and I could see her mouth move but couldn't hear her. And then it cleared. And you know what she said?' He shook his head. 'Unbelievable! She said, "Stop that! What in God's name do you think you're doing?". What the bloody hell did she think it looked like?' He started to pace now, the memories prompting movement.

Deborah forced herself to remain silent, wanting only to scream at him to get on with it, tell her what had happened next. But not too fast, not too fast... If he really got carried away, she wasn't sure her shorthand could keep up with him. She'd failed her first shorthand exam. Most people did. You had to be able to do a hundred words a minute.

He stopped pacing, huffed out air through his

mouth and looked at her.

'You know what she said next?' He gave her no room for answer. '"Put that down!" And that's when I looked at the thing in my hand and knew it was a branch. And I saw blood on the end of it. And so did she.' His lip curled. 'She was scared, then, I saw it in her eyes – just a flash, but it was there and I knew and she knew I knew. So she said, "Put that down" and I said, "Or what?" and I leaped at her.'

He leaped towards Deborah as he said the words, terrifying her as she was forced back against the wall. Their eyes locked. Deborah's heart hammered. *Please, God... Please, God...* Then he backed away, never taking his eyes from her face.

'She dodged backwards. Spoke my name – she knew my name. And she told me who she was. Mrs Richardson. As if I didn't know. Laura, she said. As if being on first-name terms would make me stop. But it didn't. Nothing could stop me.' His voice had dropped to a whisper. 'She said she didn't know what was going on, but she was sure we could work something out. Work something out!' He laughed, shaking his head. 'And she said – she said, "Helen needs medical attention". And do you know what I told her, Deborah? Do you?' His voice rose. His eyes were glittering and Deborah could see a sheen of perspiration across his upper lip. 'I told her, "Helen needs a grave, not a doctor! HELEN is my MOTHER and she's a WHORE! SHE'S A FUCKING WHORE!"' He screamed the words, rocking on his heels.

Dear God, he's mad! Completely off his head!

Deborah's mouth was bone-dry.

He drew breath, gathered himself. 'She told me again to put it down. The branch. And I went for her. Held it above my head with two hands. It was that kind of size, you know?' He mimed the actions.

Deborah wanted to lick her lips, but couldn't. No saliva left.

'How she ducked and dodged! Ducked and dodged! *Whoosh!* That was the sound the branch made when it missed her. How many times did I miss her? Two? Three? I really wasn't counting. I laughed at her then. Can you believe that? I laughed. Told her she was good. All that T'ai Chi shit. She was better even than that – balletic. Poetry in motion. And the next time I swung, I hit her. Not a thwack, like mother. This was a crack. *Crack!* The sound of splintering bone, Deborah. I broke her arm.'

Deborah swallowed convulsively, willing herself not to cough, right hand still on automatic pilot as she scribbled the shorthand cipher of his terrible words.

'She gasped, then. Not a scream. A gasp. A big one, like all the air had gone out of her. And she did the sensible thing – or so she thought. She turned on her heels and ran.'

He sat down then, glanced at the notebook to see if she was keeping up with his account. Satisfied, he continued. 'I had her in seconds. Hit her broken arm again – she did scream that time, but by God, she tried to keep her feet, tried to stop herself from falling forward. And I was screaming at her, telling her about it. "You stupid cow! You stupid fucking cow! Why did you try to help her? She's screwing your old man!" That's what did it to her. It was like some split-second paralysis, but it was all I needed. I hit her again. Only this time, I got her clean on the back of her skull.'

There was no sound in the cellar save for the two of them breathing.

He leaned forward, tapped the notebook with his index finger. 'That's when I knew I was in trouble. Two women on the ground. Both dead, as far as I knew. And the noise. It was only then that I noticed the noise. I can't believe it hadn't sunk in before. Maybe that's why I couldn't hear Laura to begin with, but it didn't register until I stood there suddenly calm and clear-headed and with two women on the ground. Music, Deborah. Loud music. Coming from the Farmhouse. So I followed it. Followed the noise. In the house, up the stairs, straight into Doc's study. I hadn't even consciously thought about a story, about what the hell I was going to tell him, but it was all there, ready and waiting. He never heard me come in. Had his back to the door. He was sitting in his swivel chair – I can see it now. And I rushed across the room and started gabbling at him and he couldn't hear a thing until he'd jumped up and switched the music off. I must have scared the pants off him. Sweating. Blood on me. Oh, but he took it in his stride. Grabbed his medical bag. I told him Mrs Richardson had attacked mother, accused her of sleeping with her husband, and that I'd tried to intervene, had hit her with a stick and killed her. He was down those stairs like lightning. And you know what, Deborah? You know what was the very worst thing? When we got outside, my mother was still lying on the ground, but Laura Richardson was gone.'

Silence hung in the air between them, the enormity of the word resonating like an echo.

'Gone?' How had she managed to speak?

'Gone. Nowhere to be seen. And Doc was down on the ground beside mother, fingers probing, doing his doctorly bit, and he said, "But where's Laura? I thought you said you'd hit her?" And I told him I had! That I thought I'd killed her! And I left him to it and went after her.'

He was agitated now, pacing again, his head rolling from side to side as he continued to speak. 'Have you any idea how I felt? How afraid I was? I had to find her. She'd got much further than I would have thought. You know the track between the dry-stone walls? She'd headed for that. God knows why. Disoriented, I suppose. She was still this side of it, though. Had collapsed in a heap, scrabbling about, trying to haul herself up, only her arms and legs weren't working properly and she couldn't see straight. Blood in her eyes. She was dying, you do understand that, don't you, Deborah? I knew she was dying. You can feel the life-force ebbing out of people, do you know that? I would have helped her if I'd thought...'

His voice tailed away. Deborah hardly dared breathe.

'...but it was too late. The decision was taken out of my hands. I'd hauled her upright. Surprising how heavy people are when they're not in control of themselves. We stood there, swaying.

Swaying like lovers. And that's when I heard it. This voice. Chanting. And I glanced round and saw a child – her child. Caitlin. Oh, she was still some way away, but she was heading in our direction. Skipping up and down the banks like there was no tomorrow. I thought I'd have to kill her, too. There was nothing else for it, really. I dragged Laura down, trying to hide her, and still I could hear this bloody chant and knew she was getting closer and must have seen us and she would ask questions and... I only did it to shut her up, you know. I didn't think about it, I just did it. She was moaning, you see. Laura was moaning. And I thought of Caitlin, thought of what she'd say, and I think Laura must have heard her, too, because she said her name, said, "Caitlin! Caitlin!" Kind of moaning. So I had to do it. I had to. You must understand that. I just held her face into the earth to shut her up. Held her face there. Until she stopped breathing.'

Chapter Thirty

As Deborah's hand finished moving across the paper and his voice fell silent, she let out the air that remained in her lungs and closed her eyes. For how much longer would *she* continue to breathe, imprisoned by the madman who had taken not only Laura's life but that of so many others? She had to survive. She had to find a way to save the Richardsons. His plan could not be

379

allowed to succeed. How far could she push him? Dare she try?

There was no sound in the cellar save the hum of the fluorescent tube lighting. Without looking at Alex, head still bent over her notebook, she finally spoke her first response to his account.

'So why do you blame Caitlin, Alex? Why does she have to die?'

'Because she saw us.' She felt, rather than saw, the shrug and spreading of his hands, told by the rustle of his clothing.

'Bullshit.' She spoke quietly but forcefully.

'What?'

'Bullshit. Don't you think she would have said? If I had just seen my mother murdered, I would have run off screaming to the nearest adult I could find.'

'Laura was not murdered!' Alex's voice was raised, sharp with rebuke. 'I had to kill her. Caitlin *saw!*'

'You would have killed Laura whether Caitlin was there or not! Who are you trying to kid, Alex? Laura saw you attack your own mother – you couldn't afford to let her live to tell the tale.'

'That's not true!' He jumped up, knocked over the chair he had been sitting on.

Deborah's heart was hammering against her ribs. How far could she afford to push him? She forced herself to hold his gaze before deliberately going back to her notebook and flicking backwards through its pages. Here it was. She read aloud from his account, ending the extract with, 'Those are your own words, Alex. You said them to me just moments ago.' She slapped the

380

notebook shut and stared him in the eye. 'You can't have it both ways – either you killed Laura Richardson to keep her from telling about the attack on your mother, or you killed her because you were seen by her daughter after you had already attacked her, an attack which may have proved fatal even if you hadn't finished her off by suffocation.'

She fought to suppress any outward sign of the revulsion she felt at the relish with which he had recounted the blows he had delivered, the horror she felt at the matter-of-fact way he had described his final act of snuffing out the woman's life.

'Caitlin Richardson was thirteen years old, Alex. A child. She told her family and the police that she hadn't seen her mother since half past one when they had had lunch together. *You* may have seen *her*, Alex. She *didn't* see you. You said yourself that she was quite some distance away, running up and down the banks along the path.' A sudden thought struck her. 'How did you know it was her? How did you know of her relationship to Laura?' She opened the notebook again, hand poised to write.

He was on edge, confused, trying to make sense of his own riddles. 'Of course I knew! I spoke to her, teased her, called her names. That's what Ronnie Walters told me off for.'

Deborah's shorthand transformed his words into lines and squiggles across the page. Even as she wrote, she was asking another question. 'If you knew her – teased her – then how come she doesn't recognise you now? You've been bragging to me about being in her T'ai Chi class – how come she hasn't put two and two together?'

His laugh was more of a bark than anything. 'Because she never *saw* me! That was her first sin – *not* seeing me. Her second sin was seeing me when she shouldn't have. And nowadays... I already told you I was a skinny kid. Ginger-haired. Look at me now, Deborah. No one knows me now. I had a late growth spurt. Gained height and breadth. I colour my hair. Had a nose job. None of them recognise me now.'

Deborah's mind was still on the issue of seeing. What in God's name was he on about? 'How could you tease her and she didn't see you?'

Alex rolled his eyes as if pained by her stupidity. He flung out an arm and began ripping pictures off the wall, thrusting them under her nose, waving them at her, finally banging them down on the table and thumping them with his fist.

'BECAUSE I WAS UP A TREE AND SHE SAW NOTHING BUT MY LEGS!'

It took every ounce of nerve she possessed for Deborah not to flinch under his onslaught. 'So that's what the eyes are about, then? In these pictures?'

'Seeing and not seeing. Seeing and being seen. That's the key to everything, Deborah. Absolutely everything. He who sees and is not seen has the ultimate power.'

'I see.' She didn't, but wrote down his words anyway.

His voice was suddenly quiet. His hand shot forward, grasped her chin.

'Sometimes I think you see too much,

Deborah.' How could a voice as soft as silk instil such fear? 'If you didn't need these to write...' The index finger of his other hand traced her eyes with a touch that lingered like that of a lover '...I would put them out right now.'

She thought she was about to faint. *God, give me a voice. Let me pull him away from this...* It was difficult to speak with his hand on her jaw, but she forced the words out. 'Two things have always puzzled me, Alex.' He relaxed his grip. 'They've puzzled everyone for nearly twenty years.'

He let her go, stepped backwards, picked up the chair and straddled it, facing her.

'What did you do with her body? And what did you do with her car?'

Daniel and Caitlin had bought a Christmas tree, a real one. They had struggled to get it through the door, and dissolved in helpless laughter at Daniel's attempts to trim it. Finally, they had it potted, its truncated tip brushing the ceiling, and were now about to dress it.

'Bags you go up the stepladder!'

'Gee, thanks, sis!' Daniel shook his head as he heaved the metal steps apart, slapping the locking mechanism into place. He turned and grinned at her. 'Remember doing this at home?'

They were quiet for a moment, remembering. When Caitlin next spoke, her voice was quiet. 'Maybe I should see him. Give him a chance.'

'Dad?' Daniel exhaled heavily. 'It's up to you, Cait. But – he's not a nice person. I know that's an awful thing to say about your own father, but... Look, like I said, it's up to you, and I'm not

383

trying to do the heavy big brother act or anything, but – if you *do* decide to see him, do me a favour – don't do it on your own. He's erratic, Cait. Drinking again, despite his Twelve-Step Programme. Just think about it carefully, OK?'

She nodded. 'I will. Daniel – he didn't kill Mummy, did he?'

'No.' Daniel shook his head. 'He's responsible for a whole lot of other shit, but not that, I think. No. Still...'

'What?'

'I can't help thinking – you know – if he'd have gone home instead of screwing Helen Latimer, maybe whatever happened to Mum wouldn't have happened. I can't forgive him that.' He smiled crookedly. 'Hey, I'm sorry! We start off putting up a Christmas tree and get into the heavy stuff. *Mea culpa.*' He put his arm around her.

She hugged him before moving to the box of decorations he had brought down from the loft. 'Up the ladder then, you! I'll hand these up, OK?'

'OK. Right. Pass the tinsel.'

Daniel's voice was muffled now, his body half-hidden as he stretched behind the tree. Caitlin kept a firm hold on the ladder. 'We ought to have music while we're doing this.'

'What did you say?'

'Music!'

He laughed at the sight of her upturned face. 'Hey, remember when I thought you were talking to a tree just before Mum... Sorry. I'm at it again.'

Caitlin's eyes were like saucers. Her mouth was open.

Shit! She looks like I've slapped her in the face. Trust me to...

'No, that's alright. That's ... oh my God, Daniel – that's it! That's *it!*' She shook the ladder in her excitement and Daniel jumped down before he was dislodged.

'What, Cait? What are you talking about?'

'That letter – not the latest one, the one before ... Cats? "Caitlin Cat" and all that stuff? That was *it*, Daniel! The voice in the tree – the *boy* in the tree! He was the one who called me "Hellcat" and all that other stuff!'

'...and I thought you were nuts until I got closer and heard it myself, and Ronnie Walters walked past on her way to work and, without missing a step, just shouted up at him to leave you alone...'

'...and once she'd gone, *you* told him to carry on because I was just your squirt of a kid sister...'

They looked at each other, fired with excitement. At exactly the same time, they spoke the same words, equally baffled by the central issue of the incomplete memory.

'What was his name?'

Nina had had a nap before getting ready for the evening's party with some of Mike's friends. As she stood under the shower, turning her face towards the jet of hot water, she closed her eyes, allowing her mind to empty. Something was trying to surface; she could sense it, and the best way to allow it through was not to focus on it but to give it space.

Flash! An image jumped forward, hovering behind her eyelids like the frozen frame of a

385

photograph. The palm of a hand, its lines as clear as day. Nina acknowledged it wordlessly, breathed in, breathed out. It was obliterated by a curtain of blood, then all was dark again.

Flash! Image number two. A line of palm trees on an ocean-front. A hurricane began to blow and the trees, whipped by rain and wind, fell like a line of dominoes. All save one – the smallest. As Nina observed it, still standing despite the lashing of the elements, the earth around its base became transparent to her vision, enabling her to see that its roots were rotten. Again, the curtain of blood wiped the image from view. Again, Nina wordlessly acknowledged it, breathing in, breathing out.

Flash! Image number three. A map. What...? Long experience enabled Nina to resist the effort to focus on it. Just let it come... Closer, closer, closing in until the map became larger, the outline clear, its markings visible. *Palma de Mallorca*... The map wavered, faded, until in its place loomed the huge Gothic Cathedral of that city. Nina had visited it many years ago. A house of the Christian god; a sacred place. The image now behind her eyelids was the same, yet different, as if it had been somehow corrupted. It was so real, she could smell it. Corruption, death and decay...

Gasping, she opened her eyes, groped for the dial and turned the water off. Despite its temperature, she was shivering as she stumbled from the shower cubicle. What the hell was this all about?

Terry Richardson had booked a self-catering

cottage in Prestbury, on the outskirts of Cheltenham. It hadn't been easy, finding accommodation over Christmas at such short notice. It had a downstairs cloakroom and kitchen with a flight of wooden stairs leading to the upstairs sitting room and bedroom.

Unpacking his things now, he began to question his actions. Maybe he should have gone back to the Retreat House after all. He would have had support there, as well as three decent meals a day, not to mention all those little extras. He thought longingly of the cakes and biscuits to hand, tea and coffee-making facilities, space for meditation... What a fool! This didn't seem like such a good idea now. He should have waited until afterwards, after New Year, even, and contacted Katie then.

Bloody hell! Can I not get anything right? A wave of confusion swept over him and he teetered, in limbo, unsure whether to laugh or to cry. He had a sudden image of a picture from his schooldays, where a poor sinner, i.e. Everyman, had a Guardian Angel whispering in one ear and a little red devil in the other. *I know, I know! Do I push it or do I go easy? Do I drink or do I not? Do I allow myself to be bitter and twisted and push for my own way, or do I respect other people's wishes even if it hurts me?*

Jesus God, it was like some cosmic battle was being played out in his own life, his own mind and feelings. He felt swamped. Long years of being away from the Church, of loneliness, had caused anger and self-pity to eat him alive. Only Father Mac's understanding had brought him back, shown him new ways of dealing with things, new possibilities.

Why, though, do I seem to have to fight every inch of the way? It's such an uphill struggle and I just don't have the strength. He saw again the priest's face, felt something of the atmosphere that had surrounded him. *Father Mac. He died after doing me a favour. I can't let him down.*

He paced the room before picking up the telephone directory. Finding Caitlin's clinic had been easy, once he knew she was an aromatherapist. What about her home number, her address? Suppose she was ex-directory? *I should have thought this through, gone about it properly.* His hands shook, this time not through alcohol, but nerves, as he leafed through the pages. There were forty-six O'Connors in the residential section of the Cheltenham & North Cotswolds telephone directory. Only one had the initial 'C'. Terry didn't know it yet, but he had struck paydirt in one easy go.

It was already dark as Colin Walters drove slowly along Northfield Terrace. He was unsettled, not having heard from Ronnie yet, and unsure of what he was doing here. To his surprise, Deborah's car was still parked outside her flat. *But she was supposed to have gone to her parents on Tuesday. Tuesday...*

A clammy feeling swept over him, making the hairs on the back of his neck prickle. *Ronnie went to Scotland on Tuesday. Or was supposed to have done...* Colin pulled in behind Deborah's vehicle, noting that the street was unusually free of parked cars. People had probably gone away for Christmas.

Suppose Ronnie had done something rash? He daren't articulate his thought more explicitly than that. Not yet. He sat for a moment, pondering his next move. Decision made, he left the Land Rover and walked purposefully towards the front door. No point looking suspicious. Just go for it. He pressed the entry phone but there was no response. Pressed again and again, with the same lack of result. Damn it! He tried buzzing the other residents. Surely to God someone was in? Too early, maybe. Some people might still be at work, if they hadn't gone away already. *Bloody hell!* Where was Deborah if her car was still here? More to the point, where was Ronnie?

Frustrated, he walked back to the Land Rover, looking at Deborah's car as he did so. Could she still be at the office? It didn't make sense. She hadn't gone to her parents, that much was obvious, but if she were still working, surely she would have taken the car? The office was certainly not within easy walking distance.

His stomach growled as he fought conflicting emotions, closed off half-formed thoughts before concrete concepts emerged from their nebulous beginnings. That wouldn't do. Therein lay the seeds of madness if he were not careful. Maybe they hadn't been able to fix her car in time and she'd hired one. Gone home anyway. That would explain her car still being here, but what about Ronnie?

He couldn't wait any longer, surprise or no surprise. *What a bloody fool! She could have had an accident ... anything could have happened.* He pulled the mobile from his pocket, punched in his daughter's number. *Of course she's there. Of course she is. Just tired after her journey.* Nicky answered after the second ring.

'Hi, Dad! How lovely to hear from you!' He could hear sounds in the background, the excited squeals of his grandchildren. 'I hope this doesn't mean you're not going to phone on Christmas Day – don't tell me, you're taking Mum away on some exotic cruise!'

Oh dear God. She's not there. She's not there...

How he managed to make small talk, he didn't know. It was as if he were somehow detached, listening to himself carrying on an apparently normal conversation while another part of him was frantically running through all the other, dreadful possibilities. He would have to phone hospitals. Phone the police, even.

The idea came to him after he finished speaking to Nicky, but he got into the Land Rover and drove around the corner before putting it into action. *Stay calm. Be logical. Use a process of elimination.* Another vacant parking space welcomed him and he slid into it gratefully. He picked up the mobile again, punched in a different number. This time his call was answered on the third ring.

'Hello there, is Deborah Harvey available?'

'I'm sorry – I believe she's finished now until New Year. Can anyone else help you?'

'Derek might, if he's in – tell him it's Colin Walters from the Darrowdale Community.' Impatient seconds seemed to drag as he was put on hold. At last, the voice he had asked for came on the line.

'Hello, Colin! What can I do for you?'

'Oh, probably nothing – I think I've made a balls-up.' Colin forced a laugh. 'I was trying to get hold of Deborah – found something she needed for the piece on Laura.'

'Ah, she's gone home for Christmas.'

'That's what I thought, but I was just on my way to the supermarket and happened to be passing where she lives – it's just round the corner – and I noticed her car was still there. Couldn't get any reply, and thought she might be working after all.'

'No, Colin. Are you sure it was her car?'

'Oh yes.' Another forced chuckle. 'Told us she'd had trouble with it – the head gasket, wasn't it? Maybe it's not fixed, then, and she hired a car instead?'

Derek frowned. One of the lads had picked up Deborah's car from the garage and driven it to her place while she was in Cheltenham, he knew that.

'Sorry, mate, I wouldn't know. She'll be back on the twenty-ninth. Anything urgent?'

'No. No, it can wait. Well, er, Happy Christmas, Derek.'

'Same to you, Colin. Take care, now, and love to Ronnie.'

Derek sat for a moment, thinking about the call. Deborah wouldn't normally tell people where she lived or give out her home phone number, but he could understand her doing it with Colin and Ronnie, being so central to the update on

Laura's disappearance. The car, however, was a different matter. Colin was probably right, of course. Maybe she'd hired a car after all. Still... A couple of phone calls wouldn't hurt. He pushed buttons for an internal connection.

'Paolo? Derek here. Was it you or Raj picked up Deborah's car for her?'

'Raj. Why? Is there a problem? Don't tell me it's not right!'

'No. Just put Raj on, will you?'

'Sure.' There was the sound of the receiver changing hands.

'Hi, boss. What's up?'

'You picked up the car for Deborah – was it running alright?'

'Sweet as a nut. And I put the keys through the door, as arranged. Bloody thing hasn't conked on her, has it?'

'Not as far as I know. Which garage did she take it to?'

'Maltby's. Hey – your car's not on the blink is it, boss?'

'My car's been pristine since the day I bought it, thank you very much.'

Derek hung up and Raj was left wondering what that was all about; at the same time, his boss dialled Directory Enquiries and got the number for Maltby's garage. The car was fine as far as they knew. She certainly hadn't called them to say there was a problem with it. He called the carhire firm next. Yes, Miss Harvey had returned the car, no problems. No, she hadn't booked one with them since.

It was probably nothing to worry about. She

must have been tired, put her journey off for a couple of days. *You're a bloody old fool, man.* Yet despite his admonitions to himself, Derek phoned Deborah's home number. All he got was the answering machine. *OK, so she's out somewhere. Leave the lass alone. She deserves a break, won't want you breathing down her neck.* Of course she was all right. Of course she was.

The tree was dressed, food and mulled wine prepared and suitable Christmas music on the stereo system. Caitlin ran down the stairs, freshly showered and changed, looking hopefully at her brother.

'Any luck getting hold of the Walters?'

Daniel shook his head. 'No. They could have gone away for Christmas, I suppose. I left a message on the machine, though. Left one with Deborah Harvey, too, and with Chris Farmer. As soon as he's back, I'll get him to liaise with Colin and Ronnie. Someone has to remember who that boy was. He should be in the guest book, too.'

'Did they have one back then? And would they still have it?'

'Hopefully. We'll find out soon.' He smiled and hugged his sister, willing her to share his optimism. 'Are you sure you're up to this evening? You could phone and put them off, you know. Cancel it.'

She had been so pleased to have last-minute volunteers for the Shelter that she was giving them supper tonight and going to run through things with them one last time.

'And waste all my hard work? No way! I

promised them, and besides, it will take our minds off this wretched business. I'm fine, Daniel, really.'

'As long as you're sure.'

'I'm sure.'

Alex Palmer made an extra visit to Deborah before leaving the house.

'Will I pass muster?' He paraded before her, a picture of elegance in suit, tie and waistcoat.

'For what?' She was puzzled. Why would he seek her approval?

'Didn't I tell you?' He smiled, knowing full well he hadn't. 'I have a supper invitation this evening. With Caitlin.'

Mike and Nina were on their way to The Sleeping Dragon, the venue for the evening's party. It was the last thing Nina wanted to do after her experience in the shower. Palm. That was what was common to each of the visions. Palm of hand, palm tree, the cathedral in Palma de Mallorca. What did it mean? Palm. Palma. She had been pronouncing it in her head the Spanish way, sounding the '1'. It was only as Mike changed down a gear as the car struggled up a notoriously steep and twisting hill that she found herself putting two and two together. Palm. Palm. Palmer. Not Palma. *Palmer.* She felt a surge of energy, knew the connection was right. Palmer. Before the evening was even underway, she was desperate to get home and check out the names on Caitlin's T'ai Chi class list. She would lay money on the fact that that name was there.

Terry made two false starts before finally holding his nerve and going through with the phone call. What if Daniel answered? What if they'd gone away for Christmas? His journey would have been wasted.

The phone was answered on the second ring. A man's voice. Not Daniel. A boyfriend, maybe?

'Hello – do I have the right number for Caitlin O'Connor?'

'Indeed you do, but I'm afraid she's a bit tied up at present. Can I take a message for you?'

Terry could hear music, voices, laughter. She was having a party.

'Yes, please. Would you make sure only Caitlin gets it? It's a surprise, you see. We don't want her brother to know.'

'Certainly. Christmas surprise, eh? That's nice. What's the message?'

'This is her father speaking. Would you tell her I'm sorry about the other day – she'll know what that means – and that I'm at the Highfield Holiday Cottages, Carnegie Road? Ivy Cottage, number two.' He took a deep breath before giving the phone number. 'Would you ask her to give me a call, please?'

'Absolutely. And her brother is not to know?'

'That's right. Don't want to spoil the surprise. Thank you very much.'

'My pleasure.'

Alex Palmer put down Caitlin's phone, his heart beating like a trip hammer. *Oh yes. Oh yes.* It had been wonderful enough tonight when he had found Daniel staying with Caitlin, a Daniel who neither recognised him from years ago nor from the recent Open Day. *I was right to steer clear of him there. My intuition was correct. I am aligned! Aligned!*

But now Terry, too? Here in Cheltenham? All of them in the one place? It has to be a sign. The green light. At last! At last! I have all of them now...

Chapter Thirty-one

Christmas Eve

He was manic. Exultant. Reporting on the previous evening's supper party, he was almost glowing with some kind of perverted religious fervour. Deborah was afraid, growing more heartsick with his every word.

'Don't you see? It all makes sense, now. They have been delivered into my hands. All three of them *here*. All three of them at the same time. Not only does *she* not have a clue, neither does Daniel. We were at the Community Open day together just weeks ago. He didn't recognise me then. Doesn't remember me now. I am protected, Deborah. Invisible to their scrutiny. And all are here now. Delivered into my hands! The plan must be changed. I no longer have to wait. I can do it now. Kill all three of them.'

The sign had come! That wonderful moment when the phone had rung, Daniel and Caitlin both in the kitchen with their hands full and he had called out, 'Shall I get it?' He had got more than he could ever have bargained for. Terry Richardson. He smiled at Deborah, rocking on his heels in exultation.

'I know where he is. This changes everything, Deborah. No more spaces between them. No more waiting. Caitlin shall be tomorrow, as planned, but why not the others, too? Or maybe Terry or Daniel tonight... Maybe both of them! No, no. Nothing to upset Caitlin. I couldn't do that, now, could I? I shall have to think about this. Plan it carefully. There can be no margin for error now I have them all together. Cheer up!' He shook her by the shoulders. 'It will soon be over, Deborah. Just imagine that!'

She could. All too well.

It was so clear to Nina now. She was floating above it all, the new perspective putting things into place, revealing that which had been hidden. She had been right. Palmer was Alex Palmer, a member of Caitlin's T'ai Chi class. She could see his demons, his torments, the sick train of his reasoning. She could see Caitlin and Daniel. Someone else, too, who she knew, without knowing how she knew, to be their father. He was in Cheltenham, now. Alex was the predator. They were his prey. There was a rippling, a kind of hushed sigh through this place where she was that was no-place. Deborah Harvey. Where was she? How did she fit into the images she saw now with such ease? She called to her. Called again.

Nina was jolted by a falling sensation. How odd. She was not in the least bit afraid, even though the falling had confirmed for her that it was not her body that had been jolted. She was not in her body. What had happened? She did not allow herself to pursue the matter further for, at that moment, Deborah Harvey came into view. Captured. Imprisoned. And somehow, at the hub of things.

Nina was floating again now. It was very nice to float. She forced herself to focus. Danger. She had to get help. And who was this other woman she now saw? Not one woman, but two, the first like a tramp, down there, far below, in Cheltenham; the second, somehow in this place that was no-place, here with Nina. Ah. Of course. Laura. Nina had never realised that Caitlin looked so like her mother...

When the nurses changed shift, there were murmurings and mutterings about the evils of drink-driving joy-riders. The police had been in pursuit and said the Shawcross's oncoming vehicle hadn't stood a chance of avoiding the collision. Bad enough at any time, but at Christmas... Mr Shawcross was a lecturer at the University and had been airlifted, unconscious, to a specialist unit with severe spinal injuries. His wife, Nina, was fighting for her life, in a coma in ICU.

There had still been no word from Ronnie. Colin had phoned just about every hospital he could think of between Darrowdale and the Highlands. No one fitting his wife's description had been admitted as a result of an accident.

Caitlin was still as efficient in her arrangements as when she was a child. Hours to go, and already she was checking her sleeping bag, bringing down a pillow. Daniel smiled to himself, thinking back to happier days. There was another plus, of course. While she was fussing about, he had the kitchen to himself, and that had given him the opportunity to set his mind at rest – or otherwise. He rummaged in the rubbish bin, distaste over-ridden by his need to know. He'd seen one of the volunteers scribble a phone message last night, seen him pass it to Caitlin and watched as she'd read it. Had he imagined the tightening in her face? It was gone as quickly as it had appeared, the mask of normality slipping back into place so smoothly it had made him question the reality of what he thought he had seen. Imagined or not, there was no mistaking his sister's next action. She had slipped past Daniel and a couple of their guests, graceful as a ballet dancer, and, scrunch-ing the paper into a ball, had thrust it into the bin. Never said a word. It was if the whole thing had never happened. Surely it could not have been a message from the letter-writer? She would have told him. Christ – she'd have been livid.

Ah! Here it was. While stained from the detritus among which it had nestled all night, it was, at least, not too soggy. Daniel smoothed it out, saw his father's name, the message he'd left. It was a shame there was no mirror. It would have shocked him to see the same expression he had witnessed on Caitlin's face take hold now of his own.

The hall that had been taken over by the Shelter for the Homeless had been transformed from its usual drab functionality into as welcoming a place as it could ever be. It was festooned with Christmas decorations and a very large real Christmas tree stood in the corner by the front door, bearing, along with the usual baubles and tinsel, a sign welcoming the guests who would be spending time here over the holiday period. Mattresses were piled against the walls to make more space during the day, and one of the small side rooms held two tables now stacked high with men's and women's clothing, all donated, clean and in good repair, to be given free to those who needed it. A large television set stood against the back wall, and had barely been switched off at all since the Shelter had opened its doors. To its left was the open door which led through to the kitchen and eating area, from which mouth-watering smells emanated, making many a stomach growl in anticipation of the fare to come. Tea and coffee were constantly available, two large urns keeping water forever on the boil. People sat in chairs, gathered at tables, watched TV, talked and dozed against a background of quiet, cheerful efficiency from the volunteer staff.

Mags's eyes followed as Lucy, a young volunteer, pinned a notice to the board by the kitchen doorway. For want of anything better to do, she ambled across the hall to look at it when the girl disappeared. It was a list detailing the names of the Shelter volunteers and the hours they would be working. First names only, but one, at least, caused Mags to flinch internally. Caitlin. *Even here, I can't get away from what I did. It's no good running, but then I never thought it was. But here. At Christmas. Hardly the time or place I would have expected a reminder of Caitlin Richardson.*

Deborah was sweating with fear. He had gone upstairs for a while, but had come back, icy cool and detached, with everything planned down to the smallest detail. *In triplicate. Plans A, B and C. No stone left unturned. Oh God, never mind stones, put a boulder in his way! Do something! Help me to do something! I don't want to die. I'm too young to die.*

How did people turn themselves into killing machines? How did they come to feel so detached from other human beings that they had not a second thought about the taking of another life?

Despite the perspiration, she was cold, chilled by the horror of what Alex Palmer was planning to do, struck, as if for the first time, by the knowledge that she herself would soon be dead unless she did something to prevent him taking that action. Deborah was calling forth parts of herself she never knew existed, parts which, despite the increasing terror she was coming to feel – or maybe because of it – were pulling plans from the hat of her resourceful unconscious which shocked her. One part of her felt sure she was going mad. Another part assured her she had never been so sane. Alex Palmer had to be stopped. And she was the only one who could do it.

Josh Middleton's face creased into a smile as Daniel Richardson called his sister to the phone.

'Hi, there – I wanted to catch you before you go off for Night Duty at the Shelter. How are things? How's living with your brother? And what's the situation with the letters?'

Caitlin laughed. 'What is this? Twenty Questions?'

'No. Rampant curiosity. Because I love you.'

'I love you, too.'

'I can't tell you how happy I am to hear that. Talk to me, Caitlin.'

'Well... Living with Daniel is fine, except he's overprotective, but I can understand that. To a degree. The letters ... well ... they've taken a weird turn. Really weird. But, Josh – I think it's caused a breakthrough. That is, we think we know who's behind them, except we don't actually know his name. Daniel's left messages with Colin Walters – with any luck, his records will put the final piece in the jigsaw puzzle.'

'Thank God for that!'

'I knew you'd be pleased. Nina will be, too.'

'You haven't told her yet?'

'No reply. I've rung her a couple of times. She's probably doing last-minute shopping or something. Sooner her than me!'

Colin Walters was more than a little irritable. What the hell was Ronnie playing at? Come to that, what was Daniel Richardson playing at? He'd listened, baffled, to the answer phone message asking who the ginger-haired boy was who'd been staying with the Latimers the summer Laura had disappeared. What the hell did he want to know that for? Momentarily diverted from his growing frustration at the mystery of Ronnie's silence, he allowed his mind to skip back. Could he remember him? Skinny, foreign – foreign name, at least, even if he couldn't now remember it. He snorted, giving up the effort. Fat chance. And he'd destroyed the records. Oh well. It couldn't be that important.

Deborah had all the pieces of the past. All that Alex was willing to give her. Was there anything more? She doubted it. She rubbed her eyes. Would Derek ever get these notebooks? Would she still be alive if he did? She'd had a hard time keeping up with Alex's account on more than one occasion. It wasn't only the shorthand; it was the mental gymnastics necessary to understand his perspective on life, his convoluted logic. How, for instance, had he managed to live such an apparently normal life for so many years? He even ran a business, although he had no financial need to do so. He had been perturbed by her questions on that front.

'Why work when I don't need to?' He had frowned. 'But I *do* need to – not for money, no. But because I love computers, Deborah. They're my life. If only people were so easy to fix, to programme...'

She rubbed her face in frustration, considering the possibility that he may never have killed again, after Laura, had it not been for – what? A couple of factors, at least. Once his mother and stepfather had left the Darrowdale Community, they had eventually settled in Gloucestershire. By his own admission, Alex had not visited often

403

until his mother had developed terminal cancer. Then, in long conversations with Doc, the secrets of their marriage had been revealed. One set of fears – drink or drug addiction – had been allayed. Others had been confirmed. Terry Richardson had not been her only lover.

'They didn't talk about sex addiction years ago, Deborah. She'd open her legs for anybody and you know what? The terrible irony, from Doc's point of view? He, who couldn't father children, wound up aborting the evidence of her liaisons. By Christ, I'd have killed her, had she been mine.'

Deborah's mind had whirred, replaying an early conversation with Ronnie Walters. 'People in the Community thought she'd had a miscarriage the day of Laura's disappearance, brought on by the shock.'

He'd laughed then. 'Tied in nicely, didn't it? She slipped on the stairs, Doc said, in her eagerness to join the search party. That accounted for the bang on the head, too – not that she remembered that. After all my efforts...'

Why couldn't they have moved to some other part of the country? At least then maybe Alex wouldn't have found Caitlin. That, apparently, was the trigger that had set him off.

'I thought it was over, Deborah. Even watching my mother die by inches left me curiously...' He had pondered the correct word, always a stickler for accuracy. '...detached. I no longer wanted to kill her. Not then. But it was meant to be, the resurrection of it all. Pre-ordained. How else do you account for my move to Cheltenham? My

404

visit to the Complementary Health Centre?'

His voice had grown dangerously quiet. In the long silence which followed, Deborah knew better than to interrupt. He was thinking, putting together the pieces of the jigsaw puzzle before presenting her with the completed picture.

'It was just after my mother died. I wasn't sleeping well. Nightmares. Nightmares I hadn't had since I was a child. I'd heard one of my clients talking about the benefits of Reiki and thought I'd give it a go. Why not? Better than drugs, eh? So I went to the Clinic, and they have photographs of their practitioners in Reception. I couldn't breathe, the shock was so great. She's so like her mother, you know – for one absurd moment, I thought it was Laura. Then I saw her name. Caitlin. The surname was different, but I thought she must be married. But that name. That face. My whole body buzzed, Deborah. It was like an electric current, tingling, flowing. I was reconnected.'

He had drawn a deep breath before continuing. 'I never did book for Reiki. Once I'd seen her picture, I had to know. I joined her T'ai Chi class. Even the fact that she taught T'ai Chi was another confirmation, but I had to be absolutely sure. And then I was. And I knew she had to die. That they all had to die. They were what tied me to the past, a past I'd worked so hard to overcome, to put behind me. Do you think I'm mad, Deborah?'

The question had thrown her. What could she say? She had hedged her bets. 'Not necessarily. Maybe...'

'What? Sick? Evil? Who is mad and who is well? Surely only time will tell...'

He had chanted those last words like a rhyme, and that had signalled the beginning of another manic phase. So much had been pent up for so long, it had tumbled out of his mouth like a flash flood in a river. What was it, Deborah wondered – some sort of unburdening?

Recounting the disposal of Laura Richardson's body had been a part of it. Caitlin had been chanting, he said, though he couldn't make out the words. Hearing her voice recede, he had risked a glance over the wall, only to see her cutting across the other field. The long way. She was taking the long way home. There was still time to cover his tracks if Doc would co-operate. He had rushed back to the Farmhouse, told Doc that Laura was dead.

What had gone through Stephen Latimer's mind? Whatever it was, it hadn't impaired his thinking. He'd run across to Laura's car, seen the keys in the ignition, shoved Alex into it and told him about the break in the hedge at the far boundary with the monk's land. She reread Alex's account.

'He said he'd used it once himself – never said why – perhaps I should have asked him. That's when I was most afraid, you know. Driving back to the track, but the other way round. I was thinking of Caitlin. Thinking how she must have been on her way home when she saw ... I couldn't risk it a second time. And the exposure ... have you seen the land there, the dirt track, the wall, before the tree line starts? Of course you have.' He had stopped talking then and she had looked up, seeing him close his eyes for an all too brief moment before looking at her again, smiling, for God's sake.

'So many risks, Deborah. So many ifs, ands, and buts. But no one saw me put her body in the car. I covered her up with her own work. A blanket first, then that stuff she'd made, slate work. Fitting, don't you think? I do so like things to be fitting. My stepfather was right about the break in the hedge, but it had been disguised so well, I thought I'd never find it. That was my only moment of panic. Once through, it was easy. I followed his instructions to the letter. It was quite a drive to the old gravel pit. He was right about the depth, too. Everything sank without a trace. They still haven't found them, have they? Her body or the car.'

How had he and his stepfather held their nerve? Alex had said it had taken him several hours to walk back to the Community and sneak in the way he'd left. A Community search party had been called by then, but Stephen Latimer hadn't taken part, telling everyone that his wife had slipped on the stairs and suffered a miscarriage. Alex had joined in, however, moving from one group to another, no one suspecting anything for a moment.

He had slid an envelope across the table to her at that point in his account. It contained an Ordnance Survey map.

'X marks the spot,' he told her. It was his idea of an attempt at humour.

Deborah's own had disappeared long ago.

407

It was dark when Colin Walters drove back into Darrowdale. There was still a light in Deborah Harvey's window. Her car was still parked outside the flat. He drove past and made a left turn. He couldn't go hammering on her door again. Wearily, he pulled into the car park behind what had been the Tulip Cinema many years ago and was now just a derelict shell. He had to get his head straight. He had to– *Oh my God...*

He stared in disbelief at the vehicle illuminated by his headlights. It was Ronnie's car.

Daniel closed the front door after waving goodbye to Caitlin. He'd been talked out of taking her to her shift himself, and one of the volunteers had collected her, a Mrs Hordern. At least she should be safe at the Shelter. Meanwhile, he had things to sort out. She had been unable to raise Mike and Nina on the phone, so he would keep trying, in order to finalise arrangements for tomorrow. There were other things, too, like wrapping her presents and trying to sort out the unwelcome problem of their father.

'I'm Liam. What's your name, then?' The man was tall, gaunt, had probably once been good-looking. Living rough had ravaged his face and blackened his teeth.

'Caitlin.'

She smiled. They shook hands, Liam apologising for the grimy state of his own.

'Caitlin? I've got your name tattooed on my arm.'

'Really?'

'Really. That's why you and me are going to bed together, later.'

Anne, one of the other volunteers, a veteran of many years, laughed.

'Wow, Caitlin! It's your lucky day!'

'No, darlin' – it's her un-fuckin-lucky day!' Liam shook his head, thinking about the wife he'd left behind long ago, the children he'd tried to phone yesterday, pretending he was Father Christmas. That's when the thugs had pounced, young muggers, three of them, no more than thirteen or fourteen years old. A few years ago and he could have handled them, no sweat. Knocked their fuckin' heads together. He closed his eyes and coughed, a spasm that made a sound like his ribs were rattling. Caitlin brought him a mug of tea and a plate of toast.

'Thank you, darlin'.' As he stretched out his hands, she glanced at the flesh that showed beneath the too-short sleeves. He was right. He really did have 'Caitlin' tattooed on his arm.

Colin was in a cold sweat. He and Ronnie had always carried a spare set of keys for the other's vehicle, and he had jumped out of the Land Rover and opened up Ronnie's estate with shaking hands. What if she'd had a heart attack? A stroke? Those headaches she'd been getting... She wasn't there. But what the hell was the car doing here? It was cold. How long...? He searched it thoroughly. Everything was as it had been when he'd waved goodbye to her. He laughed aloud at the incongruity of such a miracle. No one had stolen the car. No one had broken into it. It was crazy. He locked it again, brain having to adjust to the only thing that made sense. The only reason he could think of why she would have parked here. A flash of fear coursed through his body so strongly that his thought processes ceased to be logical. He didn't even jump into his own vehicle and drive. Just broke into a run with only one goal in mind. Deborah Harvey's flat...

It was a neighbour over the road who phoned the police to say that a man had forced entry into the flats opposite. By the time they arrived on the scene, Deborah Harvey's front door had been kicked open and the smell of blood and decay was pervading the whole of the vestibule area. They could get no sense at all out of the dishevelled man who, by the look of him, had done all the kicking. He was whimpering like a baby and quite unable to speak.

It was late. Alex told Deborah that he would be gone for some time, promising only that he would be back before going to the Shelter to give Caitlin her promised lift home early on Christmas morning.

'I shall report in before picking her up. Leave you a tape to transcribe.'

'A tape?'

'Oh yes. I have decided. So far, you have only my account. The Richardsons shall each give their own. My innate generosity, you see.' He held up the miniature recorder. 'I have a good supply of tapes. Not sure how long they last, or, come to that, how long *they'll* last.' He laughed. The sound made Deborah want to vomit. 'When I come back, Deborah, you can transcribe while I'm collecting Caitlin, taking her to her date with destiny. I shall give you the tape and you shall hear it all for yourself. Terry Richardson's death.'

Chapter Thirty-two

Christmas Day
Part One

Christmas Eve turned to Christmas Day with the mellow chiming of the mantel clock in the corner of the hall. Most of the Shelter's guests were already asleep, many having arrived late on Christmas Eve in a state of near exhaustion, one new female included. The lanky kid with dreadlocks was one of the few exceptions. He turned to the withered-looking old man in the chair on his right, face alight with pleasure.

'Mornin', mate – Happy Christmas!'

'Happy Christmas! Has he been?'

'Who?'

'Whaddya mean, who? Santa fuckin' Claus!'

Another voice entered the conversation, face hidden in the semi-darkness. 'Don't be daft – they got no fuckin' chimney here, you cunt!'

Terry Richardson had watched the clock with sinking spirits. Technically, it was now Christmas

411

Day, and he had heard nothing from Katie. He had so hoped, after having left that message... He shook his head, trying to ignore the tears that squeezed their way between closed eyelids. He sniffed, but it didn't help. He retrieved a grubby handkerchief from his trouser pocket and blew his nose. *I'm not going to drink. I'm* not. *It won't solve anything.*

He stood up, unsure of what to do. He couldn't phone now. Knew he couldn't sleep, either. She could be at a party. She could be – but wasn't it more likely that she simply didn't want to contact him? He swallowed hard. *I'm not going to drink. I'm* not.

He struggled to remember Father Mac's goodness, Father Richard's advice. *Maybe I should have gone to Midnight Mass. Confession. Maybe God is waiting for me to make a proper move. Be reconciled, like the priests said. Oh God! I'll do it. I'll go to confession as soon as a church is open. I'll do anything you like. Just please,* please, *give me back my daughter.*

Derek Kenny was in bed, awake but relaxed, when the phone rang. He rolled over and reached out to switch on the lamp before answering it.

'Boss, it's Tim. You'd better get over here. We had a tip-off.' Tim Reynolds' words were shaky. The hairs on the back of Derek's neck bristled at the sound of his reporter's voice.

'What's up, lad? And where's "here"?'

'The police will need to speak to you. It's about Deborah. I'm at Deborah Harvey's flat.' Reynolds pulled himself together with the effort of being precise.

Derek's stomach lurched. 'Deborah? Oh my God. Tell me straight – is she alright?'

'No one knows. She's not here. But there is a dead woman and ... Boss – just get the hell over here, will you?'

Derek was out of the door faster than an athlete off the blocks.

Caitlin raised her head. She was sitting in an overstuffed armchair and must have been dozing. The television had been turned off long ago and the only sounds were breathing and snoring, punctuated by an occasional, incoherent mumbling made by one or other of the guests. The women's lavatories had flushed twice in quick succession and she could hear the taps running. That must have been what had roused her. Which was fine, but she had not been aware of any women going past her to use them. Could she actually have been asleep? Still ... maybe it was best to check. She got up silently, padding towards the toilets, glancing at the sleeping figures she passed on the way. There were, apparently, three women in the shelter, but Caitlin had met none of them so far. They had retired for an early night, she had been told, in one of the side rooms. Here, in the main hall, the near darkness made illegible mounds and fantastic shapes of the men zipped up in sleeping bags on top of mattresses.

She moved in slippered feet, careful not to tread on anyone, heading for the now light entrance to the Ladies' toilets. She passed Rod, an older man, head of the Night Shift, who looked at her questioningly. She indicated where she was going and he smiled as she passed. Two guests, lying not far from the doorway, were tossing restlessly in the light. Caitlin stepped into the entrance, closing the door behind her. The short passageway opened to the right, revealing two cubicles ahead and two behind. She could now hear a quiet humming, but the figure who emerged from a cubicle was not what she had expected.

'Oh!' She let out an involuntary gasp.

'Sorry, Caitlin – didn't mean to scare you, mate!'

'Fixit! What on earth are you doing in the Ladies' loos?'

They were both speaking in whispers. Fixit was a regular at the Shelter, a small, wiry man with a shock of greying hair, who had kept Caitlin entertained for hours with tales of the travelling he'd done in France and Spain in his younger years.

'Nothin' pervy, darlin' – honest!' He took her arm and gently pushed open the toilet doors one by one. 'I was thinkin' about the ladies, see – not often we get ladies 'ere, is it? And I got to thinkin', like, 'ow it might be good to smarten things up a bit. Scrounged some of them runner things what Grannies used to 'ave on their sideboards and chair arms, and I bin puttin' 'em on the cisterns, like. Make it a bit more 'omely, if you see what I mean?'

Caitlin could see. She could also see that he had been doing a spot of cleaning, too. Tears blurred her eyes for a second. 'That's brilliant, Fixit. Really... Thank you.' She didn't trust herself to speak further. He beamed at her happily.

'Thanks, Caitlin. Merry Christmas.'

'Merry Christmas, Fixit.'

She watched as he walked out, then went into one of the cubicles to get paper on which to blow her nose. She heard the outer door open, wondered if he had forgotten something and come back for it. Walking out of the cubicle, she opened her mouth to speak, but found it wasn't Fixit after all. It was a woman. A woman who crossed herself, the colour draining from her face as she whispered, 'Holy Mother of God! Laura!'

Derek felt a million years old. Dried out. Fossilised. He hadn't felt this bad since Laura disappeared. He splashed his face with cold water, looked at the dripping image he presented to himself in the washroom mirror. He looked grey. It was worse even than he had feared. The dead woman was Ronnie Walters. The still-gibbering man the neighbours had seen kicking the door down was her husband. Derek had had to give the police details of Deborah's family. She wasn't there. Hardly surprising, since, as Colin had told him earlier, her car was still parked in the street. No way could Deborah have killed Ronnie. No way. Which made things far more serious. Who *had* killed Ronnie? And where the hell was Deborah? The logical assumption, to him, at least, was that Ronnie's murderer had taken Deborah with him. Derek suddenly felt very, very sick.

Caitlin stared at the woman, concern mingling with disbelief.

'What did you call me?'

The woman staggered, clutching at the door of the nearest cubicle.

'Laura ... God forgive me!'

Blinking rapidly, Caitlin stepped forward, took her arm and manoeuvred her backwards, lowering her onto the lavatory seat.

'Not Laura. Caitlin. My mother was Laura. Laura Richardson.' She peered into the woman's face, struggling for some clue to her identity. 'Do I know you?'

The woman returned her gaze, eyes brimming with tears. 'God forgive me, you do. I'm Mags now, but that wasn't my name then...' Never taking her eyes from Caitlin's face, she reached up and pulled off the hat she had insisted on wearing, even indoors. A long, thick plait, black streaked with grey, fell loose.

Caitlin's face lit up with recognition. 'Rosie! Rosie Dwyer!' She reached forward to hug her, but was pushed away.

'No! No! You don't know the truth! I betrayed you – all of you. It was all my fault!'

Caitlin backed away, baffled. 'I don't understand. What was your fault, Rosie?'

'Mags. My name is Mags. Margaret Rose Dwyer. I dropped Rosie when I left Darrowdale. Your father called me Rosie and I never let anyone do it again.'

Oh God... Not Rosie? Another one of Dad's conquests? Caitlin bit her lip and reached for toilet paper. 'Here. Blow your nose.' She helped Mags to her feet and led her to the washbasins, watching as she splashed her face with cold

416

water. Rosie Dwyer had not been among the names her father had given to Daniel and Deborah. Why not? What else had he been hiding? A ladder-backed dining chair stood near the hand dryers and Caitlin sat Mags on it before perching herself in the space between the sinks .

'Why don't you tell me about it? I take it you were sleeping with my father.' Her voice was gentle as she added, 'You weren't the only one, you know.'

Mags choked back a sound like barked bitterness. 'You don't need to tell me that! I found him. The day your mother disappeared.' Tears slid down her cheeks. 'Oh God, how could I have done it? I loved you and your brother. Your mother was my friend. Oh God...'

'What's done is done, Rosie – Mags. Daniel and I have learned a lot about our father of late.' Caitlin paused. 'He's not exactly what you'd call a very nice man.'

'Maybe not. Maybe not. But it takes two to tango. I was willing enough. Not at first, mind. I was a virgin, you know. I don't think he'd ever had a virgin.' Her voice tailed away.

'So you were having an affair. But what did you mean about finding him the day my mother disappeared?'

Mags gave a low moan. 'It was terrible. Judgement on me, that's what it was. I shouldn't even have been there – we used the broken down croft near the monks' land...'

'We know.'

Mags flushed scarlet. 'I shouldn't have been there. We didn't have an arrangement for that

417

day, but somehow ... thinking about him ... I found myself nearby and...' She closed her eyes, face creased with pain. 'He was with someone. Naked. Doing it.'

'Helen Latimer.'

Mags shook her head. 'I didn't see her face. His neither, come to that. But when she'd gone, I flew at him.' She laughed, a terrible empty sound. 'Can you believe it? The pot calling the kettle black? I thought he loved me, you know. Stupid, stupid woman...' She thumped her fists on her thighs.

'You flew at him, you said?'

'Yelled at him. Called him everything from a pig to a dog. Told him he didn't deserve anyone. He didn't answer me. Never said a word. I grabbed his arm – I meant no harm, just wanted him to talk, but no ... and he pushed me, tried to make me let go. Shook me off like a dog with a rat, he did, and I fell and hit my head...'

'Good God! But why didn't you tell anyone? It's not as if you were married, like Helen Latimer. You could have told the police he was there.'

Mags laughed again, hollowness ringing on the hard surfaces around her.

'I would have done. I meant to. He can't have killed her, you know. Your mother. He drove off, across the edge of the monks' land – he had his car hidden away behind the hedge. I watched him with my own eyes, heading back to town. And when Janet Wilkerson said she'd seen Laura walking away from the Farmhouse around twenty past three – well, it doesn't add up, does it?'

Caitlin's brain seemed numb as she tried to

418

calculate time and distance in her head. 'But you could have told – in fact, if anything, you could have given him an alibi. The police nearly crucified him, you know.'

'Oh, I know. And he nearly crucified me. Didn't want it coming out about him and Helen Latimer. Nor me, though for different reasons. He said if the police thought he was a serial adulterer, they'd see it as a motive for wanting rid of your mother.' She rubbed her face and shook her head. 'He said a whole lot of things. Threatened to expose me, if he had to. Oh, it all seems so stupid now, but I was so afraid. So *ashamed.* We had rows. Each had the dirt on the other, if you like, but he always swore blind he never touched Laura. Never even saw her. And I did believe him, because of Janet seeing her. She was supposed to meet you at half past three, wasn't she?'

Caitlin nodded. 'You remember? After all this time?'

'Don't you? Seared into my mind, it is. Every detail of that day. I've carried it with me. I've...' She stopped herself. 'What I'm trying to say is, if Janet saw your mother at twenty past three and she was supposed to meet you at half past, then whatever happened must have happened in those next few minutes. And your father wasn't there.'

Caitlin closed her eyes, visualising the landscape. 'Could he have looped round, do you think?'

'Not if we're talking a few minutes, he couldn't. I watched him all the way down the track and onto the main road. He turned left, back towards town. And if he had come back, surely someone would have seen him – seen the car. It's not as if

419

your mother went missing and her car was left behind, is it? If your father had driven back and done something to her – well, he could only drive one vehicle at a time, right? But he couldn't have come back on foot in less than twenty minutes or more, from where I saw him.'

There was silence. *Mummy was seen near the Farmhouse, heading home. Less than a five-minute walk. Then nothing. As if she – and her car – vanished from the face of the earth. What in God's name happened?* Caitlin brought her attention back to the woman before her.

'I'm so sorry, Caitlin. I'm so, so sorry. I couldn't live with myself. I had to leave.'

'We thought you'd gone to another Community.'

'Oh, I did. For a while. But the headaches got worse, and I got sick...'

'Headaches?'

'After I fell – when your father pushed me – I had headaches off and on for years. Off a lot, until of late. I couldn't settle at the new Community. Thinking of your father. Your mother. All of you. The way I betrayed you. I tried to make my peace, but the priest, he ... never mind. I got sick. I've never settled anywhere since. Not for long.'

She stood up, splashed her face again. 'I found myself up there, you know. A couple of weeks ago. Near the Community. They were having an Open Day...'

'Daniel was there.'

Mags nodded. 'I saw a newspaper. That's when the headaches came back. When I was near Darrowdale again. Bad, they've been. I didn't mean to go back there, I didn't! I promised Our Lady. I've avoided it like the plague. Punishment, that's what it is. Guilty conscience.' Her weeping now was unrestrained. She looked fit to collapse.

Caitlin looked at her, remembering the Rosie she had known and loved as a child, how she had envied her plait, her easy way with the animals. To think she had been brought to this. Whatever she had done, she did not deserve this. *Right now, I could kill my bloody father...*

'Rosie – Mags – I'm sure Our Lady wouldn't punish you like that. You've been punishing yourself, all these years...' Silently, she moved forward and enveloped the weeping woman in her arms.

Nina was floating again, effortlessly sending and receiving wordless information to and from Laura Richardson, to and from others. She so wanted to help. She had been to the Light. Been and come back, to float for one last time, making her goodbyes before returning to her body. Not goodbyes. She would see them again. Would eventually enter that Light to be embraced by it and transformed into a new mode of being. But not now. Not yet. There was work to be done. Her mission was not yet accomplished. First, she had to go back to her body, go through the pain and out into consciousness once again. She felt a strange falling sensation, not unpleasant in itself, but accompanied by an increasing feeling of heaviness, as if she were somehow becoming denser, more contained. It was... It was agony. Being back. She felt swamped by physicality and the sensations that accompanied it. Now she had to fight. Before it was too late...

Terry Richardson was lying on the sofa, slippered feet hanging over one end. He flicked through TV channels with the volume set on mute, before a sudden thought struck him. He changed to Teletext, then sat frozen before the screen, rubbing his eyes in disbelief. *Jesus God!* He fumbled for his jacket, pulled his spectacles from the inside pocket to check, to make sure his eyes were not deceiving him. His mouth went dry. *Jesus God! Jesus God! I'm not seeing things. I'm not!*

He fumbled in his pockets for something else, heart hammering, as the entryphone buzzer sounded, cutting through the silence, unscrambling his thoughts. The door! Katie! It had to be Katie! His prayers had been answered! *All* his prayers had been answered!

Jumping to his feet, he headed for the stairs.

Breakfast was being served in shifts at the Shelter from six o'clock onwards, and its guests were stretching, yawning, coughing and hacking as they were awakened by others around them. The smell of toast and bacon filled the hall. Stomachs growled and a queue began to form in the dining area.

'How do I look?' Trev, a ratty little man, did a perfect pirouette. Those who knew him, smiled. Those who didn't, stared. Fixit laughed.

'Very nice, Trev. Just your style. Not so sure about the colour, though.'

Trev looked doubtfully at the silver-grey ladies suit he was wearing, plunging neckline showing the concave hollow of his ribs, the fitted skirt barely reaching his knobbly knees. He had had his eye on it since yesterday and had pulled it from the pile of donated women's clothing and saved it specially for this morning. He pulled a face, disappointed.

'Never mind, eh? I could tart it up a bit.'

'You're already a tart, you sad git!' someone offered.

'Leave 'im alone!' Fixit shot a warning glance at the offender.

'Anyone seen Caitlin?' Rod, glad to have got through the night without incident, was looking around hopefully.

'Not for a while. I seen her in the middle of the night, like, but not since then. Why?' Fixit was frowning.

'Oh ... it's nothing. Just need to prepare for the handover report.' Maybe she was in the toilets. Or outside, having a cigarette. No. That couldn't be right. She didn't smoke. Never mind. She couldn't be far away.

Deborah Harvey had been busy during Alex's absence. Now, with everything planned and in place, she was strangely calm. She had used the sticky backing strips of sanitary towels to attach the notebooks to her body and tucked her clothing in well. She had to live to tell, and those notebooks held the tale. He would surely be back soon, and that would be it. Only one attempt could be made to get out, and it had to succeed. There could be no dress rehearsal, save within her head. There would be no second chance.

She focused every ounce of concentration on the image of the door at the top of the cellar stairs, the door that led to freedom. She held it, visualised herself getting through it, getting out of this house, getting help. She was still holding the image when she heard Alex snapping open the padlock to her prison...

Daniel looked at the number pinned to the cork board in the hallway and punched it into the phone.

'Christmas Centre for the Homeless. Rod speaking.'

'Good morning, Rod, and Happy Christmas! Can I speak to Caitlin O'Connor, please? It's her brother.'

He waited while she came to the phone. 'Hi, Daniel! Happy Christmas!'

'Happy Christmas, Cait! I was just phoning to check you're still alright for your lift. I went to Mike and Nina's last night, but there was no one home. Must have been out partying.'

'Let's hope they're up now, then! Oh damn – we'll need to contact them to let them know... Daniel, something so bizarre has happened – are you ever in for a surprise!'

'What? Cait, you're rambling!'

'No I'm not – I just don't want to spoil it. I'll phone Mike and Nina when I get home – there'll be an extra person for lunch! And before you start worrying, yes, my lift is still on. Alex should be here any minute.'

Several streets away, Alex Palmer stepped

through the doorway of his cellar, calling, 'He's dead, Deborah! Terry Richardson is dead and—'

Whatever else he was about to say was cut off as Deborah brought a chair down over his head, letting out a howl of concentrated fury as she did so. As Alex pitched onto his knees, she leaped over him, out of the door, and, taking the stairs two at a time, surged upwards towards escape. She was almost at the top when he flung himself on top of her, sliding down her body as she squirmed, but managing to grip her ankle. She let out a scream and kicked desperately, making a contact that sent him crashing down the stairs. Without looking back, she lurched up the last few steps towards the door, bursting into the ground floor of his house. She'd made it.

Muriel and Jenny had arrived early for their Christmas Morning stint at the Shelter, beaming and bustling around the kitchen as they arrived. Rod and Caitlin stood chatting happily, glad their shift was over. It had been a long night for all of them.

'Looks like some of the relief's early, if you want to go, Caitlin.'

'Thanks, Rod, but Alex Palmer is giving me a lift home – he'll be joining Muriel and Jenny afterwards.'

'He's one of the volunteers from your T'ai Chi class, isn't he?'

'Yes. Nice man. Very graceful. He's been with me just over a year now.' Her eyes followed Fixit as he took mugs of tea through to the main hall.

'Thanks for your help, Caitlin.'

'Anytime. At least it was nice and quiet this year!'

They both laughed their relief. Last year had been marred by drug-related violence, and several guests and volunteers, Caitlin included, had been slightly injured before it was brought under control.

'No having to leg it out of the back door this time, eh?'

'No,' Caitlin agreed. 'Knife-wielding thugs are not my idea of what Christmas should be about!' She glanced at the clock, said her goodbyes, and went in search of Mags.

Deborah's fingers felt three-feet thick as she struggled with the locks and bolts of Alex Palmer's front door. Her heart was hammering as she finally pulled it open, all too soon hearing the sound of his feet on the cellar stairs. This part she hadn't thought about, and there was no time now. The door opened straight onto the street. She was free, but he wasn't far behind her and she dare not stop to hammer on a door. At the end of the row of Regency houses, white light gleamed. A phone box. *Run, Deborah! Run!* It was her father's voice she was hearing, yelling louder than any other parent at the Junior School Sports Day. Super-human strength seemed to be pouring through her body, her feet never before as fleet as this...

Daniel chided himself for not having had the sense to ask his sister whether or not she would be eating breakfast at the Shelter before she came home. He'd really gone over the top, knowing that Mike and Nina ate Christmas lunch late, but she could be home any minute now, already full. Never mind. He was hungry as a horse. If she didn't want it, he'd eat it himself.

Deborah realised that she was gabbling when she was put through to the police, but couldn't stop the words pouring out. No, this wasn't a hoax. She was a journalist, Deborah Harvey, and Alex Palmer had killed a woman in her house in Darrowdale, held her captive, killed others, and was right now planning to kill a woman called Caitlin O'Connor who was working at the Homeless Shelter right here in Cheltenham. She was nearly hysterical when they asked where she was. How the hell did she know? The calm voice on the other end of the line told her the phone box would have a sign stating its location. She found it, read it out, nerves at screaming pitch as she kept her eyes on the street.

Oh shit! He had got into a car. The ignition fired, and she watched in awful fascination as he drove towards her, engine breaking the silence of the road, bathed, as it was, in the sullen glare of orange street lamp light. A half-cry escaped from Deborah's parched lips.

'He's in a car!' She forced herself to focus, to read aloud the number plate, readying herself for the turning of the wheel that would aim the car at the telephone box in which she stood.

If he was aware of her at all, he gave no sign of it, indicating left and moving away.

'Caitlin!' she shouted into the phone. 'He's going for Caitlin! The Homeless Shelter!'

Oh God, I've left it too late... Dropping the handset, she raced desperately after him.

Caitlin shivered in the frosty morning air, thrusting her hands deep into her coat pockets. At least it was clean and fresh. Probably not really, but it certainly felt and smelled that way after the central heating of the Shelter, thick with cigarette smoke and the fug of unwashed bodies and damp clothing. Back inside, the kitchen was the best place to be, where the smells of cooking overcame other less welcome odours. She had come outside to wait for Mags, hoping to clear her head and gather her thoughts before Alex arrived. They had talked further during the night and she had been stunned by much of what she'd heard. What a mess. What a Godawful mess.

She longed for a hot shower before going with Daniel and Mags to Mike and Nina's. Who would have thought it? Having her brother with her for Christmas after all these years? And poor Mags – well, she had more valuable pieces of the jigsaw. The least they could do was feed her. She had been reluctant to come, saying she'd be fine at the Shelter, but Caitlin had insisted, promising to bring her back later, reassuring her that Daniel would not sit in judgement on her.

She let out a deep sigh of satisfaction. Life was good. She had Daniel back. She had friends, and a special friend in Nina. She had Josh and they were planning to talk about the future when he came back from his parents. Despite the cold, a little glow spread across her heart as she thought of him. She – they – had a future together. She glanced at the still dark sky and whispered a heartfelt prayer of thanksgiving.

A passageway cutting between houses flickered in the corner of Deborah's eye and she swerved to enter it, feet flying along its uneven surface. *Yes!* It was the short cut she had prayed for, and as she glimpsed Alex's car, she ran for all she was worth, cold air stinging her nose, burning in her lungs. And she saw, too, in the middle of an empty car park, a large, makeshift sign, illuminated by dazzling white light that said 'Christmas Centre for the Homeless'. A large arrow pointed to the right. Alex was going left. Deborah whooped with renewed hope as she realised he was following a one-way system. She still had a chance...

Everything was ready. The table was set, candles lit, even if it was for breakfast. The teapot was warming, as were the plates, and breakfast was being kept hot in the oven. All Daniel needed to make it complete was his sister.

Alex Palmer's mind was icy cold and crystal clear as he turned into the street housing the Hall. Deborah Harvey had escaped. She would, by now, have contacted the police. He had to get Caitlin and get away, as far and as fast as possible. As he drew up outside the building, he shook his head, blinking rapidly to check that he wasn't imagining things. Caitlin was waiting, yes. But there was someone with her. *Nothing can go wrong now. I won't allow it.* He lowered the window. She stepped forward, smiling.

'Alex! You won't believe what happened! This is an old friend of mine. She's coming home with me. Hope you don't mind one more!'

'Of course not!' He got out of the car unsteadily, opened the back door for the other woman.

'Alex! Are you alright?'

'Yes. Well no, not really. I had a bit of an accident on my way out. Slipped on the stairs.' He lurched, Caitlin having to brace herself against his weight. There was no way she could get him to the front of the car, so she helped him into the back with Mags, who manoeuvred her backpack, with difficulty, between the front seats to make room for him.

'I'll drive you to the hospital. You shouldn't have come!'

He handed her the keys, wincing with pain. *How well I act...* 'I didn't want to leave you stranded. It's still dark, after all.'

'Someone else could have run me home. My brother could have picked me up. I could have walked, for heaven's sake!'

She moved Mags's backpack properly into the passenger seat and started the car, closing the window against the chill morning air. 'Let's get you to the hospital.'

Deborah's eyes had conveyed information to her brain, but it had seemed like some sort of surreal fantasy. She had seen Alex getting into the back of the car and Caitlin get into the driver's seat. Had screamed at her, for all she was worth, startling the man who had got out of another vehicle, but failing to halt Caitlin. The hall was well lit, and, as she'd run further, she had glanced at the parked vehicle, seen the keys still in the ignition. The next moment, she was inside and in pursuit of the Alfa Romeo.

Dave Phillips had pulled up in front of the hall, switched off the ignition and got out of his car, carrying two large cool boxes towards the front door. His partner, Mark Chambers, had been doing the Christmas Eve Shift and he had come to pick him up, dropping off more sausages and bacon at the same time. There wasn't enough room in the fridges there to keep everything needed for breakfast, so it had seemed like a good idea to do this. A good idea at the time, anyway. As he told the police later, yes, it was stupid leaving the keys in the ignition, but he'd hardly expected some mad woman to be about at that hour of the morning, to come screaming down the street, jump into the car and steal it right from under his nose...

Chapter Thirty-three

Christmas Day
Part Two

Nina was floating again with a new urgency and even more startling clarity. She saw exactly what Alex Palmer had in mind but was aware that it was only one possible reality. Other realities were also possible, their availability shimmering, pregnant, ready to burst forth, just waiting to be called into being. She prayed with all her heart, directing energy to Caitlin, willing Caitlin to call it down herself, realising that she was not yet aware of the need. Once she was, anything was possible. As for Deborah – she was focused as a laser. Nina could see light, like arrows of prayer, emanating from her. Nina channelled energy back to her, a willing go-between in the place that was no-place, the sacred space between life-death-life.

Caitlin glanced at Alex in the rear-view mirror and smiled reassuringly .

'Thank goodness it's not far. I don't want to rush, providing you're OK – I expect the police will be out looking for drunk drivers.'

How alike we think. That's why I refused to be panicked by Deborah's escape. No point drawing attention to oneself. Especially not today.

'Like vultures,' Alex agreed. 'No, just take it steady, Caitlin. Thank you.'

Caitlin turned into the one-way system, already having figured out the shortest route. There were two more sets of traffic signals to negotiate before she needed to make a right turn. She had slowed for a red light, watched as it turned to red and amber and accelerated as it turned to green, when she glanced in the mirror again and frowned.

'Oh God – looks like there's at least one on the road with us.'

'What?' Alex's voice was sharp as he followed her eyes and turned in the seat to look out of the back window of the car.

'Drunk driver. Or a boy racer, more like. Coming like a bat out of hell and flashing his lights.' Caitlin shook her head. 'What does he think this is? A bloody race track?' The second set of traffic lights loomed. They were on red.

'Go straight over.' It was a command.

'What? We need to turn right – the hospital...'

'Forget the hospital. Do as I say.'

'Alex!' Caitlin looked in the mirror as she made her protest, her eyes widening as she saw the expression on his face.

'Do exactly as I say unless you want me to kill her.'

Alex had Mags's head gripped firmly in his left arm. His right hand held a shining blade inches from her face.

'Put your foot down!'

Caitlin had inadvertently slowed with the shock of what she had seen.

'The light...'

'Jump it!'

'But the police...'

Mags gave a half cry, half scream, as Alex drew the blade down the side of her face, opening up her cheek. Caitlin jumped the light.

Daniel smiled when he heard the doorbell. All that forward planning and Caitlin had forgotten her key! The smile melted from his face when he opened the door and found two uniformed police officers on the step.

The arrows flashed upwards like beacons of light

433

to Nina's non-physical eyes. Yes! Now Caitlin knew. Now they all knew. Nina felt a sense of expansiveness such as she had never experienced before. There were no limits. She and the Universe were One. Power. Vibration. Raw energy. The battle was on.

Shit, shit, SHIT! Deborah's plan had backfired and she hammered the steering wheel in frustration. She had hoped, by flashing her lights but not using her horn, to alert Caitlin to danger. Instead, she had accelerated away, streaking through a red light and forcing Deborah to follow. Deborah, unfamiliar with the place except for her brief trip of a few days earlier, knew only that they were heading out of town. What she needed to know was where they were going to.

'Alex...' Caitlin's mouth was dry with fear. 'Alex, whatever this is, we can talk about it...'
'We certainly shall. When I'm ready. *Drive!*'
'I'm doing my best. This is your car, remember, and I'm not used to it. And it would help if I knew where we were going.' How was she keeping her voice so steady? *I've dealt with worse than this. It will be alright. It will be alright...*
'You'll know that when we get there. For now, head for Blacksmith's Hill. And put your foot down.'
Mags squealed. Caitlin did as she was told.

Deborah swore as the Alfa accelerated away, changed gear and prayed for all she was worth. The road ahead lay empty and straight as far as she could tell, but she would never normally do anything like this speed in the dark. Where the hell was a police officer when you needed one? She must have imagined the sound of sirens as she had turned into the one-way system back in town, for there was no sign of any help now. How fast could an Alfa Romeo go? She couldn't think, but would have laid money on the fact that it could outstrip the Peugeot she was driving.

'GOD HELP ME!' She screamed her anguish aloud as the red tail lights disappeared from view.

Caitlin had been aware of the lights behind them all the way until her last acceleration. *Damn, damn, damn!* From Alex's reaction, it was possibly help. Dare she allow a drop in speed? How quickly would he notice? And dare she risk more damage to Mags? She took a deep breath.

'Alex, whatever it is – please – I'm willing to listen – to help.'

'Help?' He laughed. 'I'm past help, Caitlin. And so are you.' He began, then, to chant.

> *'I know where she is*
> *I know where you are*
> *Caitlin-cat, Hellcat*
> *You thought it was over*
> *but it's just begun*
> *I sleep not nor slumber*
> *till everything's won*
> *But do not try thinking*
> *that you can outrun,*
> *for vengeance is mine,*
> *little hellcat.'*

Up until then, the thought had never crossed Caitlin's mind that Alex's behaviour was in any way connected with her. Now, her skin prickled and the hair on her scalp stood on end.

'You! It was you!'

'Oh yes. *I know where she is. Your mother...*' He was unaware of the gasp from the woman whose head was still gripped in his arm.

'How, Alex? How?' Her eyes flicked to the rear-view mirror. 'You were the boy in the tree... Who *are* you?'

It was the question he had been waiting for. He began to tell her.

'Yes!' Deborah shouted with relief as the red rear lights of the Alfa Romeo came into view again. 'Thank you, God!'

Had Caitlin slowed down or had she, Deborah, speeded up? Was it her imagination, or were the first glimmerings of light seeping into the sky to her left? *Let it be a sign. Please bring the light. Bring HELP...*

He was taunting her now, telling her so much, but withholding what she most wanted to know.

'Please, Alex. I've waited so long. Please.' How was she coping with this? Her anguish and fear were real, yet it was as if she were simultaneously operating on another level, observing herself quite objectively, knowing she had let her speed creep down; not too much, but she knew it had been enough. She had glimpsed those lights again, seen them dip. She had to keep Alex's

436

attention, keep him from noticing. Keep him talking. Bluff it. Anything to keep him from noticing those lights... She cleared her throat, tried a different tack.

'This is all so weird. Mags – that's Mags, in the back with you. She was at the Community, too. I didn't realise – it was only last night at the Shelter...'

'You too?' He squeezed the woman exultantly. 'A bonus! Another devil from the den of iniquity! Tell me about yourself, Mags. I'm not sure I remember you.'

Mags's voice was croaking, barely audible. 'I can't – my throat.' Alex loosened his grip. Slightly. 'I remember you. That summer. The boy with the foreign name. Always up trees.' *Jesus, Mary and Joseph, I give you my heart and my soul...* 'I haven't told anyone my real name in years, until last night. I've been Mags for so long.' *Jesus, Mary and Joseph, I put all my trust in thee...* 'My name is Margaret Rose Dwyer. Rosie Dwyer, I was called in the Community. I looked after the animals.'

Alex laughed, squeezing her so hard she gurgled, having to fight for breath.

'The animal keeper! Was that the human or the four-legged variety? I remember you now! The pretty, rosy-cheeked woman with the long plait.' He moved his attention from her to Caitlin, talking to the back of her head. 'Your father liked undoing that plait, Caitlin. Undoing her clothes, too. I bet you didn't know that!'

'Not until last night, no. My father used Rosie like he used so many women. It's why she is as

437

she is today.'

'A crazy vagrant?' He laughed again, hatred filling the interior of the car with its sound. 'That's his fault, is it?'

'He has a lot to answer for.' *And answer he bloody well will. If we ever get out of this...*

'But not your mother's death, eh, Caitlin? Not that. That was *your* fault. Yours, do you hear? I'll tell you about it in a minute. When we get there. In every beautiful, Technicolor detail. Put your foot down, why don't you? Don't you want to hear? Don't you want to know?'

They were climbing now, the hill not only steep but snaking.

'It's so winding... I can't risk driving any faster. We could go over the edge.'

'Over the edge? Ha!' He gripped Mags harder and she squealed again, the sound of her pain turning Caitlin's stomach into a screaming knot. 'Rosie and I did that long ago. Turn left here.'

'Left?' Caitlin slowed, peering in frustration, seeing no entrance.

'That's right. Turn left. Just after the crumbling stone pillar. Tell her, Rosie.'

Mags moaned this time. Caitlin fought down bile as she turned, praying to God that whoever was behind had seen what she was doing.

Daniel was beside himself. *It's all my fault. I should have gone to the police as soon as it started. They blame me. And they're right.* The police had descended on the Shelter moments too late. Rod, the man he'd spoken to on the phone, had remembered that Daniel was staying with Caitlin and had given them her address. *Oh God – it wasn't meant to be like this...* The female police officer asked, 'Is there someone you'd like us to contact? Someone who could be with you?'

'Mike and Nina – Caitlin's friends.' He struggled to remember their surname, grabbed Caitlin's address book, tearing through the pages, showing them. 'I tried to phone them last night, but they weren't home. We're going to them for Christmas lunch. We *were...*' His face crumpled. He didn't see the glance exchanged between the police officers as they read the name and address he had pointed out. The male officer took a deep breath.

'I'm terribly sorry, Mr Richardson. I'm afraid there's something you need to know. There's been an accident...'

Caitlin's mind and body felt completely divorced. Her mind was icy clear, one part driving the car, on automatic pilot; another part analysing information with dispassionate detachment. *The scrabbling noises behind the dry-stone wall – not a dog or a fox or a cat. Mummy. Dying. I walked within feet of her and didn't know.* Alex's voice was like the hum of a generator, incessant, hypnotic, drip-feeding the poisonous truth that finally bound the pieces of the jigsaw puzzle together. *Walking back. Not lovers. Alex finishing her off. Suffocating her. My mother. He killed my mother...*

Her body, too, was split. One part driving the car, on automatic pilot; the rest overwhelmingly alive and conscious. She could hear the blood pounding in her ears, squishing, circulating, coursing through every artery and vein. Fire burned within her, radiating from her heart to the farthest extremities of toes and fingers, giving awareness even to each hair on her head, crackling now with electric current, like living antennae. *My mother. He killed my mother...*

Where had they gone? Deborah had been driving on dipped headlights, had had the rear lights of the Alfa firmly in view when – pouf! They had vanished. It didn't make sense. She lowered the window, listening as her eyes searched the road ahead. They couldn't have carried on. She would have seen them. Dammit all to hell – where *were* they? She was crawling along now, desperate for a clue. No right turns were possible – the road was edged by stone wall, behind which the ground fell away in a sheer drop. Left then. They had to have turned left. She screamed her pent-up frustration, thumping the steering wheel in her anger. All she could see were trees. No. Wait. What was that glimmer? As her headlights picked up the broken stone pillar, a sound reached her ears, shattering the countryside beyond her metal shell. It was a car horn, long, loud, and coming from her left.

Oh God – don't let me be too late! She swung the steering wheel, scraping the half-hidden wall as she turned, put the headlights on full beam and trod hard on the accelerator.

Mags's mind had become oddly clear. It seemed, in fact, to have become more clear with each injury inflicted upon her body by this madman

440

who had whisked them away from their lives. He was set on killing Caitlin. She herself was just so much extraneous baggage, a useful tool with which to beat Caitlin into compliance. She couldn't allow that to continue.

I betrayed her – and her brother – all those years ago. Being their friend and sleeping with their father. I betrayed Laura. Fornicating with her husband, making him an adulterer. I let them down, keeping silent and moving away after Laura disappeared, allowing myself to go mad through self-centred guilt. It's up to me now. I have to face up to my responsibilities.

It was time. She had been given an opportunity to atone. Her nerve must not fail now. *Mother of Mercy, pray for me. Sweet Jesus, receive my soul...*

As the car bounced over the uneven furrows in the dirt track, she acknowledged the irrevocability of her decision. *Jesus, Mary and Joseph, assist me in my last agony...*

Briefly, she closed her eyes, gave thanks for the life that had been given to her, a life she had not, in her own estimation, used well.

'Pull up over there.'

Mags felt the car swing right at Alex's command, felt the slowing down, knew she had to make her move. Her right arm was trapped beneath her body, but her left was free. She had been feigning limpness for the past few moments.

I know I shall die, but please God, let it give Caitlin a chance. Mustering every ounce of strength, she lashed up at Alex, twisting her body as she did so, attempting to drive her head, still gripped by his left arm, into him. She was unaware of the roar she let out, so loud and primeval it startled Caitlin and Alex both.

'No!' Caitlin screamed as she brought the car to a halt, jolting forward and hitting the horn as hard as she could. The car rocked with the frenzied thrashing from the back seat.

'Run, Caitlin – run!' Mags's voice was hoarse.

Oh GOD! Caitlin was out of the car, almost tumbling onto the frosted earth. In an instant, she was up and running for her life.

Deborah's headlights picked out a scene from hell as she approached the top of the rutted path. The Alfa Romeo was stationary, two doors open, and from one of them sprawled the body of a woman. Involuntarily, her eyes slid away, seeking signs of life. There! She swung the car off the track as she made out the figures of Caitlin and Alex, both running across open ground towards stunted bushes. She hit the horn, swinging the car again in an effort to cut Alex off, to put herself between him and Caitlin, realising fractionally too late that beyond the bushes was nothing but a sheer drop. *SHIT!* She overcompensated, back wheels spinning, rear end sliding. Her heart hammered as she brought the car to a halt. Caitlin was beside herself, pointing, screaming.

'What?' Deborah shouted.

Caitlin had turned at the sound of the horn, seen Deborah's manoeuvre, seen what Deborah had not, fixated as she was on avoiding the drop and avoiding Caitlin. The back end of the car had slid across the ground, lifting Alex clean off his feet and sending him in a strangely beautiful arc

442

of loose-limbed grace over the edge of a hundred-foot drop.

'The car clipped him – he's gone.'

Deborah jumped out, running to Caitlin, grabbing hold of her and clutching her fiercely. 'Thank God you're all right!' They clung to each other wordlessly.

'He killed my mother! He killed my mother!' Caitlin was sobbing, shaking, gasping for breath. Abruptly, she stopped. 'Mags! Oh God – Mags – Rosie...' She pulled away from Deborah and started running back towards the Alfa, stumbling like a drunk.

Reaction had set in for Deborah, now, too. Without Caitlin to hold onto, her legs were shaking so badly she could barely stand. She leaned forward, sliding her hands down to her knees before pitching face down onto the ground. It was only as she finished being sick that she heard the voice. Alex's voice.

'Deborah!'

Every hair on her body seemed to rise in fear. Her head jerked up, eyes searching for him as she moved first to her knees, then to her feet as a new surge of adrenaline spread through her body. The sky was streaked with orange and pink as she looked towards the gap in the wall.

'Deborah!'

Slowly, she walked towards the edge.

Nina could resist the pull no longer. She was going back. Back to her body. Caitlin was safe, but Deborah ... and what had Laura meant by drawing her attention to the pool? Not a pool – a gravel pit? She was becoming heavier, losing the clarity of revelation. She understood that Laura's remains were there, but what else had she seen? It was as if she herself had been under the water, moving freely, quite able to breathe. Yes. That was it. The car. Laura's skeleton.

She had moved again, sleek as an otter, seeing through weed, under gravel, seeing other skeletons, some large and some tiny – no more, surely, than babies? She struggled now, sensing the imminent return to her body and pain. What was the last thing Laura had said? A name... Isabella. Something about a window... She could no longer make the effort to understand. Heavy. Everything was heavy. She was back in her body now. Finally, she was back.

The nurse on duty saw the signs. *Good news at last!*

Alex saw Deborah before she saw him. He grabbed at her ankle, the loose stones and earth giving way beneath her feet. She screamed, twisting as she fell, hands scrabbling, grabbing at anything, everything, to try to stop her fall. The drop was sheer. God knows how he'd survived, hung on. She clawed her way to the top, shouting for Caitlin, heaving herself up, swinging her legs, feet flailing to find a grip.

As she lay on the top, hands still holding the edge, one of his hands slammed down onto hers. Then the other. He had her by the wrists. *Dear God! He means to take me with him!*

Eyes wide with terror, she could see him clearly now, bloodied, broken, skin hanging from his

444

face. He looked at her, lips drawn back in a caricature of a smile. He was mind-reading again.

'No, Deborah. I need you to be my scribe, remember? Accuracy.' He coughed blood. Released one hand from hers, swinging perilously as she found herself fighting to hold onto him.

'What are you *doing?*'

'Accuracy,' he repeated. Deborah let out a cry of fear as his weight dragged her closer to the edge. He was using his free hand to fumble in a pocket. 'Terry. I didn't do it.'

The Dictaphone? All this for the Dictaphone? What in God's name? He was slipping now, trying to give it to her.

'Take them!'

Them? 'I can't! There's no way I can hold onto you!'

'You don't have to.'

He smiled then, the first genuine smile he'd managed in years. Oblivion was calling. Peace at last.

'Take them, Deborah, and let me go.'

Their eyes locked. She gave way first, moving her gaze to the Dictaphone in his free hand. She looked back at him. He nodded. She reached for it, grasped it and felt him slip soundlessly away.

'Mags – Rosie – is still alive! I've phoned the police – ambulance – everything. He had a mobile in the glove compartment.'

Deborah, now sitting sideways in the driver's seat of the Peugeot with her legs out on the grass, nodded wordlessly.

Caitlin looked at her. 'Are you alright? I have to go back. Be with her.' Deborah nodded again. Caitlin threw her one last glance before running back to the Alfa.

From where she was sitting, Deborah could see the sunrise in all its glory.

The Dictaphone was in her lap. In her hand, the crumpled piece of paper Alex had given her with it. She shook her head, rewound the tape and listened again.

The sound of an entryphone buzzer. A clicking whirr as the door was unlocked and pushed open. Terry hadn't asked who was there. Then came his voice – too late, too late – excited, calling, 'Katie? Katie?' Alex's quiet laugh, cut off abruptly by a jumble of noise.

Skidding.

A series of bumps.

A final cascade, culminating in a sickening crack.

Silence.

Alex's voice. Incredulous. 'He slipped on the stairs! He slipped! Waving...'

She switched off the tape. Looked again at the piece of paper in her hand.

Terry had died for it, carried away by excitement.

Alex had died for it, seeking accuracy.

She smoothed it out.

A Lottery ticket.

Lifting her face to the rising sun, Deborah Harvey began to laugh.

The publishers hope that this book has given you enjoyable reading. Large Print Books are especially designed to be as easy to see and hold as possible. If you wish a complete list of our books please ask at your local library or write directly to:

Magna Large Print Books
Magna House, Long Preston,
Skipton, North Yorkshire.
BD23 4ND

This Large Print Book for the partially sighted, who cannot read normal print, is published under the auspices of

THE ULVERSCROFT FOUNDATION